"If anyone asks why I've changed, I might mention a certain earl in a certain castle."

She didn't say anything further and neither did he. When he took a few steps towards her, she didn't move back. She only continued to smile, her eyes widening a little.

He bent his head, even as he told himself that what he was doing was unwise, and slowly placed his mouth on hers.

This was what he'd wanted to do for a very long time.

It didn't matter that she was an American, that her home was thousands of miles from here. It didn't matter that in weeks she'd be gone and he'd never see her again.

Nothing mattered but these seconds when he held her in his arms . . .

By Karen Ranney

To Wed an Heiress

❧ AN ALL FOR LOVE NOVEL ❧

KAREN RANNEY

AVONBOOKS

An Imprint of HarperCollinsPublishers

Excerpt from *To Love a Duchess* copyright © 2018 by Karen Ranney LLC.

TO WED AN HEIRESS. Copyright © 2019 by Karen Ranney LLC. All rights reserved. Printed in the United States of America. No part of this book may be used or reproduced in any manner whatsoever without written permission except in the case of brief quotations embodied in critical articles and reviews. For information, address HarperCollins Publishers, 195 Broadway, New York, NY 10007.

First Avon Books mass market printing: April 2019
First Avon Books hardcover printing: March 2019

Print Edition ISBN: 978-0-06-284106-3
Digital Edition ISBN: 978-0-06-284107-0

Cover design by Patricia Barrow
Cover illustration by Patrick Kang
Cover photographs © Catuncia/solarus/Shelli Jensen/Aleksandr Nizienko/ Heidi Besen/sumroeng chinnapan/Anna Anisimova/Shutterstock (seven images)

Avon, Avon & logo, and Avon Books & logo are registered trademarks of HarperCollins Publishers in the United States of America and other countries.

HarperCollins is a registered trademark of HarperCollins Publishers in the United States of America and other countries.

FIRST EDITION

19 20 21 22 23   QGM   10 9 8 7 6 5 4 3 2 1

To Vicki Branson
For her friendship and courage

To Wed an Heiress

Chapter One

"$\mathcal{I}$t's a monster!" Ruthie screamed. "One of those Scottish monsters, Miss Mercy, just like the stories we heard."

"It's nothing of the sort, Ruthie," Mercy Rutherford said, trying to calm herself and, by extension, her maid.

Ruthie, however, was having none of it. She grabbed Mercy's right arm with both hands and was practically atop her, straining to see out the window on the left side of the carriage.

It might not be a monster, but it was one of the oddest things she'd ever seen. A boat with wheels and a tail hanging from a massive sail. The most surprising and alarming thing was that the contraption was aloft like a giant misshapen bird and was now headed straight for them.

"I knew it, Miss Mercy. I knew it. Didn't I tell you when I saw those three magpies that something terrible would happen?"

Ruthie saw omens in everything.

"If it isn't a monster, Miss Mercy, then what is it?"

Mercy didn't know. She'd never seen anything like it.

"Is it a dragon?"

That was as good a name as any.

"It's going to hit us, Miss Mercy."

It certainly appeared that way. Ruthie wasn't the only one becoming agitated. The horses were screaming and the coachman Mercy had hired in Inverness was shouting, trying to control them.

She wanted to close her eyes and pretend to be asleep. In a moment she would awaken because the maid was at her bedside with the morning tray, complete with coffee, toast, and a rosebud from their greenhouse in a vase.

Her day would be like a thousand other days. "The jeweler is here with some new designs for you to see, Miss Mercy." Or: "There's a final fitting for your ball gown, Miss Mercy." Or: "The cook has prepared some sweets for you. Shall I fetch them?"

Inconsequential details marking her life, one crafted to be without a care. One from which she'd escaped weeks ago.

Was she going to die because she wanted her freedom?

The carriage stopped, then lurched forward as the horses panicked. She truly couldn't blame them, especially after she looked out the window again. The dragon was getting closer. At another time she might've marveled that something that looked nothing like a balloon was somehow managing to stay up in the air. Not right now, however, when it was a very real danger.

If the horses continued to be uncontrollable they could end up off the road entirely and over one of those cliffs they'd passed earlier. Below them was a lake, or what the Scots called a loch. She didn't think Ruthie could swim and she didn't know about Mr. McAdams.

If screaming would do any good, she would join

her voice to the horses and now Ruthie. It wouldn't do for everyone to lose their minds. Someone had to remain calm.

The dragon was lower and closer now, directed by a man seated in the boat-like part of the craft.

"Turn," she said. Of course he couldn't hear her, but perhaps God could. "Make him turn."

The man was still headed directly toward them.

Would anyone be able to convey the information that she'd perished to her parents? She'd written them a letter explaining this forbidden journey, but if she failed to return home would they be able to find out what had happened to her?

How odd that she'd never thought to die in Scotland.

LENNOX CAITHEART SWORE as he pulled one of the ropes controlling the tail of his airship. There wasn't supposed to be a carriage in the road. There was never a carriage on this road.

The road was the unofficial boundary between his land and the Macrorys', and he was careful never to venture on the other side of it.

Ben Uaine didn't count. The mountain belonged to Scotland, not the Macrorys, although they'd claimed dominion over everything they saw.

No, the carriage shouldn't have been there and now he was heading directly for it. The wind gusts had been exactly what he planned. He'd kept the air sock and pennant in place for weeks now, measuring the difference in the wind between the morning, afternoon, and evening.

One simple errant carriage might be the difference between his first true success and utter disaster.

If he tried to avoid them, he would head straight for the loch, which wouldn't be bad from a landing point of view, but he wouldn't be able to retrieve his Cayley replica if he landed in the water. He aimed for the glen, just as he'd planned, and it would've been almost successful if the blasted carriage hadn't been between him and his landing site.

MERCY BEGAN TO pray. That's what people did in the midst of a crisis, wasn't it?

She wasn't Roman Catholic like Ruthie. Nor did she have a rosary, but she no doubt sounded as panicked to the Almighty.

Perhaps I shouldn't have embarked on such a foolish errand, God. But it was born out of compassion. Does that excuse me?

Probably not. Doing the right thing for the wrong reason was almost as bad as doing the wrong thing for the right reason. Either way, she didn't doubt that God preferred two positives to a positive paired with a negative.

It truly had been an errand of compassion for her aunt and grandmother. They'd lived in North Carolina during the Civil War. Granted, she and her family had experienced war as well, but not as personally since they lived in New York. Their home hadn't been razed. Their crops hadn't been burned. They hadn't been nearly starved for the past year.

When her father's messenger returned from North Carolina with news that her grandmother and aunt were no longer there, Mercy thought her mother's heart would break. The valise, filled with greenbacks, hadn't been a lifeline after all. The messenger had reached North Carolina after her grandmother and aunt had left. They'd gone to Scotland where her grandmother had been born.

Mercy had decided to bring the money to Scotland, to ensure that her mother's family was provided for just as her mother had intended. In all honesty, she would have found any reason to escape, but she never thought to be sitting in a carriage waiting for a man-made dragon to land on her.

He was almost atop them now, his descent muted beneath the sound of the screaming horses and Ruthie praying in her ear.

Suddenly, the roof of the carriage sounded as if it was being torn off. This time she did close her eyes, pulling her arm free of Ruthie's grip to embrace the other woman. The maid had been with her since Mercy was seventeen, nearly eleven years now. If she must die in a strange land, then at least Ruthie was with her.

Scant comfort for both their families.

She hoped her mother would forgive her and that her father would understand.

The carriage lurched to the side as Ruthie prayed in her ear. She didn't understand half of what the maid was saying because it seemed to be in Latin, but Ruthie never missed Mass. Perhaps God would look upon both of them favorably because of that. Mercy went to church every Sunday as well, but Presbyterians didn't seem nearly as fervent.

With her left hand she reached up and grabbed the strap over the window, her right arm still around Ruthie. A horrible groaning noise was the last thing she heard before the carriage overturned.

Chapter Two

Something was wet on her face. Mercy tried to move her head, but it seemed like it weighed twenty times more than it had just a few minutes earlier. She pushed something off her head, finally realizing that it was the seat cushion.

The carriage had overturned. They were on their side and everything that had been on the floor was now tossed willy-nilly, including the hamper that had been prepared for them this morning. A large chunk of pungent-smelling cheese was only inches from her nose. She suspected that one of the bottles of wine had broken open and that's what she felt on her face.

Ruthie was crumpled on the other side of the carriage. One of her arms was outstretched and her head was pillowed on it, almost as if she were asleep. But she was entirely too pale and when Mercy called her name she didn't respond.

Mercy managed to inch to the other woman's side.

The roof of the carriage abruptly opened, almost as if it had been peeled back by a gigantic hand. No, not a giant. Only a man.

"Are you all right?" he asked.

"I don't believe so, no."

"You're an American," he said.

She squinted at him. "Was it you flying the dragon?"

"The what?"

"Dragon. Monster. Whatever it was."

"It's an airship."

"Whatever it was, you're insane."

He didn't respond to her comment. Instead, he frowned. "You're bleeding."

She raised her hand and placed it on her cheek. When her fingers came away, they were bloodied. Not wine after all.

"Are you going to faint?"

"If I do it's what you deserve," she said. She was intensely furious at him, but the effort of saying so seemed suddenly too much.

"You've killed Ruthie," she said. "You're not only insane, you're a murderer."

"Hardly that," he said. "She's still breathing, but we do need to get her out of there."

He pulled off the remainder of the roof easily, dragging it away from the rest of the carriage.

Ruthie, thankfully, surfaced from her faint as he and the coachman were pulling her free of the wreckage.

Mercy had decided to refuse his help, idiot that he was, and make her own way out of the vehicle. She was reminded of her mother's words a few minutes later when she realized that she couldn't pull her foot free.

Your father's pride gets him in trouble, sometimes, Mercy. It's a good thing to be proud. But it is not a good thing to be excessively prideful.

The stranger returned for her a moment later.

"I can't move my foot," she said, annoyed at having to ask for his help.

He didn't say anything, just crawled into the carriage, removed part of the frame, then grabbed her under her arms, dragging her unceremoniously out of the carriage onto a grassy area not far from the road.

She lay looking up at the clear Scottish sky. At least it wasn't raining.

"How do you feel?" he asked.

"How is Ruthie?"

"I think her arm is broken."

She closed her eyes.

"I must get her help," she said.

"I have some experience in setting bones."

She opened her eyes and moved her head slowly until he was within sight.

"You broke her arm and now you want to fix it?"

"I don't see any alternative."

"I really don't want you to treat her," she said.

"I don't care what you want."

"Are you always so boorish?"

"Yes."

"You should apologize," she said, pointing her finger at him. "For both your attitude and crashing into us."

He didn't pay her any attention. Instead, he turned to the coachman and was indicating something at the bottom of the hill.

"I'm going to take your friend to my home," he said, glancing once more at her. "I can treat her there. You'll be safe here with the coachman until I return."

Of course she would be safe. Mr. McAdams was a very nice man, one she'd interviewed in Inverness. He had been exceedingly polite and willing to take them this far. Of course, she'd paid him a small fortune so the decision had been an easy one.

Ruthie was lying on the grass with her eyes closed

as if she'd fallen into a faint again. Without another word, the man scooped Ruthie up from the grass and cradled her in his arms. Then he was gone, walking down the hill toward the loch.

She watched them until they were out of sight, then lay back down on the ground. Her head was pounding and must be bleeding again.

A few minutes later Mr. McAdams came to stand at her side.

"The carriage is done for, I'm afraid, Miss Rutherford. Mr. Caitheart said he has a carriage we could borrow, miss."

"Is that his name?"

Mr. McAdams nodded. The coachman was a large man, but then she had never seen a coachman who didn't have a burly shape. They needed muscles to control the strong-willed horses that pulled carriages. If Mr. McAdams was fond of his dinner, that seemed a small sin when compared to the ones he could have possessed.

The sin of pride, for example.

She turned her head slightly. To her left was the monster Mr. Caitheart had been riding. It didn't look remotely like a dragon now, only a crumpled bit of wood with fluttery fabric in two places. A dragonfly, that's what it reminded her of—a wounded dragonfly resting on the ground before it healed itself. Or perished.

She'd been a fool to come to Scotland, even if it had been a compassionate errand. She'd made the whole situation worse by bringing Ruthie with her. Not that she would've left New York without the other woman. First of all, she had her reputation to consider. Secondly, Ruthie was her only true friend. Yet now she had something else on her conscience, Ruthie's well-being.

Mr. McAdams had already unfastened the horses from the ruined carriage. He went to them now, sliding his hands over their flanks, examining each leg with care. Mercy did the same for herself as discreetly as she could. She was wearing a dark blue traveling dress and the crinolines beneath her skirt were a great deal more comfortable than trying to wear a hoop inside the carriage.

She sat up after having determined that there was nothing wrong with her arms—unlike poor Ruthie. Nor did she seem to have any injury of her legs or feet. Her head still ached, however, but that was all.

A half hour passed and it didn't seem as if Mr. Caitheart was going to come back anytime soon. Nor was Mr. McAdams interested in anything but his horses.

Very well, it was up to her to find out how Ruthie was faring. Mercy had come to Scotland to demonstrate her independence and she would begin right now.

She stood, feeling a little bit wobbly. After a minute or two the scenery didn't tilt. Grabbing her skirts, she made her way over the grass, taking care to avoid the tall purple flowers that looked spiky and almost dangerous. She had never seen a thistle up close before, but she knew what they were. There were carvings of thistles and other Scottish plants on the mantelpieces in their summer home. A way of her father honoring her mother's heritage, though her mother had never visited Scotland.

Her grandmother was a different story. She might have lived in North Carolina for forty years, but you wouldn't know it to hear her speak. Nor, from the stories she told, had she ever lost her longing for Scotland.

Mercy went first to the carriage where Mr. McAdams had retrieved all their belongings and placed them to the side of the road. After finding her reticule and the valise she'd guarded ever since New York, she made her way to the coachman's side.

"Are your horses all right, Mr. McAdams?"

"They seem to be, miss. Scared more than anything."

She reached out and rubbed a nose close to her. She'd never excelled at riding, although they had horses at their summer home, but she'd always liked being around them.

"I'm going to go check on Ruthie," she said. "Mr. Caitheart doesn't seem to be returning anytime soon. I just want to make sure she's all right."

He nodded.

She hesitated before leaving. Whether it made any sense or not she felt responsible for Mr. McAdams's carriage. If he hadn't been taking them to her grandmother, he would never have encountered an idiot like Mr. Caitheart.

The crumpled vehicle looked as if it had been squashed like a bug, with only the wheels intact.

Mr. Caitheart had not offered an apology for his actions. Nor had he seemed to possess the least concern that he'd disrupted their lives.

A few large rocks were arranged together on the side of the road. She wasn't sure if it was natural or something built by man, but she went and sat on the largest rock, dug into her reticule, and pulled out one of her calling cards. She wrote instructions on the back, then returned to the coachman.

"Take that to this company in Inverness," she said. "It's one of my father's shipping companies. They'll see to it that your carriage is replaced."

She would pay her father back for the carriage out of her own money.

Mr. McAdams took the card, looked at her, then the card, then her again.

"Thank you, miss."

"I am sorry about all this, Mr. McAdams."

"Whit's fur ye'll no go past ye," he said.

Fortunately, she'd heard that expression before and knew it meant something along the lines of whatever happens will happen.

She grabbed the valise and her reticule, left the coachman, and started walking across the grass. Once she rounded a small hill she stopped, staring. She'd thought that Mr. Caitheart lived in one of those cottages they'd passed ever since leaving Inverness. The white walls and the thatched roofs were exceedingly picturesque, but the homes weren't very large.

Mr. Caitheart, however, lived in a castle. They'd seen one or two of those, as well, but they'd been ruins, stark against the horizon.

This castle stretched out before her, an immense fortress of salmon-colored brick built on a promontory jutting into the loch.

Surrounded on three sides by water and a narrow bit of land, the castle featured a tower at least four stories high. The curtain wall at the farthest point of the castle, close to the knoll that began to taper up toward the glen, was damaged in places but mainly intact.

The castle stretched between the tower and the wall. Part of the original roof looked to have fallen in because it was now clad in unfinished timber. Something so obviously old that was still in use seemed almost magical, but then the land on which she walked was settled long before her own country was discovered.

The road down to the castle led to a bridge over a

gushing river. She crossed it, grateful for the iron railings on both sides.

The castle had a second tower, but the structure had collapsed, leaving only waist-high rounded walls. The road curved in a circle in front of it, no doubt for carriages to turn around.

The closest she'd ever come to being in a castle was a house in upstate New York owned by a friend of her father. He'd claimed that most of the bricks had been taken from an ancient fortress in Ireland and that the house had been built to replicate that castle. There was no resemblance between that luxurious home and this place.

There was no door inside the ruined tower. Instead, it led to a space that looked to have once been an anteroom. It was dark, the sunlight only penetrating a few feet. The smell of damp brick mixed with dust assaulted her nose. That could have come from the stone floor that looked as if it had never been swept. A few more feet in was a bronze-colored metal door with a tarnished brass ring hanging by a rope down the middle of it.

She pulled on it and heard the distant peal of a bell.

Chapter Three

Lennox frowned at the sound of the bell and dismissed it a second later. He knew who it was, the arrogant American who'd called him insane. She wasn't the first. Nor would she be the last.

People didn't understand what he was trying to do. Nor did he waste any time attempting to explain it to them. He corresponded with a few men on the matter, but otherwise it was simply easier to keep his experiments to himself.

He focused his attention on the young woman in front of him, grateful that his housekeeper was at the market. Otherwise, Irene would have been fussing at him for placing Miss Gallagher on her kitchen table.

The woman's hair was the sort of red that reminded him of autumn leaves just before they fell to the ground. Her bright green eyes were the shade of the grass in the glen and her pink cheeks brought to mind a child's delight in winter snow.

She'd been silent during his palpitation of her arm. The only sign that she was in pain was when she bit her lip. Otherwise, she occupied herself by staring at Connor.

Connor was tall, towering over Lennox by a head.

But, then, Connor towered over most people. He was known for two things: his height and being a peacemaker. Connor disliked conflict of any sort.

He'd been with Lennox for four years, ever since being hired from the nearby village. Some of Lennox's inventions had sold, which meant that he'd been able to cobble together enough money to purchase the supplies he needed, do a few repairs to the castle, buy some creature comforts, and pay a salary of sorts to Connor and Irene.

Connor reminded him, strangely enough, of a swan. Despite his height he moved gracefully, his hands performing a ballet as he reached for the exact part he needed or tightened a screw. He glided through his tasks with a tranquility despite any obstacles he faced. Except that he had acted differently ever since seeing Miss Gallagher, witnessed by the fact that he refused to leave her side.

Connor had steadfastly stood beside the table, holding Miss Gallagher's free hand. To offer support, he had said. From the moment they'd seen each other, it was as if they were meeting once again after having been apart.

Lennox had never seen anything like it, but he knew, from the expression on Connor's face, that there was no way the other man would leave the kitchen.

The bell rang again. Lennox ignored it and finished tying off the bandage that would keep Miss Gallagher's arm straight until it healed.

"Would you like some tea?" Connor asked as Lennox helped her sit up. "Lennox has a tincture that can help with the pain," he added. "It tastes bad, but you might not be able to tell in a strong cup of tea."

Connor had never been so solicitous, but then they

didn't often have female visitors. Other than Irene's sister, of course, but both women were in their fifties.

Lennox hoped Miss Gallagher declined. Now that he'd splinted her arm, the faster she left, the better. She was a stranger on her way somewhere, not someone Connor would ever see again.

"I've offered our carriage to their coachman," he said to Connor. "Would you mind going along and bringing it back after they've gotten to their destination?"

He had a few Clydesdales, working horses that he'd purchased from a friend. They weren't as well matched as Mr. McAdams's pair, but they would do the job.

Lennox didn't know if he was doing a favor for Connor or making the situation worse. Despite the fact that Connor and the maid had an instant rapport, he doubted anything could come of it. She was a visitor to Scotland with nothing to root her here.

He put up his supplies, turning his back on the couple deliberately. If they wanted to gaze soulfully into each other's eyes, he didn't have to see it.

Love made a man lose his mind. Even instant attraction dulled his wits somewhat.

As he opened the cupboard, the bell rang again. He had to answer the door. No doubt the American woman would call him insane again. Or call him names because he'd almost killed Miss Gallagher. He hadn't, but he did bear a sizable measure of guilt. He should have asked Connor to stand watch and ensure that no one was traveling on the road from Inverness.

A carriage accident had killed his brother. Lennox had nearly caused the same catastrophe, albeit because of an oversight.

He doubted if it would be wise to apologize, however. The American woman—and she was only the third

American he'd met, not counting Miss Gallagher—
didn't look the type to appreciate an apology. Instead,
she would probably consider it an admission of his
insanity.

She was attractive, but a fair face didn't necessarily accompany good character. Beautiful women were
difficult, mainly because they knew they were beautiful. Instead of viewing their looks as an accident
of birth, they seemed to think that it was a boon be-
stowed by God. As if it made them somehow different,
better, and special among other women.

He would much rather prefer a plain woman with a
kind heart than someone like the American who was
evidently well versed in sounding arrogant and behaving the same.

This was Scotland and he was a Scot. She evidently
didn't realize what that meant. He didn't obey orders
well. Nor did he appreciate someone calling him names.

The bell rang again, and this time he closed the
cupboard with a bang and left the kitchen.

MERCY RANG THE bell four times and wondered, despite the fact that she could hear it, if it was audible to
anyone in the castle. She could always walk around
and head for the curtain wall and see if there was a
door there.

The door finally opened and *he* stood there. She
hadn't truly noted his appearance earlier. No doubt
that was due to the accident and her shock at what had
happened.

Mr. Caitheart was extraordinarily attractive. His
face was square, his chin well defined, and more
than a little stubborn. His nose reminded her of a Roman general's bust she'd once seen in a museum. His

cheekbones were prominent, but again the impression she got was of obstinacy, even in his features. His black hair was still mussed as if he hadn't taken the opportunity to put himself to rights after the accident.

He had the most direct and intense blue eyes she'd ever seen, and as he wordlessly stared at her, she had the absurd desire to explain herself and apologize for disturbing him.

Instead, she asked, "How is Ruthie?"

"She's fine," he said stepping back as if he expected her to enter his home without an invitation.

She remained where she was.

"And her arm?"

"I've set it," he said. "I've used a splint and bandages. When you get to where you're going you should have it examined again."

His voice was interesting, deep and compelling, especially with his accent. She almost wanted to ask him to keep speaking, if he could do so without being boorish.

"You're still bleeding," he said, frowning at her.

"It's only an annoyance," she said. "The cut isn't that large."

"Head wounds bleed." He reached out and grabbed her arm, surprising her.

"You sound as if you are a physician yourself, Mr. Caitheart."

"We live in the Highlands, miss. You need to be a master of many trades here. There aren't doctors around every corner. You need to be treated."

With that, he pulled her into his castle. Hardly a gracious invitation, but she had no choice but to go with him.

Chapter Four

The anteroom—she hesitated calling it a foyer—had been dark. The room she entered was lit by the sun and much larger than she expected.

She pulled her arm free of Mr. Caitheart's grip, allowing her gaze to travel up the various arches and to the stained-glass windows high up on one wall. For a moment she thought this space might have once been a chapel, but then she realized that the windows didn't depict any kind of religious images. Instead, they showed scenes of battle and all the red in the windows must represent blood.

On the walls were various pendants and flags along with cudgels, swords, and instruments of war that looked as if they could deliver a painful death.

She doubted if either of the fireplaces on opposite sides of the room would warm the area much. Summer in the Highlands was like autumn in New York. Even now, in the middle of July, the space was chilly. She could only imagine what it would be like in the depths of winter.

The sun streaming in through various spots in the roof created patches of bright white light on the stone floor. Other than a few benches along the wall and two throne-like chairs in front of one fireplace, the cavernous space was unfurnished.

"What is this place?" she asked.

"It's the Clan Hall," he said, striding away from her.

She had no recourse but to follow him. He led her down a covered corridor with windows open to a pleasant summer breeze before entering a large kitchen smelling faintly of fish.

The room was dominated by an enormous fireplace on one wall. A wrought-iron frame held cauldrons, a tea kettle, and various pots, all waiting for the fire to be lit. The logs were at least six feet long and looked as if they would burn for a week. This was probably the warmest spot in the castle during the winter months.

Two windows lit the space, each on opposite walls. The east-facing window held a dozen or more clay pots bearing a selection of plants. The west-facing window was bare and faced the loch. The sight of the sunset over the water must be magnificent.

A rectangular table sat in front of the fire along with an assortment of chairs and stools. Ruthie was sitting at the table, her right arm bandaged and held close to her body in a sling made from a piece of leather.

As they entered, the man who'd been sitting beside Ruthie stood and smiled at Mercy. He was very tall, with dark brown hair, and warm brown eyes.

She couldn't help but smile back.

"Connor Ross," Mr. Caitheart said in a begrudging tone.

Did he never cease being rude?

"Welcome to Duddingston Castle," Connor said.

At least now she had a name for the place. She smiled in response and walked toward Ruthie.

"How are you feeling?"

"Much better, Miss Mercy," Ruthie said. "Connor has given me the most bracing cup of tea."

"And a tincture," Connor added. "Something to dull the pain."

"Oh, Ruthie, I am sorry," she said.

Glancing over at Mr. Caitheart, she willed him to add his apologies to hers. After all, they were here because of him and his outlandish dragon of a machine.

He remained silent, but not immobile. Before she could ask what he was doing, he grabbed her arm again and forced her onto a chair at the end of the table.

She was about to tell him that he didn't have the right to manhandle her, thank you very much, when he bent low and peered at her head. She had no choice but to put both her valise and reticule on the floor beside her.

"It's only a small cut," she said.

"It's larger than you think."

"I'm fine," she said.

"You're not."

He went to a cupboard, gathered up a few items, then returned to her side where he laid a bag and a bottle of whiskey on top of the table.

"It's not necessary, really," she began, only for him to cut her off.

"You have a gash on your head, Miss Mercy," he said.

She really should have told him that her name wasn't Miss Mercy, at least not to him. The proper way to address her was Miss Rutherford. Yet the sound of her first name uttered in a Scottish accent was so intriguing that she kept silent.

"Lennox, I'll take Ruthie out to the garden for a little while. The sun will be good for her."

Lennox only nodded, being involved in pulling Mercy's hair out by the roots.

"Could you be a little more gentle?" she said.

"Could you be a little less critical?"

She really did like the way he spoke even if she disliked what he said. If he tried, just a little bit, to be agreeable, he might be excessively charming.

However, his demeanor was none of her concern. In a short while, as soon as Mr. McAdams borrowed his carriage, they would be gone from here. She would never see him again.

For that reason and because she was determined not to say a word no matter what he did, she remained silent when he brought a basin of water back to the table. He pulled out a chair and sat entirely too close to her before taking a few squares of white cloth, wetting them, then blotting her head.

"It's a good thing you don't have a mirror," he said. "You're bloody."

"I do have a pocket mirror," she said, "and I have examined myself, which is why I know it's only a scratch."

He didn't say anything in response, only shook his head.

Lennox Caitheart was an entirely disagreeable man. What a pity he was so handsome.

"I'm truly all right," she said.

He wasn't content to simply bathe her forehead. Now he was examining her scalp, a good two inches from where she'd been wounded. When he touched one spot, she let out a gasp.

"That's what I'm talking about, Miss Mercy. You have another cut here."

"Oh, for heaven's sake, either call me Miss Rutherford or Mercy. You're not my maid."

"Indeed I'm not," he said. "I'm not your servant at all. You might take note of that fact."

She had closed her eyes in the past minute and now she opened them again. He was still entirely too close. She could feel his breath on her cheek.

"This is really not necessary. As soon as we get to our destination, I'll have my wound taken care of."

"That might be too late," he said.

"What do you mean?"

He meant to disturb her, she was certain.

"You need to get the wound stitched," he said. "Otherwise, it's going to continue to bleed."

Without waiting for a response, he stood, went to the other side of the room, and grabbed the handle of the pump. After he washed his hands and dried them, he returned to stand in front of her.

"I'm going to have to cut a little of your hair," he said.

She would have clamped her hand over the area, but it was hurting now. Just as he'd said, she could feel the wound bleeding more profusely, thanks to his ministrations.

"Well?"

She was proud of her hair. It was dark brown with hints of auburn, thick and easy to manage. Yet here he was, claiming that he needed to cut it. Not just anywhere, but at the crown. She was going to look absolutely ridiculous with a bald spot at the top of her head.

"Must you? Cut my hair, I mean."

He stared directly into her eyes, his blue gaze giving

her the impression that he could see right through her, viewed her vanity, and found her wanting.

"It's not that I'm vain, Mr. Caitheart. It's just that I'm on the way to visit my family. My mother's family. I've never met them, except my grandmother and my aunt and it's been years since I've seen them. I'd much rather not be bald."

"I'll make you a promise," he said. "I will only cut what absolutely must go. You won't be bald, I can assure you."

She nodded, which he evidently took as agreement. The next thing she knew he was standing even closer.

He really should have warned her about what he did next. He took the whiskey bottle and poured it on the wound. Despite herself, she let out a yelp.

"It's just a little whiskey. Do you want something to chew on while I do the rest?"

"Is it going to be worse than that?" she asked.

"It's entirely possible. How brave are you?"

Up until this moment, she'd honestly thought she'd demonstrated a fair amount of courage. After all, she and Ruthie had crossed the Atlantic Ocean by themselves. They had traveled from Inverness. This had been a grand adventure and it had taken some amount of bravery to attempt it, but he was challenging her ideas about herself.

"I don't know," she said honestly.

"Well, then, I guess we'll have to see."

$\mathcal{H}$E SHOULDN'T HAVE teased her, but he found it almost irresistible to do so.

He'd been wrong. She wasn't simply beautiful; there was something different about her. Her face was an oval, her lips a perfect size. Her eyebrows seemed to be designed to call attention to her wide-set brown eyes and their long lashes. As he watched, her camellia-like complexion turned rosy, and her lips firmed in irritation.

He liked the way she spoke, her accent one of sharp corners and crisp consonants.

If he could have avoided it, he would have, but he was going to have to hurt her. His question about her bravery had been sincere. Her answer had startled him because she'd considered the matter for several seconds.

She was a stranger to his country, to his home. Once this act of charity, and expiation of guilt, was done, he would never see her again. He found himself strangely remorseful about that fact and gave a fleeting thought to asking for her address. Perhaps he could write her.

About what? His desperation to keep a roof over his head? His need to find the answer to flight? His loneliness? What in hell could he tell her, that he was worried about paying Connor's and Irene's wages next quarter? Could they discuss his lack of a vegetable garden? His vigil on sleepless nights as he walked from one room to another in his castle?

He was feeling out of sorts. The carriage accident had reminded him of another, that's all.

The sooner he was done here, the sooner she would be gone, and he would banish her memory as quickly as he could.

Chapter Five

Lennox parted her hair with his fingers, pressing down on what felt like the edges of the wound.

Mercy kept silent only through force of will. The very last person she wanted to whine in front of was this man. He would label her weak. Or something even worse.

He reached into the bag again, withdrawing something that looked like a sewing kit. She closed her eyes and vowed not to open them again until he finished.

She heard something liquid being poured into a bowl and couldn't help but open her eyes again.

"What's that?"

"Whiskey. I'm soaking the thread in it."

She closed her eyes again.

"Do you sing?"

"Do I sing?" she asked.

"If you do, I certainly don't mind if you occupy yourself by singing."

"While you stitch my wound closed?" she asked. "I have quite a good voice." She slitted open one eye to find him glancing down at her. "You're going to say that you do, too, aren't you?"

He shook his head. "No. I can't carry a tune. Now close your eyes again."

She took a deep breath and did exactly as he asked.

She heard him cutting her hair, each snip sounding as loud as a thunderclap. True to his word, however, it didn't feel as if he was cutting very much. At least she hoped he wasn't.

She was going to have to come up with some kind of explanation for her grandmother, something that didn't include having an accident. She could just imagine the lectures she was going to receive.

You were foolish to leave New York.

You've been impulsive and stupid and you're lucky you weren't killed.

Thoughts of that nature kept her occupied while Lennox drenched her scalp with more whiskey. She clutched her hands together and hoped she was brave.

The first stitch, even dulled somewhat by the whiskey, felt like a spear going into her head. She made a sound, but Lennox merely kept working.

She was bleeding again, if the warmth on her forehead was blood. Or it could be whiskey. Heaven knew he had poured enough. She would appear before her grandmother not only nearly bald but smelling of spirits. Poor Ruthie was sporting a sling and a bandaged arm.

How could she possibly explain the situation without admitting to the accident?

He stepped back. She opened her eyes and looked up at him. "Are you finished?"

"Almost."

She took another deep breath and forced herself to relax.

"You've been exceedingly brave," he said, blotting at her face with the white cloth again.

"Thank you, but I don't think I have been. Not truly."

"You didn't scream."

"I don't think I've ever screamed," she said. "Screaming doesn't come naturally to me."

He took another step back and studied her.

She wanted to ask him if he disagreed with her assessment. Instead, she remained silent, a difficult feat since he hadn't stopped staring at her.

"I'd thought you were an imperious sort of woman," he said. "But I don't think you are. I think, perhaps, that you get angry when you're frightened. People probably interpret that as being arrogant."

She didn't know what to comment on first, the fact that he had called her imperious or that he'd realized she had been frightened.

"Of course I was frightened," she said. "Your dragon was heading right for us."

"It's not a dragon."

She sighed. "Very well, your airship. Still, it was very scary seeing it nearly on top of us. I thought that I acted quite well in view of everything that happened. I certainly haven't been arrogant."

Yet she had called him insane. Perhaps that's what he was referring to.

"I apologize for calling you names," she said. "I never thought to see an airship in Scotland."

"We are not the backwater of the world, Mercy. Scotland abounds with men of vision and enterprise."

Here she was trying to make amends for her earlier comments and all she'd accomplished was to annoy him further. She'd been schooled in tact from her earliest memories. Why, then, was it so difficult to talk to this Scotsman?

"You are not hearing me," she said, deciding that their problem with communication was because of him.

"I beg your pardon?"

"I was attempting to be conciliatory and you inferred that I was insulting you. You couldn't be further from the truth."

He was gathering up his materials on the table, but he took the time to glance at her and smile. She hadn't seen that smile before and if she had, she might have been a great deal more polite.

He wasn't just handsome. Women no doubt threw themselves at him. Or pined after him. Or made up stories about how much he would adore them if only he gave them a second look.

"Then I should be the one to apologize," he said.

"In all honesty, your airship does look something like a dragon."

"Perhaps it does," he said. "It's designed along the lines of a governable parachute."

"Whatever you call it, it's very dangerous, isn't it?"

"It has an element of danger, yes. But doesn't everything? Your traveling from America, for example. Wasn't that dangerous as well?"

"Not until you crashed into our carriage."

He only smiled at her again.

She studied him for a moment before speaking. "Thank you for your ministrations on my behalf."

"You're welcome. Be careful when you wash your hair and have the stitches removed in a few weeks."

"Did you cut very much?"

"You probably won't even notice that it's missing."

She honestly doubted that, but he was trying to be nice. She could at least be the same.

"I'm sorry if I appeared arrogant or imperious. I didn't mean to be."

"It was my fault for thinking of you that way. I have a tendency to view beautiful women with a somewhat jaundiced eye."

Talking with him was not very easy. He threw her into constant confusion. First, he was rude and boorish. Then he'd called her arrogant and now he labeled her beautiful. If his aim was to keep her off-kilter, he was certainly accomplishing that.

No one had ever called her beautiful before. Oh, her parents, yes. And Gregory, of course, but he was trying to marry her. As James Rutherford's daughter she could have been as plain as a rock and he would have called her magnificent.

She could feel her cheeks warm and it wasn't the stitches, the whiskey, or the accident. Embarrassment and determination kept her silent. She wanted to ask him why, exactly, he thought she was beautiful. What was it about her appearance that made him think such a thing? Such questions would be unwise and immodest.

Now was the time for her to gather up Ruthie and be about their journey again.

This morning Mr. McAdams had said it wouldn't take very long to reach her mother's family home. Before the accident they had been on the road a good three hours. Perhaps she needed to speak with the coachman and find out what he considered "very long." She had no idea where they were or how much longer it would take to reach Macrory land.

Strangely enough, she wanted to tell Lennox that

she would never forget him, that this interlude at his fascinating castle would be a tale she would tell everyone when she returned to America. Depending on her audience, she might confess to how handsome he was. She certainly wouldn't tell people that they had grated on each other at first.

"Thank you for everything," she said. "I misjudged you as well. Perhaps I tend to look at handsome men with a jaundiced eye."

"Then it's good that we won't see each other again," he said.

She was foolish to feel disappointed at his comment. Of course they weren't going to see each other once she left his castle, but he didn't have to seem so pleased about the fact.

"You're right," she said. "We must be gone. Thank you for the loan of your carriage. I'm sure it won't be long to our destination. This morning Mr. McAdams said we should reach Aultbean in a matter of hours."

"Aultbean?" he asked, walking to the sink once more.

She nodded. "It's the closest village to my mother's family. The Macrorys."

He turned and faced her. His smile was gone and in its place was the same intense look he'd given her earlier.

"Your mother's family? You're a Macrory?"

"In a way, I guess. I'm a Rutherford, but my grandmother was a Macrory. Before she married, of course."

"Then you'll need to leave here as soon as possible," he said.

Without another word he strode from the kitchen, leaving her staring after him.

Chapter Six

$\mathcal{M}$ercy sat there for a few minutes, trying to figure out what had just happened. Evidently, Lennox knew of her mother's family and didn't approve of them.

Very well, the faster she left the castle and was about her journey, the better. She stood, a little too quickly because she was suddenly dizzy. Grabbing on to the table she waited until the room steadied.

The door opened and she turned, prepared to question Lennox about his aversion to the Macrorys. Instead, Connor stood there with Ruthie.

"If you're looking for Lennox," Mercy said, "I've no idea where he's gone. He seemed to take affront when he realized our destination."

"Macrory House," he said, glancing at Ruthie then back at her. "I knew the minute I heard that he wouldn't be pleased."

"What on earth have the Macrorys ever done to him?"

"His older brother fell in love with one of the Macrory women. They eloped and were killed in a carriage accident."

"Both of them?"

He nodded. "Either way, the families haven't spoken to each other since then."

What a sad tale.

"By being related to the Macrorys, even distantly, I guess I'm unwelcome at Duddingston Castle."

"He doesn't mean to be that way, miss. It's just that Robert was his older brother and he raised Lennox after their parents died."

She didn't answer Connor. There was nothing she could say, after all.

The sun had done Ruthie some good, because she didn't look as pale as she had earlier.

"Are you going to be all right?" Mercy asked. "Do you feel up to a carriage ride?"

"You haven't far to go," Connor said. "You're almost on Macrory land."

"Truly?"

"You could easily walk it on another day," he said, glancing at Ruthie again. "Not today, of course, not with you injured."

Ruthie didn't say anything, merely gazed up at Connor with worship in her eyes, her cheeks pink with emotion.

At another time Mercy would have cautioned Ruthie about revealing her emotions so readily. It was never a good idea to be vulnerable, especially in such a strange place. Besides, nothing could come of any relationship with Connor. He was a Scot. Ruthie was an American.

Yet who was she to give advice about love to anyone?

She had gotten carried away by the madness surrounding the start of the Civil War. She'd watched as Gregory went off with his regiment, his blue uniform pristine, his vow to protect the Union still ringing in her ears. She'd been determined to wait for Gregory, to be one of innumerable women who monitored the newspapers for information about a loved one's regiment, made bandages, knitted socks, and prayed for their soldier to come home safely. After a while, however, the heady excitement of the potential for war had faded to the reality and horror of it. Then, as it had continued to drag on for four long years, she realized she'd made a terrible mistake.

She didn't love Gregory. She wasn't even certain she liked him. Yet she couldn't reject a suitor who was fighting for the Union. Nor would it have pleased her father if she'd done so.

Once the war was over, however, all their differences came to the forefront. He'd come home, expecting that they would wed shortly without any type of courtship. She was a fait accompli, a mission he'd already accomplished. Why should he continue to pay her any attention when it was certain she was going to be his wife?

He hated the South, yet her mother had been born and reared in North Carolina. He was obsequious to her father, which made her wonder if he was marrying her for her or because of who she was, the only daughter of James Gramercy Rutherford. He was not affectionate with his own family, claiming that his mother was too interested in his life and that his sisters were occupied with foolish pursuits. Having met them, Mercy found Gregory's family—including his father whom he rarely mentioned—to be lovely people. The fact that Gregory didn't feel the same was concerning.

Gregory was ambitious, witness all the times he met with her father to discuss plans for one or another of her father's companies. He knew there wasn't an heir who could step into her father's shoes and he'd already decided that he would be that person by virtue of marrying Rutherford's daughter.

She might have gone along with the marriage had it not been for something Gregory had said, a simple statement that was an indication of her future and made her reconsider everything.

She'd come down to greet him one evening and he'd frowned at her.

"I prefer the blue dress, Mercy. I don't like the one you're wearing. Have you changed your hairstyle? It isn't flattering."

His comment had been an indication of things to come. She wouldn't have a choice about anything in the marriage. The way she wore her hair, the color of her dress, the people with whom she'd associate, or how she spent her days would be subject to the whims of her husband. Where once she'd followed the dictates of her parents, now Gregory would be in charge.

The war had changed a great many things. She'd read that women were expected to take on duties they'd never before assumed. They kept businesses running while their husbands went off to war. They planted crops, went to market, and formed associations of women helping women. Gone were the days of women having to remain subservient or without a voice.

Yet change, progress, and growth had skipped Gregory somehow. All he wanted in a wife was an obedient female.

Her parents had never seen her as grown and Gregory would always view her as his puppet.

The seeds of her rebellion had been planted that night.

When she'd told him that she no longer wanted to marry him, Gregory had lost his temper. No doubt because he envisioned all his ambitious plans being destroyed. He wasn't mollified by her reassurances that her father wouldn't dismiss him from his position just because they were no longer engaged.

She'd never anticipated that he would refuse to accept her decision.

Badgering her hadn't worked. Neither had his incessant calling on her or bringing her gifts. Unfortunately, her parents saw his new attentiveness as proof of his affection.

She'd talked to her mother one morning, bringing up the subject of her engagement.

"I don't want to marry Gregory," she'd said, the words difficult to say.

She'd never disobeyed her parents and rarely challenged them. She didn't want to hurt her mother or cause her any pain. Life had not been easy for Fenella Rutherford, despite the fact that she was married to a wealthy man.

Her mother had looked surprised, but hadn't said anything right away. The unexpected silence had been a void Mercy felt compelled to fill.

"It's not that he's not an admirable man, Mother. Or that he wouldn't be a good husband."

"Then why do you feel that way, Mercy?"

She looked down at her hands nervously twisting together. "He and I don't suit."

"You were very supportive of Gregory during the war."

She nodded. She had been. What kind of woman

would have broken an engagement to a soldier fighting for his country?

"Nor does Gregory seem to feel the way you do, Mercy."

How did she tell her mother that Gregory truly didn't care about her, that he would have married her if she'd had two heads as long as she was James Rutherford's daughter?

She tiptoed among the words, picking the right ones. Her mother had to understand.

"I don't wish to marry him, Mother. I can't envision living the rest of my life with Gregory."

"That's only silliness, Mercy, and you're not a silly girl. It's natural for a young woman to feel as you do. Marriage is not as frightening as you think it is. You'll see."

"I don't want to marry him, Mother. Truly."

Her mother had shaken her head and smiled. Reaching over, she'd patted Mercy's arm.

"Your feelings will go away the minute you marry him, Mercy. I'm sure of it. It's only fear that's making you say these things now."

Perhaps it was fear, but not the type her mother thought. She didn't want the life her parents and Gregory had planned for her.

"We won't hear any more of this, all right? You'll be fine. What you're feeling will go away in time. You'll even smile at what you're feeling today."

She'd known, then, that her mother didn't understand. By extension, neither would her father. The marriage would happen whether she wanted it or not.

Coming to Scotland had not only been a way to obtain some freedom, but it had been a respite, of sorts, from Gregory. The freedom wasn't going to last, of course. Sooner or later she'd have to return, but when she did, hopefully he would have finally understood that their engagement was over.

No, she wasn't the one to give advice of the heart to anyone.

Less than an hour later—the time no doubt expedited by Lennox's wishes—they were on their way. The coach was more luxurious than she'd expected, the springs such that Ruthie didn't suffer any jarring movement. Still, Mercy had taken advantage of Connor's offer and propped a pillow beneath Ruthie's arm.

Mr. McAdams's horses followed, their reins tied to the back of the carriage, an act that necessitated the vehicle's slow speed. Even so, less than a half hour later Connor looked out the window and announced that they had arrived.

They truly were close to Duddingston Castle, neighbors in this isolated part of the Highlands. The carriage pulled into a graveled drive and Mercy looked out the window.

For the next few moments she stared, incapable of speech.

Macrory House was built of red brick in the shape of an E, with the circular drive facing the middle part of the letter. She'd never seen such an ill-named structure in her life. It wasn't a house. Instead, it was a series of buildings linked together by porticos and extensions. The whole of the complex was easily the size of a city block.

At least two dozen chimneys topped the sloping roofs and at least that many white-framed windows faced the approach.

She truly hadn't considered that her mother's family

might be wealthy enough to build the palace that was Macrory House.

"Is that it?" Ruthie asked, her voice faint.

Mercy glanced at Connor for confirmation.

"That it is," he said.

When they stopped in front of the impressive two-door entrance framed by carved white stone, two servants emerged from the house, one to hold the horses and the other to open the carriage door. Each was dressed in identical green shirts with black trousers.

She hadn't expected livery, either, but she had a feeling that she should be open to anything from this point forward. Nothing had been as she'd anticipated from the moment they left Inverness this morning.

Connor left the carriage first, holding out his hand for Mercy and then Ruthie. It wasn't at all proper for Connor to grip Ruthie's waist in an effort to assist her down the steps, but that was another comment Mercy wasn't going to make.

"Welcome to Macrory House."

She turned to find that they were being greeted by a white-haired man standing at the top of the steps. He was attired in a black coat, green waistcoat, and cravat. His somewhat amenable expression immediately faded as he stared at the carriage.

"Does that belong to Caitheart?"

Connor answered. "It does, McNaughton, and I'll be moving it as soon as I can."

The older man, whom she assumed was the butler, turned his attention to her. His mouth thinned, his bushy white eyebrows lifted, and his hazel eyes hardened. All because of Lennox's carriage. Evidently, the antipathy between the families was equally shared.

"I'm McNaughton, miss," he said in a voice as cold as ice. "How can I be of service?"

The inference being, of course, that he couldn't possibly help anyone who'd arrived in a Caitheart carriage.

Mercy had given a great deal of thought on how to announce herself to her relatives, except that she'd never considered that she would have to do so through a servant. She'd envisioned a tearful reunion with her grandmother and her aunt. Then, they would introduce her to her great-uncle and other relatives.

That vision had been turned on its ear.

"I'm Mercy Rutherford," she said. "I've come to visit my grandmother."

McNaughton tilted his head slightly, but before he could ask, Mercy said, "Mrs. Ailsa Macrory Burns."

If the butler was surprised, he didn't show it. Instead, he nodded and stepped aside.

"If you'll follow me, miss," he said, his tone still icy.

She only nodded before turning back to Connor and the coachman.

"I'm so sorry about everything, Mr. McAdams," she said. "I quite enjoyed the journey before the accident."

He nodded and pulled on his hat, bowing a little.

"Thank you for your help," she said to Connor. "You've been very kind."

She gave Ruthie a chance to say her farewells in relative privacy as she grabbed her valise and reticule and followed McNaughton up the steps.

Chapter Seven

$\mathcal{M}$ercy was led to an understated room with a circular table in the middle adorned with a bouquet of summer flowers. A large fireplace sat on the opposite wall. Other than a bench in front of the fireplace, there was no other place to sit.

McNaughton bowed slightly and removed himself, no doubt to alert her grandmother to her presence.

She placed the valise beside the bench and rubbed the marks on her left palm. Soon she would give it to her grandmother and be rid of it. She wouldn't have to worry about the money anymore. Or carry the heavy thing everywhere she went.

There was no doubt of the artistry around her. The overmantels were friezes of female figures dressed in diaphanous garments. The ceiling was similarly carved with cherubs and angels. Two deep-set windows with a view of the drive were framed with burgundy curtains. Between the windows sat small tables, each topped with a tall mirror, their white frames carved with vines and small flowers.

As she waited for Ruthie she realized that she should have sent word somehow. She shouldn't have assumed that her relatives—people she'd never met and only had a brief correspondence with over the years—were living in poverty.

At the very least she should have warned her grandmother. Ailsa was not a young woman and the journey from North Carolina had probably been a difficult one.

Ruthie entered the room and Mercy went to her side.

"Come and sit down," she said. "You've had a tumultuous morning."

Ruthie only nodded.

Her lack of speech coupled with the fact that she hadn't uttered one of her superstitions since the accident was worrying Mercy. She wanted to say something uplifting, but nothing occurred to her. Was Ruthie in pain? Was that why she wasn't acting herself? Or did her somber mood have something else at its root? Was it Connor?

It might be possible for Ruthie to see Connor again, but nothing would come of it. They weren't going to remain in Scotland. There was no sense involving yourself in a romance with no future.

McNaughton entered the receiving room, bowed slightly, and asked, "May I offer you some refreshments, miss?"

At least the butler hadn't said anything about their deplorable condition, although he was looking down his very long nose at both of them. According to the mirror she kept in her reticule, she had spots of blood on her white collar. Her hair was matted at the crown with dried blood and she no doubt smelled of whiskey.

Ruthie looked even worse with her bandaged arm and her pale face.

They needed beds, something to eat, and a warm welcome, not necessarily in that order. That was not a comment she was going to make to the butler, however.

"Thank you, no."

"I've conveyed word to your grandmother that you are here," McNaughton said.

That was all. He didn't say anything further, leaving her to imagine their reception. Hopefully, her grandmother would appear soon. Otherwise, she had the feeling that they were going to be left here for hours.

Would they be turned away? If they were refused what would they do? They didn't have a carriage. For that matter, they didn't have a driver. From the conversation on the way here, Connor was going to see Mr. McAdams back to Inverness.

Perhaps she could borrow a carriage from the Macrorys to take her and Ruthie to Inverness as well. Except that she wasn't altogether certain that Ruthie could make the trip until she had a chance to rest.

No, her relatives were just going to have to allow her to stay for a few days.

How odd that she'd never doubted her welcome. Perhaps she shouldn't have made that assumption.

She wasn't feeling all that affectionate toward the Scots right at the moment. Other than Connor and Mr. McAdams, she hadn't met very many of them whose acquaintance she would like to pursue. Certainly not Lennox Caitheart. Or McNaughton who looked down his nose at them.

She doubted if the butler could have handled the events of the morning any better than they. In fact, McNaughton looked like the type of man who would quail in the face of adversity. Or blame his problems on some other person.

Or perhaps she was just out of sorts because she was tired and her head was aching.

"Mercy?"

She turned at the sound of her name to see her aunt Elizabeth striding toward her, her arms opening in a hug and her smile so welcoming that tears peppered Mercy's eyes.

"When McNaughton said you were here, I couldn't believe it. What are you doing in Scotland? But I'm so glad to see you. It's been so very long. How is your mother? And your father? They are well, aren't they?"

She didn't know which question to answer first, but it wasn't necessary to talk at all as she was being warmly embraced.

A moment later, Elizabeth pulled back and studied her.

Her aunt was ten years younger than her mother, but all the Burns women looked alike. In fact, they were so close in appearance it was like seeing a younger version of Fenella Rutherford in Elizabeth. Both women had dark brown hair, deep brown eyes, and fine features in an oval face.

Mercy was shocked at the change in her aunt. The last time they'd seen each other, five years ago, her aunt had had a sparkle about her, an enthusiasm that seemed dampened now, no doubt because of the privations she'd suffered in the war. Or it could have been simply grief that had aged her. The black dress she wore was no doubt in honor of her fiancé.

"I was so sorry to hear about Thomas," Mercy said.

He'd been a tall, robust, and handsome man with a deep voice and a laugh that made others want to join in. The world—Elizabeth's world—must be different without Thomas in it.

Elizabeth only nodded, her wan smile acknowledging Mercy's words.

"What are you doing here?" Elizabeth asked.

She'd forgotten about her aunt's voice. Her accent was of North Carolina, just like her mother's was occasionally when she was either tired or moved in some way. Her grandmother, or *seanmhair* as Mercy had been taught to call her, spoke with an accent made up of a Scottish lilt combined with a North Carolina cadence she'd acquired after living in America for the past forty years.

"We'd heard that you moved to Scotland," she said.

She would talk about the valise of greenbacks later. It didn't seem appropriate to discuss money right at the moment.

"Mother was concerned that you were all right."

"And she sent you here to ensure our well-being, is that it?" Elizabeth asked, her voice filled with doubt.

"In a way."

Elizabeth frowned at her, but the expression was fleeting.

"Now tell me what has happened to you. McNaughton said you came here in a Caitheart carriage. Is that true? And why do you look as if you've been coshed on the head? And that poor girl? What has happened to her?"

Ruthie had stood at Elizabeth's entrance, but Mercy waved her back down.

"This is Ruthie," Mercy said, going to the other woman's side. "She and I traveled together from New York. We had a bit of an accident this morning and our carriage was damaged. Ruthie suffered a broken arm."

"What on earth happened?"

She gave her aunt an expurgated version of events. She couldn't eliminate the flying machine entirely, but when she explained how the accident happened, her aunt pressed her lips together and looked exactly like Mercy's mother when she was incensed and at a loss for words.

She didn't have any doubt that news of their adventure would be transmitted to New York, as soon as the postal service could deliver the letter. If her aunt didn't write her mother, her grandmother surely would.

"Mr. Caitheart doesn't seem to have a great deal of fondness for the family, Aunt Elizabeth."

"That's all right. We don't like him any more than he likes us. Most of the time we can ignore each other." She sighed. "It seems as if, by moving here, we've only traded one war for another. But never mind that. Come, we will get both of you settled. I'll give the housekeeper instructions to prepare a room for both of you. In the meantime, McNaughton is very good at handling injuries. Could he look at your arm?" That last question was addressed to Ruthie who nodded in response.

Mercy wasn't in the position to refuse.

A few minutes later Ruthie had her arm examined by the butler in a room off the kitchen. He frowned a good bit, then announced that Lennox's handiwork was acceptable and that Ruthie's arm lacked only time to heal correctly.

As for herself, she was subjected to McNaughton's look of disapproval once more as he poked and prodded her head. Finally, he sat back, announcing that she needed a bandage until the wound had a chance to heal.

He wrapped a wide linen bandage around her

head, frowned, then looked to Mrs. West, the house-keeper.

"Have you any hairpins?" he asked, his tone almost polite.

The housekeeper nodded, opened a drawer, then handed him a few hairpins. Evidently, Mrs. West was prepared for every contingency. McNaughton fixed the end of the bandage to Mercy's hair, gouging her scalp as he did. She thought he was finished, but he kept wrapping the linen around her head until half her forehead was obscured.

When he was finally done, the butler frowned at her once more, accepted Aunt Elizabeth's thanks with a small smile, and left the room without saying a word to her.

As soon as he was gone Mercy pulled the mirror from her reticule and sighed inwardly at her reflection. She had scratches on her face and was developing dark circles beneath her eyes. Coupled with McNaughton's mummy-like ministrations, she was a sorry sight.

"You've been injured, Mercy," Aunt Elizabeth said. "No one cares what you look like right now."

Mrs. West led Ruthie away to her room. Mercy promised to come and check on her later. Ruthie only nodded again, her uncharacteristic silence worrying.

"Shall we go and see Mother?" Elizabeth asked.

No, she really didn't want to see her grandmother right now. She wanted to go hide under the covers somewhere, or have a day or two to prepare.

Instead, she forced a smile to her face, picked up the valise, and followed her aunt.

Chapter Eight

All of the furniture at Macrory House was made by Chippendale, the information passed along by Elizabeth. Mercy didn't know who Chippendale was, but it was obvious he was a master at carpentry. Every piece of furniture was beautifully crafted for its intended purpose.

Even the banister of the massive staircase in the middle of the house was lovely. She'd never seen anything like the various shades of carved wood twisting to follow the incline of the stairs.

Mercy gripped the valise with her left hand and the banister with her right.

"Why don't you let one of the servants take that to your room?" Elizabeth asked, glancing at the bag.

"It's something I've brought for Seanmhair," she said.

Elizabeth didn't ask any further questions.

At the second-floor landing, her aunt turned left and walked to the end of the corridor. There, a set of double doors stood like a wall between Mercy and her grandmother.

"I think you'll find Mother a little changed, Mercy. These past years have been difficult for her."

Mercy nodded, understanding. Her grandfather had

died four years ago, at the start of the war. It had been
up to her grandmother and her aunt to keep the farm
going. In the months preceding the end of the war,
their house had been burned to the ground and all
their crops, such as they were, torched. They'd been
left with nothing, difficult enough when one was
young and resilient. But her grandmother was in her
sixties.

"It's all right, Mercy," Elizabeth said.

No, it wasn't, but her aunt was kind to say so. Mercy
managed a smile, clutched the valise tightly in her
hand, and followed her aunt inside the room.

A massive four-poster bed sat in the center of the
room. The wood dome and frame were covered in
royal blue silk, the fabric worked into the design. The
mattress looked to be twice as thick as normal.

Two bookcases—no doubt made by Chippendale—
sat on either side of the bed and held a selection of
books, glass flowers, and gilded boxes.

The painting over the white fireplace was of lush
flowers, the pinks, greens, and golds of the artwork
echoed in the carpet and upholstered chairs.

This bedroom was the perfect backdrop for her
aristocratic-appearing grandmother, who now sat in
one of the wing chairs before the fireplace like a queen
expecting one of her subjects.

Before the war, Mercy's family had made an annual
pilgrimage to North Carolina. Her childhood was
marked by such visits. They stayed for a few weeks,
and it was always with a sense of relief that they returned home.

During those visits her grandmother never lost an
opportunity to lecture Mercy on various aspects of
womanhood. There was such a long list of things she

should or should not do that over the years she had written them down in a journal and always took care to reread her notes before leaving for North Carolina. Whenever she made a mistake, such as laughing too loud or running when she should have strolled, her grandmother didn't criticize her. Instead, Fenella was the focus of her irritation.

"What are you teaching that girl? Do you act that way in New York?"

That had been the refrain during those childhood visits.

Mercy was her father's daughter and because of that she could never win her grandmother's approval.

Fenella had married James Rutherford after meeting him at The Patton in Hot Springs. Her father had brought his mother to the resort, thinking that the North Carolina spa would help the older woman's arthritis. At the time, Ailsa and her husband had approved of the marriage, especially since James Rutherford was exceedingly wealthy. Over time, and especially in the years before the start of the Civil War, their feelings had changed. Her father was now an enemy and, by extension, so was anyone related to him.

"She has a set of standards, Mercy," her mother had said. "She insists that everyone follow those standards."

"Is she very unhappy?" Mercy had asked that day.

Her mother looked surprised, then pensive. "I don't think she is," she answered.

"She seems unhappy."

She thought the same thing now.

Ailsa Macrory Burns was tall for a woman and rather formidable despite being so slender. Her beautiful hair was snowy white and swept up into a coronet at the top of her head. Her blue eyes were probably her best feature, large and cool, capable of freezing the object of her irritation to the spot. Her chin was pointed, her entire face too thin, no doubt a result of the conditions she'd had to endure before coming to Scotland. Her nose, aquiline and regal, however, regrettably reminded Mercy of a beak.

Overall, the impression Mercy had was that Ailsa was a force of nature, someone with whom you dealt with care.

She went to greet her grandmother, kissing her cheek as she had always done. Ailsa's cheek was papery and tasted of powder. Her perfume smelled of lavender and something else that reminded Mercy strangely of grass.

Pulling back, she smiled and said, "You look well, Seanmhair."

"You look abominable," Ailsa said, frowning at her. "What are you doing in Scotland, Hortense?"

Mercy tried not to cringe.

Her grandmother was the only person who called her that. Her full name was Hortense Abigail Paula Sarah Gramercy Rutherford. She bore the name of her father's mother, that of her two deceased sisters and the feminized version of her deceased brother's name, as well as her father's middle name. Her parents had acquiesced to calling her Mercy when she was old enough to announce that she hated the name Hortense.

"Mother wanted you to have this," she said, putting the valise beside her grandmother's chair.

Ailsa ignored the bag. Instead, she studied Mercy as if disliking everything about her. At any other time, she would never have dared to appear before her grandmother wearing a soiled dress, but what did it matter now since she was wearing a turban and she looked so abysmal?

"What have you done, Hortense?"

"She was in an accident, Mother."

Ailsa glanced at her youngest daughter with a frown. "Was I asking you, Elizabeth?"

Elizabeth only shook her head. Mercy was grateful that she hadn't had to travel from America with her grandmother. She could only imagine what that journey had been like for her aunt.

"Well?"

"There was a carriage accident," Mercy said.

Her grandmother didn't ask if she was hurt or the reason why she was wearing a bandage. Nor had she asked one question about Mercy's mother, as if her eldest daughter was no longer any of her concern.

Had the war burned away any trace of maternal affection?

Mercy bent and opened the valise. Elizabeth gasped at the sight of all the money, but her grandmother didn't say a word.

"What is this, Mercy?" her aunt asked.

"We'd heard how difficult it was in the South. Mother wanted you to have this, but you'd already left for Scotland."

Elizabeth looked like she was blinking back tears. Her grandmother, on the other hand, appeared to have been carved from marble. Her face was frozen in a rictus of expression. She might look the same the moment after she died. Only her eyes bore any sign of life and they were fixed on Mercy.

"I don't want anything from James Rutherford," she said, the words forced through thinned lips.

"The money isn't from my father. It's from my mother. Your daughter."

"It's one and the same," Ailsa said. "Do you think

I would take charity from the man responsible for the deaths of my friends and the ruination of our farm?"

She stared at her grandmother, not one word coming to mind. Her father had only a small interest in an armaments company. Other than that, most of his businesses were focused around shipping. Did her grandmother think that he was responsible for the blockades of the Southern states? Or that he had done something directly to impact the outcome of the war?

"Take your blood money. I don't want it. And you can tell your mother that I am not yet pitiful enough to take her charity."

"It's an act of love," Mercy said. "Not charity."

"Don't you talk back to me, child. I'm not yet infirm, either."

Nor was she very likable. Four years had changed her grandmother. There was a bitter edge to her now that hadn't been there before. She could remember her grandmother laughing, but the woman seated in front of her now didn't seem capable of amusement.

"I can't take it back," she said. "I've come all this way to give it to you."

"Then you've been extraordinarily foolish," Ailsa said. "Go home, Hortense. You're not wanted here."

Mercy glanced at her aunt. Elizabeth grabbed the valise, closed it, then reached out and took Mercy's arm.

They didn't say anything as they left. Nor did her grandmother speak.

Charity? It hadn't been charity. Nor was her father's money somehow tainted. Ailsa Macrory Burns, however, didn't want to hear contrary thoughts or protests.

Her grandmother was right. She'd been extraordinarily foolish.

Chapter Nine

When Elizabeth opened a door in the middle of the corridor, Mercy saw that her baggage had been delivered to her room. A young girl, attired in a green dress with a white apron and cap, was finishing unpacking Mercy's trunk and hanging up her garments. No one but Ruthie had ever touched any of her things and it was an odd experience having a stranger go through her clothing and personal articles. But Ruthie shouldn't be working until she was feeling better.

"This is Lily," Elizabeth said.

The girl curtsied to her, the first time anyone had ever curtsied in Mercy's presence.

"If you need anything at all you have only to ask Lily."

Mercy nodded. "Thank you, Lily."

Inwardly, however, she vowed to do things for herself. After all, she hadn't always had Ruthie. Nor was she helpless.

When Lily left, Mercy went to the chair in front of the vanity and sat heavily.

"Seanmhair hates me, doesn't she? And Mother? Does she hate her, too?"

"She hates the world right now, Mercy. She lost everything she knew. Thankfully, Uncle Douglas welcomed us with generosity and affection. She isn't treated as a poor relation here, but as a member of the family who's finally come home. For the first time in a long time, it's given her some kind of position."

Her aunt had been forced into the same situation, with the added loss of her fiancé, yet she hadn't descended into bitterness. The events Ailsa had endured had only whittled down her sharpness. It had always been there, ready to be a weapon.

"If Father's messenger had found you in North Carolina, would she have taken the money then?"

"I don't know," Elizabeth said. "I hope she would have. Things were awful there, Mercy. It would have been an act of foolishness to refuse, but Mother has her pride."

Mercy nodded. She'd met her share of prideful people today.

"I can't leave right now," she said. "Ruthie needs a chance to recuperate."

"Of course you can't. If nothing else, I want to spend some time with you. Besides, Mother didn't really mean what she said."

Mercy was certain that her grandmother had meant exactly what she'd said.

"Did Fenella really send you here?" Elizabeth asked.

She couldn't lie to her aunt. "No." Her mother would have been terrified by the idea.

"I think it was a very generous gesture to bring the money to Mother, but I suspect it is not the true reason you're here."

Elizabeth returned her gaze and it was almost like

seeing a younger version of her mother. Both women had suffered losses. Both had a look on their face that said they were anticipating being hurt again.

How could she explain, without sounding ungrateful, that she'd desperately wanted her freedom?

She'd been cosseted, protected, and wrapped in bunting for fear that something might happen to her. If she wanted a new book one was delivered to save her a trip to the bookstore. All manner of people came through the doorway of their house to offer a multitude of products to the Rutherford heiress: sweets, dresses, hats, gloves, shoes, lace, hairpins. She didn't need to lift a finger and anything she wanted was provided.

How did she tell her aunt about the guards who accompanied her everywhere? Or when she had the sniffles, five physicians were called in to treat her? It was as if her parents were terrified she was going to be stolen or was going to die at any moment.

"Freedom," Mercy said. "I needed to get away."

"Couldn't you have settled for something easier, instead of crossing an ocean?"

She didn't answer that question. It wouldn't have worked to simply visit another town or state. She needed to get far enough away that her father couldn't send men out looking for her. She didn't have any doubt that he would have done exactly that and that she would have been returned home within days.

"Was your life so bad that you would do something so dangerous, Mercy?"

"I felt like I was in a prison, Aunt."

"We're all in some kind of prison, my dear niece. Life itself is a prison. We're all expected to behave in certain ways," Elizabeth continued. "Society dictates our behavior. Decency, honor, loyalty—they are not just traits that men possess."

"Why can't you possess all of those traits and still have some control over your life?"

"It's not that easy," Elizabeth said.

"I should think it would be no more difficult than a decision. How do I wish to live my life? In accordance with someone else's notions of it? Or doing what I want to do?"

"Isn't that a selfish way to behave?"

"Is it? I know men who behave that way, Elizabeth, and they're heralded as having their own minds, of being trailblazers."

"Are you talking about Lennox Caitheart?"

She'd been thinking of Gregory, who did exactly what he wanted to do at any time he wanted to do it.

"I wasn't," she admitted, "but he might well be an example."

"You would be foolish to model your behavior after his."

"Would I? I envy his freedom." She smoothed her hands over her knees then clasped them again.

For most of her life she'd been a dutiful daughter. She tried to be as perfect as any person could be. Not once had she spoken for herself. If she had she had no doubt about her father's reaction. *You wouldn't want to cause your mother any pain, would you? She's suffered so much already.* She couldn't even allow herself thoughts of rebellion, not until the day she actually rebelled.

"You do realize, don't you, that you've done something that must surely be worrying your parents."

Mercy nodded. "I know and I'm sorry for it."

She should've spoken up years ago, but nothing

was ever as important as her parents' feelings. Hers certainly weren't. Living in the enormous gray house had been like being encased in glass.

"What made you decide to leave?"

She didn't know how to explain that, either. One day the glass had simply shattered. She knew she had to escape for a little while. The money was only an excuse, a rationale she'd given herself, but if it hadn't been there she would've done something else, gone somewhere else. If life was the prison her aunt thought it was, she'd become an escaped prisoner.

"You have to go back. You know that, too, don't you?"

Mercy nodded. "There's a price you pay for everything you do," she said. "My father taught me that. I'll go back and be dutiful once more." There was no other alternative, but even as she said the words she felt a cloud descend over her mood.

Her aunt sat on the edge of the bed and regarded her somberly. "They must be frantic."

"I left them a letter, telling them where I was going."

She'd also told them that she'd taken the valise and intended to convey the money to her aunt and grandmother as her mother had originally wanted. She'd also asked them to stop planning the wedding. She hadn't wanted them to incur any additional expense because she was determined not to marry Gregory.

"I booked passage on one of Father's ships, which was tantamount to being chaperoned by the captain and his first officer. They were very kind and promised to take word to my parents that I'd arrived safely."

"Only to have a carriage accident on the way here," Elizabeth said, surprising her by smiling.

"I sincerely hope that no one tells them," Mercy

said. "Otherwise, they'll think that they were right all these years."

"I won't tell them," Elizabeth said. "I can't speak for Mother."

That meant her grandmother was going to lose no time telling her mother everything. Yet she was no longer a child. She hadn't been a child for well over a decade.

"I understand why I live the way I do, Aunt Elizabeth. I just don't want to live like that anymore. Even Gregory was their choice."

"Gregory?"

"The man they want me to marry."

She didn't tell Elizabeth about Gregory's heroic reputation, that he'd dispatched a number of Southern soldiers in countless battles. Not when Elizabeth's fiancé had been killed in the war.

"My parents planned for Gregory and me to live with them. Father had already given orders to start renovations on the second floor."

Even after she became a wife she wouldn't be able to escape her protective parents.

"And you don't want that?" Elizabeth asked.

"No."

"How does Gregory feel about it?"

"He's very ambitious. When James Gramercy Rutherford wants you to marry his daughter and live with him in his house, what man would refuse?"

Elizabeth didn't say anything, but her soft smile spoke volumes. Perhaps a man who wasn't so ambitious or who chose his own path in life.

Her aunt stood and came to her, bent down, and gave her a hug.

"I'm sorry. I wish I could change the situation for you."

"Me, too," Mercy said. "Not just my situation, but yours, too."

Elizabeth smiled at her. That simple expression eased Mercy's discomfort from the verbal flogging she'd received from her grandmother. And maybe from being banished from Duddingston Castle by Lennox Caitheart.

"I'll leave you to rest for a while," Elizabeth said. "I'll come and get you for dinner in a few hours. Unless you would like a tray here."

"I'll go down to dinner," Mercy said.

She doubted she was going to look any better in the next few days and wasn't about to spend all that time in her room, although it was a lovely place. The wealth that had created Macrory House was evident in this guest chamber as well.

Lemon-colored silk fabric lined the walls and upholstered the chaise, the headboard, the bed hangings, and the window curtains. Watercolor paintings of flowers and herbs in gold frames hung in various places on the wall. In addition to the four-poster bed, the room was furnished with a vanity, a small secretary, a bureau, and an armoire that looked wide and deep enough to accommodate all the clothing she'd brought with her.

After Aunt Elizabeth left, she put the valise with the money at the bottom of the armoire. Coming to Scotland had been a fool's errand, but at least she'd obtained some freedom for herself, however short it might be.

Mercy removed her traveling dress, grateful that the cuffs and collar were detachable. She would just replace them rather than try to remove the spots of blood on her collar and the dirt on the cuffs.

She'd never needed Ruthie's help in undressing and she removed her traveling dress and crinolines with ease. Her corset was never tight and she merely unfastened the busk at the front, placing the garment in one of the bureau's drawers.

Lily had hung her wrapper just inside the armoire. Mercy put it on before going into the bathing chamber adjoining the bedroom, grateful for the natural light in the large mirror.

Her eyes looked dull and the dark circles were more pronounced now. Her skin appeared waxy and as pale as Ruthie's had been. Even her lips looked odd, nearly bloodless.

McNaughton had not stinted on the bandaging material. She looked exotic. Or exotic and injured.

Lennox Caitheart had a great deal to answer for. What a pity she'd never see the man again to tell him that to his face.

Chapter Ten

$\mathcal{I}$t took only a matter of seconds for Mercy to fall asleep on the comfortable mattress. When she woke it was to find that three hours had passed. She quickly donned a green-striped dress over two crinolines and her kid slippers—a welcome respite from her traveling shoes.

She used a little rouge on her lips, but it made her complexion look even more pale in contrast. She wiped most of it off and decided against applying any color to her cheeks.

Like it or not, she looked as if she had been in an accident.

Elizabeth knocked on the door a quarter hour later.

"Were you able to get any rest?" her aunt asked.

"I was," she said. "But I still feel like I could go to bed and stay there for a week."

"I felt the same when we arrived in Scotland, but we didn't have to suffer through an accident. Are you certain you feel well enough to go down to dinner?"

"I do, but would it be possible to check on Ruthie first?"

"Of course," Elizabeth said, leading the way to the back stairs.

She was glad to see that the rooms occupied by the servants at Macrory House—or at least Ruthie's room—were large, well lit, and quite attractive. She found Ruthie sitting up in bed, Lily sitting on a chair beside her. The two women were eating their dinners and looked as if they were engaged in an animated conversation.

Mercy didn't mean to eavesdrop, but after a second or two it wasn't difficult to ascertain that they were talking about Connor. There might be a feud between the Macrorys and the Caithearts, but it evidently didn't extend to the servants.

"How are you feeling?" she asked.

"Much better, Miss Mercy. I've been treated like a princess."

"Is there anything that you need?"

"Are there donkeys roundabouts?"

"I'll ask," she said.

Ruthie nodded, evidently satisfied. "I'll do for you in the morning, Miss Mercy. I'm sure to be feeling fine."

"No, you won't," Mercy said. "You've been hurt and the most important thing is for you to feel better."

Ruthie looked as if she wanted to argue, especially when Lily spoke up and said, "If you ring, Miss Mercy, I'll be glad to help you."

"Thank you, Lily. As for you, Ruthie, I'll check on you in the morning. But I don't expect you to be out of this bed."

Once they left the room, Elizabeth spoke. "Donkeys?"

"Donkey hair," Mercy answered. "Ruthie believes that donkey hair will stave off a cold, an infection, and in this case, probably help her arm to heal."

When Elizabeth didn't say anything, Mercy smiled.

"Ruthie has many folk remedies and sayings to go along with them. The fact that she wants donkey hair is a good sign."

"It is?"

Mercy nodded. "That means she really is feeling better. She hardly said a word to me all afternoon."

It felt odd going down to dinner when it was still light outside. But, then, it didn't get dark until nearly midnight in the Highlands in summer, a fact Mercy had discovered on arriving in Scotland.

As they descended the main stairs, Elizabeth spoke about the people she would soon be meeting.

"Your great-uncle, Mother's brother, is a very strong-willed man. Uncle Douglas will question you endlessly, Mercy, but don't take it to heart. He does the same thing to everyone when he first meets them."

Her father had a similar questioning style bordering on interrogation.

"And then there is Flora," Elizabeth said. "She's your cousin and Douglas's granddaughter."

They didn't have any more time to speak because they'd reached the dining room.

The Pink Dining Room, so called because of the color of the walls, was surprisingly restrained in decor given the remainder of Macrory House. The small room was furnished with a large square table with wooden chairs and upholstered seat covers.

True, there were carved cornices representing a variety of fruits and vegetables and sideboards constructed of the same wood as the table. But the lamps weren't overly large. Nor were there any cavorting imps and goddesses on the ceiling.

Her grandmother, great-uncle, and cousin were already seated, all of them looking fixedly at her. She didn't blame them for staring. She hadn't been able to improve her appearance in the past few hours.

A male servant helped her to her chair in the middle of the table, opposite her cousin and next to Elizabeth. She thanked him, which was no doubt the wrong thing to do, earning her a frown from her grandmother.

Ailsa was sitting at the foot of the table while Uncle Douglas was at the head.

Her great-uncle was tall and portly with a mane of white hair that stuck out in different directions on the top of his large head. Mercy got the impression of a Scottish lion with a roar of a voice, one that boomed out at her as she sat.

"Welcome to Macrory House, lass. It's happy I am that you're here. We've more Americans here now than Scots." He extended a large hand toward the woman opposite Mercy. "This is my granddaughter, Flora."

Flora looked to be a few years younger than her with an appearance unlike the rest of the women in the family. Her eyes were blue, her hair a shade of dark red Mercy had rarely seen. She was exceedingly pretty, one of those females who looked lovely despite the circumstances. She would appear as presentable first thing in the morning as she would drenched in a downpour, crying or laughing, and sick or well.

No doubt she would wear a turban of bandages with aplomb and look gorgeous while doing so.

Mercy instantly felt ugly and clumsy.

"That Caitheart fool caused the accident, I hear," Uncle Douglas said. "Him and that infernal machine of his. Damn idiot. Hasn't got a bairn's sense. Always said that he would come to no good."

She had the curious compulsion to refute her great-uncle's words, although she was certain that Lennox would not welcome her defense. Still, he wasn't quite an idiot. Nor was he insane as she'd called him. If anything, he was brave. She wouldn't have the courage to jump from a mountain like he had in an airship.

"I think what he's doing is quite exciting, myself," Flora said.

Mercy witnessed the most amazing transformation, something she'd only seen in one other person. Her great-uncle's face changed when he looked at his granddaughter. It was like everything inside of him softened, smoothed the lines of his face, and prompted his smile.

Her father looked the same way when he was with Jimmy. In his case, however, she thought it was more sadness than love that prompted the change.

"You be sure to mind yourself, lassie," Douglas said to Flora. "You'll not go near that place and you'll stay off the road. I'll not let another Caitheart harm a Macrory woman again."

At least she'd learned about the reason for the feud at Duddingston Castle. She doubted if her relatives would have told her otherwise.

She decided she would focus on her dinner because she was genuinely hungry. Better that then say something that would be taken wrong. Besides, it would be a good way to avoid her grandmother's eagle-like stare.

At least she hadn't been banished from the table and the house. She had a feeling, however, that she hadn't found a haven at Macrory House.

Chapter Eleven

"If you don't come and eat your dinner now, I'll give it to the pigs."

"We don't have pigs," Lennox said, glancing up at Irene.

Connor and Irene were the only servants at Duddingston Castle, if that label was entirely fitting. Irene had taken over the position of housekeeper, cook, maid of all work, busybody, and his mother.

She'd been in the village this morning or she would have inserted herself into the drama as usual.

He returned to his examination of the tail structure of his airship. It had been damaged in his controlled crash this morning. Before he went up again, he was going to have to repair it as well as the damaged sail.

"I mean it. I haven't stood over a hot stove for hours for you to ignore what I cooked."

"How could I possibly ignore it?" Lennox said. "I've been smelling onions all afternoon."

Irene put her fists on her hips and sent him a familiar glare, but she didn't look like she was going to move anytime soon. Most of the time their confrontations ended in a draw. Evidently, Irene was all for winning tonight.

"It's tatie scones and fish skink," she said. "Your favorites."

It was except for the fact that he had eaten it entirely too much in the last month. Beggars, however, couldn't be choosers. He'd spent a good deal of money on his airship. Too much, actually, and now he had to pay the price by eating fish until he was certain he was growing gills.

He put down his tools, looked up at her, and surrendered.

"Just bring it in here," he said.

He'd taken over the Laird's Room, a small chamber off the Clan Hall that allowed him some privacy. Here his work was shielded from prying eyes. Not that he had all that many visitors. He'd gotten a reputation for being a recluse and a grumpy one at that. Or maybe it had been Irene who scared off any visitors. She was as protective of his time as he was.

"I'll not do that," she said. "You're alone too much as it is."

"You do remember that I pay your wages?"

"That's something else entirely," she said. "We'll be talking about an increase there. Jean earns more than I do and doesn't do half my work."

Her sister worked for the Macrorys. If he hadn't liked Irene so much, he would have dismissed her the minute he learned that. The familial relationship, however, had proved to be helpful over the years. He had some insight into the family's actions, thanks to Irene and her sister.

"I'm not made of money like the Macrorys, Irene."

"Then you'd better get busy and invent something else," she said.

That admonition was new.

"I'll take my dinner in the kitchen, then."

He had no intention of eating by himself in the dining room. The place was a gloomy cave and he avoided it as much as possible.

Besides, this way, Irene would join him for dinner. Duddingston was large but empty, a catacomb of memories and ghosts, whistling winds and strange noises. No doubt she wanted the company as well before she went home to her cozy little cottage.

"I'll be there in a moment."

She took that for the capitulation that it was and nodded.

He folded the torn sail and wondered if it could be mended. Irene had known of a seamstress who'd helped him fashion the cloth around the wooden struts. Could tiny stitches make it air worthy again or did he have to start with a new sail? Cost was a factor, but so was safety.

He'd review his finances and see if he could afford a new sail. Otherwise, he'd have to stay on the ground and make theoretical assumptions rather than actually flying.

Maybe he was as insane as Mercy said. Normal people, however, didn't change the world and he was all for doing a little changing. There were ideas that needed to be explored. Inventions that needed to be made.

Sometimes he felt that the world was filled with cupboards, some of them open but most of them closed. All a man had to do was to choose a field and open the cupboard. It's why they were laying transatlantic cable. Why it would soon be possible to send a telegraph from London to New York. It was why the roads were paved with a smooth surface that made it possible to travel long distances in relative comfort.

Why the steam engine had been invented and why there were almost daily advances in medicine. Science was only one of the cupboards that was being opened.

He wanted to be among the first to understand the principles of flight. That meant actually being up in his own aircraft and not on the ground.

Maybe he'd even prove to Mercy that he wasn't insane but merely a visionary.

Had she been warmly welcomed by her relatives? No doubt they were filled with indignation about the accident. He could just imagine the conversation.

He'd enjoyed talking to Mercy, even liked their sparring, at least until he'd found out who she was. After that, he simply wanted her gone from Duddingston.

Perhaps he was insane, after all. Otherwise, why would he remember the look on her face when he told her to leave? It wasn't indignation or humiliation. She hadn't been embarrassed. No, he had the errant thought that he'd hurt her feelings. That was so ridiculous an idea that he pushed it from his mind as he left the Laird's Room.

Walking through Duddingston was like visiting the past four hundred years ago. The castle had been built for defense. Comfort hadn't been a consideration which meant that succeeding generations had tried to make the structure more habitable. For the most part it had been a battle between the castle being a home or a fortress. When the west tower had crumbled, there hadn't been money to repair it. The same with parts of the curtain wall. He had spared the time and money, however, to replace the roof where it had fallen into the Clan Hall.

When Duddingston was still intact there had been plenty of clan members, people who needed to be sheltered in times of trouble and protected in times of plenty. The Caithearts had never turned their backs on their clan, but the numbers had dwindled over the years, people choosing to emigrate or move to the south of Scotland where the living was easier. They hadn't been like the Macrorys who'd made members of their clan little more than serfs and then, when the land couldn't support them, tossed them from their homes and replaced them with sheep.

His title of laird was only ceremonial, carrying with it none of the very real responsibilities of his grandfather and those before him.

As he passed through the Clan Hall, he could almost hear the protests, the raised voices, the clamor from gatherings far into the past. If the laird proposed something unpopular there would've been raised fists, red faces, and Caithearts who stood with legs spread apart and hands on hips, ready to do battle.

But there would have been raucous laughter as well, music played by fiddlers and pipers to celebrate one of life's milestones.

Now there was only silence broken by the cawing of birds or the soughing of the wind around the castle. Occasionally, an adventurous squirrel would scramble over the roof he'd repaired, the sound loud enough to wake a dozen ghosts.

He was like a spirit himself, the sole product of all those Caithearts who stretched back four hundred years. Had they any idea that their bloodline would narrow until only one of them would be left?

That was a thought he didn't wish to have and he walked faster, reaching the kitchen with a feeling too much like relief.

Chapter Twelve

"$\mathcal{I}$ hope you will express your displeasure to him," Ailsa said. "The man mustn't be allowed to escape the consequences of his actions."

At first Mercy thought her grandmother was talking to her, but then realized that Seanmhair was speaking to Uncle Douglas.

From the conversation around her, she gathered that the families didn't communicate. Even if Douglas unbent enough to talk to Lennox, it might well be a wasted effort. She didn't think that Lennox would care what the older man had to say.

Although he hadn't expressed any regret that the accident had happened, he'd treated Ruthie and her with care and had loaned his carriage to them. He didn't have to do any of that. In fact, he'd been charming for long stretches of time. However, it didn't seem wise to mention that to her family.

"How did the accident happen, lass?" Uncle Douglas asked.

She gave them all a quick account, eliminating certain details from her explanation such as calling Lennox's airship a dragon. How foolish that sounded now.

"He set Ruthie's arm and tended to my head," she added. He should get credit for that, at least.

"As well he should," Seanmhair said. "The man is a menace." She directed her attention to Flora. "You'll be wiser than my granddaughter, my dear. Don't go anywhere near Duddingston Castle."

"I didn't know where I was when the accident happened," Mercy said in her own defense. "I didn't know anything about your feud with the Caithearts, either."

"It isn't a feud, lass," Douglas said.

It sounded like a feud. Lennox couldn't tolerate her presence because she was a Macrory. Douglas acted as if there was something unclean about the Caithearts. What was it, if not a feud?

She looked to Elizabeth for support, but her aunt was busying herself with her napkin, staring down at her lap as if it held the most interesting view. Mercy had often done the same at home, especially when her mother and father were arguing.

If her father was firm about a topic and her mother disagreed, it didn't mean that Fenella remained silent. Occasionally, her father would appear to goad her mother into speaking her mind, almost as if he wanted to be challenged. There were plenty of times when she heard her mother do exactly that.

According to her grandmother, who had adopted many of the ways of Southern women, a proper female never raised her voice in anger. The frontal assault, as she termed it, was never preferable and made a woman look less than gracious.

It seemed to Mercy that the frontal assault was the only way for a woman to survive in Scotland.

"I'll not have your parents thinking that you have a haven here, Hortense. I've already written them, telling them I've no liking for the situation."

Mercy looked at her grandmother. She hadn't expected anything less of this new Ailsa.

It was obvious that there was nothing she could say that would soften Seanmhair. She certainly wasn't going to explain that she'd wanted a little freedom from her situation at home. Ailsa would only frown at that explanation and tell her that she was acting in an unladylike manner. Nor would she tell anyone that the prospect of marriage to Gregory was like a huge black cloud on the horizon.

The Rutherford-Hamilton wedding was planned for the next spring and was going to be ostentatious. She wouldn't be surprised if a parade down Fifth Avenue was arranged. It wasn't so much a rite of passage as an announcement to the world that James and Fenella Rutherford's only daughter was marrying. For that, all of New York needed to stop, if just for a moment, to acknowledge the day.

She'd already seen the white carriage that would carry her to the church. The frame, roof, and wheels of the vehicle were gilded. The interior was upholstered in tufted white silk. No doubt it would be pulled by two pairs of magnificent matched horses.

The bridal gown had been ordered from Worth. The flowers had also been reserved in advance in such quantities that blooms would probably be picked from all over the country and shipped to New York.

In other words, if money was no object then anything was possible.

She truly hadn't come to Scotland to hide. Nor had she envisioned her grandmother's ancestral home as a permanent refuge. The journey here, the journey back, the days—or weeks—she would remain at Macrory House only constituted a temporary respite, a short stint of freedom before she returned to the life already carefully mapped out for her.

"Do you understand what your grandmother is saying, lass?" Uncle Douglas asked in his booming voice. "We can't be seen to agree with your foolishness."

"I do," Mercy said calmly.

"We're happy to offer you hospitality until your maid heals, but I don't want your parents to think that we approve of the situation."

"Or of your journey here, Hortense," her grandmother said. "In my day such a thing would have been scandalous enough to ruin a girl's good name."

"Have you nothing to say for yourself, then?" Douglas asked.

Mercy shook her head, uncertain what words would pacify the older man.

He scowled at her, an expression matched on her grandmother's face. Elizabeth was still looking down at her lap, but Flora was staring at her with wide eyes. Perhaps everyone cowered before Uncle Douglas, but she was James Rutherford's daughter. She didn't cower before anyone.

"You've got a head on your shoulders, Flora," he told his granddaughter. "I'll not have you act the fool like this cousin of yours."

"No, sir," Flora said, smiling prettily.

She was to be seen as an example, then. Someone not to emulate. How very strange since she'd been exemplary most of her life. The sensation was almost heady. Mercy Rutherford, unbiddable, wicked, and recalcitrant.

The first course was served and she occupied herself with eating the fish soup and ignoring the side-eyed glances from her relatives. Conversation swirled around her, dealing with Lennox Caitheart, a new litter of puppies, and Flora's upcoming visit to Edinburgh.

The feeling of being isolated was a new one, but not entirely unwelcome. At home, her parents hung on to her every word. Sometimes, she had the feeling that even her breathing was monitored both awake and asleep. Being ignored was almost a gift.

She wasn't required to speak until dessert. She'd eaten all the other courses in complete silence. That had never before happened and it was such a novel experience that she thoroughly enjoyed it.

"Why haven't you married, cousin?" Flora asked.

The question took her off guard. She glanced up to find everyone at the table looking at her.

"Is it normal for American women to be so old before they marry?"

Granted, she was a few years older than she might have been if the war hadn't intruded. Still, she was hardly ancient.

No one seemed to think Flora's question intrusive or rude. Even her grandmother looked merely curious. Not once did she send a censorious glance in Flora's direction.

It was a strange sensation watching someone else being treated as she was at home, as if she was special and could do nothing wrong. Mercy couldn't help but wonder what other people thought when viewing her parents' behavior around her.

"I'm going to be married next spring," she said. Even to her own ears her voice sounded dull and lacking in enthusiasm.

"Why so far away? If I was to be married, I'd be clamoring for my wedding to be held immediately."

Mercy only smiled in response. She wasn't going to mention the complicated arrangements, the hundreds of people involved in ensuring that the Rutherford-Hamilton wedding was the event of the season.

With any luck it wouldn't happen.

Nor was she going to tell anyone how she felt about Gregory.

How odd to feel a spurt of kinship for Lennox Caitheart. They'd both earned the ire of the Macrorys, albeit for different reasons.

Chapter Thirteen

"What's she like?" Irene asked.

"What is who like?"

"The Macrory girl. The new one from America. The one you nearly killed."

Lennox looked up from his soup and stared at her across the table. She would have had a fit if she'd known that he'd treated Miss Gallagher on this same table this morning.

"Who told you that?"

No doubt it was Jean. The two sisters had a remarkable way of communicating. If anything important happened at Macrory House, Irene heard about it within the hour. He often suspected they had runners between the two homes. But her ability to ferret out knowledge wasn't limited to Macrory House. Irene hadn't been here this morning, but she already knew the details of what had happened.

"She's female," he said.

"Is she pretty?"

He took a bite of crusty bread and made a point of chewing slowly.

Irene wasn't the most patient of people. By the time

he was ready to answer, she had already started frowning at him.

"I suppose she is, if you like that sort of woman."

"What sort of woman would that be?" she asked.

"Used to getting her own way in all things. Insistent. A barnacle."

"How long were you with her?"

"What does that matter?" He reached for his bread again, frown or no frown.

"She seems to have made an impression on you in a short time."

"It was a difficult situation. You can tell a great deal from people in difficult situations."

"So," she said, standing and taking her empty bowl and plate to the wash stand, "are you going to see her again?"

"Why on earth would I want to?"

"To ensure her health, perhaps. To check on her wound. McNaughton has put quite a bandage on it, I hear."

"He shouldn't have," Lennox said, annoyed. "It will heal faster if it's exposed to the air."

"Why don't you send a note explaining that?"

"I doubt McNaughton would listen to anything I have to say."

"Not to McNaughton. To the Macrory girl. Or are you going to let all that fancy education go to waste?"

Irene was the only person in his life who made a point of bringing up his medical training as often as she could. He'd returned to Duddingston Castle after Robert had died, a necessity as it turned out. If Robert hadn't died, Lennox had planned to finish his education and set up his practice in Inverness.

Things happened. Plans sometimes went awry. He couldn't live in the past, however much Irene brought it up.

"She'll be fine," he said.

"They don't like her."

He put down his spoon and stared at her. "What do you mean, they don't like her? They have to like her. She's a Macrory."

Irene shrugged, went to the stove and retrieved the kettle, pouring boiling water into the dishpan.

"Not according to what Jean said. That block of ice of a grandmother didn't have much good to say."

"What about Flora and Elizabeth?" he asked, as familiar with the residents of Macrory House as Irene. She related tales of their exploits, flaws, and failings nearly every day. At first he told her that he didn't like to listen to gossip. After a while, however, and especially after she divulged how often he was a topic of conversation, he found himself waiting for Irene's stories.

"Flora hadn't met her yet and poor Elizabeth just wanders around the house like a ghost herself."

He knew her tale, too. Her fiancé had been killed in the American Civil War. Of all the people in the house, he was inclined to like her the most, for all that they'd never met.

"She'll be fine," he said again, but the first niggling doubt entered his mind. "Are they going to send for the physician?"

"Not that I've heard," Irene said. "Why should they? A physician has already examined both of them."

"I didn't finish my training, Irene."

She waved a hand at him as if to dismiss his words. "Yer bum's oot the windae! You and I both know that you were nearly finished. What you missed probably doesn't matter. If you weren't determined to become a bird."

He really didn't want to start this conversation. He knew that Irene's starchy comments were because of her affection for him. For that reason, he tried to ignore what she said on the subject of his airships. He couldn't convince her. She was of the mind that if God had wanted man to progress in such a way He would've filled his arms with feathers.

"If I send her a note," he said, before she launched into a full tirade, "will you take it to her in the morning?"

She smiled, an expression that always startled him. Irene had a utilitarian face, broad and long with lines that had been carved by years and experience. Yet when she smiled, time fell away and he could see the girl she'd been, eyes alight with mischief.

"That I'll do," she said. "You go on and write the note."

He shook his head, knowing that she would badger him until he did so. A good thing he'd already finished his dinner.

The castle's library had seen better days. The roof over the room had been damaged and a number of the books—some of them valuable—had been irreparably damaged in his grandfather's day.

He used the library as an office, but not that often. Most of his sketches and his calculations were performed in the Laird's Room where he'd devised a sloping table that allowed him to see a drawing at a different angle. Sometimes all he needed was a different perspective to figure out a problem.

Now he sat at the desk and looked around him, wondering how long it had been since he'd entered the library. Robert had used this desk, that pen. The silver inkwell was his favorite, as was the silver blotter, two items Lennox could never bring himself to sell.

His older brother had epitomized family to him. Although he'd lived a number of years in Edinburgh, knowing that Robert was at Duddingston had always been reassuring. They'd been separated by seven years, but together they'd faced the deaths of their parents. First their mother, then their father less than a week later, both of influenza.

Even so, he'd never considered that Robert would die.

After Robert's death everything fell apart. The Macrorys wouldn't honor the grazing agreement that Robert had made with them. Their herds had to be sold. The seaweed contracts weren't renewed. Nor were the pacts Robert had made with the fishermen in the village. He saw Douglas's fine hand behind all those events.

Within a matter of months, he was out of money.

That first year had been difficult. He'd never shouldered the responsibility that was suddenly thrust on him. To get out of his financial difficulties he could have sold Caitheart land, but he'd balked at that. Instead, he'd taken another course and found a buyer for his design of a new chimney flue. The money from that sale had lasted them almost a year. Before the year was over, however, he'd gone back to his notebook of ideas and constructed a strongbox that opened in the middle, allowing the two sections to part.

He'd never sold one of his airships, however. Those felt like part of him, a segment of his identity. Although he wouldn't be the first man to fly—that had already been accomplished in a glider and a hot-air balloon—he did have an idea that might be revolutionary if he could prove that it worked. The air itself could power an aircraft.

The first time he'd successfully piloted his governable parachute design and landed without incident, he'd come to the library. Here he felt closer to Robert than anywhere at Duddingston. Robert had brought in some of the artifacts from the Clan Hall, arranging them on a few of the bookcases, as if he wanted the history of Duddingston Castle around him as he worked.

What would Robert have thought of his efforts in the past five years? A question he'd asked himself numerous times. He didn't know. He would never know. The elder brother he thought he knew had changed. Robert had fallen in love. A woman had dictated Robert's actions. A Macrory woman.

He pulled out a piece of stationery from the middle drawer, dipped the pen in ink, and began to write.

The Macrory woman had told him her last name, but he couldn't remember it. He was sure that Irene knew it, but he just wanted to write the note and get it over with. So he addressed it to Miss Mercy, feeling a little foolish for doing so.

I have heard that your wound has been bandaged. It will heal much faster if you leave it open to the air. I realize that such an action may challenge your vanity, but rest assured it will not be for an extended time.

He frowned at the words he'd written. Perhaps he could've been less didactic. Or more gracious. He could have wished the rest of her visit to Scotland to be uneventful and pleasant. However, being at Macrory House, he couldn't imagine how that would happen. He could take out that remark about her vanity. She hadn't struck him as excessively vain.

She'd been genuinely concerned about her maid. In that respect she was unlike most of the Macrorys, at least according to Irene through Jean.

Maybe he should reword the whole thing. Better yet, he shouldn't send her a note at all. The sooner everyone forgot about the accident, the better. Besides, she'd called him insane.

Yet he couldn't help but remember the look on her face when he told her to leave. He'd never been that rude to anyone before, but the accident and the fact that she was a Macrory summoned forth all sorts of memories and emotions.

He wanted his brother back and that was impossible. He wanted someone to be punished for what had happened to Robert and that was impossible, too. No one was at fault. The carriage accident had been caused simply by too much speed.

Before he talked himself out of it, he sealed the letter, writing her first name on the flap. There, that should both assuage his conscience and silence Irene.

Chapter Fourteen

$\mathcal{M}$ercy would have been tempted to stay in bed if it hadn't been for the knock on the door.

She was in no hurry to encounter the inhabitants of Macrory House this morning, especially her grandmother. The passage of years had softened her memory of Ailsa. She'd had nothing but empathy and compassion for the desperate times her grandmother and aunt had gone through, yet it was all too obvious that those emotions weren't wanted or appreciated.

All she'd accomplished by coming to Scotland was injuring Ruthie.

She slid from the bed and went to the door barefoot.

"Good morning, Miss Mercy," Lily said, bobbing a curtsy. "It's a fine day, it is. With a breeze blowing from the north, giving us a hint of the autumn."

Mercy expected Lily to enter the room, but she stepped to the side and grabbed a large silver tray.

"Is that my breakfast?" Mercy asked, staring at the tray piled high with food.

"Cook and I didn't know exactly what you wanted, miss, so we thought a little bit of everything was called for."

Mercy closed the door behind the young maid and

watched as she placed the tray on the small table beside the chair.

While Lily arranged everything, Mercy put on her wrapper.

"Tomorrow morning, miss, if you'll tell me what time you'd like to get up, I can come and open the draperies for you. That way, you can greet the day with a beautiful view of Scotland itself."

"Thank you," Mercy said, a little overwhelmed by such a bright and bubbly manner first thing in the morning.

Usually, she and Ruthie merely nodded to each other until they were each sufficiently awake. She wasn't an early riser, especially if she'd been to an event the evening before, but neither was she known to lay in bed until midmorning. Normally, the sounds of the household woke her.

"You really didn't need to bring me a tray," she said. "I can come down to breakfast tomorrow."

"None of the family does, miss. The only meal they take together is dinner."

How odd, but the practice might be a blessing. She wouldn't need to undergo her grandmother's scrutiny until this evening. Unless, of course, she was summoned beforehand. That was entirely possible. Ailsa liked to lecture.

After visiting the bathing chamber, she returned to the bedroom, sat, and tasted her Scottish breakfast. Blood pudding was something she would avoid in the future, but the scones were wonderful. The eggs were excellent, as well, along with the buttered toast. Cook made bread each Wednesday, she was told, and the butter was churned from cream from their own cows.

"Have you worked here long, Lily?" she asked as

Lily bustled around the bed straightening the sheets and bedspread.

"The better part of three years, miss. Still, I'm the newest here."

She finished eating while Lily flew through the room dusting all the surfaces and rearranging the items on the bureau, nightstand, and vanity, chattering all the while. Mercy answered all her questions as she ate.

Yes, New York was large and filled with people. No, she had never before visited Scotland. Yes, she thought the scenery was awe-inspiring. She'd never seen the like. No, she wasn't chilly and didn't need a fire lit.

When she was done with breakfast she thanked Lily for bringing the tray as well as straightening the room, but declined any help dressing.

Once the maid was gone she went to the armoire and selected a blue-striped silk dress with a snug bodice and puffed sleeves. Her grandmother couldn't say that she was improperly attired. Except for hats. She hadn't wanted to bring along her collection of hats—that would have been too much luggage. As it was, she had a trunk and three valises while Ruthie had only one small bag.

After dressing she worked on her hair. There was nothing she could do about the bandage, but she gathered the rest of her hair into a dark blue snood. She was just going to have to look odd for a little while.

At least the circles beneath her eyes weren't as dark as they'd been yesterday. Plus, her face seemed to have a little more color.

She gave herself a final look in the pier glass, made a face, and opened the door, heading for the servants' stairs, hoping she could remember which room was

Ruthie's. She found it on the second try, grateful that the first room had been empty of an occupant.

Ruthie called out for her to enter and when Mercy did she found the other woman sitting up in bed, her head tilted back against the headboard, eyes closed.

She blinked open her eyes and smiled wanly at Mercy.

"You're in pain," Mercy said.

She'd forgotten, until just this moment, to ask if the Macrorys owned a donkey and hoped Ruthie didn't remember. She would rectify that oversight the minute she left the room.

"Just a little, Miss Mercy."

"Were you able to sleep at all?"

"Some."

The breakfast tray on the nightstand was barely touched.

"I should send a message to Lennox that we need some more of his tincture," Mercy said.

Ruthie closed her eyes again and leaned her head back. "That would be nice."

"Perhaps Mrs. West has something for pain. Is it your arm?"

"I'm sore all over, Miss Mercy."

"I'm going to find you something and then I'll come back."

Ruthie only tried to manage a smile again.

Mercy found her way down to the kitchen, thanks to two friendly maids she encountered along the way. Each of them greeted her with a smile and answered her question with a beautiful lilting accent. She wanted to engage all of them in further conversation just to hear them talk.

She peeked into the housekeeper's office, found it

empty, and went to the small dining room attached to the kitchen.

Two women sat there.

Mercy blinked, but it was no use. There were two Mrs. Wests sitting in front of her, both of them with brown hair, their blue eyes watching her with an expression of puckish humor.

"We're twins," both women said together.

She nodded, having come to that conclusion.

"We've met before," the one on the right said. "Mrs. West."

"She's Jean," said the woman on the left. "I'm Irene."

Even now she could barely see any differences between the two women. Their smiles were identical. They had the same strong faces, the same square jaw and prominent noses.

"How does anyone tell you apart?" she asked.

Both women smiled at the same moment.

"I don't work here," Irene said. "Only Jean does. I work at Duddingston Castle, but I've come today because of you."

"Me?"

The other woman nodded before pulling the letter out of her dress pocket. Mercy walked forward and took the letter.

"Lennox wanted me to give it to you," Irene said.

Both women looked at her expectantly, so she opened the letter in front of them, read it, folded it back up, and placed it in her own pocket.

Instead of talking about the letter's contents, she said, "Does the family own a donkey?"

The twins looked at each other and then back at her.

"I don't believe so," Mrs. West said. "What would you be wanting a donkey for, miss?"

She explained Ruthie's belief in folk remedies and added, "She's in pain this morning."

"We've no donkeys, but we do have some medicine she could take. Would you like some of that?"

"I would. Thank you."

Mrs. West stood and left the room, leaving her alone with Irene.

"He's a good man," she said, looking at Mercy's pocket. "Once you get to know him you'll figure that out well enough. It's getting to know him that's the difficult part."

"I can assure you that I have no intention of getting to know him."

Irene sighed. "He's offended you, then. Now that's a pity. I'm thinking that you could go back to America with tales of the handsome Scottish earl you met."

"Earl?"

Irene nodded. "He's the Earl of Morton. I forget if it's the eleventh or the twelfth. It's one of those. A lot of history behind that title."

"He certainly doesn't act like an earl," Mercy said, having met her share of titled Englishmen. New York was occasionally visited by aristocratic young men eager to be feted and adored by a title-loving American population.

They pranced, these English dandies, affected a certain manner of speech, and were filled with knowledge of their own uniqueness.

Lennox Caitheart had been as dissimilar as a bird was from a fish.

She was torn between wanting to know his story and being irritated at the man. He'd insulted her in his three-sentence letter. How dare he call her vain?

"He was very concerned about your wound, miss."

"I don't know why," she said.

"He studied as a physician in Edinburgh."

That was another surprise. First an earl and now a doctor?

"Why doesn't he practice?"

"He didn't finish. Robert died and he came home."

She pulled out a chair and sat, giving in to her curiosity.

"Why does he hate my family so much?"

"I don't think he actually hates them," Irene said. "Maybe he's jealous. Or a touch resentful. It's an old story, one you hear often enough. Mary Macrory and Robert knew each other as children. She went off and married a man by the name of Thomas Shaw. They had a daughter and when he died Mary and Flora came back to Macrory House. That's the way of the Macrorys. When there's trouble, they come home just like your grandmother and your aunt."

She didn't say anything, mulling over Irene's words.

"When she returned, Robert visited that very day to express his condolences. Soon enough they fell in love."

Mercy remained silent. She was not going to beg for the rest of the story, however much intrigued she was.

Thankfully, Irene continued without being coaxed.

"Douglas was all for Mary remaining a widow, I think. Flora might have felt the same, but I'm not sure. Mary had other ideas, however, and the two of them left one spring morning without a word to anyone. They never came back."

"What happened to them?"

"The carriage overturned. A common enough tale.

A sad one in this case. Robert died immediately, but Mary lived a few days. Long enough for Douglas and Flora to reach her."

"I'll never forget how they looked when they returned," Mrs. West said, entering the room carrying a dark brown bottle. "It was as if life had been sucked right out of them."

"The two of them weren't just eloping," Irene said. "They were escaping."

"Escaping?" Mercy asked.

Irene nodded. "What other people wanted them to be. Robert had always been known as a man who was responsible for raising his younger brother, for caring for the castle. He was responsible to a fault and yet in this one thing, this one act, he wasn't."

"And Mary didn't want to remain a widow," Mrs. West said. "Love changed them."

The two sisters looked at each other.

Thankfully, they didn't expect her to comment because Mrs. West handed her the bottle and gave her instructions as to its use.

"I wouldn't leave it in her room, miss. People get confused when they're in pain. She might take another dose before it's time and that would be dangerous."

Mercy nodded. "Thank you, Mrs. West. I'll keep it with me." She looked at both women. "Thank you for telling me the story, too."

She was almost to the door when Irene spoke again.

"Douglas and Flora had each other, but Lennox lost the one man who'd been a rock and an example to him. When Robert died, I thought Lennox would never stop grieving. It's only been in the past few months, with his airship, that he's been more like himself. I think you would like him, miss, if you got to know him."

Mercy only nodded. Lennox was blessed to have someone who believed in him the way Irene did. But he hadn't sent Irene a nasty letter, one that irked Mercy the more she thought about it. She was going to dispense with the turban of bandages and perhaps her wound would heal faster.

He didn't have to know that she'd taken his advice, however.

Chapter Fifteen

After spreading out the sail on the floor of the Clan Hall and examining it in minute detail, Lennox decided that it was better to err on the side of caution and replace it. He didn't want to end up crashing on his next flight. It had been a small miracle that he hadn't been injured last time.

Thoughts of his landing led to thoughts of *her*. He wished the woman would stay out of his head. He had more important things to think about.

"I don't know what you wrote in your letter," Irene said when she returned to Duddingston a week ago. "But it didn't please her one bit."

Maybe he should have taken out the part about Mercy's vanity.

"Don't worry, Irene. She won't be here long enough to make an enemy out of her."

Irene huffed. "She's not leaving all that soon. She has a care for that Ruthie of hers. She hasn't let the girl do a thing this past week. So Ruthie stays in her room except for a few hours when she comes down to the kitchen."

"Where Jean solicits information from her," he said.

Irene looked like she was considering various ways

of answering his question. Her brow was furled and her lips pulled to the side. He almost rescinded the question when she spoke.

"Aye, she does, but Ruthie's as loyal to Miss Mercy as Miss Mercy is to Ruthie. We've learned a bit about the house in New York, though. Ruthie called it a mansion and it sounds equal to or bigger than Macrory House."

"So Miss Mercy is a wealthy American."

She nodded. "That she is, but she doesn't act it. I've never heard her talk about money like some do."

Like Flora, for example, who knew how much each of her dresses cost and lost no time telling anyone who would listen.

Surprisingly, Irene hadn't said a word about Mercy in the past week. The silence was unlike Irene who had a comment about almost anything, from the morning fog to his red eyes when he chose to work late into the night.

Summer in the Highlands encouraged you to stay awake longer. By the time it got dark it was early morning. Sometimes, he simply stayed awake, especially if he had an idea for a new wing or an invention or two.

He went ahead and wrote the seamstress in Inverness, ordering a new sail. The replacement wouldn't be ready immediately, which meant that he had an opportunity to test out another design. This one was potentially more dangerous than his first airship. For that reason, he made copious notes. Connor could forward those on to the men with whom he communicated if anything happened to him.

This morning would be a perfect time to carry out the test of the new airship. That is, if he could get Connor's attention.

The other day, when he and Irene had gotten into a spirited discussion about Irene's claim that she needed another frying pan, Connor hadn't injected a calming note into the conversation. Nor had he appeared to hear anything they said. Instead, he sat staring off into the distance—in the direction of Macrory House—with a lovelorn look on his face.

Lennox and Irene had stopped talking about the frying pan, the truce brought on more by their confusion over Connor's behavior than any agreement. Yet Lennox knew he'd lose that battle eventually, like all the battles Irene championed. He was only a thrall in Irene's kingdom. When he said as much to her, she only laughed, agreeing without a word spoken.

Whenever Irene returned from Macrory House Connor made a point of asking about Ruthie. Lennox had a suspicion that Irene was acting as a go-between for the young maid and Connor.

According to Irene, Ruthie was healing well. The pain she'd experienced in the first few days had disappeared. She would, no doubt, be pampered until it was time to remove the bandaging from her arm. Perhaps he should offer to do that. At least, then, he could be assured that it was done correctly. From what Irene had said, McNaughton had a habit of being ham-handed.

Ruthie wasn't a Macrory servant, but he wasn't sure that Connor would be allowed to call on her once she was feeling better. Not that anything good could come from the situation, but just because Lennox was a hermit didn't mean Connor had to be.

THE FRESH, MOIST breeze blew Mercy's hair back from her cheeks, bathing her skin with the scent of morning in Scotland. This, this is what she'd wanted when she left home. A sense of peace. Moments in which she could be alone, be herself, perhaps even discover who she was down deep.

She'd escaped Macrory House with a sense of desperation.

Flora had followed her around for most of the past week engaging Mercy in conversation at every possible juncture. She'd heard the girl's plans for her trip to Edinburgh, her hopes to meet with a famous seamstress and milliner, not to mention all the entertainments planned for her by Douglas, who seemed not only a fond grandfather but an indulgent one.

Not once had Flora asked her a question. Mercy served as a listener and only that. If she responded to a remark Flora made, the girl simply ignored her comment like it was so much wind and nothing else.

Macrory House was a stage on which Flora performed. The other inhabitants were merely ancillary characters of little importance to her cousin. Even Douglas, doting as he was, merely acted to satisfy Flora's wishes and wants.

The other woman would probably be surprised to discover that Mercy considered her exceedingly boring. The only topic Flora wanted to discuss was herself. Or, when she was coaxed to talk about something else— like the history of Macrory House or the Macrory clan—she did so only until she could turn the conversation back to her plans, her wardrobe, or her hairstyle.

"I can't believe you came all that way from America by yourself," Flora said just this morning. "I would have been terrified."

"I wasn't actually by myself," Mercy said. "I had Ruthie with me."

"I would still be terrified. And to think you had an accident when you were almost here. I would have been terrified about that, too. Not to mention having to deal with the Earl of Morton."

"He was very nice to us," Mercy said.

"My grandfather thinks he's quite daft."

She hadn't had a rejoinder to that, but her participation was rarely required in a conversation with Flora.

"Just think, my mother would have been a countess if they'd lived. I would have been the daughter of a countess."

She stared at Flora, amazed that the girl had been able to make Robert and Mary's deaths about her, too.

"I am sorry," she finally said. "It must have been awful to lose your mother."

Flora's smile slipped. "It was. She was the loveliest person, Mercy. Always laughing or smiling. She shouldn't have died that way."

Mercy expected Flora to speak further about her mother, but her cousin only shook her head, causing her red curls to tumble over her shoulders, then paused in front of a mirror they were passing.

"Oh, well, grieving is not good for the complexion, is it?" she asked, smiling at herself. "Grandfather says I have the most beautiful complexion. Don't you think it's lovely?"

Mercy murmured something appreciative, enough to appease her cousin.

Unfortunately, Flora was the only person who made an appearance in the morning hours. Aunt Elizabeth remained in her room until afternoon, telling Mercy that she preferred to work on her needlework, a task that required concentration.

Seanmhair preferred her room in the morning as

well, never venturing out until the day was well advanced.

Thankfully, their paths never crossed.

However, her grandmother held court at dinner, pronouncing her opinions on a variety of topics. For someone who kept to herself every day, she was extraordinarily conversant with what happened at Macrory House.

When she could escape Flora, Mercy headed for the kitchen or the housekeeper's office, either spending time with Ruthie or Mrs. West or both of them with the addition of Irene from time to time.

Unlike her conversations with the rest of her Scottish family, these talks were often lively, filled with laughter, and questions and answers from both sides.

Ruthie was feeling better, to the extent that she had begun quoting superstitions once more. She told Mrs. West that burning two lamps in the same room was a bad omen—someone would die by the second night. A whistling woman pushed away good fortune.

Mercy had heard them all and more. Mrs. West, thankfully, had a kind heart so she never lectured Ruthie about the foolishness of her beliefs. Her only comment was that the Irish had as many sayings as the Scots.

It was Mrs. West who pushed Mercy outside this morning.

"It's a fair and lovely day, Miss Mercy. Go and take a walk through the glen, see the wildflowers. Greet the sun with a smile and Ben Uaine with a nod."

She had taken the housekeeper's advice and now she was glad she had. It truly was a lovely day.

According to what she'd been told, the road acted as a barrier between Macrory land and that belonging to the Caithearts. Although wide and paved, it was barely traveled. Her carriage had probably been the only vehicle for days.

Now she crossed the road slowly, following the glen that sloped down to the loch. The earth was almost wild here, with deep gullies and rolling hills that hid the rest of the scenery from her. The loch, shiny silver in the morning light, stretched out before her like a crooked finger, disappearing into the horizon. On the far side, thick woods hid any settlement from view. On this side of the loch, Duddingston Castle guarded the land at one end while the mountain they called Ben Uaine was the sentinel to her left.

Lennox had flown from that mountain like an enormous eagle, swooping down on her carriage. She could still hear Ruthie's screams.

It had been the act of an insane man, yet everything she'd heard about Lennox made her believe that he was as sane as anyone. Did no one realize that he was simply a man of science? Why, though, had he changed from studying to be a physician to trying to fly?

What the Earl of Morton did was none of her concern. An admonition she'd told herself often enough in the past week. The truth was, however, that the Scottish earl fascinated her much more than he should have.

Every night at dinner he was a topic of conversation. She'd learned that he was considered a hermit by the villagers, rarely traveling away from Duddingston Castle. He never asked for help. Nor did he ever participate in village events. The castle, once known for its entertainments, especially at the holidays, was now dark and somber. People weren't invited there and those who had occasion to visit told a tale of being kept at the door instead of being asked inside.

At least she'd seen the interior of Duddingston Castle, or the Clan Hall and the kitchen.

Why was Lennox living nearly alone? None of the conversations at dinner mentioned a sweetheart or a wife.

Her interest was innocent enough. She wouldn't be remaining in Scotland long and a little curiosity about a Scottish earl didn't seem amiss.

Still, it wasn't something she was going to mention to her Scottish relatives. Flora would ask her how she could possibly want to know something about another man when she was due to be married. Her grandmother's words would be even more cutting.

No, it was better if she kept her questions to herself.

Chapter Sixteen

$\mathcal{T}$he morning was bright and sunny, the breeze off Ben Uaine smelling of growing things and Loch Arn. For some reason the wind was always stronger in the morning than the afternoon.

As a child Lennox had played on Ben Uaine, disobeying his parents as he pretended to be the conqueror of the world. Robert had come in search of him, lecturing as was his habit. It hadn't worked. Lennox had explored all sides of the mountain, including the south face where he stood now.

He'd always come to the mountain to think. Ben Uaine gave him distance, lent him perspective, and healed him.

There was a spot near the top that was hollowed out as if God had reached down with a giant fist and scooped out part of the rock. He often sat there watching as the clouds skidded across the sky. Most of the thorny questions of his youth had been pondered there.

When his parents had died he'd come here, looking out over Caitheart land. He'd felt the pull of history in this spot, something that had oddly comforted him at his loneliest. The mountain had been the first place he'd come to when he'd moved from Edinburgh, reluctantly taking over his role as the Earl of Morton, assuming the yoke of Duddingston Castle with grave reservations, knowing that he wouldn't be as good as Robert at preserving and protecting their ancestral home.

Somehow, he'd managed. Over the years he'd learned to anticipate problems, seeing the castle like it was a diseased organism, something needing to be healed. He'd repaired the roof over the Clan Hall himself, cleaned out the chimneys in the intact wing with Irene looking on in terror. He'd removed dozens of years of refuse from the courtyard so he could use the space to build his airships, and had generally been as good a steward for his home as he could manage.

From here Duddingston Castle looked almost whole, a four-hundred-year-old fortress standing resolute and strong against any invader. The castle was impotent against time itself, however. The eroding years had done their damage. The Caitheart home would never be what it had once been.

Perhaps that was right and good and proper.

He could not reverse time or circumstances. If he could, he'd bring Robert back to life. He would transport himself to Edinburgh except for periodic visits home. Perhaps he would have still been fascinated with the idea of flying and his inventions. Or the press of his work might have pushed those other interests to the back of his mind.

"You're all for doing this, then?" Connor asked, helping him push the airship to the edge of the pad.

When he'd originally thought about launching one of his airships, he'd remembered this area of Ben Uaine. It was like the Almighty had flattened part of the mountain, leaving a wide square that was a perfect takeoff point.

"I am," he said. "I know this is a new design, but it's stable. I don't think it will fight the wind and it should be easy to pilot."

Connor still looked skeptical, but that was fine. He didn't have to approve.

"You haven't worked on this one as long as you have the other."

He clapped Connor on the shoulder. "You worry too much. I promise not to crash into any carriages."

They'd put up a barricade on the road, wide enough to stop a vehicle if one were turning toward Duddingston Castle. In that way he was reassured that he wouldn't cause another accident.

Connor didn't say anything further, probably because he knew it would be a waste of time.

He'd taken precautions. After all, he had no wish to die in the name of science. Yes, there was always an element of risk in doing something few men had tried. Other men interested in flight had recruited either their servants or volunteers to fly their airships, but that seemed like a cowardly move. If he'd built his airship right and used the correct calculations, he'd be fine. If not, no one else would have to pay the price but him.

He climbed into the basket. Using a tool he'd created for just this purpose, he reached up and turned the wheel holding the upper sails, relieved when it rotated easily. Two massive square sails jutting out on either side of the airship would act as stabilizers while the fins on the tail would allow him to change direction. He was hoping that the rotating sails would keep him aloft for longer, but the idea was currently unproven. He'd discover if he was right—or wrong—with this test flight.

"I'll be fine, Connor."

The other man didn't say a word. If the only thing Connor had to say was a warning, then maybe it was better if he kept silent. Irene had already scolded him for being too adventurous.

Was he supposed to sit in his castle, surrounded by goose down for fear that he might hurt himself? Even as a physician he would be in occasional danger—from a disease he couldn't cure or an epidemic that would rage out of control despite his best efforts.

"It's time," he said.

The aircraft was close to the edge of the platform. The basket was equipped with wheels on the bottom, less for landing than for the takeoff. All it would take was a small push and he would be airborne.

Leaning forward, he gave Connor the signal. The next second, he was over the edge, into the air, excitement overwhelming any nervousness he might have felt. In that space of time, that long minute or maybe two, he was more than a man. He was Icarus, a godlike creature challenging nature itself.

His stomach dropped a little as it always did, but the feeling was also accompanied by a surge of exultation.

The airship descended, a little faster than he'd anticipated, but at least the upper sails were catching the air.

A second later he glanced up, realizing that the wheel wasn't turning. None of the side sails were billowing, either. The airship wasn't gaining grace in the sky. Instead, it was lumbering toward the ground like a wounded creature.

He pulled hard on the right paddle that controlled the tail, anticipating that he would be turning slowly right, heading for the road. The airship didn't respond. He could hear the sound of the wind in his ears, the creak of the wood as it strained to obey.

If the right paddle didn't work, maybe the left would. He pulled hard on it, saying a prayer at the same time, hoping that God would forgive his arrogance or whatever stupidity he'd demonstrated. Somehow, he'd made a mistake. Otherwise, the design should have worked.

The side sails finally caught the air and his rate of descent lessened a little. He held on to the paddle with both hands, pulling with all his strength. The airship responded in infinitesimal degrees.

The snap, then crack of one of the upper supports was something he almost expected. The feeling of plummeting to earth wasn't.

The airship swung slightly to the left, heading for Loch Arn. A water landing was preferable to hitting the ground so hard that the airship shattered. At least he stood a chance of surviving.

SOMETHING FLICKERED AT the far left of Mercy's vision. She turned to see what had attracted her attention, but all she saw were tall grasses and a punch of orange, purple, and pink from the occasional flower.

There it was again.

Turning, she faced Ben Uaine. Maybe it was a bird. No, she wouldn't have been able to see a bird from here unless it had a massive wingspan.

Not a cloud marred the perfection of the clear blue sky. As she stood there, the wind blew her hair back from her face.

There it was, slightly to the right of Ben Uaine and growing nearer.

Frozen, she watched as the airship came closer. This one was different from the one Lennox had piloted a week ago. This creation was ungainly like a many-tentacled monster.

The sails weren't catching the wind. Nor was the airship soaring with the current like a bird. Instead, it was descending too fast.

Mercy couldn't look away.

She'd never thought to see someone fall out of the sky, let alone someone she knew. She wanted to do something to help him, but short of having the power to levitate objects or render the earth as soft as a feather, she was powerless.

For the first time she wished that screaming came easily to her. Or fainting. Anything but standing there and watching as Lennox crashed to earth.

Her hands were clenched at her waist and she felt too close to nausea.

Nothing seemed real, just like the accident a week ago. Everything was taking longer than it should. Yet the sensation of time slowing didn't prevent the disaster from unfolding in front of her.

Lennox had to do something. He couldn't crash.

Suddenly, pieces of the airship began to fall, a few of them hitting the ground vertically with such force that they looked like swords spearing the earth. Another piece fell. Then another. As the airship neared her, she grabbed her skirt and began to run, trying to avoid the shards of wood.

If she wasn't fast enough she wouldn't be just a witness to Lennox Caitheart's crash, but a victim in the disaster.

Chapter Seventeen

At first Mercy thought Lennox was going to hit the ground not far from where he'd landed a week ago, but then he slowly began to turn, heading for the loch. Another piece of wood fell off the aircraft, missing her by only feet. It looked as if his invention was going to come apart in midair.

He was over the rocky shore now, only inches from impact.

The craft hit the water almost soundlessly, sliding beneath the surface with only broken pieces of wood marking where it landed.

The rocks on the shore were large but rounded and not sharp enough to cut her shoes. She made her way to the edge of the water, her gaze fixed on the spot where Lennox had gone down.

He hadn't surfaced.

She toed off her kid slippers and removed her two petticoats, wishing her dress didn't have such full sleeves. Her skirt would also drag her down, but she was a strong swimmer. After tossing her petticoats onto the rocks, she entered the water, propelling herself forward, feeling the drag of her skirt and sleeves. The lake was surprisingly clear here, a calming blue-green color. Twenty feet out she could finally see the wreck, a collection of wood pieces and waterlogged sails that was sinking fast.

Lennox still hadn't surfaced.

Fear made her kick hard as she dove.

A few seconds later she realized why he wasn't leaving the airship. His hand was caught in one of the ropes. She followed the rope to a wheel that had come loose and was under the craft. Uncoiling it, she grabbed the end of the rope and showed it to him, then pointed upward.

A few moments later they got to the surface together.

Connor was suddenly there, reaching for her.

"I'm all right," she said, her lungs straining for air. "Help Lennox."

She watched both of them as they made it to shore, taking care to stay close. Lennox looked to be a more experienced swimmer than Connor. By the time they made it onto the rocks, she couldn't tell who was helping whom.

A few minutes later she made her way gingerly over the rocks, reaching the grass between the loch and the castle. She sat there, her arms wrapped around her knees. It might have been July, but the waters of Loch Arn had been frigid. The tower loomed over her, casting a shadow.

Neither Lennox nor Connor was talking, so she could only assume that they were as out of breath as she was.

Closing her eyes, she concentrated on just breathing for a few minutes.

"Are you all right?"

She looked up to find Lennox standing there, his hand outstretched toward her. His face was cut in a dozen places. There was a wide red spot over his left cheek that she suspected would be a bruise later. His shirt was torn and it wasn't until she took his hand and stood that she realized there was a nasty gash running from his shoulder to his elbow.

"You're bleeding," she said.

He looked at his arm. "I am at that. We need a fire and some whiskey, not necessarily in that order."

She pushed her wet hair away from her face. "I've never tasted spirits before."

"Well, I don't know a better time than now to start," he said.

Connor was on one side and Lennox the other as they walked toward the tower, as if the men were suddenly afraid she would collapse. Lennox stopped beside a door so short that she had to duck to enter. Straightening up, she looked around her, the space illuminated by the small slitted windows.

She'd expected to be able to see to the roof of the tower, but the stairs built into the curved wall led up only a short way. There was a floor directly above her.

"The tower was converted to a bedchamber," Lennox said. "A change made by my father."

What a pity that she wouldn't be able to explore further. A single woman did not ask to see a man's bedchamber.

"I'm dripping through your house," she said as they entered a carpeted corridor and headed toward the back of the castle.

"We all are."

"I'll go fetch us some towels," Connor said.

Lennox nodded and led her to the kitchen. He headed toward the massive fireplace on the opposite wall and began building a fire.

For long minutes they didn't talk. She simply stood there watching him as he knelt in front of the fire, his wound dripping blood on the stone floor.

Connor entered the room with an armful of towels and handed her one. She thanked him, then dried her face and blotted her hair. There was nothing she could do about her dress, but she placed the towel in front of her in an effort to maintain some type of modesty.

Lennox had seen her bare legs. She hadn't been able to keep her skirt from billowing around her hips in the water. In those seconds underwater, she'd been as close to being naked as she possibly could be while still clothed. Even worse, when she'd emerged from the loch her dress had been plastered to her body.

She sat at the table, grateful that the fire had caught. She felt cold from the inside out.

"I'll be going to change," Connor said, placing the rest of the towels on the end of the table.

She wished she could do the same.

Unlike Connor, Lennox didn't leave to change his clothes. Instead, he went to the cupboard and took out a leather bag she recognized. He placed it on the table before turning to her.

"I need your help," he said. "My arm needs tending to."

It was bleeding freely now, turning his white sleeve red.

She had helped her mother's garden club roll bandages. She'd even knitted a credible volume of socks, mittens, and scarves for the troops, but she'd never been a nurse.

"You'll do fine," Lennox said, as if he heard her thoughts.

She doubted that.

"Couldn't Connor help?"

"He gets a little green around blood."

So did she, but there wasn't a choice. Someone needed to help Lennox.

"We need some whiskey," he said, going to another cupboard, retrieving a bottle of whiskey and returning to her side. "Medicinal reasons," he added, placing it on the table.

Pulling out a chair beside her, he sat and emptied the bag of its contents, then pushed the squares of cloth and a small brown bottle toward her.

"Now you get to reciprocate for any discomfort I caused you."

"What do you mean?"

She was in the process of reaching for the cloth when he asked, "Can you sew?"

Horrified, she stared at him. "You can't be serious."

"The wound is deep. It isn't going to heal without some help."

"I can't sew a person," she said.

"I'd much prefer you than Connor. His sewing skills are negligible."

He seemed to take her silence for assent, because he removed his shirt, turning so that his wounded arm was close to her.

She'd never before seen a half-naked man, let alone one with such a distinctive-looking chest. He had muscles everywhere. She wanted to sit and look at him for a moment, to fix him in her memory. A water droplet rolled down the middle of his chest and she wanted to pat him dry.

Seanmhair would be horrified. Her grandmother would begin to lecture her about all sorts of rules Mercy was having trouble remembering right now.

He grabbed one of the cloth squares and began to blot at his wound. When he poured a little whiskey down his arm, the only sign that it was painful was a tightening of his mouth.

The cut was beginning to bleed more. She grabbed a cloth, batted his hand away, and pressed gently on the wound.

"It really doesn't look that bad," she said. "Not something that needs to be stitched."

"Mercy."

She liked the way he said her name, even if it was an admonition.

"The faster I get sewn up, the better. Delaying it will only cause me more pain."

With his good hand he pushed the sewing kit over to her.

"Very well," she said crossly. "It serves you right if I make a mess of everything. I've never done anything like this before."

He only smiled.

She frowned at him again and reluctantly threaded the needle, even though her hands were shaking. She was still cold and now she was terrified.

Before she began he doused his wound again with whiskey.

"Do you just want to cause yourself more pain?"

He shook his head. "No, but I've found that wounds treated with whiskey first tend to heal faster."

"I'm certainly not going to argue with you. After all, you're the one who studied medicine. But it seems to me that there should be a better way. One that doesn't sting as much."

He took another cloth, doused it with whiskey, and began to blot at the cuts on his face.

"You're missing a few spots," she said. "Your face is a mess."

"And you're delaying."

She was, and it annoyed her even more that he'd called her on it.

Chapter Eighteen

"Do you realize that the only time we've seen each other is when one of us is hurt?" she said.

He didn't respond.

Taking the whiskey-soaked cloth, she placed it at the widest part of his wound, hoping that it deadened the skin a little. Unfortunately, she had some experience with being stitched up and she could attest that it was not a painless process.

"Either you're sewing me or I'm sewing you," she said. "I would much rather have met you at a dinner party or luncheon."

She made the first poke into his skin with the needle, feeling nauseated when he flinched. The best thing to do in this situation was to simply finish this task as quickly as possible.

She made two stitches, blotting with the cloth as she went. She felt each stitch as if it were her own flesh she was sewing.

"Or a ball," he said, surprising her. "I used to attend quite a few of those in Edinburgh."

"Did you?" she asked. "Were you a man-about-town?"

He smiled. "Hardly. Normally I was always the

one to even out a dinner party. Or I followed along with a bunch of friends. However, if I'd had my way I would've spent my time studying."

"Who pushed you to be more social?"

"Friends," he said. "One in particular, the mother of a fellow student. She's a lovely woman but I've never met a more interfering female."

She'd made a total of six stitches, each one making her tremble more.

"How many more should I do?"

He studied his arm. "About six more, I think."

For the next few minutes she didn't speak. She bit her lips, focused on pulling his skin closed, trying to pretend that it was cloth she was stitching, or leather, not Lennox's arm.

"You're doing well. I couldn't have done better myself."

She'd never thought to be praised for performing such a terrible task, but then she'd never been in this situation before. Her life had been carefully prescribed and she'd never ventured beyond its boundaries. Her journey to Scotland had been the first time and stitching up Lennox's arm the second.

"How are you going to explain why you're drenched?" he asked, the white line around his mouth the only sign of his discomfort.

An idea had occurred to her, one that was slightly shocking but less so than appearing at Macrory House in her current condition.

"Could I prevail upon your kindness, Lennox? And Connor's as well? Would it be possible for him to go to Macrory House and ask Mrs. West to fetch one of my dresses? I can't imagine going back there looking as I do. I think Mrs. West would keep the matter private.

Only Flora is up and about until late afternoon, but she's excessively curious and wouldn't hesitate to tell everyone."

If her grandmother learned about Mercy's actions this morning, Ailsa would dedicate hours to telling her how disgraceful she was and how much shame she'd brought to the family. She'd probably be restricted to her room until such time as she and Ruthie left Scotland.

"You dispensed with the bandage, I noticed," he said.

"Someone recommended that I do so." She gathered up the squares of cloth then began to put the other items inside the leather bag. "There was my vanity to consider, after all."

"I shouldn't have said that," he said. "I apologize."

She glanced at him. If anyone should be vain it was him with his impressive chest and striking face. And those eyes. She felt like he could peer inside her with that direct blue gaze.

"I appreciated the advice. Besides, it was a relief to get rid of all that wrapping around my head."

"Bend down," he said.

"What?"

He reached out, grabbed her arm, and gently pulled her to stand in front of him. "Bend down so I can see your head."

She felt exceedingly strange doing so, but his touch was gentle around her wound.

"You can hardly see it," he said. "But you should bathe it with whiskey after being in the loch. Would you like me to do it or would you prefer to do it yourself?"

She opted to do it herself, sitting and blotting sparingly. It didn't matter, the whiskey still stung.

"In a few days, you can have McNaughton remove your stitches."

She'd attempted to avoid the crusty butler for the past week. However, McNaughton was everywhere. When he looked at her it was always with disapproval, especially the morning after she'd removed her turban-like bandage. She'd ducked into Aunt Elizabeth's room rather than endure a lecture from the man.

"I'd much rather come to you," she said. "That way I don't have to endure McNaughton's sniffing."

"He doesn't approve of you?" he asked, smiling.

"I don't know if it's because I'm an American. Or a woman. Or the fact that I was foolish enough to get myself injured. Or that I arrived at Macrory House in your carriage."

"If it makes you feel any better, I don't think McNaughton approves of anyone. He's been a crusty old codger since he was young, or so I've been told. He and Irene once stepped out together."

She put down the whiskey-soaked cloth and stared at him. "Surely you're jesting."

He raised his right hand, palm toward her. "On this I don't jest. Evidently, it was quite a serious romance."

"What happened?" A moment later she waved her hand in the air as if to erase the words. "Never mind. It's none of my concern. I shouldn't engage in gossip."

"Then you're doomed to boredom in the Highlands," he said. "There aren't that many of us still here. We have a tendency to talk about each other. You should hear what they say in the village."

"What do they say about you?"

Taking another cloth square, she dampened it with

the whiskey and began blotting at the cuts on his face.

He looked at her, his blue eyes intense. Her stomach felt hollow. He really should look away. Or she should, but the sensation was so unique that she kept her gaze on him.

It felt as if they spoke in that moment. Words weren't necessary or would have been superfluous. Their initial antipathy was gone as if it had never been. Lennox was, in some strange way, a friend. Or perhaps more. She felt as if he were someone she could trust with her secrets, her worries, and perhaps even her fears.

How very odd to have that thought.

"Much the same as what you've said, that I'm insane."

"It's my turn to apologize," she said. "I think you're foolishly brave, but I don't think you're mad."

"That's progress," he said, placing his hand over hers. "I'd be happy to remove your stitches."

It was a perfect moment of accord with another human being. One of a different country, culture, background, family, and future—yet she couldn't help but feel that they were linked somehow, despite all those things that separated them.

If so, what connected them? She didn't know, but she realized in those silent moments that she very much wanted to figure it out.

"I'm sorry about your machine," she said, pulling her hand away.

"So am I. I've never crashed before. Not and lost an entire aircraft." Lennox stared into the fire as if he could see the ruin of his dream in the flames.

His voice was very calm and matter-of-fact, almost

as if he were discussing something of no importance to him at all. Yet there was an undercurrent if you listened hard enough. Not sadness as much as a touch of anger.

"It was an accident," she said.

"No," he said. "It wasn't an accident."

"Do you think someone sabotaged your airship?"

He shook his head. "Nothing like that. It was incompetence, pure and simple. I did something wrong. My calculations were wrong. Without the lift from the sails, I was doomed. The aircraft didn't have the shape to glide." He glanced over at her. "Actually, I was lucky I made it as far as the loch."

"Surely you're being too hard on yourself," she said. "Maybe it wasn't anything you did. Maybe it was just that there wasn't enough wind."

"Or the day was too humid or the wood was bad." He smiled. "Even if all of that had been true, it would still be my fault. It was up to me to check all of those things."

She was left without anything to say. Perhaps he assumed too much responsibility and blame, but she knew people who were the opposite and refused to accept any accountability for their actions. Or, even worse, blamed others for their misfortune.

Lennox wasn't like that. He was honorable, a word she'd thought she knew the meaning of, at least before the war. All the men who'd marched off in proud splendor had been honorable, heeding the call to protect the Union. Yet she knew now that honor was more than patriotism, more than loyalty or beliefs. It was standing for what was right, even when it was difficult to do so.

Lennox had come home, abandoning his calling as

a doctor, recognizing a greater responsibility to his clan and his family. That, to her mind, was honorable. The highest form of honor because it also demanded sacrifice.

He was an admirable man. It wouldn't do to let him know that she felt that way about him. Or maybe something even more. That was such a troubling thought that she pushed it away and concentrated on her task.

Chapter Nineteen

Mercy began to bandage Lennox's arm, following his instructions. First she applied a noxious thick yellow mixture over the cut. It smelled of onions and other spices and was so thick she had to dab it on with another cotton square.

"What is this?"

"A concoction I devised," he said. "It aids in healing."

"You didn't use it on me. Did you?"

He shook his head. "I didn't dare. You were already furious with me. I didn't want to send you on your way smelling of onions and painted yellow."

She smiled. "That was probably wise."

Connor returned to the kitchen, only his damp hair a sign that he'd been swimming in the loch.

Lennox explained Mercy's idea about going to Macrory House and asking for Mrs. West's help. Connor agreed that it would be wise to speak only to the housekeeper about his errand.

After Connor left them, Lennox stood, going to the fireplace and stirring the blaze with the poker. She could feel the warmth of the fire from here and was grateful for it.

"You're very good at building fires," she said.

"Needs must," he said. "My lodgings in Edinburgh were almost always cold. There I only had coal. I missed a wood fire. I like the smell of them." He turned to look at her. "Irene says that they're the best way to cook, better than our stove."

"Where is she now? At Macrory House?"

He shook his head. "At the market. She goes there every week around this time."

"Is there any coincidence between her being gone and your flying?"

His grin was boyish and utterly charming. "Perhaps."

"Has she been with you long?"

"With the family, yes. Fifteen years, now, ever since our parents died. She was very fond of Robert."

Irene was also very fond of him, but surely he knew that.

Her curiosity about this man didn't surprise her in the least. Lennox was unlike anyone she'd ever met. He was fearless, iconoclastic, and so much his own man that he was almost a king in his castle.

"Who taught you to swim?" he asked.

"Fred Brown," she said. "One of my guards. I always loved the water and swimming brought me some freedom. Fred was always nearby, but sometimes I forgot about him."

"Why a guard?"

She debated how to answer him. She could always just smile or change the subject. How odd that she wanted to tell him the truth.

"Two reasons. My father is very wealthy. He worried that I might be stolen away and held for ransom."

"And the other reason?"

"My parents had five children. Three of them died in infancy. I even carry their names. Other than me, there's only my brother, Jimmy, and he . . ." Her words trailed off. She'd never spoken to anyone outside the family about Jimmy.

Lennox studied her. She wondered what he saw.

"Are you spoiled as well?" he asked, surprising her.

"What a very strange question," she said, grateful that he hadn't asked anything about Jimmy. "If I say no, will I be forced to prove it in some way? If I say yes, what does that say about me?"

"That perhaps you're honest. Are you?"

"Honest? Or spoiled?"

"One doesn't presuppose the other," he said.

"Are you as direct with everyone, or only females who save you from drowning?"

"I would've extricated myself," he said.

She smiled at him, recognizing bravado when she saw it.

"I promise I won't tell anyone."

His smile startled her.

"Very well," he said. "I'm in your debt, Mercy. Connor does not swim as well as you."

"That's something that should be rectified, especially since you live on the edge of a lake."

"Yet he's in no danger of falling in."

"Unless you take another tumble. Is there somewhere else you could fly your machines?"

"Nowhere where the wind is as strong," he said.

When she didn't respond he continued. "I'm not taking that many chances, Mercy. I calculate everything, from the angle of the wings to the rotation of the upper sails. I know exactly where I'm going to land with relative assuredness of my velocity."

"Yet something went terribly wrong today."

He nodded. "Which is why it's a shame that I won't be able to recover all of the pieces. Without them, I can only guess at the problem."

"I would think that a man skilled in trying to save the lives of other people would have more care about his own."

"You've been talking to Irene, haven't you?"

"She's at Macrory House quite often," she said.

"Sometimes I think she would be happier working there than here."

"You're wrong about that. She talks about you a great deal. How smart you are. How clever. About all of your inventions."

He looked away.

"Have I embarrassed you?"

"It's my turn to ask. Are you as direct with everyone?"

She took a moment to honestly consider his question. "I don't think so. You're very easy to talk to, which is surprising given our first meeting."

"I was exceedingly cordial, as I recall."

"Until you learned about my mother's family," she countered. "Then you couldn't get me out of your castle fast enough. Have you changed your mind about me?"

He turned his head slowly, regarding her like he must stare at his airship, with an eye to changing it or improving it in some way.

"I owe you thanks for saving my life."

"I believe you were right in that you would have extricated yourself soon enough."

"Hopefully before I drowned."

He stood and walked to the cupboard, pulled out

another bottle before retrieving two glasses and returning to her side.

"That one is for medicine," he said, nodding at the bottle of whiskey on the table. "This one is for drinking."

He poured a few inches into each glass and handed her one.

She debated drinking it or choosing the more prudent course, refusing with a smile.

When she hesitated, he dragged two chairs in front of the fire and invited her to sit next to him.

"I was wrong to ask if you were spoiled."

"No, I don't think you were," she said, raising the glass to her lips. "I have lived what most people consider a privileged life. I've never had to worry about anything. Other than my lack of freedom, it's been idyllic."

"Lack of freedom?"

She nodded. "My every movement was monitored. I used to think my mother wrote everything about me in her journal. 'Today Mercy woke at seven, partook of breakfast of toast and coffee, asked about the weather and the Donaldsons' dinner party two days hence. Color is good. Mood seems normal. All is well.'" She glanced at him. "Until it wasn't, of course. I had the sniffles or a headache or was out of sorts. I've been irritated a great deal in the past year, so I'm sure that went into her journal."

"Why irritated?"

She didn't want to discuss Gregory right now, not when she was feeling so content. Instead, she shrugged. "Perhaps that's the answer to your question. I am spoiled."

The smell of the whiskey seemed to burn a passage

through her nose. The small sip caused fire to race over her tongue and down her throat. She'd never thought to be warmed from the inside out. When she said as much, Lennox only smiled.

"Why do you think whiskey was born in the Highlands?"

"You really should go and change," she said, taking another few sips. "You don't need to keep me company."

He smiled again and she wished he wouldn't. Whereas once she found him to be the most aggravating man, now she could see that he was entirely too attractive. Almost dangerously so.

He could probably charm a mouse out of its hole. She got the strangest image, then, of Lennox standing on the edge of the loch and simply commanding the fish to come to him. All the female fish would obey with a flip of their tails, sailing out of the water to land at his feet.

Did he have that power with women, too? He probably had been overwhelmed with female company during those years in Edinburgh.

A man has needs. Gregory had told her that once, when she'd refused to kiss him after they'd become engaged. She didn't particularly like the way he kissed, but how was she supposed to tell him that?

How did Lennox kiss? Was that a question she was allowed to ask, even in the privacy of her own mind?

She took another sip of her whiskey, then held the glass up to the light streaming in from the kitchen window. There was only a tiny bit left.

"It's quite a lovely color, isn't it?"

"Indeed it is," he said, taking the glass from her.

"But I haven't finished."

"That's enough for your maiden voyage, Mercy."

She was feeling delightfully warm and not the least bit tipsy, if that's what he was implying. Still, perhaps he was right.

"I didn't like you at first," she said.

"And now?"

"Now I think you're entirely too handsome for your own good."

"That wouldn't be the whiskey talking, would it?"

She shook her head emphatically. "I didn't drink that much whiskey."

"Then thank you, I think."

"You should go and change," she said again. "I'll stay here and guard your kitchen. I'll wait very patiently for you."

He chuckled and she had the fleeting thought that she needed to tell him that it was rude to laugh at someone who hadn't made a joke.

The fire was making her comfortably warm. Or maybe it was the whiskey. She closed her eyes to rest them just for a moment, thinking that she heard him say something but couldn't rouse long enough to ask him to repeat himself.

Instead, she smiled, utterly at ease for the first time in a very long time. Perhaps she was tipsy, after all.

Chapter Twenty

Lennox's arm was burning like blazes, but the discomfort wasn't enough to distract from his thoughts.

He had lost his aircraft and nearly his life. But for Mercy, he might have drowned.

He'd never met anyone like Mercy. Most women he knew—which was, he would admit, a small number—would have stood on the shore when he crashed, probably screaming. Mercy had, without any thought to her own safety, helped pull him free of the rope. Not once had she made a comment about her appearance. She hadn't whined about her dress, the fact that she was barefoot, or soaked to the skin.

Even though she hadn't wanted to stitch his arm, she'd done it without complaint. He'd known how difficult it had been for her. Her face had turned white and she'd trembled the entire time.

People were easier to figure out when he could put them in categories. He didn't know where to put Mercy.

He liked her. In addition, there was something intriguing about Mercy and he always had the urge to solve a mystery. She'd come all the way from America for some reason. He didn't know what it was any more than how long she was going to remain in Scotland.

She was unlike any heiress he'd met and he'd had the occasion to be paraded in front of a few of them in Edinburgh. As the brother of an earl, even an impecunious one, he'd been sought after as a guest. After a while the women he'd met had all seemed the same. Their appearance might differ, but not their character. Mercy didn't preen. Nor was she coy. He couldn't imagine her flirting. She was too direct for that. Nor did she talk about her wardrobe, her hats, or what she owned. They hadn't discussed the weather and she hadn't batted her eyelashes at him once.

After stripping off his clothes and putting them in front of the cold fireplace—less to dry them than to avoid a lecture from Irene—he finished toweling himself off before dressing again. He slid his hands into the leather grips of his brushes, making short work of his hair.

When had he become so concerned about his appearance that he stopped in front of the mirror to judge himself?

He turned away from his reflection, left his room, and with uncharacteristic enthusiasm, went to rejoin the woman who'd saved his life.

"MISS MERCY! MISS MERCY! What is wrong with her?"

"Nothing. She's asleep."

Mercy surfaced from a delightful dream to find Ruthie standing in front of her clutching the petticoats she'd removed on the shore of the loch. She was accompanied by Connor, but that wasn't the worst of it. Lennox was also standing there, humor lighting his eyes.

How on earth had she forgotten about her unmentionables?

She closed her eyes and wished herself back asleep again. She would never survive the embarrassment of this moment.

"I found your slippers, too, Miss Mercy. And I brought your blue dress, the one with the flowers embroidered on the cuffs."

She forced herself to open her eyes and look at Ruthie. "Thank you, Ruthie, but I didn't expect you to come. You really shouldn't have bothered."

"Who else would you expect, Miss Mercy? I've only broken my arm. I've never been as bored as I have this past week. What I can't manage I'll ask for help with, but otherwise I'm not going to let anyone else do for you when I can."

Had Ruthie always been so stubborn? Perhaps it was being in Scotland that brought out that trait in her.

"If you'll come with me," Lennox said, "I'll show you where you can change."

She half expected him to lead her into the tower, but he turned right outside the kitchen and down a corridor she hadn't seen before. They came to a wide set of stairs leading to a second floor.

Mercy glanced backward to find Ruthie behind her, still gripping the offending petticoats. Connor was beside her, carrying a valise. The two of them were smiling at each other. If they weren't careful, both of them would take a tumble down the stairs.

The corridor on the second floor was wide, carpeted with a beige runner heavily embroidered with a red-and-green flowered pattern. The walls looked to be made of the same stone as the floor throughout the castle.

"It's the oldest part of Duddingston," Lennox said. "Once, the family used to be large and these were all bedrooms. Now Irene is hard-pressed to keep them dusted."

He opened one of the doors in the middle of the corridor and stepped back.

She preceded him into the room, stopping and looking around her. It would be possible to believe that she had stepped back into time itself. Perhaps even to when the castle was first constructed and still smelled of newly quarried stone and fresh mortar.

The spread and the hangings on the four-poster bed were emerald, the color of a forest on a bright summer day. The predominantly green tapestry hanging on the far wall was of a serpentine road leading to a knoll where a blonde woman was petting a small white unicorn. The only windows in the room were high up and without curtains, letting in the early afternoon light. An armoire and a small desk and chair completed the room's furnishings. On the opposite wall from the bed was a fireplace, the mantel surround of black marble.

There wasn't a speck of dust anywhere. Everything was perfect and pristine as if a guest had been expected at any moment.

Connor put down her valise on the chair in front of the desk, smiled at Ruthie, and left the room.

"If you need anything," Lennox said, "there's a bell pull beside the fireplace."

"Thank you," she said as he moved to close the door.

He only smiled in response, leaving her to fervently wish that he'd instantly forget about her petticoats.

Within a matter of minutes, Mercy was stripped of her damp garments.

"I didn't think to pack a shift and another corset," Ruthie said.

"At least my petticoats aren't wet," she said. "Besides, it doesn't matter at this point. My hair is damp. They'll know that something happened."

"Did you really save his life, Miss Mercy? That's what Connor said. I wouldn't have been as brave."

"I didn't think," Mercy said. "I just knew he needed help." For a moment she relived the terror she'd felt as she watched Lennox's airship slide beneath the waters of the loch. "Besides," she added, "I think you're very brave, Ruthie. You didn't say a word when I told you that I wanted to come to Scotland. I couldn't have made the journey without you."

Ruthie's cheeks blossomed with color.

"I think we made each other brave, Miss Mercy."

There was enough truth in that statement that Mercy only smiled.

She wished she could dispense with her corset and damp shift, but there was nothing she could do about those. Ruthie helped her don the dry dress. Outwardly, she looked presentable, as long as her damp garments didn't soak through the fabric.

She hadn't brought a reticule, so that meant she didn't have a comb available. Nor had Ruthie brought one, an oversight for which she apologized profusely.

"Never mind," Mercy said. "I didn't think this through. I forgot about my hair. I doubt I'll be able to enter Macrory House without someone asking questions. Flora, if no one else."

"You can tell them that you tumbled into the loch, although I think you should tell everyone what really happened, Miss Mercy. It's nothing to be ashamed of."

"I doubt the Macrorys would feel the same, Ruthie. I can just imagine my grandmother's comments."

She hadn't said anything to Ruthie about Ailsa, but the other woman still gave her a sympathetic look.

"Is she a tyrant to the staff?" she asked.

"Your grandmother has her ways. That's what Mrs. West says. The housekeeper has to rotate the maids assigned to her room. No one seems to fit."

That's exactly how she felt. As if she hadn't fit. Her mother's family wouldn't approve of her actions regardless of the explanation. Nor would they be happy that she was once again arriving in the Caitheart carriage.

She was just going to have to handle one problem at a time.

Chapter Twenty-One

When they came down the stairs, Ruthie saw Connor and murmured some excuse for needing to speak to him, such a flimsy pretense that Mercy could have easily refused. Instead, she watched as Ruthie and Connor walked down the corridor together, each smiling at the other.

One day soon Ruthie's heart would break. Would these moments be worth that pain? Mercy couldn't answer that question. She'd never looked at a man the way Ruthie looked at Connor, as if he held all her happiness in his smile.

Irene was the only one in the kitchen when Mercy entered. Evidently, she'd been told about the accident because the older woman came to her, grabbed both of Mercy's upper arms, and did a silent scrutiny from the top of her head down to her feet.

At least Irene hadn't seen her petticoats.

"Are you sure you're all right, then?" Irene asked. "Nothing broken?"

Mercy shook her head.

"Nothing cut?"

Mercy shook her head again.

"Fool man," Irene said. "Thank you for saving him."

"I didn't, really. He saved himself."

"That's not what I heard. His Lordship told me what happened. He gives credit where credit is due."

Mercy could feel her cheeks warm.

"Fool man. He had no business going up in that fool contraption, but will he listen to me? No."

Mercy couldn't help but wonder if Irene pinned Lennox's ears back when she objected to what he was doing. He, in turn, probably took the occasion to slip free of her criticism whenever he could. Some people would have simply dismissed Irene or insisted that she mitigate her comments. The fact that Lennox didn't do either added another level of complexity to what she knew about him.

Where was he now? She kept herself from asking because she didn't want to betray her interest. Irene might tell Jean and by nightfall the story could be wafting through Macrory House. She didn't need any tales to reach her grandmother.

No one had to know that Lennox fascinated her or that she appreciated his looks. She even liked the way he walked, in a loose-limbed gait as if he'd mastered the ground beneath him.

She'd never met a man as confident. Not even Gregory, who'd come home a hero.

"Lennox is very kind," she said.

"You're the kind one, Miss Mercy."

She really didn't deserve all that praise. She'd done only what anyone would do confronted with the same circumstances. When she said as much to Irene, the older woman clucked her tongue and shook her head.

"'Modesty is the beauty of women.' One of my mother's quotes."

Mercy hadn't the slightest idea what she should say to that. Luckily the kettle began to make an odd warbling sound.

Ruthie entered the kitchen, alone this time. She stopped at the door and tilted her head. "What's that sound?"

"That would be the newest invention," Irene said with a smile. "Lennox has put a whistle on the top of the kettle and when it's ready it lets me know."

"It sounds like a cricket," Ruthie said. "When a cricket whistles on the hob, it's a bad sign."

Everything was a bad sign to Ruthie.

"I think it sounds like a bird," Irene countered. "I will admit it took a few days for me to get used to the sound. At first I thought I needed to check the chimney for another nest. The birds do like to make their home there."

Irene moved the kettle to the back of the stove. "I'll be making you some tea and when the carriage is ready Lennox will let us know."

Mercy reluctantly sat at the table, wishing she'd left before the offer of tea. Scottish tea was unlike anything she'd ever tasted. It was so strong that most people added milk and sugar to it, making it much too sweet for her. The alternative was to drink it straight. In the few times she'd done so, she couldn't rid herself of the metallic taste in her mouth for hours.

One of her earliest memories was traveling to North Carolina with her parents. Her mother had impressed upon her that it was always necessary to adapt to their destination. Therefore, when she was given grits, she never said a word in protest. Or when she was expected to eat something called hush puppies or breaded fish, she only thanked the cook, never commenting that the foods were heavy and nearly tasteless to her.

So in Scotland, she would drink what the Scots drank and keep silent. To do otherwise would be rude and disrespectful.

Still, she much preferred coffee. Or maybe another taste of whiskey. What would her family think to learn that?

Lennox came into the kitchen, greeting them with a quick smile.

"Did you find everything you needed at the market?" he asked Irene.

"Aye, I did, and most of it dear enough."

Irene looked as if she'd like to say more but Mercy and Ruthie's presence kept her silent.

For the first time since Mercy had arrived at Duddingston Castle, she felt uncomfortable, especially since it was easy to assume that the castle and its owner had fallen on hard times.

"When did you invent the tea kettle?" she asked, hoping to dispel the awkward silence.

"I didn't invent it," Lennox said. "I just improved upon it. About a year or so ago."

"It's very clever."

They looked at each other across the room. Now it was Mercy who felt constrained by the presence of other people. Yet if they had been alone in the kitchen, she wasn't quite sure what she would say next. Perhaps thanks for their conversation and how easy it had been to talk to him. Or thanks for not caring that she was related to the Macrorys. A final thanks for the experience of drinking whiskey and, despite the accident, feeling lighthearted for the past few hours.

"I'll walk you to the door," he said. A reminder that she needed to leave.

She nodded and said goodbye to Irene, turned, and followed Lennox down the corridor to the door she had opened a week ago, Ruthie behind her.

This time, she studied details of the Clan Hall that she hadn't seen earlier. Here, too, there was a tapestry mounted on the wall, this scene of a battle taking place on a hill. She wanted to ask him to stop and allow her some time to study the needlework. Instead, she tucked the wish into the back of her mind, along with the desire to inspect those interesting bronze bowls and artifacts on a series of shelves.

Duddingston Castle was like its owner, revealing itself a little at a time. She couldn't help but wonder if it would prove as fascinating as Lennox.

The carriage was directly outside the door, Connor acting as driver.

Ruthie made a little wave with her good hand and Connor smiled back at her. There was most definitely a romance blossoming there.

"Is this the door you came in, Miss Mercy?" Ruthie asked.

Mercy had already heard this superstition. "No," she said, "but we're in Scotland so maybe it doesn't matter."

"It matters, Miss Mercy. If a person comes in one door, they should go out the same door if they don't want to take the luck with them."

Lennox looked amused when Ruthie narrowed her eyes and stared at her.

"We can't go out the door we came in, Ruthie," she said patiently. "It leads to the loch."

Ruthie didn't appear convinced, but she finally nodded.

Mercy turned to Lennox. "Thank you," she said. "You've been very kind. I hope that I haven't taken your luck with me."

"After today I think you've probably brought me luck."

He smiled at her and she got that feeling again, that strange, disconcerting sensation that her stomach was falling. It was suddenly difficult to breathe and her pulse was racing.

There was no reason she should be thinking how handsome he was or how charming he could be. Instead, she should be praying that he forgot the accident as quickly as possible, especially her near-naked appearance in the water as well as the sight of her petticoats.

She was strangely thankful that they weren't alone. If they had been, she had the feeling that she might do something entirely improper and shocking, like standing on tiptoe and kissing him. The image of doing that very thing was so startling that she took a step back, then turned and entered the carriage as fast as she could.

Chapter Twenty-Two

*T*he carriage ride back to Macrory House felt even shorter than before, but perhaps that was because Mercy was becoming familiar with the route.

She turned to Ruthie. "We'll be leaving as soon as you feel up to the journey. That's only going to be a matter of a week or two at the most."

Ruthie turned her head, surveying the scenery as if she'd never seen pine trees.

"I know," she said in a voice that sounded as if it had lost all its life.

They didn't talk for the remainder of the journey, the silence uncomfortable and unusual.

The view of Macrory House was as awe-inspiring as it had been the first time. Since she had explored the majority of the rooms in the past week, she knew, first-hand, how large the house was. It probably equaled Duddingston Castle in space. Not in history, however, or appeal.

No, she shouldn't be thinking about the castle at all. Or its owner.

She would banish him from her thoughts completely. She wouldn't worry about the next time he went up in the air, and she knew there would be a next time because men like Lennox didn't see obstacles. They went around them or over them. He wouldn't be deterred by his failure. It would only add to his determination.

Nor was she going to think about how terrified she'd been or how relieved when she'd known he was safe. And she most certainly was not going to think about the way he looked at her, as if his gaze were somehow tied to her heart.

"SHE'S A BEAUTY," Irene said. "Not only that, but she has a good heart. Plus, she's brave as well. I think there's more Scottish in her than just the Macrory blood."

Lennox hesitated in the doorway. He had work to do. He was going to go back to his drawings and try to figure out what had gone wrong this morning.

Irene arranged the vegetables she'd purchased on the cutting board. He liked watching her. The angle of the knife there, the way she lined up the carrots and onions. Every movement of her hands seemed like it was planned and carried out with militaristic precision.

The vegetables didn't stand a chance.

"We need to work on the kitchen garden," he said.

She glanced at him. "That's the first time you said anything about that. And why would that be now?"

"It seems to me we should be able to grow our own vegetables."

"And who would be doing the weeding? And the cultivating? And the planting? Are you planning on hiring someone else?"

"There is that," he said.

"Tommy grows the best vegetables and he charges a fair price for them. I've not the energy nor the time to be hoeing and digging. Never mind getting on my knees to weed. And I doubt that you're willing to give up your puttering to become a gardener."

"Puttering?"

She rolled her eyes at him. "Whatever you call what you do in the Laird's Room. It puts coins in our pockets, Your Lordship. Gardening wouldn't."

"I hate it when you call me that," he said.

"That you do," she said, smiling. "But it was very clever of you to get me started on gardening so I wouldn't talk about the American girl."

It was his turn to smile. Irene had always been an intelligent woman. He didn't want to talk about Mercy with anyone, even Irene.

However, it seemed as if Irene wasn't finished.

"You need to call a truce," she said. "Make up with Douglas."

"I wasn't the one who started it all, Irene."

"I swear, the two of you are bairns. It doesn't matter who started it. It's who finishes that counts. Be the bigger man."

"I'm fine without Douglas Macrory in my life. I've managed the past five years. I can manage the rest of it."

"The old man might not have five years."

"Then the problem will resolve itself, won't it?"

"If you think that sister of his is more reasonable, I'm here to tell you that you're wrong. I've never seen ice in a human shape before, but there it is."

"Irene. Let it go."

She sliced the end off a carrot with more force than was necessary, then looked up at him with a frown.

"Mercy isn't your enemy," she said. "If you gave her half a chance she might be a great deal more."

He didn't know how to respond to that, so he turned and left the room. He needed to involve himself in his work. That way, he could banish all thoughts of Mercy.

WHEN THE CARRIAGE stopped in front of the house, a servant opened the door and stepped aside. Mercy was about to exit the vehicle when McNaughton stepped up.

He extended his arm and she had no choice but to take it, descending the two steps to the gravel.

"Miss Rutherford."

"McNaughton."

"I take it that you've had another misadventure," he said, his stare encompassing her damp hair. At least he couldn't see the state of her corset or shift.

The servant who'd opened the door helped Ruthie from the carriage.

All four of them mounted the steps, entering the reception room just as they had a week earlier.

"I believe the family wishes to speak with you, Miss Rutherford."

"Why?"

"The carriage was spotted on the approach to the house, miss. There are questions as to where you've been and why you've returned in the Caitheart vehicle again."

She sighed inwardly, wishing there was an end to this idiotic feud. The two families were fighting because of people who were long dead. Wouldn't their deaths have been cause enough for them to band together?

"They're waiting for you in the family parlor, Miss Rutherford."

She couldn't help but wonder how much pleasure

McNaughton received from the idea that she was about to be lectured.

Mercy turned and addressed Ruthie. "Thank you, Ruthie," she said. "Will you go and rest now?"

"You don't want me to go with you, Miss Mercy?"

Mercy shook her head. "No. There's no need for you to be there. I really want you to go rest."

Ruthie nodded.

Mercy turned and looked at McNaughton. "I'm not certain where the family parlor is. Can you give me directions?"

He looked down his narrow nose at her, gave her a grim smile—the kind undertakers must surely wear— and said, "If you'll follow me, Miss Rutherford, I will take you there."

She had no choice but to trail along in McNaughton's wake. A few minutes later she was grateful that she'd done so, because she was certain she would never have found the room without help.

The butler stood aside, opened one of the double doors, and bowed slightly. The glint in his eyes, however, was anything but obsequious. He was thoroughly enjoying her discomfort.

"The family parlor, Miss Rutherford," he intoned.

She was surprised that he didn't announce her in that same officious voice. Mercy took a few steps inside the room and was assaulted by the color blue. The sofa and two flanking chairs were upholstered in blue silk. The curtains on the four north-facing windows were made of the same fabric. The room would be naturally dark, given that several trees had been allowed to grow close to the house, but the color scheme made it seem even gloomier.

The whole family was there: her grandmother,

Great-Uncle Douglas, Flora, and Aunt Elizabeth. Only Elizabeth smiled at her, an expression that seemed filled with pity. Flora was wide-eyed and no doubt grateful that she wasn't the person being watched so carefully. As far as Ailsa and Douglas, she doubted if even Mount Olympus had had such strict and cold judges.

There wasn't anywhere for her to sit, unless she chose the opposite side of the room where four chairs and a gaming table had been set up in front of the fireplace. She chose to stand in front of the sofa where Douglas and her grandmother sat, grateful that a wide rectangular table was between her and her older relatives.

When she was a child, her grandmother had slapped her on occasion, claiming that Mercy had misbehaved. The infractions had been so small that she'd never re-membered them, only the punishment. Mercy didn't have any doubt that Ailsa would resort to such behav-ior now if she was annoyed enough. The past four years might have aged Seanmhair, but she was neither frail nor feeble.

Mercy's shift was nearly dry, but it was itching. She wanted to go change her clothes, bathe, and consider the events of the morning. Instead, she stood before her relatives in an impromptu tribunal.

They must truly be angry to venture out of their rooms before dinner.

The irritation Mercy felt was a slow-burning thing, a tiny fire lit by a solitary, rebellious thought. Who were they to pass judgment on her?

"What have you done now, Hortense?" Ailsa asked. "I never thought to see the day when my own grand-daughter behaved with such shocking lack of decorum."

"You evidently have no care for the family's wishes," Douglas said. "Or you would not be in that man's company."

"Is it because he's an earl?" Flora's eyes were wide, her cheeks pink. "Americans quite like titles, I hear. He hasn't any money, however."

"That doesn't mean anything," Douglas said. "A man is who he is. Not a title he inherited."

"Is that why you're sniffing after him?" Ailsa said.

Her grandmother had never sounded so crude in the past.

Mercy had come into the room determined not to say a word about what had happened this morning. She'd known, because of their antipathy toward Lennox, that they wouldn't understand. They didn't disappoint. The only person who hadn't said anything to her was Aunt Elizabeth. Nor did she say anything supportive.

"There was an accident," she said. "Rather than walk home soaking wet I dried myself off at Duddingston Castle. Irene was very kind."

There, the kernel of the truth if not the exact telling of it.

All four of her relatives looked as if they were trying to decide whether or not to believe her.

"And the carriage?" Douglas asked. "Was that Irene's doing? Or did Lennox summon his carriage for you?"

It hit her then.

"Are you worried that history will repeat itself? A Macrory woman and a Caitheart man?"

Uncle Douglas didn't answer, but he didn't meet her eyes, either. Her grandmother had no such difficulty. That unblinking gaze would have been disconcerting if she hadn't had practice meeting it.

"Your blood is diluted," Ailsa said. "You're hardly a true Macrory."

Diluted because of her father, of course, a wealthy Yankee who had the temerity to offer her compassion.

Mercy didn't respond. From past experience, the best way to behave would be to say something conciliatory, admit her flaws, beg for forgiveness, or otherwise grovel.

She didn't feel like groveling at the moment.

Flora looked mildly disappointed and Mercy couldn't tell if it was because she hadn't been verbally whipped or confessed to something salacious.

Aunt Elizabeth was watching her, her aunt's gaze as direct as Ailsa's.

"If you don't mind," Mercy said, taking a step back, "I'd like to go to my room now."

"I think that would be best," Ailsa said.

"And I think you should remain inside Macrory House until such time as you return to America," Douglas added.

Her grandmother nodded. "Since you've proved to have little common sense or decorum, Hortense, that sounds like an excellent idea."

No one said a word as she turned and left the room.

It was entirely possible that her grandmother would discover the truth about her adventures of this morning and that she'd been alone with two men while in a state of undress.

Ruthie might not get a chance to recuperate. They might be banished back to America any moment now.

She'd never disobeyed at home, being a dutiful daughter so as not to cause her parents more grief. Coming to Scotland had changed her. Maybe it was because she'd made a bid for freedom. Or because she'd made a choice not to accept the life doled out to her. For whatever reason, she wasn't the same person she'd been even a short time ago.

She reached her room to find Ruthie sitting there.

"What am I going to do with you? You should be in your room resting, Ruthie."

"Will we really be going home when my arm heals, Miss Mercy?"

She had a feeling that Ruthie wasn't homesick as much as dreading the day they would leave Scotland.

"Yes," Mercy said. "We weren't meant to stay here long."

Perhaps she should tell Ruthie that she was feeling a similar reluctance, but it wouldn't help for both of them to be foolish.

Ruthie nodded. "Let's get you out of that dress, Miss Mercy. That corset and shift must be uncomfortable."

"It's beastly, Ruthie, but I would feel better if you rested. Truly."

"I'd much rather be doing something, Miss Mercy. When I'm alone in my room, all I can do is think and all that does is make me sad."

She hugged Ruthie, fervently wishing she could do more.

Chapter Twenty-Three

$\mathcal{F}$or a week Mercy remained inside Macrory House, only venturing as far as the walled garden. At least she wasn't bothered by her cousin since Flora had departed for her Edinburgh trip with her grandfather.

With the exception of her relatives and McNaughton, who looked down his long beak of a nose at her, everyone at Macrory House was warm, friendly, and curious. The servants asked her questions about America or her journey to Scotland. Numerous times she'd been told about a relative who'd emigrated and now lived in Chicago or New Jersey or a half dozen other places.

Conversation in the kitchen was lively, never malicious, and always sprinkled with laughter.

After dinner she'd grabbed a book and left the house, intent on the garden. All she wanted to do was sit on one of the benches and read.

"May I join you?"

Mercy looked up to find that her aunt had followed her.

Other than dinner, stiff uncomfortable events where her grandmother and aunt rarely spoke to her, Mercy hadn't seen Elizabeth. Although her aunt had said that she'd wanted to spend time with her, it felt like Elizabeth was avoiding her. Mercy couldn't help but wonder if that was on orders from her grandmother. She hadn't known Ailsa to be petty, but the war might have changed her.

She moved aside so that Elizabeth could join her on the bench. Her aunt's skirts were wider than hers, but then Mercy had the advantage of a newer wardrobe. She rarely wore the wide hoop Elizabeth favored. The only exception was when she donned a gown for formal events. The latest styles were accentuating a bustle, but Elizabeth wouldn't have had access to a new wardrobe.

They sat silently together for a few minutes. Elizabeth looked over the garden with an expression that indicated she truly didn't care what she saw. The view wasn't very inspiring. This part of the garden led to a maze and the hedges were precisely trimmed and over their heads. No flowers had been planted. Nor was there anything of interest, like a bit of statuary to catch the eye. The garden was, however, a lovely place to escape to if you wanted to avoid Flora.

Mercy waited, certain that her aunt had sought her out for a specific reason.

"You spend a great deal of time in the kitchen, Mercy."

She was right, she had been sought out for a reason, evidently to be lectured about her behavior.

"Did Seanmhair send you to find me?"

Elizabeth looked away rather than answering.

"I know that things are different here than in America, Mercy, witness the relationship you have with Ruthie. Here the line between staff and employer is well drawn. It breaks down the barriers when a member of the family socializes with the servants."

She had never known her aunt to be a prig. Nor did the words Elizabeth was saying sound like something she would say.

"Tell Seanmhair I'll be gone soon enough," she said, trying to mitigate the irritation in her tone. Weren't there more important things for her grandmother to be concerned about than whether she spent time in the kitchen?

Elizabeth finally looked in her direction.

"Your face lights up when you talk about him."

"Who?" she said, even though she knew to whom Elizabeth was referring.

"Lennox. When his name comes up in conversation, you seem eager to defend him."

Mercy put her book to the side, clasped her hands in her lap, and stared down at her fingers.

"It isn't, as Flora thinks, because he's an earl. I admire him. I didn't, initially. I thought he was boorish and arrogant. He does things that other people think are foolhardy, yet he doesn't seem to care about their opinions. If there's something he wants to do, he simply goes forward with it."

"That might be considered obstinacy."

"Or determination. Or being his own man, without regard to whether other people approve."

"He's also a very handsome man."

She glanced at Elizabeth again to find her aunt studying her.

"He is at that," Mercy said. "But I don't understand why you refer to him so often at dinner. As if he's some hideous and horrible person. I've never found him to be so."

"As you said, Mercy, you'll be gone from here soon enough and life will return to what it has always been."

"Are you living the life you want, Aunt Elizabeth? Here, in Scotland? Is this where you wish to be?"

Elizabeth was staring at the hedges again, but this time she looked like her thoughts were far away from Scotland and perhaps years distant.

"I'm sorry," Mercy said. "That's not a question I should have asked."

Mercy reached over and placed her hand atop her aunt's. She wanted to say how sorry she was, how much she wished that Elizabeth hadn't had to endure the pain of losing the man she loved. Instead she remained silent because there were times when words seemed useless.

ROBERT HAD INSTALLED a telescope between the merlons on the tower's top. Lennox had covered it with an oiled tarp years ago, more out of respect for his brother than to protect the equipment. Now he put down the lantern and removed the tarp, shaking it over the edge to get the dust off before dropping it at the base of the telescope.

He'd never been a romantic like Robert. He'd never felt about a woman the way Robert had Mary, or been willing to make a fool of himself for love. Living at Duddingston had probably been as lonely for Robert as it was for him. Whenever Lennox had thoughts about such things, he buried himself in his work. To do otherwise would be foolish.

When he'd first seen the telescope, he'd known why Robert had put it here. Not to see the stars or the scenery. No, he'd probably somehow communicated with

Mary. Maybe by lantern light or some other type of signal.

Now here he was, doing something almost as idiotic.

He tilted the telescope toward Macrory House, looked through the eyepiece, and tried to focus it. All he could see was fog, as if the lenses needed to be cleaned. He tried a half dozen more times before he finally gave up and put the tarp back. If he wanted to continue to be as foolish, he would have to disassemble the telescope and clean it thoroughly.

That wasn't going to happen. Robert might have been lovelorn, but he wasn't.

It was almost midnight. On a normal Highland summer night it wouldn't yet be full dark, as if the land was reluctant to surrender the day. Tonight the sky was black with rolling clouds. Loch Arn was no more than an inky stain without moonlight reflecting on the water.

The air smelled clean, mixed with the scent of dusty stone. Somewhere, a bird called, no doubt announcing that a storm was coming.

He might be the only person awake for miles. The only one whose thoughts reached out far beyond his own body. Had Robert felt like this? Had his older brother willed Mary to light a lamp, to stand in front of her window, to wait for his signal?

He gently pressed his hand against his upper arm. He could almost feel Mercy's touch on his skin. Or hear her indrawn breath when he'd flinched. He'd wanted to remain immobile for her sake, but her stitching had been more painful than he'd anticipated. He'd no doubt caused her as much discomfort. He'd ask her the next time she came.

A warning voice whispered in his ear. Perhaps

it wouldn't be wise to see her again. The better course would be to send word to Mercy that McNaughton should remove her stitches. The man could do a good enough job. Perhaps he should also tell her that there was no reason for her to ever return to Duddingston Castle.

The sooner she went back to America, the better.

For whom? How strange that the question was uttered in a voice that sounded too much like Robert.

Chapter Twenty-Four

"You're up early, Miss Mercy," the housekeeper said, looking up from her small desk in the office next to the kitchen. "Shall I ring for your breakfast?"

"Thank you, no, Mrs. West. I'm not hungry. Perhaps just a cup of coffee."

Mrs. West stood. "Of course. Let me get it for you myself. Shall I bring it to the family dining room?"

"That's not necessary. Perhaps I could sit with you for a few minutes?"

The older woman smiled and nodded toward the chair beside the desk.

She quite liked Mrs. West. First of all, she reminded her, not unexpectedly, of Irene. Secondly, the woman was possessed of an incredible practical nature, no doubt because of her position. Thirdly, she was exceedingly kind, evident in the way she treated her staff. No one was ever subjected to criticism in front of another person. She didn't demean the people who worked at Macrory House. Even her conversation was carefully directed toward the good in a situation or a person. She was filled with compliments about the two new maids she'd recently hired. Or the young stable boy who'd prevented a fire because he'd been paying attention one night.

Mercy sat, folded her hands, and tried to maintain an aura of calm. Ever since yesterday, she'd been thinking about her conversation with her aunt. The longer she mulled over Elizabeth's words, the more annoyed she became. She was tired of everyone trying to mold her into a perfect person. She wasn't one. Nor did she have the least desire to be.

Coming to Scotland had been an act of rebellion, shocking and unusual for her. Being here in the housekeeper's office was another rebellious act and would, no doubt, annoy her grandmother and aunt.

Wait until they learned what she was going to do next.

When Mrs. West returned with the coffee, she thanked the older woman and took the cup from her.

The next few minutes were spent discussing various innocuous topics, such as the garden, the staffing requirements, and the menu for the next week. When her coffee was nearly done, she put the cup on the edge of the desk and smiled at Mrs. West.

"Lennox has offered to take out my stitches. I would very much like them gone, Mrs. West. My head is itching abominably, and I haven't been able to wash my hair correctly ever since the accident."

The housekeeper didn't say a word which surprised her. She'd expected Mrs. West to offer that McNaughton would be happy to remove her stitches. She had her explanation ready for the housekeeper. McNaughton had made no secret of his contempt for her. For that reason, she'd rather anyone else do the job.

"Is there a way to get out of the house without any-one noticing? I want to go to Duddingston Castle."

"Miss Mercy . . ." Mrs. West began.

Mercy held up her hand. "Please do not lecture me, Mrs. West. I know what I want to do."

"I would not venture to do such a thing, Miss Mercy. I was only going to say that you're not dressed for crossing the glen. It rained last night and the ground is soggy. I'm guessing that you've no boots for the purpose."

Mercy shook her head.

"Then, if you'll allow me, I'll loan you mine. They'll no doubt be a might big, but they'll work well enough."

"Thank you. I'd be very grateful."

"If you don't mind I'll send a bit of tablet over to Irene by way of you." She smiled. "It's a bit of a sweet treat that Irene likes and I made it yesterday."

"Of course," Mercy said.

Before she left, Mrs. West surprised her by saying, "I'll just spread the word to a few of the maids, miss. It's a little misdirection, but it's harmless enough. One will say they've seen you in the library. Another heading toward the garden. It will only give you a few hours, though, until someone goes in search of you in earnest."

Mercy nodded. Armed with the pan of something that looked like a light-colored grainy fudge, she left the house, heading for a narrow door near the kitchen gardens. Trees close to the house shielded her departure, plus she had directions to a door in the garden wall. She would be out of sight of anyone in the house and could make it across the glen with no one the wiser.

The ground was solid until she left the walled garden by the secret door. Without Mrs. West's help, she would never have found it, tucked as it was behind rose bushes and hidden by ivy. Once on the glen, she followed the housekeeper's instructions and looked for the beginning of a drover's trail, shortening the distance to Duddingston Castle.

The boots were too large, but she made them work by slipping them on over her shoes. More than once she sank nearly up to her ankles in the spongy earth, but after she was on the trail it was easier.

The morning felt damp, a residual from the storm last night. The woods at the foot of Ben Uaine were shadowed, the diffuse sunlight not able to penetrate the thick pines.

She climbed a small hill, stood there, and looked over the scenery, feeling a curious sense of belonging in this strange place. She felt as if she'd always known the mountains in the distance, the glen undulating before her, even the sight of the loch in the distance.

At first she'd been unable to decipher the Scottish accent. Now she could understand most of what was said to her, although there were still some sayings that were unfamiliar, like *haud yer wheest, gie it laldy*, it's a *dreich* day. And the word for Ruthie's splint: *skootie*.

Coming to Scotland had been an act of freedom, but it was turning out to be so much more. She felt different, more herself than at any time in her life. She wasn't forced to wear a polite and stiff mask or endlessly guard her words.

Perhaps she could take this new person she was becoming back to America. Perhaps she would even have the courage to speak up for herself and explain that she wasn't going to break. She didn't need a guard twenty-four hours a day. Nor should her life be a prison.

Her parents would be upset about her decision not to marry Gregory, but she hoped they would eventually understand.

He may have come from a fine family. He may be ambitious and intelligent. He was not only regarded with respect by several of her father's friends and business acquaintances, he had been lauded as a hero. He was handsome, polite, and exceedingly cordial to her parents.

Yet life with Gregory wouldn't be a blessing. She would be expected to obey him, to be molded and coached, to be all the things he wanted in a wife. She would be expected to continue to strive for perfection, only with Gregory being the arbiter of her behavior.

She couldn't imagine a more hideous future.

Of course, there was every possibility that she would cause a scandal that echoed throughout New York because she'd broken the engagement. No doubt rumors were floating now about her behavior. She'd probably be ostracized and people would gossip about her for years.

Let them say whatever they wanted.

If nothing else, this trip to Scotland had taught her that people will think what they will, because their own prejudices fueled their opinions. Her relatives had been guilty of that.

From here she could see Duddingston Castle spread out before her. Her heart beat a little faster at the thought of seeing Lennox.

She wasn't going to lie to her relatives. If she was asked where she'd been, she was going to confess that she'd disobeyed their wishes and returned to the castle, but only to have Lennox remove her stitches. Very well, perhaps not simply to have Lennox remove her stitches. Perhaps for another reason, less easy to understand. She wanted to see him again.

After descending the hill, she stopped at the bridge to watch the water cascading down to the loch before entering the shadowed alcove that led to the castle's front door. She pulled the bell, hearing it ring deep inside the house. Was he home? Or was he out experimenting with his flying machine?

He really should take more care than he'd shown on the two flights she'd witnessed.

It struck her then, hard enough that she stared at the iron door in front of her. She was worried about Lennox.

During the four years Gregory had fought in the war she'd been concerned about him, but in a way she suspected was different from what she was supposed to feel. She'd never cried into her pillow or sent words of longing through the mail. She'd worried about him because he was a human being, but she'd never once thought her heart would break because he hadn't come home for so long.

She knew that she wouldn't feel the same if Lennox had gone to war.

Chapter Twenty-Five

To her surprise, Irene answered the door.

"I was told that you were kept at home for your own good," she said.

"Your sister helped me escape. The price for her assistance," Mercy said, handing her the pan.

"I'm thankful that you're here, then, for more than one reason. His Lordship has a liking for tablet, too."

"Is he here?"

Irene studied her for a moment. It was an uncomfortable examination. She wanted to tell Irene that the reason she was here was only for Lennox to remove her stitches. That was all. She had no interest in the man. However, she wasn't willing to lie to Irene.

"Aye, he is at that. He's in the courtyard, working on one of his machines. Go straight through the Clan Hall, turn right and out the big door, and you'll find him."

Mercy smiled her thanks and followed Irene's directions. The Clan Hall was larger than she realized, the noise of her borrowed boots clomping on the stone made her sound like a horse tromping through the space. Before she opened the door, she stopped, pulled off the boots, and held them in one hand.

Most of her upbringing had been geared to understanding what was right and proper, first within the confines of her own home and then in society. She was a Rutherford and that dictated she act in certain ways. Her father was a benefactor to several charities and more than once she'd accompanied her parents to events saluting his generosity. She was expected to be gracious at all times, cordial, and conversant in a variety of subjects regardless of who engaged her in conversation.

She spoke French and enough phrases in four other languages to make people of several nationalities at ease in her company. She'd been given an extensive education in art so as to appreciate the Rutherford Wing of the New York Art Institute. She'd been schooled in etiquette since she was five and in how to manage a household since she was ten.

Yet she'd never been coached about what to say when a man was half-naked in front of her.

Lennox was bare to the waist again. This time she was going to look her fill.

She had no idea that a man's chest could be so well defined or muscular. She had the most curious compulsion to run her fingers through the hair there. Then she wanted to drop her hands and press them against his midriff.

He was reaching above him, tightening something on a piece of wood that was fastened to another crosspiece, and hadn't seen her yet, giving her ample time to study him.

When he turned away from her, she saw that his back was almost as impressive as his front.

Should she retreat or announce her presence? She honestly didn't know what to do, but the decision was taken from her when he turned and noticed her.

"You're three days late," he said, giving her no more greeting than that.

"I couldn't get away," she said.

"Irene said you'd been confined to the house. How did you escape?"

She really shouldn't smile at his comment or feel so proud of herself.

"I went to Mrs. West. The price for her help was to bring something to Irene."

"Tablet?" His eyes lit up like a child's.

She nodded and began walking toward him, still carrying the boots. To her disappointment, he reached over and grabbed his shirt, putting it on as she approached.

"Forgive my attire," he said.

She almost wanted to apologize for staring, but kept silent.

"Why were you confined to the house? Was it because you'd come to my aid?"

She smiled. "I think my family's afraid that I'll shame them in some way."

"Will you?"

"I've never shamed anyone before. I've been the epitome of perfection. Yet I've broken all sorts of rules by coming to Scotland with only Ruthie as my companion."

"Why did you?"

As she was framing her answer, he said, "Forgive me, it's none of my concern. I was simply curious."

She stopped what she was going to say and looked at him. "No one's ever been curious about me."

"Why not?"

She thought about it. "Probably because I've never

been very interesting. Everything about me has been known. I'm James Gramercy Rutherford's only daughter. That says it all."

"On the contrary," he said. "That doesn't even begin to describe you."

The strangest feeling of warmth was traveling through her body.

"You didn't have that idiot McNaughton remove your stitches, did you?"

She shook her head.

"Good. Come, we'll get it done now." He turned and walked back to the door, glancing over his shoulder to see if she was following.

This time as they walked through the Clan Hall she stopped more than once to look at the objects on the wall. Lennox didn't seem in a hurry, so she asked him questions about what she saw.

She knew more about American history than she did that of Scotland, but she recognized the names of some of the battles he listed. Evidently, the Caitheart clan had participated in almost every confrontation occurring in Scotland for the past four hundred years. Either their weapons or their banners remained as a testament to the clan's courage.

"You never talk about being an earl," she said, stopping in front of a large framed painting of the Caitheart clan badge.

"It was always Robert's title. Not mine."

"You must have loved him very much," she said. "I envy you."

"I thought you said you had a brother."

She nodded. Jimmy was a subject that was rarely mentioned, even at home. Her parents didn't discuss him in front of her. It was as if Jimmy existed on the third floor but nowhere else, not even in their conversation.

"Jimmy isn't like most people," she said, violating a long-held unwritten rule. No one spoke about Jimmy outside the family. "He will never be older than a child. He doesn't really recognize people other than my mother and father."

"He doesn't know you're his sister?"

She shook her head. "I used to visit him every day, but every day I had to introduce myself all over again. The nurse finally asked me not to come so often, because it upset him."

"That must be exceedingly difficult for your parents," he said.

Her mother visited Jimmy every morning and every afternoon, always returning from the third floor with a look of resolution.

Her father treated Jimmy as he did everything, like a task that must be performed. Every night he went up to the third floor by way of the elevator he'd had installed. Every night he returned the same way, pushing Jimmy's chair before him. The father and the son spent an hour in the large study before her father retraced his steps, talking to Jimmy about his day or plans he'd begun for another merger before returning his son to his modified living quarters.

Mercy went out of her way to avoid the two of them at those times, only because it hurt too much to hear her father's conversation, knowing that her brother wouldn't be able to respond or even understand. Her father wouldn't have welcomed her pity. Jimmy's condition—the result of a difficult birth—had never gotten better. Mentally, he would never be more than a child. The only change over the years was that her brother grew larger, the chair was replaced with a bigger one, and the nurse now had a male attendant to help her wash and move Jimmy.

"Yes, I think it is."

"It's difficult on you, too," he said, surprising her. "I'm sorry."

"And I'm sorry for your loss," she said. "I'm guessing that you loved your brother a great deal."

He nodded. "Robert raised me after our parents died. He was the one who insisted that I go to school in Edinburgh."

"What would he think about your adventures now? Would he be angry that you didn't finish your schooling?" Before he could answer, she asked him the one question that had truly intrigued her. "Why did you go to school to become a doctor when you've invented all those things?"

"I needed a profession," he said. "Tinkering was not a suitable occupation."

"I think you do more than tinker, Lennox."

He glanced at her.

"Your airships," she said. "They're quite involved and intricate."

He nodded, then led the way down the corridor to the kitchen.

Irene wasn't there, but the pan of tablet was on the table under the window. Lennox ignored it, going to the cupboard for his bag.

"Will we need whiskey again?" she asked.

"To drink or for medicinal purposes?"

"I think I should avoid drinking it from now on," she admitted. "It put me to sleep."

"I don't think we need it."

To her surprise, removing the stitches took only a moment.

When he was finished she said, "I thought it would hurt."

"Did it?"

"No. It was just a pinch."

Lennox combed his fingers through her hair, an intimate gesture she should have rebuffed.

She should've pulled away, too, when he placed his hands on either side of her face and tilted her head back.

"There you go, Miss Mercy. All healed and as good as new."

"Thank you, Your Lordship."

"If I agree not to call you Miss Mercy, will you simply call me Lennox?"

She nodded.

His grin startled her. "Would you like to see what I'm working on now?"

"In the courtyard?"

He nodded.

Would he remove his shirt again? That was a question she wouldn't ask, but she hoped he did.

Why was it permissible to look at a statue of a Greek or Roman, to admire the form, the sculptor's talent, and not feel admiration for a living body?

Not that her interest in Lennox's form was purely for artistic reasons. That was not a lie she would tell herself.

Chapter Twenty-Six

$\mathcal{L}$ennox put up the bag and together they walked back through the castle and out to the courtyard. The deep blue skies promised a fair day with no rain. Yet even if it had stormed for hours, Mercy wouldn't have cared.

The curious thing about being in Lennox's company was that she felt lighthearted around him. It was as if a smile began deep in the core of her and happiness radiated outward. It was such an unusual feeling and one she'd never experienced.

"Connor has gone to Inverness to pick up the new sail," he said. "I'm missing an assistant. Would you like to help?"

"Yes, but I've no experience in airships."

"I plan to use you for painting," he said.

It didn't matter whatever he wanted her to do. As long as she was here she would do what she could to help him. That turned out to be applying a noxious yellowish substance to various pieces of wood and then placing them in the middle of the courtyard to dry.

"What does it do?" she asked, holding the jar up to the sunlight.

"It seals the wood. It doesn't make it entirely water-proof, but it protects it enough that if I land in the loch again I can salvage the craft."

"Must it smell so atrocious?" she asked, holding the jar away from her. The odor was one of rotting onions and fish.

"It's almost perfume next to the liquid I use to pre-pare the sails."

"What are these for?" she asked, picking up one of the narrow lengths of wood.

"They're struts to support the wings."

Once she'd been given her task, he returned to the other side of the courtyard.

She was probably not as fast as he would have been at the same task, but she managed to finish one stack of struts, taking care that she painted the wood just as he'd demonstrated.

From time to time she glanced in his direction. It looked as if he was building the framework of an-other airship. At the moment it appeared almost like the skeleton of some giant mythical beast. Without its sails, it seemed to be flimsy, almost fragile. How could he entrust his life to a few pieces of wood and cloth?

Lennox might have escaped unscathed the last two times, but he'd been lucky. Next time he might not be so fortunate.

He was standing on a crate, reaching overhead to string something that looked like copper wire from the edge of the wings down to the boat-like structure where he sat and controlled the aircraft.

She was certain that if she hadn't been there, he would've removed his shirt again, taking advantage of the warm summer sun.

"Why?"

He glanced over at her.

"Why do you want to fly?"

"Because it's possible. Because men have flown in balloons for decades. Because a man flew in Cayley's glider twenty years ago. Because the next great thing won't be a glider at all, but something powered by steam. All that's left is to figure out the formula."

She held up the jar. "Like this?"

He shook his head. "No," he said. "Like lift, weight, thrust, and drag. What makes a successful glider. I think velocity will have to be part of the formula as well, but I haven't yet figured out a way to compute that. It's only a matter of time, Mercy. Every day, we're making advances somewhere across the world. Why not here? Why not in this one spot in Scotland?"

"So you want to be the first?"

"I don't care if I'm first," he said, surprising her. "I just want to contribute. I want to be part of it."

"I should think that all of you would get together, whoever you are across the world, and form some sort of club or association."

"I do correspond with a few men. We exchange ideas and theories."

They lived in two different worlds, not just New York and Scotland. He was a man fighting to protect his legacy while following his interests. She was a woman expected to conform to a certain role. Of the two of them, he had the more exciting life and it was one he had crafted himself.

She couldn't even conceive of a circumstance in which she was given a chance to follow her interests. If she even had an interest in anything beyond herself.

The thought brought her up short, made her turn

and apply herself to the task that she'd been given once more.

Was she that insular? Yes, she had been. Her entire life, from the first moment she'd drawn breath, had been lived inside a luxurious bubble. Nothing was as important as she was. Life revolved around her.

Lennox was willing to put himself in danger to prove something. She had nothing that meant enough to her to fight for—except for her freedom.

She'd read newspaper accounts of women who'd been heroines during the war. They'd been nurses or operated as couriers or spies.

Even Ailsa had kept her farm going in the middle of a war with Elizabeth helping. They'd only come back to Scotland after they'd been burned out.

The only thing Mercy had done was leave America. Her freedom had been important enough to brave censure and the endless lectures she would receive in the future from her disappointed parents, but it hardly seemed as significant as the actions of those other women.

Each of them had believed in something outside themselves that was more important than their own safety. Even Lennox's single-minded pursuit of flight wasn't for himself as much as to prove that it could be done.

Her life had never expanded beyond the big gray house in New York. If nothing else, this time in Scotland had taught her that and one thing more: she wouldn't be able to live in such a narrow world again.

"Why don't you get along with the Macrorys?" she asked, desperate to change the tenor of her thoughts. "You both lost someone you love. Wasn't that enough to bridge any gulf you might've felt?"

"I didn't know your family," he said. "I rarely had anything to do with them when I was a boy and then I went to Edinburgh to study and live. I didn't come back to Duddingston very often. Robert always came to Edinburgh."

She turned and looked at him, wanting to know more and hoping that he'd continue.

"Robert made arrangements with a variety of people," he said. "Most of them refused to honor any contracts once he was gone. I saw your great-uncle's hand in that. Our cattle were grazing on Macrory land. I had to sell the herd because I had no way of feeding them. There was a right-of-way your great-uncle forbid me to use. Robert had developed a new way to dry seaweed. That stopped. Even the fishing contracts he made with the villagers weren't continued."

"And you think Douglas was behind all those things? Why would he do something like that?"

He shook his head. "I don't know. No, that's not true. I suspect I know, but I've never gotten corroboration from him. I think he blamed Robert for Mary's death. It's always neat and tidy if you can blame someone for acts of nature or accidents. So he was determined to obtain his own form of justice. If he could ruin me, all the better."

"Do you think him that petty?"

"He loved his daughter. He couldn't see that I loved my brother. For some reason, or because I was a Caitheart, I had to be punished, although I wasn't responsible for the accident. No one was."

He remained silent for a moment and then spoke again. "There are times, Mercy, when things happen. There isn't anyone to blame. You can't wrap everything up in a nice little bundle and put a bow on it and say *this* is why that happened. Life doesn't work that way. Douglas doesn't understand that. He's a scales kind of man. Everything has to be balanced in his world."

She hadn't known her great-uncle for long, but from their conversations at dinner, she got the impression that he and her grandmother were alike. They each had a penchant for blaming others for their ills. In Ailsa's case, it might have been appropriate to blame the war and the Union soldiers—especially those who'd set fire to her home—for her current situation. But it seemed unfair to hold Lennox accountable for the tragedy that had befallen both families.

Now it seemed as if both sides were deeply entrenched in their respective positions. She wasn't going to solve anything in the time she would be remaining in Scotland. That thought joined the others, succeeding in ruining the happiness she felt by being here with Lennox.

Chapter Twenty-Seven

$\mathcal{L}$ennox hadn't expected her to want to help, but once again Mercy surprised him.

When she asked a question, he felt compelled to give her the truth. It was genuine curiosity he saw in her eyes. Or a wish to understand him.

It was a heady experience having a beautiful woman look at him in such a way.

He should've banished her the moment he tended to her wound. Instead, he'd lifted up her face, studying her. He'd wanted, in those moments in the kitchen, to kiss her. A forbidden yet exciting compulsion, one he hadn't acted on but that still lingered in his mind.

For the last hour, he hadn't paid enough attention to what he'd been doing. Instead, he'd been watching her, how she was intent upon brushing the solution on each side of the struts, then carefully moving them to the table in the middle of the courtyard.

He should have given her an apron, but she didn't seem concerned about her dress. She was an heiress, a fact that he needed to remember. She probably had never been given such a mundane task to perform. Yet she hadn't balked. Nor had she spoken for the past quarter hour, intent on what she was doing.

"Why did you come to Scotland?" he asked, letting his curiosity escape.

She didn't look at him. Instead, she finished painting the strut she was working on, put the paintbrush back in the jar, and carried the strut to the table.

Only then did she come and stand next to where he was working on the wing assembly.

"I escaped," she said. "I ran away from home. I never thought to do such a thing, but my life was all planned out for me. No one ever asked me what I wanted."

"What do you want?"

She looked startled, and then began to smile. He'd never been affected by a smile before, but something about Mercy's expression made him want to smile in turn.

"I'm not quite sure," she said. "Isn't that terrible? I've spent all that time being certain that I didn't want what I had. But what do I want? I don't know."

She glanced away and then focused on the ground as if the courtyard held some kind of answer.

"I don't have an airship," she said. "I don't want to nurse anyone. Or carry dispatches. Or shoot anyone."

He didn't know what she was talking about, but rather than interrupt, he kept silent.

"I wanted my freedom, but why?"

"Why freedom?"

"Why bother?"

"You're asking a Scot that? We fought for our freedom for centuries."

She pointed one finger at him. "You see, that's exactly what I'm talking about."

"Mercy, I have to confess I'm totally confused with this conversation. I don't understand."

"Of course you don't," she said.

She didn't speak for a moment and he wondered if she would continue.

"It just occurred to me that I have nothing to believe in," she finally said. "I don't have a cause. I don't have some abiding interest. There is nothing that fascinates me." She pointed to the frame of his airship behind them. "That's your cause. That's your abiding interest."

"Is it important that you have one?"

She nodded slowly. "I think so. Everyone I know has one. My father's is his business empire. Douglas's might be the feud with you, if you're right about him. My grandmother even has one. Once it was her home in North Carolina. Now it's hatred. She grooms it and holds it close as if it's a pet. Even my mother has one: me."

"Perhaps you'll find one," he said. When she didn't speak, he continued. "What do you *not* want?"

"To be a puppet."

He hadn't expected that answer. "How so?"

"To be told what to do and how to do it every hour of every day. To have my schedule made for me. To dictate where I'll go, with whom I'll meet, and what I'll say."

"Is that how it was with you?"

"To some degree, yes. But plans were being made for me that would make it even worse. I decided I didn't want that."

"So you came to Scotland."

She nodded.

"But not to stay."

"No."

"So what will change once you go home?"

"Me," she said. Another answer he hadn't expected.

"If anyone asks why I've changed, I might mention a certain earl in a certain castle."

Once again, she surprised him.

"Why would I be credited with such a metamorphosis?"

"It started with you," she said. "And now you've made me think. Although I'm not pleased with my thoughts, I should probably thank you."

"For giving you uncomfortable thoughts?"

She smiled once more and this time he returned the expression, feeling buoyant in a way that startled him. He had that same feeling in his stomach when he took off from Ben Uaine, as if his insides were ascending as he dropped.

She didn't say anything further and neither did he. When he took a few steps toward her, she didn't move back. She only continued to smile, her eyes widening a little.

He reached out one hand, curved it around her waist and drew her forward. The other he placed flat on her back, feeling the fabric of her dress where the sun had warmed it.

He bent his head, even as he told himself that what he was doing was unwise, and slowly placed his mouth on hers.

She sighed against his lips and it wasn't an expression of surrender as much as it was satisfaction. As if she felt what he did at this moment, a curious sense of homecoming, of welcoming. This was what he'd wanted to do for a very long time.

It didn't matter that she was an American, that her home was thousands of miles from here. It didn't matter that she'd soon be gone and he'd never see her again.

Nothing mattered but these seconds when he held her in his arms and she melted against him like pliant wax.

She smelled of sunlight and the formula he'd made to coat the struts.

He smoothed his hands up and down her back, pulling her even closer. One of his hands went to the nape of her neck, his fingers trailing through the tendrils of hair that had come loose from the bun she wore.

He wanted to see her hair down, spread across her shoulders. He wanted her in his bed, naked, so that he could kiss her everywhere. His lips would memorize the texture of her skin at the juncture of her neck and shoulders, smooth over her breasts, dance across her nipples.

None of his thoughts were sensible or proper. He'd lived alone for so many years that he'd grown accustomed to his solitary state. He told himself that companionship didn't matter and, for the most part, he'd been correct.

Until Mercy came. Until she pointed her finger at him and demanded that he apologize.

"I'm sorry," he said, pulling back.

"Sorry?"

She blinked up at him and he knew that he would always remember the sight of Mercy at that moment, a becoming flush on her cheeks, her eyes soft and lambent.

"For nearly landing on you that first day," he said.

"But you're not apologizing for the kiss?"

"I'm not a fool, Mercy."

She smiled at him and that feeling was there again. He'd never expected that being around her could make him feel like he was flying.

She placed both hands on his shirted chest.

"Lennox . . ."

He had no idea what she was going to say, because the door to the Clan Hall abruptly opened. Ruthie and Irene stood there.

"Oh, Miss Mercy! You'll never believe it," Ruthie said, the look on her face one of barely contained terror. "He's just arrived at Macrory House. Him, Miss Mercy. Mr. Hamilton."

Mercy dropped her hands and turned.

"Gregory?" she asked.

Ruthie nodded.

"Who is Gregory?" Lennox asked, concerned that Mercy's face had lost all of its color.

She looked up at him. "The man who thinks he's my fiancé."

Chapter Twenty-Eight

$\mathcal{M}$ercy said her farewells in seconds. She didn't want to recall the look of incredulity on Lennox's face as she left the courtyard. They'd been kissing only minutes earlier and suddenly a fiancé appeared.

No, just Gregory, who refused to accept her decision.

She and Ruthie began following the trail back across the glen. Ruthie asked only one question and it revealed the heart of her concern.

"Why do you think Mr. Hamilton came to Scotland, Miss Mercy?"

Although she'd communicated with her parents, she hadn't written to Gregory. Evidently, her parents had sought his help in retrieving her.

"He's come to get me," she said. "As if I'm a parcel that's been sent to the wrong destination."

The two of them shared a glance.

Gregory had no qualms ordering Ruthie about or even being critical of her. More than once she'd heard him being cutting in his remarks to the maid—behavior that was unnecessary.

It was as if Gregory put everyone around him on a ladder and ranked them depending on their status in life. Those people who weren't his equal he felt comfortable in ridiculing while those like Mercy's parents he treated like gods.

Ruthie never allowed her gaze to alight on anything but the floor when she was in Gregory's company. When he gave her a command—which he did often—Ruthie only nodded and carried it out swiftly. It hadn't been difficult to determine that her maid disliked Gregory, even though Ruthie had never said as much.

Mercy's thoughts should have been on her coming reunion with Gregory, but as they followed the drover's path, she was thinking less of him and more about Lennox. And their kiss. He'd kissed her. Lennox had kissed her.

Her heart had been in her throat. Fire had raced through her at Lennox's touch. She'd wound her arms around his neck, not conscious of anything but him.

She'd never felt that way before. When Gregory had kissed her—or tried to—she hadn't liked the experience. His lips had been too wet and he'd pressed too hard. But kissing Lennox had been a gateway to another world, one in which pleasure speared through her.

She hadn't retreated or rebuffed Lennox. Nor had she slapped him. She certainly hadn't lectured him on his effrontery. Instead, she wanted him to kiss her again. Time had meant nothing in his arms. Until Ruthie had spoken, she hadn't even realized that the two women had entered the courtyard.

Now they made it through the door in the garden wall and only then did Mercy think about the coming confrontation.

At least Flora and Uncle Douglas weren't here. But her grandmother was and so was Aunt Elizabeth. McNaughton probably hadn't waited to inform them of Gregory's arrival. Perhaps all of them were comparing notes about what she'd done wrong now.

"Did he seem angry?"

"He seemed the same as he always is, Miss Mercy."

A polite answer that revealed nothing of Gregory's mood.

"Thank you for coming and getting me, Ruthie."

"Only Mrs. West knows where you were."

"I don't think it matters now," Mercy said.

Ruthie said nothing about finding her in Lennox's arms. Nor did Mercy offer any excuses. If this had been New York and something similar had happened, she might have been embarrassed. Or she could possibly have begged Ruthie to keep silent. Now? She didn't care if everyone knew.

At the kitchen door, Mercy turned and faced her maid. "Well, it's time, I guess."

"Your cheeks are flushed, Miss Mercy."

No doubt Gregory would comment on it. He rarely gave her a compliment unless her parents were in attendance. When they were alone he lost no time in critiquing her appearance. Too bad he hadn't seen her in the turban bandage she'd worn. He missed the opportunity to tell her how hideous she looked.

"Would you like me to come with you?"

Mercy shook her head. "No, that's not necessary." She gave Ruthie a quick hug and entered the house.

McNaughton was in the hallway outside the kitchen. No doubt he'd been waiting for her to appear.

"Mr. Hamilton is in the Green Parlor," he said, all stiff and frosty.

He probably approved of Gregory because he never noticed servants. McNaughton wouldn't have intimidated him. On the contrary, Gregory could freeze anyone to the spot with a simple look.

How odd that she'd never realized that McNaughton and Gregory had some traits in common.

By the time she made it to the parlor, her heart had started beating thunderously. She stopped more than once and placed both hands against her midriff, trying to quell the fluttering sensation inside her stomach.

She hadn't expected Gregory to come to Scotland, but perhaps she should have. He was a determined person, the reason her father was so impressed with him. Gregory had started as a junior executive in one of her father's companies and had advanced at a startling pace to upper management. His meteoric rise was duplicated in the army. He had left for war as a lieutenant and returned a colonel.

Gregory never saw obstacles. Nor did he ever change his mind. She knew that firsthand from his refusal to accept her decision about breaking their engagement.

She entered the room to find him sitting in a chair beside the fireplace. Aunt Elizabeth was sitting opposite him on the settee. Neither of them was talking. Each was studiously avoiding looking at the other.

It couldn't be easy for her aunt to greet a man who'd been a colonel in the Union army. The minute Gregory heard her speak he would know that Elizabeth was from the South. Two adversaries from a war that was just barely over.

At her entrance, Gregory stood, advancing on her as if he were a hunter and she the prey he'd been stalking.

He was a foot taller than she, but so was Lennox. Gregory, however, had a habit of looming over her as if to take advantage of his height, with his broad chest and shoulders. He was a handsome man with light brown hair, blue eyes, and a smile that he used when he got his way. Otherwise, he rarely appeared genial. Instead, he was a watchful man, studying people as if to learn their weaknesses.

He was doing that now, looking for changes that might have occurred in the past few weeks. Could he tell that she'd been kissed? Or that she had participated wholeheartedly?

"Mercy," he said, stretching out both hands toward her.

Reluctantly, she put her hands in his, allowing him to pull her forward.

When he hugged her, she kept her hands at her sides, her chin hitting his chest.

He pulled back, his hands still on her upper arms, and examined her. She probably failed his inspection. Her shoes were scuffed and she hadn't asked that they be polished. The hem of her skirt was damp. She'd spilled a few droplets of Lennox's formula on her left sleeve and it had hardened into dark yellow spots. Her hair was mussed from the wind.

If she were the person she'd been only short weeks ago, she might've apologized for her appearance and made a self-deprecating remark.

Instead, she raised her head and returned Gregory's look steadily.

He dropped his hands, glanced at Elizabeth, and said, "Is there somewhere we can talk, Mercy?"

Aunt Elizabeth startled her by standing. "You can talk here." Without another word, she left the room.

"She's an odd woman," Gregory said.

Although Mercy hadn't felt all that amenable toward her aunt recently, Gregory's comment rankled.

"She's not odd at all, Gregory."

The antipathy Elizabeth felt was easy to understand. Elizabeth's fiancé had fought and died for the South. Mercy chose not to explain that to Gregory, hoping to avoid yet another lecture on how the South had been shortsighted and idiotic to secede.

She'd felt torn from the first. Her mother had been born and raised in North Carolina. Mercy had visited the state often enough to love the beauty of it. She had friends there and that hadn't changed due to the war.

Because of her reading and the conversations around the dinner table, she understood the complexities that had led to war, hating that the impasse meant men would be killed and life would change. It was more complicated than Gregory made it sound. Yet because he'd fought, because he'd been a soldier, his opinion was given greater weight than anything she might say.

She moved to sit on the end of the settee, hoping that Gregory wouldn't join her. A moment later he sat on the adjoining cushion.

"Why are you here?" she asked.

"Is this rudeness a Scottish trait, Mercy? One you've recently acquired?"

He was right. She hadn't asked about his health or his journey. An oversight that she wouldn't have made a month ago. The truth was that she didn't care. If he wished to label her rude, she didn't care about that, either.

"Why did you do such a foolish thing as come here, Mercy?"

Her trip to Scotland hadn't been foolish. She would remember it for the rest of her life. Yet she'd never be able to tell anyone why. Perhaps she should start a journal. Within the pages she could write about Lennox, reveal things that she'd never felt before, thoughts that surprised or shocked her.

"Does it matter?"

"Of course it does," he said. "Was it because of our wedding? I hear brides sometimes get nervous before the nuptials."

She looked away, focusing on a painting on the opposite wall. The man standing there was portly, bald, and smiling brightly. She thought it was one of the first Macrorys, perhaps even the one who'd begun building this house. She kept her attention on the painting rather than look at Gregory.

"My father might respect you. My mother may be fond of you, but I'm still not going to marry you, Gregory. How many times have I told you that? Twenty? Thirty? I'm not going to change my mind."

"Don't be foolish, Mercy."

She glanced at him and then away, trying not to be affected by the odd smile he was giving her, almost as if he knew something she didn't.

"I don't want to marry you. I won't marry you."

"There's nothing to be nervous about, Mercy. Your life isn't going to change."

If he knew anything about her, Gregory would know how that comment made her feel. She loved her parents, but she wanted her own life, not one shared with them. Her parents had already committed to redoing half the second floor of their New York home for her and Gregory so that they would have the illusion of their own apartment, their own space. Except, of course, that it would be just an illusion. They would be expected to take each meal with her parents, spend time each evening with them, even entertain with them. Her life would be indistinguishable from what it was now. The only addition would be Gregory as her husband and that was most definitely not what she wanted.

He reached over and covered her hand with his.

"Were you safe, Mercy?"

She turned to look at him. "Safe?"

He nodded. "You weren't waylaid on your journey, then? Nothing untoward happened?"

Waylaid? She knew quite well what *waylaid* meant. In other words, was she still pure and inviolate?

"It's none of your concern whether I was safe, Gregory. I'm not your fiancée."

He ignored her comment. "You did something foolish, Mercy, traveling by yourself. You don't realize how dangerous your journey was."

"Again, it's none of your concern."

He examined her hand. "You aren't wearing your ring."

"No. I removed it because I knew I wasn't going to marry you. I'll return it."

He smiled. "Don't be foolish, Mercy. Of course we're going to be wed. The invitations have already gone out."

Did no one ever hear her? Was every word she'd spoken ignored? Had she no ability to control her own life? Evidently not, according to her parents and Gregory. Even after she'd left they'd continued to make plans. She didn't even need to be there for her life to be arranged.

She pulled her hand free, not wanting to touch him. "Then we'll have to rescind each and every one. I'm not going to marry you, Gregory."

He reached over and pulled her close to him. Before she could move away, he placed his hand on her cheek and turned her head, leaning close until they were only inches apart.

"You will marry me, Mercy," he said softly. "It's been decided. You can try to escape, but it won't matter. I'll follow you to the ends of the earth. You're mine."

The smile he wore didn't find its way to his blue eyes. She wanted to move away except that his grip was too tight.

"Do you understand?" he asked softly. "We will be married, exactly when and where it's been planned. I promise you that, Mercy, and I never break my word."

Her hands were damp. Her heart was racing and there was an odd feeling in her stomach, almost as if she were going to be ill.

"We'll return to New York as soon as possible," he said.

She shook her head. "Ruthie can't travel yet. Her arm is broken."

"Then she can stay here."

"She can't stay here," Mercy said.

"That's the last time you'll correct me, Mercy." Gregory's smile thinned but didn't completely disappear. "Do you understand?"

She managed to pull away a little. He grabbed her arm and jerked her back, placing his hand on her face again. She closed her eyes, but it didn't matter. He was still there, still smiling that odd smile at her, his eyes holding a gleam she'd never seen until now.

"Do you understand, Mercy?"

She managed to nod.

Although there had been times when she found Gregory overbearing, he'd never before frightened her.

Until now.

Chapter Twenty-Nine

*W*hat the hell did that mean, *The man who thinks he's my fiancé*?

Lennox didn't know why he was angry. Maybe the ache in his arm was bothering him. Another week or so and he'd take out the stitches himself.

There wasn't one damn reason why he should care that Mercy had a fiancé or that she hadn't told him. The subject had never been broached.

It should have. When he'd bent his head to kiss her, she should've pushed him away, told him that she was engaged to be married. She hadn't demonstrated any loyalty toward the man who'd asked her to be his wife.

Instead, she'd not only allowed him to kiss her, but she'd cooperated fully.

What a kiss it had been.

He'd lost track of where he was, who he was, and anything other than her. The top of his head had floated off into the clouds and all he'd been conscious of was deep, unrelenting pleasure.

He'd wanted to take her to his bed, keep her there for a week or until they'd worn each other out.

One kiss and he'd nearly lost his mind.

Turning, he stared at the place where she'd worked

for nearly an hour. He'd expected her to complain, but she hadn't. Instead, she'd been intent upon her task. More than once he'd glanced over at her, admiring the picture she presented, the sun bringing out the gold and red in her brown hair. Her lips had been pursed in concentration, the movement of her hand holding the brush capturing his attention.

She hadn't uttered one word about being warm or bored.

He'd threaded his fingers through her hair and she hadn't objected to that, either. He'd never done such a thing before. Nor held a woman's face and tilted her head up to study her features.

He'd been around beautiful women before and had flirted with more than a few. Mercy was different. She had a sparkle in her eyes, a kindness in her heart, and endless curiosity. Since he, too, wanted to know the answers to various questions, he appreciated the trait in others.

No, she wasn't like other women he'd known. At least he'd thought that until her maid had appeared. There had been plenty of time for her to tell him that she had a fiancé. Why hadn't she?

He told himself that he wasn't angry. He certainly wasn't offended. Any other emotion was out of the question.

She was going back to America shortly. He was a fool to feel anything more than a mild interest in the woman, especially one who said things he didn't understand. *The man who thinks he's my fiancé.*

Yet he liked her. He was interested in her. He wanted to know all sorts of things about her. What were her thoughts about the Macrorys? What was her life like in America?

She wasn't who she appeared to be, a single woman engaging in an adventure, tempting scandal for a bit of freedom. Mercy was engaged. Soon to be married. Spoken for. Her emotions had already been involved, her future planned.

He was damned if a woman was going to hurt him, especially one he barely knew.

Removing his shirt, he threw it beside the drying struts and examined his airship. Yesterday, he'd stripped everything down to the bare bones, removing the damaged main sails and leaving only the rear ones in place. He'd investigated every single strut. He'd affixed an extra wheel to the bottom of the basket so his landings would be a little smoother. He'd done everything in his power, including going over his drawings and notes, to ensure that the craft was airworthy. He didn't want any more accidents.

In addition to picking up the new sail in Inverness, Connor was going to offer Lennox's most recent inventions to one of the companies that had purchased his designs in the past. One day last week he'd watched Irene making scones and it had occurred to him that the effort would be much faster if she had something to cut the dough into neat triangles all at one time. The resultant device looked like a metal wheel with eight spokes. The sale probably wouldn't amount to much, but any money he could bring in was welcome.

Damn it, why hadn't she told him about the fiancé?

"You'll be wanting some tea," Irene said at his elbow.

He turned, surprised that he hadn't heard her approach.

"I'll be wanting some whiskey," he said.

"There's time enough for that, but for now, drink your tea."

She held out a cup and he took it, thanking her. She was a godsend, a comment he made often. If he could, he'd pay her more, but she seemed to understand, only fussing at him whenever her sister got a raise in her salary.

"I don't know who this man is," she said, "but I would wager he isn't a good one."

He should've told her that he didn't have any curiosity about Mercy's fiancé. Instead, he took a sip of his tea, then asked, "Why do you say that?"

"Ruthie was afraid of him," she said flatly. "Any man who inspires fear is not one I want to be around."

Lennox wondered about her long-dead husband, thoughts brought about by a few of Irene's comments. She'd married when she was barely twenty and the man had drowned two years later. Both twins were widows, but Jean had been married longer.

He took another sip of his tea. "She didn't tell me about him," he said and then wondered why he admitted that.

Other than Connor and Irene, he was nearly a hermit. He'd never given much thought to his life until the past few weeks. He should return to Edinburgh and spend some time reacquainting himself with friends. Perhaps he should abandon his research into flight and spend more time inventing things. That way he could at least be solvent enough to marry.

That is, if any woman would be satisfied to live at Duddingston. He had a responsibility to the castle since it embodied the history of his family and his clan. A woman from Inverness or Edinburgh wouldn't feel the same.

Mercy had seemed fascinated by the castle, however, a thought that he immediately pushed away.

"There was no reason she should have told me, of course," he added. "She's a stranger and won't be here long."

"But you're wishing it was different, aren't you?"

He handed her the empty cup and forced a smile to his face.

"You're an incurable romantic, Irene. Seeing things that aren't there."

"Or I'm seeing what's before my eyes," she said. "Even if I'm the only one."

He didn't have a response to that.

Chapter Thirty

*M*ercy stood, taking several steps away from the settee, out of reach of Gregory.

Her face felt stiff with the effort of controlling her expression. Nor did she speak. She didn't want her voice to quaver.

It wouldn't do to let Gregory see that he'd scared her. He'd take advantage of that information, using it to further manipulate and perhaps even bully her. If she was forced to marry him, her life wouldn't be a luxurious prison where she was coddled and feted for simply drawing breath. No, Gregory would threaten, criticize, and belittle her and might even take pleasure in doing so.

She had no doubt that he meant what he said. He would follow her anywhere. Not only was his pride at stake, so was his future. He didn't love her as much as he coveted her father's wealth. He'd picked her as the easiest way to advance in life.

Her parents had been overjoyed at his attention. She hadn't agreed to marry Gregory as much as she had simply submitted to her parents' pressure. Not for the first time she wished she'd spoken up and refused to participate in the plans everyone was making for her life.

What was she going to do?

Without another word she walked out of the Green Parlor, uncaring that she was leaving Gregory alone, a gesture that would be seen by anyone as rude. She retreated to her room and, because there was no lock on the bedroom door, put a chair beneath the latch. She hoped that would stop him should Gregory want to continue their talk. He'd never been that forward, but everything had changed in the past few minutes.

There was only one way to stay in Scotland. Her grandmother and her aunt needed to support her in refusing to return to New York with Gregory.

Her grandmother believed that a woman should never strive to be independent. Instead, a woman was subservient to a man in all ways. In addition, a fiancé was almost as influential as a husband. Mercy doubted that any of the changes brought about by the Civil War would matter to Ailsa.

Still, she had to try.

Mercy changed her dress and rang for Lily to help redo her hair. She bathed her face, wishing that the sun hadn't tinted her cheeks pink. She spritzed a small amount of perfume behind her ears and added earrings and a gold brooch her mother had given her on her twenty-first birthday.

Finally, she turned slowly for Lily to inspect her. Everything about her appearance had to be perfect, in order to escape Ailsa's withering criticism.

"Will I do?"

Lily nodded, then gave her a smile.

Mercy left the bedroom, walking down the corridor with a tight feeling in her chest. At her grandmother's door, she took a moment to calm herself. One deep breath, then another before she raised her fist and knocked. When she heard her grandmother's voice, she opened the door slowly.

"Seanmhair, may I speak with you for a moment?"

"I'll not rescind my disapproval of you, Hortense. If that's the reason you've come, you can just leave again."

"I know that you consider my behavior to be unlady-like, Seanmhair," she said as she entered the room and closed the door behind her.

"I'm surprised you don't."

This conversation was not getting off to a good start.

"I'm sure you know that Gregory Hamilton has ar-rived."

"I have been informed of that fact, yes."

"He wants me to return to New York with him as quickly as possible."

She came and stood before her grandmother. Ailsa sat in her throne-like chair beside the window. Her hands, engorged with thick blue veins, rested on the arms of the chair. Her posture was perfect and Mercy wagered that it wasn't her corset that kept her so up-right, but the habit of a lifetime.

"How does he propose to travel, Hortense?"

"I beg your pardon?"

"Your maid is not up for the journey. Does he think to shame us further by traveling with you without a chaperone?"

"That would be unacceptable, wouldn't it?" she said, feeling the first stirrings of hope. Her grand-mother might save her after all.

Ailsa nodded imperiously. "Granted, the fact that he is your fiancé might provide some latitude, but it is a voyage of some time, Hortense."

Mercy nodded. "Of course, Seanmhair."

"I despair of my daughter's teachings. She was reared to be a proper gentlewoman. Perhaps marrying a Yankee forced her to discard all those lessons she learned from me. And you, Hortense, are the result."

If she hadn't needed her grandmother's help, Mercy would've turned and left the room. It wasn't the first time she'd heard criticism about her mother and it probably wouldn't be the last.

Fenella was the sweetest, kindest, and loveliest woman she knew. She certainly didn't deserve Ailsa's criticism, but Mercy bit back the words she wanted to say. Correcting Ailsa right at the moment wouldn't be a good idea.

"I don't want to return to New York with him, Seanmhair. I've already informed Gregory that I have no intention of going through with the marriage."

A white eyebrow arched. "A word given is a promise, Hortense. He might have fought for the Union and therefore be a despicable creature, but what about all the people who know of your engagement? Are you that selfish that you would bring embarrassment to the family?"

The words were said in a calm tone, but Ailsa's blue eyes were chips of ice.

According to her grandmother, women were simply to endure all that life gave them. They weren't to protest, speak up, or attempt to alter their fate in any way. Doing so was to invite shame. Shame, to Ailsa, was the worst thing that could happen to anyone, short of death.

Her grandmother had been difficult to please before the war. Now she was inflexible, her opinions set in stone.

"You don't understand, Seanmhair," she said.

Ailsa held up her hand. "Yes, I do. I understand all too well. Your parents have given you everything you wanted, and led you to believe that what you think matters. It does not, Hortense, from your name to your opinions. If the only way to get you home properly is to marry the man, that's exactly what you shall do."

"What?"

"You heard me, child. The minute Douglas returns, we will make arrangements."

"I don't wish to marry Gregory."

"I do not care," her grandmother said. "No one else will, either. You will do as you're told."

She stared at her grandmother. The situation that had been untenable five minutes ago had just turned worse.

Gregory wouldn't mind marrying in Scotland. She could almost hear his words now. *We'll simply redo the ceremony in New York, Mercy.*

She couldn't marry Gregory.

She didn't want to be afraid of her husband.

She didn't want to dread being in his company.

She didn't want to be bullied or badgered, endlessly criticized and critiqued.

She wanted to be in love and she didn't love Gregory.

Ailsa kept her gaze, never once blinking.

Mercy realized that nothing she said would make any difference to her grandmother. Nothing.

She doubted that Uncle Douglas would listen to her pleas and allow her to remain at Macrory House. He'd disapproved of her the minute she'd arrived. First, she'd traveled all the way from America with just her maid. The second, unforgivable thing she'd done was to associate with Lennox.

"I have to go," Mercy said, not even bothering to come up with an excuse to leave the room, only knowing that she had to before she said something she couldn't retract. Or uttered a comment Ailsa would hold against her.

Her grandmother only nodded again, not one word of affection passing her lips.

Chapter Thirty-One

When Ruthie came to help her dress for dinner, Mercy didn't reprimand her for trying to work. Instead, she was grateful for the presence of one of the few people in the house who liked her.

"I'm not feeling well, Ruthie. I'm not going down to dinner."

"But neither is Miss Elizabeth or your grandmother, Miss Mercy."

She doubted if either woman was ill. Gregory had served in the Union and, as such, was probably an unacceptable dinner companion for two Southern women. At least according to her grandmother.

He was good enough for Mercy to marry, however.

At any other time she would have gone down to the dining room, representing the family even if she didn't want to do so. Not now. Not after her grandmother had decreed her future. No doubt Ailsa had already informed Gregory of her plans.

She couldn't bear sitting alone at the table with a gloating Gregory.

"Perhaps you can put out that we're all ill with some malady, Ruthie."

"But you're never sick, Miss Mercy."

Mercy nodded. "I am now," she said and told Ruthie what her grandmother decided.

Ruthie's face paled. "She has a soul as black as the Earl of Hell's waistcoat."

She hadn't heard that saying before. No doubt it was something Scottish. She really should have chastised Ruthie for the comment, but she didn't do that, especially since she secretly agreed.

"What are you going to do?" Ruthie asked.

"I don't know."

Regrettably, that was the truth. Not one avenue of escape occurred to her.

"I'll tell them, Miss Mercy," Ruthie said. "But I'd get in bed if I were you. They're bound to check on you."

She nodded, but she honestly didn't care if they entered her room and saw that she was fine.

What more could her relatives do to her?

"Shall I bring you a tray?"

"No, I'm not hungry," she said. She glanced at Ruthie. "I'm fine, really. Thank you, though."

"I'd have someone bring it up, Miss Mercy," Ruthie said with a mulish twist to her lips. "I wouldn't try to carry it with only one arm."

"I know that, and it's not why I turned it down. My stomach is so upset I don't think I could eat anything right now."

When Ruthie was finally convinced that she would be fine—at least for tonight—and left, Mercy replaced the chair beneath the door handle. As a deterrent, it wasn't much, especially if Gregory or one of her relatives was determined to enter.

Her thoughts were turbulent, forcing her up from

the chair to pace around the bed and back again. The longer she walked, the more horrible her situation appeared.

There was no way out. There was nothing she could do.

Her mother was wrong. It wasn't nerves that were making her feel this way. It was revulsion. Marriage to Gregory loomed in front of her like a nightmare. She didn't want him to touch her. She didn't even like when he insisted she put her hand on his arm. She didn't think he was charming and gracious and deferential like everyone else thought. Gregory showed one face to her parents and another to her.

Before today she'd never been afraid of Gregory but maybe her fear had been there all along, lurking under the surface. She'd never felt comfortable with him. Not like you should be with the man you were supposed to marry. She avoided moments alone with Gregory, claiming a shyness she didn't feel.

Not once had she ever behaved with him like she had with Lennox. But, then, she trusted Lennox and that was not an emotion she felt around Gregory.

She went to the armoire, knelt, and retrieved the valise she'd kept at her side ever since New York. She opened it, staring at the mounds of greenbacks inside. She'd broached the subject of taking the money once more with her grandmother, but Ailsa had been adamant about not needing a Yankee man's charity.

Perhaps God had answered her prayers after all.

There were only two people in the entire house who could help her. Mrs. West and Ruthie. She didn't want to involve either one of them in her plan. Mrs. West was staff and could be dismissed. Ruthie's punishment would probably be banishment from Macrory House.

No, she would do this on her own.

THE NIGHT WAS a blustery one, filled with thunder as if God were lecturing the Highlands. Rain lashed the windows of the tower as if it wanted in.

Lennox normally liked to sleep during this kind of weather. He always felt grateful for the shelter, thinking that there had been plenty of people over the years who'd had to endure the Highland storms in barely habitable conditions.

His ancestors, for one, stalwart men and women who'd claimed this spot of land for their own, building the castle brick by brick with the help of clan members and family.

The fact that he couldn't sleep was an irritant, but his insomnia was brought about by the ache in his shoulders and the pain in his arm. He'd brought a bottle of whiskey up to his tower room in anticipation of this moment. Now he poured himself a half glass, sat back against the headboard, and contemplated the lightning show through the windows.

The storm sounded like it was chewing up the sky.

Had the thunder awakened Mercy? Was she, even now, like him, watching nature's display of might and feeling grateful that she was not out in it?

Or was she in her fiancé's arms?

He shouldn't have kissed her, but it had been an unmistakable temptation. He wasn't a saint, after all. Nor did he aspire to be. His hermit-like existence of late, however, put the lie to that thought. He truly needed to return to Edinburgh for a time, just to prove that he wasn't avoiding people. Or women, for that matter.

His friends would have more than a few plans for him, he was certain, if he let them know he was coming. They would schedule dinner parties where he was the guest of honor, tout him as being the reclusive Earl of Morton. He hated using the title. Every time someone mentioned it or called him *Your Lordship* he felt like he had usurped Robert's position and wanted to apologize to his brother's shade. Yet his friends liked it. Reflected glory, they called it.

Most of them were physicians now while he had taken an entirely different track in life. Yet he still gave in to his curiosity about how things worked. He'd improved the Mordan pencil by adding a spring inside the mechanism. When he pushed down on the top of it, the lead was advanced. He'd developed a new type of window latch that opened the window from the top. He'd created braces for his shoes that cut into the surface of Ben Uaine when he had a yen to climb a steep face. The greatest of all of his inventions, however, was his airship, a physical representation of his desire to master flight. To at least understand, as no one had been able to yet, what components were necessary for a man to emulate a bird.

Things were a great deal easier to understand than people. He could figure something out if he took it apart. For the life of him, he couldn't fathom Mercy Rutherford.

Yes, it would be a good idea to return to Edinburgh, just for a while. Long enough to dispel any thoughts of a certain American woman.

She was like a burr in his mind, something that had stuck there that he couldn't easily budge. He liked the way she smiled, the slow dawning of humor traveling from her lips to her eyes. She had a habit of spreading her fingers on her knees and then closing them again. And her voice was soft, soothing, although her accent was different from those voices he heard every day. He even liked her name: Mercy.

Irene was right, Mercy was kind. It was there in the way she talked to Connor and Irene and cared for Ruthie. The way she talked about her guard was another indication. Or how tender she'd been when stitching his wound.

Yet she'd been damn cruel in hiding the fact she was going to be married.

No, he most definitely needed to rid himself of any thoughts of Mercy Rutherford.

Chapter Thirty-Two

$\mathcal{M}$ercy heard the thunder as she waited for the household to fall asleep. A little before midnight she slipped down the servants' stairs and into the kitchen, made bright by the flashes of lightning. She hesitated at the outer door. The rain was coming down so hard she couldn't see to the walled garden. She'd only worn a light summer shawl over her dress and it would be drenched within minutes.

The question was: How desperate was she to escape her situation?

Desperate enough to brave a Highland storm.

She clutched the valise to her chest with both arms, doubting that it would become waterlogged because of the oilskin lining the interior.

The darkness was absolute, the black clouds obscuring the sky. She had followed the drover's trail once to Duddingston Castle and again on her return. She could find her way. She had to.

She made it to the walled garden, then found the secret door and headed for the trail. What she'd seen in the morning light was harder to find in the midst of a rolling storm. More than once she stopped and tried to get her bearings, but couldn't stay in one place for long because her feet started sinking into the ground. She hadn't thought to borrow Mrs. West's boots again and the ground was like a marsh.

Wind howled through the pines, sounding like the screaming banshees Ruthie talked about so often. Thunder roared directly above her, almost as if the fist of God was about to pummel her into the ground like a giant hammer.

Clamping her lips together, she battled the wind with each step. The sideways rain turned into shards poking her skin like needles. She kept her eyes lowered, determined to make it to Duddingston Castle.

Her hair escaped the bun and lashed across her face, the wet mass of it stinging her cheeks.

She was bent nearly horizontal, her head butting the wind. Twice she almost fell and twice righted herself without losing her grip on the valise. The distance felt much longer than what she'd walked only this morning, but she kept moving, one foot in front of another.

She had to reach the castle and Lennox. He was the only one who could help her.

The eerie whistling began to fade as the wind changed directions, no longer fighting her approach to the castle, but pushing her there. She had no choice but to stumble down the track to the bridge. As she crossed the causeway, the water came up to her ankles. She kept one arm around the valise as she gripped the handrail with her other hand, trying not to be swept into the loch.

She had never been so cold. It felt as if ice was coating her hands, bare as they were to the elements. If she was shivering, she was too frozen to know it.

No one had ever warned her about a Highland storm. If they had she wasn't sure she would have believed that it could feel like the depth of winter in New York. Or that she was certain she would be drowned in the deluge.

She was finally past the bridge and into the ruined tower. The wind keened around the castle like a beast who'd been stripped of its prey, but at least she'd found some type of shelter.

Would Lennox turn her away?

She had to convince him. Somehow, she had to.

It was so dark that she couldn't see her way. She stretched out her free hand until she felt the door, and then followed the rope to the iron ring. Her fingers wouldn't work the first time and curve around the ring to pull it. After blowing on her fingers to try to warm them she tried again, finally managing to hold on to it. If it rang she couldn't hear because of the booming thunder and the sound of the rain.

She was going to scandalize Irene, but hopefully the other woman would understand once she heard her story.

No one was coming to the door. Mercy wasn't sure how long she stood there, but it felt like hours instead of the few minutes it had probably been. At least she wasn't out in the rain or being thrown about by the wind. Pressing her back against the door, she slid down to sit on the stone floor. Hopefully, Duddingston Castle didn't have mice or rats. With any luck they—or other creatures—weren't sharing this dark space.

As if he'd read her thoughts, she heard an owl, so close that he must be above her in the anteroom.

She was so cold that she couldn't feel her feet. Even her nose felt like ice. What a terrible thing, to expire on Lennox's doorstep. She reached up and pulled on the ring once more. The journey here had exhausted her. Or perhaps emotions had drained her. Ever since leaving Lennox earlier she'd felt fear, despair, anger, then fear again.

A friend of her father's, a man given to pontificating whenever he came to their home, had once stated that most people were the architects of their own problems. She wasn't supposed to have overheard his conversation with her father. She was only presented to guests and then whisked upstairs to her own quarters. Nonetheless, she'd thought about what he had said often, especially in the past few weeks.

She had to agree with him. If she'd told her parents how she felt—about her life and Gregory—there was a possibility that she would never have left New York. They might have ignored her feelings. Or they might have agreed with her that changes should be made. They may have understood, as well, why she wasn't comfortable with the idea of marrying Gregory.

Yet if she'd never come to Scotland, she would never have met Lennox.

He was the only man she knew who fascinated her and yet with whom she felt so comfortable. He didn't seem to care that her father was James Rutherford or that she was reputed to be one of the wealthiest young women on the eastern seaboard, thanks to her grandfather's inheritance.

She doubted Lennox would care.

When the door opened, she fell backward, staring up at Lennox. He was carrying a small lantern that held a candle. He was barely dressed. His trousers weren't completely fastened and his shirt was open. His bare foot was only inches from her nose. His feet were very striking, long and almost aristocratic looking. The Earl of Morton's feet.

"Mercy? What are you doing here?"

She didn't have a chance to answer before he placed the lantern on the ground, bent, and picked her up in his arms as if she weighed no more than a feather. She had her father's height and wasn't tiny and delicate, but he seemed to bear the burden of her quite well.

"Hold this," he said.

This turned out to be the lantern and she grabbed it with one frozen hand.

For a moment, just a moment, she lay her head against his chest and closed her eyes. She was safe. That thought kept repeating itself in her mind as he kicked the door closed and strode through the Clan Hall with her.

"I'm sorry," she said.

She hoped he didn't ask her what for, because she had a litany of things for which to apologize. For needing his help. For calling at such a late hour. For scandalizing Irene. For being so cold and wet.

"What are you doing here, Mercy?"

She loved the sound of his voice, low and soft with the sound of Scotland in each word. She wanted him to continue talking just so she could listen.

He took her to the kitchen. She'd been here more than any other room at Duddingston Castle. Should she tell him that she'd only rarely been in their kitchen at home? As a child she had found her way there and had been promptly scolded for disturbing the work of the servants. As an adult her presence there shocked the staff. They all stood at her entrance, their hands nervously folded in front of them, the looks on their faces making her realize that they were afraid. Of her, because of her, because of what she might say to her father. Not once had she ever sat at the kitchen table and imbibed whiskey. She'd never sat in front of the fire and warmed herself.

She liked the Mercy of Scotland a great deal more than the woman who lived in New York. This woman was less constrained and more free.

He didn't say anything further, merely pulled out a chair with his foot and sat her there. She reached up and placed her hand against his cheek. He flinched at the touch and she apologized again.

He startled her by shaking his head, and then pressing her hand against his face and holding it there.

"I didn't expect you to be so cold," he said.

"I'm freezing. And I'm wet. I'm sorry."

"Stop saying that."

He turned and began to lay a fire in the massive kitchen fireplace.

"Irene is going to be scandalized," she said.

"Irene doesn't sleep here." He glanced over his shoulder at her. "There's no one here but me, Mercy."

Oh, dear. She'd just made her terrible situation even worse.

Chapter Thirty-Three

$\mathcal{S}$he slowly pushed the words past her ice-cold lips. "I have to go back."

He pulled out another chair and sat beside her.

Lennox reached over and placed his hand on her knee. She shouldn't have been able to feel the warmth of his palm through her sodden skirt, shift, and petticoat, but she did. Or maybe she just wanted to.

"Mercy," he said, his voice kind. "I'm not sending you back out in that storm. I'm not even sure you could cross the causeway by now."

"I have to try," she said. "I've made things even worse and I didn't think they could get more terrible."

"What's wrong?"

She shook her head. "It doesn't matter."

"Mercy, tell me."

She glanced over at him. "Have you ever known someone that everyone else admires, but there's something about them that puts you on edge?"

When he didn't speak, she continued. "You can't figure out what it is, but the fact that no one else seems to notice makes you think that there's something wrong with you. It's not that person at all. It's you. That's how Gregory has always made me feel. He's so charming and polite. He's handsome and personable and he says all the right things at all the right times. People like him. They seem to gravitate toward him."

"But there's still something about him that you don't like?"

She nodded. "I found out what it was today," she said. "He's cruel. He's determined. He's relentless. No one will stand in his way. And I'm the one person who's an obstacle. I don't want to marry him and if I don't marry him, he doesn't have access to my fortune or to my father's when he dies."

"Why did you agree to marry him if you don't like him?"

She stared at the fire just now catching. "I'm always in the worst condition when I'm here. Either I'm wounded or I'm wet from swimming in the loch or now when I'm near drowned from your weather."

"Except for the latter, the earlier conditions were because of me."

He didn't say anything further, which meant that he was waiting for an answer.

"Because it was easier," she said. "Because my life was already planned for me, down to the minute, it seemed. It was simpler than saying no." She took a deep breath and gave him another measure of the truth. "It was only after I left New York that I realized I'd been wrong all along. I'd had choices. I just hadn't made good ones. Staying silent, accepting what people planned for me wasn't the right choice. Ever since I've been determined to make better choices."

"And Gregory isn't a good choice?"

"He scares me." She stared down at her hands, wondering why she felt so ashamed to make that confession.

Lennox didn't say anything, which gave her a few moments to marshal her thoughts.

She looked around the chair and realized that she'd left the valise outside.

"My valise," she said, standing. "I need to get it."

Lennox gently pushed her back into the chair.

"Where is it?"

"Beside the door."

"I'll get it," he said. "You stay there and get warm."

The fire was blazing now, but she still couldn't feel the heat. She had never been as cold as she felt right at the moment, both on the outside and the inside as well. She'd made everything so much worse.

Lennox returned, dropping the sodden valise to the floor. It landed with a *thump* beside her.

He went to the cupboard, withdrew a large bowl, and used the pump beside the sink to fill it with water.

Only then did he return to her side, putting the bowl down on the floor. He retrieved a teakettle that she hadn't noticed hanging to the side of the fire and poured some boiling water into the bowl.

Still not speaking, he knelt in front of her and removed her ruined shoes. Only then did she realize that her feet were coated with mud.

"I'm sorry," she said. "I don't mean to look so disreputable."

"Don't be ridiculous, Mercy. You've come through a storm."

He startled her again by placing both of her feet in the bowl.

"Irene isn't going to be pleased if you're using one of her cooking bowls," she said.

He grinned up at her. "I wouldn't have the courage. We keep this bowl around for nights such as this."

"Do you often go traipsing through the glen in the middle of a storm?"

"I do not," he said. "I have too much sense."

Before she could offer a rebuttal to his comment, he added, "Nor have I been as desperate as you, Mercy."

She sat back in the chair, watching him wash her feet. They were beginning to prickle, almost like feeling was coming back to them. When she said as much, he only nodded.

His hands were very gentle. No one had ever washed her feet, at least since she was a baby. She wondered if his touch was due to his training as a physician or whether it was just something natural to him.

She hadn't told him the whole truth. She really didn't want to leave Scotland. She didn't want to leave him. There was no other alternative, however.

"We need to get you dry," he said.

She looked down at her dress.

He stood and went to the cupboard, grabbing a length of toweling before returning and removing her feet from the bowl. He dried them one by one, still gentle.

"Has Gregory threatened you?"

She shook her head. "No, but my grandmother is set on arranging my wedding at any moment." At his look of surprise, she asked, "Can that even happen in Scotland?"

"We have some odd marriage laws here in Scotland, but I don't know if they apply to Americans."

"Well, she'll make sure there's a way. She informed me that, in order not to shame the family, I need to marry Gregory. I'm not going to marry him, but even Gregory doesn't accept that. I've told him a dozen times that I've no intention of marrying him and he only laughs."

He came and sat beside her.

"What can I do?"

She almost kissed him again, right then and there. She was so grateful for his offer that she thought she might weep.

"I was going to ask for your help." She nudged the valise with her bare foot, then bent to open it, revealing the cache of money. "But I was more than willing to pay you."

If she hadn't been watching him so closely, she would've missed the look that flashed over his face. Had she insulted him?

"I wanted to get to Inverness," she said. "In order to book passage back to America."

"On your own?"

She shook her head. "That was the second part of what I was going to ask you. I was hoping that Irene could get word to her sister and that Ruthie could leave the house and meet me here."

He didn't say anything for such a long time that she decided she had insulted him. How did she make reparations for that?

"I didn't know Connor hadn't returned," she said. "Or that Irene wasn't here."

What was she going to do now?

Lennox stood, picked up the bowl, and went to dump out the water. When he returned, he held out his hand to her.

She stood, still holding his hand.

"At least I have a dry shirt for you," he said. "And a towel or two. We can dry your dress before the fire. If you insist on returning to Macrory House, you can do it at dawn. The storm will surely be finished by then and the causeway passable."

He bent and placed his lips on hers. She hadn't expected his kiss, but she didn't pull back.

When his arms went around her, she stepped into his embrace. Any thought of her reputation was lost when he deepened the kiss. Everything narrowed to become simply sensation. It felt as though lightning traveled through her body, racing back again to where their lips were joined.

Her mouth opened beneath his. She wrapped her arms around his neck as colors sparkled behind her closed eyelids. She'd never considered that a kiss could be magical. Or that she would want it to continue for much longer than it did.

When Lennox stepped back and looked down at her, she had the impression that he was going to apologize. She pressed two fingers against his lips.

"No," she said. "Don't say a word."

"I was going to say that I needed to show you to your room before I did something else foolish."

She could feel her cheeks warm at his words. Foolish? Was it truly foolish to feel so alive? So excited and curious? She wanted to know what came after. What would happen next? She wanted to be in his arms, and that thought was most definitely scandalous. Her body was heated, her thoughts racing from one shocking proposition to another. She wanted to see him with his shirt off again, touch his magnificent chest, stroke her fingers across his impressive back.

What would it feel like to have him touch her?

She wanted to tell him all the questions she had, all the thoughts that were cascading through her mind.

He wouldn't criticize her or condemn her, but she wasn't certain exactly what he would say.

How very odd that she had to come halfway around the world to find someone like Lennox, a man whom she admired. He was not simply kind and attractive, but she felt like she could tell Lennox anything and he would understand. She'd already divulged more to him than she had anyone, including Ruthie.

It wasn't just being in Scotland that was changing her. Knowing Lennox brought out the best in her, made her want to be more daring and less of a coward, especially now. She wanted to ask for another kiss, but she stepped back as well.

A proper woman would certainly apologize for being so forward. If nothing else, she should attempt to find an excuse for her lamentable behavior. The truth was that she would do the same thing if offered another chance. She would stand within the shelter of his arms and become lost in his kiss.

She didn't miss the world when she was with Lennox.

Chapter Thirty-Four

This was not a good situation. Mercy being alone with him in the castle would be enough to cause comment in the village and Macrory House for months, if not longer. Lennox wasn't under any delusion that they would be able to keep the circumstances of this night secret. The gossips always knew, somehow, some way.

Although the castle was large, built to house members of the clan, the space wouldn't protect them from rumor or innuendo. People would think what they would, and most of what they would think would be detrimental to Mercy.

The only thing that would save her from condemnation would be to leave Scotland. He doubted if the long trail of gossip could reach across the Atlantic Ocean.

The causeway that connected the island on which Duddingston Castle was built often flooded in a storm. By now it was impassable, which meant neither of them could go anywhere. Nor could anyone reach them.

They were just going to have to get through the night. Once dawn came and, hopefully, the storm ceased, Irene would arrive. She would serve as chaperone until he could find some way to get Mercy to Inverness.

She sat in front of the fire now, holding her hands closer to the flames.

Once back in New York, what made her think Gregory would leave her alone? Or that she could escape a marriage her parents obviously wanted?

The questions put him in a foul mood. The realization that he didn't want her to leave made him even more irritated. She'd been in Scotland only a few weeks and had already managed to disrupt his life.

Connor and Irene—those were the only people he'd needed for the past five years. Somehow, however, Mercy had inserted herself into his thoughts and even his dreams. When he wasn't looking, she'd somehow become important.

When had that happened? *How* had it happened?

"Do you have anything in your case other than money?" he asked. "Like dry clothes?"

She shook her head.

"For an heiress, you travel light."

Her smile was quick and amused.

"I was more concerned with leaving Macrory House than what I was going to wear." She looked down at herself. "I should have planned better."

"My shirt won't be the height of fashion, but at least it's dry."

"You're very kind, Lennox. Thank you."

He didn't feel kind right at the moment. He was annoyed, out of sorts, and half wishing she'd never come to Scotland. She was going to hurt him, a realization that struck him like a blow.

"Was he the reason you ran away?"

"No, not the whole reason."

"What was so terrible about your life that you felt like you had to escape it?"

"Nothing was terrible," she said. "On the contrary. I was special. I was a princess. People came to our home to outfit me, provide me with jewelry, hats, gloves, anything that a young woman could want. I had my own carriage and two guards who were with me at all times. I was never out of sight of them. I was never allowed to make a friend. She might be a bad influence. Or she might get sick and pass it along to me. All of my books were approved. If I saw a play, it was only after it, too, had passed inspection. I was their one perfect specimen, the child who lived, the one on whose shoulders their future rested. I was a hothouse flower, a perfect rose."

She glanced at him again. "Gregory was only one part of my life. I was wrong not to realize that he was determined to marry me." She turned and looked into the fire once more. "My parents were in favor of the marriage. My mother thought he was the perfect husband for their perfect child. I was told that all I was feeling was nerves, that I'd come to realize that marriage to Gregory was . . ." Her words stopped. "Maybe blessed? I think I was supposed to be overjoyed. I was left with the impression that it was for my own good, that they knew what was best for me."

"Why Scotland?"

She nudged the valise with her foot. "Because of the money. My mother had tried to send it to my grandmother and aunt, but they'd already left North Carolina for Scotland. Mine wasn't an altruistic gesture as much as a convenient one. Or a foolish one. My grandmother doesn't want the money. She sees my father as a Yankee and an enemy. She called it blood money."

"What was the catalyst? What made you leave on that day?"

"That day? It was the last straw, I think. Gregory was going to get rid of Ruthie," she said. "He didn't feel that Ruthie was a good enough companion. She giggles and she has all these superstitions and sayings. He announced that once we were married she would be gone." She glanced at him, then away. "Ruthie's been my only friend for years. I couldn't let that happen, so I enlisted the help of my old governess. I was allowed to visit her, and I did, except that Ruthie and I slipped out the back, emerged in the alley behind her house, and hired a coach to take us to the *Molly Brown*, one of my father's ships. I'd booked passage through Miss Haversham."

"You took a number of chances in your bid for freedom, Mercy."

She nodded. "Not as many as you think. It was my father's ship and I knew the captain would ensure my safety. I did, however, take the precaution of not identifying myself until we were well out to sea."

"Yet you're taking Ruthie back with you."

"I'm taking her back to New York with me. It's her home, after all. It's where her family is."

"Unless Connor asks her to stay."

She turned to look at him. "Would he do that?"

"I'm not going to speak for Connor, but it's my opinion that he feels something for Ruthie."

She looked away again, staring into the fire.

He wanted to know what she was thinking, one of the few times he'd ever been curious about another person's thoughts. Mercy wasn't like anyone he'd ever known. Perhaps that was the fascination she had for him. Or maybe it was simply because she was a beautiful woman and although he was a quasi-hermit, he was still a man.

"Let's get you to your room," he said.

He looked down at her shoes, now mere scraps of muddy leather. Going to her side, he grabbed the valise and put it on her lap. Before she could object, he scooped her up in his arms once again.

"The floors are stone, Mercy, and cold. This way you won't get a chill."

She looked as if she wanted to say something, then thought better of her words.

"What are you thinking?" he asked, finally giving in to his curiosity.

"I've never been carried before, and now you're doing it again."

"You're not that much of a burden," he said, "especially compared to one of my airships. I've hauled those up the side of Ben Uaine."

She laughed, the sound summoning his smile. He hadn't heard her laugh before and now he wished he had something amusing to say that would make her laugh again.

At the base of the stairs, she looked up at him. "I really can walk, Lennox. You can let me down now."

He didn't want to release her, so he kept silent as he mounted the steps.

"Really, Lennox."

"We're almost there," he said, and he was right. He entered the room where she'd changed before and deposited her on the edge of the mattress. "There, safe and sound and without frozen feet."

"I meant what I said earlier, about your being kind," she said as he lit the lamp on the table beside the bed.

"I'll start a fire. If you move the chair in front of the fire and put your dress there it should be dry by morning."

She only nodded at him.

Even with her wet hair she was beautiful, her eyes wide and deep as she watched him. He wanted to be as kind as she thought him, but he was having thoughts he had no business having.

He opened the flue, grateful that he always inspected the chimneys in all the unoccupied rooms once a year. Bending, he started a fire, conscious of her eyes on him.

"Marry me."

He slowly straightened, turning to look at her. She was still sitting on the edge of the mattress, clutching the valise to her chest.

"I beg your pardon?" he said, playing for time.

"Marry me. You can't deny that it would be helpful to have an heiress for a wife. You could buy whatever you needed and never have to worry about money."

He'd never considered that a woman might propose to him. That's why he was struck dumb.

"I can spend my money the way I wish."

"So, if you want to buy yourself a husband you can, is that it?" He didn't know whether to be flattered or insulted.

"It would certainly solve my situation," she said, staring at the far wall instead of him.

He should never have kissed her. He should never have given himself free rein to think about her. He should never have wondered at her thoughts or been pleased by the sound of her laughter.

"Mercy . . ." he began.

"You could finish the repairs on Duddingston Castle," she interjected. "And have any amount of money you needed for your airships."

Her face was bright pink, leading him to think that the words hadn't been easy for her to say.

"Have you never thought of marrying?" she asked.

"No."

She tilted her head slightly, her look one of skepticism. "Really? Not even to ensure an heir? Wouldn't that be important to an earl?"

Her cheeks were even more flushed after that comment.

"I don't really care what happens to the title."

"That doesn't sound like you," she said. "You care about Duddingston Castle. Why wouldn't you care about who became earl?"

"The two aren't connected."

She didn't respond to that. The silence in the room was uncomfortable. He'd never thought to have this conversation with anyone, let alone Mercy.

"What about love?" she asked.

"Love?"

"Don't you believe in love, Lennox? Do you never see yourself falling in love? Does it cost a fortune? I thought it was allowable for everyone, even paupers."

"Life is much easier when you don't have to worry about where your next meal is coming from. Or how to support a wife."

"That wouldn't be a problem if you married me."

"I hadn't considered marriage," he finally said. "Not to any appreciable degree."

"Do I disgust you?" she asked.

"I beg your pardon?"

"Do I disgust you?" she repeated. She pushed her

hair back with one hand, the other fluttering at her waist.

"Are you daft?"

Her eyes widened. "I don't think so. This is a very strange proposition, but it makes a great deal of sense, don't you agree? I'm an heiress with a problem. You're an earl needing money. I would think that it would be reasonable to give it some thought. Unless, of course, I disgust you."

Up until that moment he'd been awash in his own discomfort. With her question, he understood how awkward she was feeling.

"I kissed you. I'm not in the habit of kissing women who disgust me. You interest me. You startle me. You intrigue me. But, no, you do not disgust me."

She stared down at her knees and nodded.

He approached her until he stood only a foot or so away. Reaching out, he brushed her cheek with his knuckles.

"There are those who would say that you were blessed at birth, Mercy. Not only are you an heiress, but you're intelligent, witty, and beautiful."

"But you won't marry me."

"I'll just go get that shirt," he said, turning toward the door.

"Will you at least think about it, Lennox?"

He honestly didn't know what to say. He avoided answering her by leaving the room, hoping that by the time he returned she would have regained her sanity.

Chapter Thirty-Five

$\mathcal{M}$ercy had shocked herself by proposing to Lennox, but the more she thought about it, the more appeal it had. After all, she had to marry one day. She wanted to be a wife. She wanted to bear children. Why not here in Scotland? The notion of living at Duddingston Castle was appealing. How lovely it would be to live somewhere with history all around her.

Her money could accomplish any repairs that were needed to the castle as well as providing almost unlimited funds for Lennox to continue his inventions and his airships.

Irene could have maids to aid her in cleaning the castle and someone to go with her to market. They could have a garden right outside the kitchen and keep chickens. Perhaps they could also hire a stablemaster who could double as Connor's helper when he needed one.

She'd never before considered how much good could come from her money but now it seemed a shame not to use it at Duddingston.

She should have broached the subject with more delicacy. Hinted at it rather than coming out and asking him, but the truth was that she'd surprised herself with the words. As if a hidden nature within her knew what she wanted before she acknowledged it.

Sliding off the mattress, she grabbed the valise, and walked to the other side of the room where a screen was propped in the corner. After dropping the valise on the floor, she extended the screen, slipped behind it, and began to unbutton her bodice. She'd left her shawl somewhere, but it wouldn't have provided any warmth, being as drenched as the rest of her garments.

Thunder roared overhead as if to remind her how she'd gotten so wet.

She wasn't as cold as she had been earlier, but she wasn't comfortable, not with sodden garments clinging to her.

Why had she said anything to him? Lennox was unlike anyone she knew. He was brave, stubborn, independent, almost unbearably handsome as well as being kind and a dozen more attributes. He intrigued her, as well as interested her. Kissing him was almost magic. Perhaps she should have told him all that.

If she'd been engaged to Lennox she wouldn't have been looking to escape. On the contrary, she would have asked for the ceremony to be moved up. She could even see herself being Lennox's wife when she could never visualize herself married to Gregory.

She'd dreaded her wedding night with Gregory. She and Ruthie had discussed it and her education had expanded due to the other woman's knowledge. Ruthie had eleven siblings and they'd lived in a small apartment. She knew where babies came from and she'd imparted that knowledge to Mercy.

"I'm a good girl myself, Miss Mercy, but I know a few who aren't. They do the deed sometimes for money, but mostly for the love of it."

She couldn't imagine going to Gregory's bed for the love of it, especially after today. Or was it yesterday? She had no idea of the time.

But Lennox's bed? Her cheeks burned. Yes, she could well imagine that. And, even more shockingly, wanted it.

Was he going to return? Maybe he'd been so offended by her words that he intended to avoid her completely.

After removing her dress, she hung it over the top of the screen. Her corset was almost as damp as it had been when she'd been swimming in the loch. Her petticoats still dripped and her shift clung wetly to her skin. She peeled it off and draped it over the washbasin table.

There was a small bit of toweling next to the washbasin, but it wasn't sufficient to dry her completely. She peeked around the screen. The door was firmly closed so she went to the end of the bed, stripped off the bedspread, and wrapped herself in it.

The warmth of the fire beckoned and she sat on the rug in front of it. Tucking the bedspread beneath her arms, she leaned closer to the fire, threading her fingers through her wet hair.

A small white dish filled with potpourri sat on the mantel. As the heat rose, it carried the scent with it—cinnamon and something that reminded her of oranges.

Raindrops made their way into the chimney, hissing as the fire devoured them. Thunder still roared overhead as if this Highland storm was a beast of the clouds and sky. She couldn't see how it would simply be tamed by dawn.

She could just imagine her grandmother's comments if she could see her now. Shameful, unladylike, a disgrace, a stain on the family name. No doubt Ailsa would call her those and more.

Right at the moment, Mercy wasn't trying to be perfect or to please anyone. Sitting on the floor in front of a fire in a Scottish castle on a stormy night, she was simply warming herself.

Regardless of what she did after tonight, someone was going to disapprove of her. She was going to disappoint someone. Yet she was more than content. She was happy, a realization that startled her.

It wasn't being at Duddingston Castle. Nor was it escaping Macrory House. She was happy because she was with Lennox.

Yet it was evident that nothing could come of any relationship with him. His pride would not allow him to marry her, for whatever amount of money. That was obvious from his reaction to her proposal. Her being an heiress was a detriment, not an asset.

There was no sense involving yourself in a romance with no future. A thought she'd had about Ruthie and Connor. How sad that it fit her situation as well.

If only she could be someone else. A Scottish woman, perhaps, with a great deal more courage. Someone who lived at the castle and who faced both the hardships and the blessings of each day with a smile and an optimistic heart.

As long as she was pretending, she'd make Lennox her husband. She allowed herself to daydream about his return. Perhaps every night she waited for him and every night he greeted her with a kiss before taking her to their bed.

What would it be like to love him? To be able to touch him freely and tell him her secret thoughts? To look her fill at him without shame? She'd never know.

After tonight she'd never see him again. She'd find a way to Inverness and leave Scotland.

The country would always exist in her mind as a place of possibilities unfulfilled, of hope and sorrow. She'd always remember him. There was a spot in her heart that had already been carved out and marked Lennox.

*H*E HADN'T LIED. Lennox hadn't given any thought to marriage. Perhaps in the back of his mind he'd known that it was something he would do, sooner or later. He'd never considered that a woman would propose to him. An heiress, no less.

He descended the stairs and headed for his tower bedroom.

He'd also never considered the type of woman he would marry. It had never occurred to him to do so. Now, because of Mercy's words, he couldn't help but give it some thought.

She'd have to be loyal, that was a given. She would have to have a fondness for Duddingston since it would be her home and the home of their children. He would want her to encourage him in his pursuits. Whether or not that included flying was something he would have to consider. Intrepid—that was another quality she would have to have. Someone with a heart of courage. A woman who would jump into a loch to save him, for example.

Mercy Rutherford had twisted him up in knots from the first moment he'd seen her. Nothing had been right about his life since the day of the accident. It wasn't because his airship had nearly been destroyed. Or because Ruthie had broken her arm and it had been his fault. No, it was all because of Mercy.

She'd reminded him of those tumultuous days after Robert had died, when destiny had stood in front of him and forced him to reconsider his life.

He was the last of his family, the last of his line. He'd given some thought to simply turning his back on Duddingston Castle and the history of the Caithearts in the Highlands. He'd trained as a physician. Was he simply supposed to give up all that for the sake of a few bricks?

In the end, he had. There hadn't been any other alternative. If Robert hadn't worked so hard for so many years to keep up the family legacy, perhaps his decision would have been different. If he hadn't been the last of his line, perhaps he could have remained in Edinburgh, finished his studies, and begun his own practice.

He'd made difficult decisions before and paid the price they'd demanded. There were times when he regretted not being a doctor, but fewer than he'd first imagined. He had a duty to Duddingston, his clan, and his family. He'd find a way to ensure that the castle survived, that the Caitheart clan prospered, and that their name would not be forgotten.

Perhaps it was pride, after all. Or the calling of his clan. He could no more abandon his heritage than he could accede to Mercy's outrageous plan.

He wasn't for sale. Not even to a beautiful heiress with the ability to plant herself in his mind.

He grabbed a clean shirt and the dressing gown he rarely wore and retraced his steps. Once outside the bedroom he told himself that the wisest course would be to put the garments in front of the door, knock, then disappear. However, that would be the behavior of a coward and he'd never considered himself one.

Chapter Thirty-Six

Lennox knocked on the door and when she answered, he opened it and stared.

She'd done it to him again. Words flew from his mind, leaving him standing there with only one thought.

Mercy was naked.

He could tell that she wasn't dressed beneath the bedspread, reason enough to excuse himself, turn, and retreat.

Her face was pink from the heat, her shoulders bare and creamy in the light from the fire. Her hair tumbled over her shoulders in curls that made him want to bury his hands in them.

Strangely, he was reminded of the morning of the accident when she'd pointed her finger at him imperiously and demanded that he apologize.

He should do that right now.

Forgive me for my refusal to leave, Mercy.

Forgive me for feeling as if my feet were stuck to the floor.

Forgive me for all the thoughts racing through my mind right now, none of which I should be having. You're a guest in my home and under my protection. You should not be subject to my libidinous thoughts.

But, oh, Mercy, you are so beautiful and it has been so

long since I've been sorely tempted. I will remember the
sight of you sitting in front of the fire until my dying day.

He closed the door softly behind him and walked
across the room, placing the shirt and the dressing
gown on the end of the bed. He had performed his
errand. He'd done what he'd come to do. Now, now he
should leave.

Mercy lifted her hand toward him, palm up.

His conscience shouted at him to leave. The weight
of the past five years, the sheer solitary burden of it,
however, urged him to stay just for a moment, to take
her hand and sit beside her.

A beautiful woman was imploring him with a look.
What man in his right mind would ignore such an
invitation? Perhaps one who hadn't been a hermit for
years. Or one who was stronger, who hadn't thought
too much about her in the past few days.

"Mercy, this isn't wise," he said, the last dregs of his
honor forcing the words from his lips.

"Will you kiss me, Lennox?"

When he didn't answer, she grabbed his hand. "I
love your kisses."

"This isn't wise," he said again.

One of them had to be sensible. He wasn't altogether certain it was going to be him. He could feel
himself weakening even as she pulled on his hand.

"No," she agreed. "It isn't wise. Nothing about the
situation has been wise. Nothing about you or me has
been steeped in wisdom, has it?"

He found himself shaking his head.

"Must we be wise, Lennox? Is it altogether necessary?"

She tugged on his hand again and this time he
knelt in front of her. "I know what my future is. I can

almost foretell it. But tonight can be what I want it to be. And tonight I don't want to be wise. I only want to be kissed."

"That often leads to other things, Mercy. Especially dressed as you are. Or undressed."

She nodded slowly. "Yes."

"Yes?"

Did she know what she was saying? It seemed as if she did, because she leaned forward and put her hands on either side of his face, then rose up and placed her mouth on his.

Thunder exploded above them, but he was barely aware of it. He was too attuned to the storm inside of him, one that overpowered his conscience and made him wrap his arms around her.

He pulled her tight to him, lost in the kiss. The future, the circumstances, nothing mattered but Mercy.

Perhaps, if she called a halt now, he would still be able to stop himself. Not too many minutes in the future, however. From the moment he'd kissed her in the kitchen, he'd wanted her. No, he'd wanted her for weeks.

"Mercy." Just that, her name and nothing more. A last-minute plea for her to refuse him, to pull away, to counsel him on restraint.

"If you won't marry me, then will you take me to your bed?"

So much for restraint.

She was leaving Scotland, leaving him. He'd never see her again. He'd never again get a chance to hold her in his arms or kiss her. She'd be only a memory, another ghost of Duddingston, another regret.

He stood, but instead of heading for the door, he bent and pulled her into his arms. The bedspread fell to the floor. Mercy stood there, naked, her body tinted by firelight. She didn't gasp or shield herself with her hands. Instead, she stood there proud and unashamed.

His years in Edinburgh had not been monastic ones. Yet he couldn't remember ever seeing a woman as perfectly formed. But he studied her not as a physician, only as a man. She stood silently as his gaze swept her body, down over long and beautifully shaped legs, upward to a narrow waist and full breasts with erect nipples.

He wanted to touch her so desperately he ached with it, but first he followed her example. Under her gaze he unfastened his shirt and pulled it off. Then his shoes, his trousers, and the rest of his clothing. If she could reveal herself without self-consciousness, he had no choice but to do the same.

"Your arm," she said, placing her fingers gently beneath the wound.

"It is of no consequence." It certainly wouldn't hamper him tonight.

When they were both naked, he placed his hands on her waist, drawing her forward. She was trembling. He wrapped his arms around her, uncertain whether she was still cold or if she was frightened.

He pressed his cheek against her hair, counseling himself on restraint. A difficult task with Mercy in his arms.

"It's not too late," he said. "This is more than a kiss, Mercy. I can't say that I'll be able to stop if we continue further."

"I don't want to stop, Lennox. This is a gift."

He pulled back and looked into her face. "A gift?"

She nodded, her eyes luminous. "There will never be another time like this, don't you see? We're alone.

The rest of the world can't interfere. No one can disturb us. No one will know."

"You will. I will."

"I know what the rest of my life will be like, Lennox. There will be no more stolen moments. That's what I meant about it being a gift."

"Are you certain this is what you want?"

She nodded.

Before he could say anything else, she placed her hands on his shoulders.

"Would you kiss me again?" she asked. "I always get lost in your kisses."

"So do I."

Her lips curved as she stood on tiptoe to kiss him again. For long moments they stood there, entwined in front of the fire, two people who should have known better but in thrall to emotions more powerful than concepts like honor and propriety.

He wanted her more than he wanted to unlock the secrets of flight. He wanted her enough to ignore the whisperings of his conscience.

When she wrapped her arms around his neck, he was lost. The feel of her abdomen against his erection, the press of her nipples against his chest, the sigh she made when his tongue dueled with hers—all those things were greater than any wise thoughts that might have stopped him.

He led her to the bed, holding her hand as she took the steps and sat on the mattress. A second later he joined her.

Rain slashed against the windows and lightning illuminated the room in a bright white flash that lasted only a second.

He looked down at Mercy. "I need to ask you if you're certain, at least one more time."

"No," she said, startling him. "I'm not entirely certain. I know I'm being horribly unwise, but I want this."

"Aye, Mercy. If I were a better man I would leave you right this moment."

She reached up and entwined her arms around his neck. "Not if I won't let you leave," she said. "You have asked me enough times, Lennox. You've been honorable and decent and a man of great character. Forgive me if I'm not of the same estimable character, but I want to remember this for the rest of my life."

Must you leave? A question he didn't ask because it promised a commitment he couldn't make. Yet even as he kissed her, a voice whispered about the stupidity of pride. This surprising, enchanting, fascinating woman had offered to change his life and he'd turned her down.

He was either the world's worst fool or the proudest man in Scotland.

Chapter Thirty-Seven

*H*e shouldn't have returned to the room. Nor should he be here now. But any kind of caution Lennox should have uttered to himself was useless at the moment. His baser self had taken over, the entity who lectured him endlessly and was heartily sick of his hermitage. The same creature who'd spent countless moments adrift in thought about the woman in his arms.

His hands were shaking. His fingers trembled as they slid over Mercy's skin. She was warm, yet her flesh pebbled at his touch.

He kissed the sigh that emerged from between her lips.

"Forgive me," he said, his better nature surfacing from beneath his need.

She pulled his head down for a deeper kiss, silencing any further words he might've said. In that second he was truly lost, given over to the feel of her beneath his hands.

It had been some time for him, yet he couldn't remember when the act had ever been painted with a sense of wonder.

He kissed his way down her throat, across her

shoulders, and between her breasts before giving attention to both of them.

Her gasp was an indication of how shocking all of this was to her. Another reminder, perhaps, that he should stop, excuse himself, and retreat to his tower room. Instead, he kissed her again, growing familiar with the delicacy of her mouth and the sound of her sighs.

Perhaps she had some imperfection, but he couldn't find it. Everything about Mercy was flawless from the curve of her shoulders to the slenderness of her ankles.

She was a virgin, deserving of patience. He wasn't sure if he could restrain himself. Every moment touching her ratcheted his desire up even further.

Her kisses became wild things, her breathing nearly the match of his. His hands stroked her intimately, found proof that she was ready. Even so he should have waited perhaps.

He wasn't a god, only a man.

If she rebuffed him he would somehow find the strength to leave her.

All she did was smile up at him, wind her arms around his neck, and pull him down to her.

$\mathcal{S}$HE SHOULDN'T BE doing this. Every rule she'd learned from her mother, her nurses, and her governesses was geared toward this one act. She was to be treated as inviolate, the Vestal Rutherford Virgin. She was to act pure, hold herself up to a higher standard than most women, and be without blemish or flaw.

No one had ever embraced their downfall with as much enthusiasm as Mercy felt right now.

Lennox was touching her, kissing her, causing remarkable sensations throughout her body. Her skin felt heated, even her breathing was different as if she were running a race.

Her breasts felt as if they were swelling to meet his touch, her nipples hard. Each of his kisses had left an impression on her lips. She'd never feel another kiss like his, never experience the wonder at the simple touch of a mouth on hers.

Her hands gripped his shoulders, then flattened against his impressive chest.

His manhood was hard against her stomach and she wanted to touch it, but held back. A second later she dared herself and when her hand brushed against it, Lennox made a sound in the back of his throat.

"Have I done something wrong?" she asked, wishing she knew more.

"No," he said, before kissing her again. Permission, then, to keep touching him.

Time meant nothing. In one sense it was racing. In another, each second was elongated, pulled thin.

He kissed her neck and she shivered at the sensation. The inside of her elbow, between her breasts, even her wrists were especially sensitive. His lips on her nipples were tied in some magical way to a place deep inside her.

When he raised himself over her, she pushed back her momentary fear. She knew this next part might be painful at first, but how could that be when everything felt so wondrous?

He hesitated, kissed her, and said her name. Just her name, but it was a question, permission sought.

She nodded and then she was no longer a virgin. It pinched, but that was all. Just a momentary pinch, not pain.

She'd never imagined that the act of love would

make her feel part of another person. She was joined to Lennox physically, but it was more than that. She'd always remember this moment when she was no longer innocent and unaware.

The discomfort was gone, the pinch eased. He bent to kiss her as he entered her again. She raised her hips as he left her, then sighed at the feeling of him once more deep inside.

Her body felt as if it was preparing for something. Her breath caught, her pulse was racing, her heart thundering in her chest. Pleasure began deep inside her like a tiny explosion, one that grew bigger with each movement Lennox made. She extended her arms around his shoulders, her hands flat against his back. She wanted to call out his name, ask him what was happening, but she remained silent as the sensations grew.

When Lennox bent to tongue her nipple, the pleasure magnified like the fireworks she'd once seen in New York. In those seconds she lost her sense of herself. She wasn't simply Mercy. She was part of Lennox and he was part of her.

He murmured her name before collapsing on top of her. A moment later he kissed the area just in front of her ear. His breath was harsh; his heart beating as rapidly as hers. She closed her eyes tight, feeling the rhythmic beat inside her body where they were still joined.

This was sin.

This was bliss.

MERCY WOKE BECAUSE something tickled.

She blinked open her eyes to find Lennox smiling down at her. He was using a lock of her hair to brush the end of her nose.

"How do you feel?" he asked.

She glanced away, embarrassed by the question. Still, she did a quick inventory. Her breasts ached a little and she was sore in other places. She pressed her fingers against her chin.

"It's a little red," he said, brushing her hand away and replacing it with a kiss. "No doubt it was my beard."

He had always been clean-shaven before, but then she'd never seen him at dawn, either. He looked almost swarthy this morning, and when she said as much to him, he smiled.

"I probably look like my ancestors," he said.

"Do you wear a kilt?"

"Not really."

"I'd like to see you in a kilt," she said.

He didn't answer. Instead, he sat up on the edge of the bed, his back to her. He had marks on his skin, faint red lines that made her wonder if she had gouged him with her nails. Should she apologize for that?

"The storm has finally stopped," he said, standing and finishing dressing.

"Good."

"We should see about arrangements to Inverness."

She nodded. She shouldn't be disappointed. Lennox wasn't suddenly going to claim undying love for her simply because he had taken her virginity. No, that wasn't right. He hadn't taken it as much as she'd given it to him.

Draping her legs over the side of the bed, she reached for the bedspread. He must have retrieved it from in front of the fireplace early in the morning. She wound it around herself, shielding her nakedness, but not her vulnerability.

He came to stand in front of her.

"Are you all right?"

She nodded.

He looked as if he wanted to say something else, but remained silent.

"I don't regret last night," she said when he turned and headed for the door. He glanced over his shoulder at her. "If you were wondering."

It was his turn to nod.

She watched as he closed the door behind him. Her emotions were all jumbled up like yarn in a basket. She was afraid that if she started to pull on one piece, it would lead to another skein.

All she felt was sadness. That was normal enough, she supposed, given the circumstances. She'd expected to feel sad leaving Lennox, but she hadn't thought it would be this great, gaping hole where her heart used to be.

She had to leave.

The thought had occurred to her last night and time had only solidified the idea.

She didn't want to be guilty of behaving the same way she had for most of her life. She'd always been a coward. A coward who'd lived a privileged existence. Not once had she said anything to her parents about how she wanted to be treated. Instead, she'd taken their care and protection and secretly railed against it.

Last night she'd been a coward again. Instead of fending for herself, she'd expected Lennox to save her. She wasn't Lennox's responsibility. If she wanted to get to Inverness she'd do it herself. Or maybe she wouldn't run away again like she had a few weeks ago. Maybe this time she would face her problem.

No one could force her to marry Gregory. Her grandmother held the sword of approval over her head. Do as she said or risk being shunned. She doubted there was anything she could do to gain Ailsa's approval at this point. The same with her parents. She wasn't without options. She had the ability to set up her own establishment. It would mean that she'd live on the fringes of society, something she would never have considered before coming here. Yet she would be able to live her own life as she wanted.

Scotland had changed her.

Or maybe it was Lennox.

Chapter Thirty-Eight

$\mathcal{M}$ercy made it down the stairs and through the Clan Hall without being seen. She hesitated at the kitchen door when she saw Irene at the stove.

She couldn't very well walk to the village or to Macrory House without her shoes.

"You'll be needing boots to cross the glen," Irene said without turning.

Mercy nearly jumped a foot.

"Your shoes are ruined." Irene pointed to the back door where a pair of boots sat. "Take those. You can give them to Jean."

Mercy entered the kitchen and grabbed the boots, then sat on one of the kitchen chairs to put them on.

"Thank you," she said.

Irene only shrugged in response.

She turned and left the kitchen, walking through the corridor and into the Clan Hall. Here she slowed, looking around her, knowing that she'd never see this fascinating place again.

When she made it to the iron door, Irene startled her by coming up behind her silently as if she walked on cat feet.

"I'll be seeing you to the glen," Irene said.

"That's not necessary."

"It isn't for you. I'm doing it for Lennox. He'd want to know that you were safely on your way."

Mercy stopped herself from asking where he was, suspecting that Irene wouldn't answer her.

The causeway was flooded, making her grateful for the loan of Irene's boots. The older woman wore a pair of sturdy black shoes. If she felt any discomfort from the water seeping in through the leather she didn't mention it.

"You've not said goodbye to him. Was that your plan, then? Sneaking out like a mouse who'd got her cheese?"

She glanced at Irene. In the past few hours Mercy had ceased to be a friend, or even an amusing visitor from New York. Now she was the enemy.

"It was easier," she said, giving the older woman the truth. She hadn't wanted to say goodbye to Lennox. She'd never come back here. She'd never see him again. She had wanted to spare herself a little pain.

The older woman merely glanced at her and then away, her gaze fixed on the wet path before them.

"That grandmother of yours is a harridan," Irene said. "I wouldn't be surprised if she banishes you."

"It doesn't matter. One way or another I'm leaving today."

"No doubt the Macrorys would loan you a carriage. They have three of them."

She exchanged a glance with Irene. "You think that's what I should've done last night."

"No one would have gone anywhere last night with that storm."

Mercy remained silent.

"They can put two and two together at the house

just like I did," Irene continued. "But I'll not have the judgment come down on Lennox's head. You're the one responsible. You're the one who showed up at the castle. He didn't come after you."

Irene's mouth was thin with anger and there was a look in her eyes that said she wouldn't believe anything Mercy said.

"I'll make sure they don't blame him."

"Now that would be impossible. You know they're going to regardless."

"They shouldn't."

Irene sent her a glance that ridiculed her comment. "What do you feel for my earl?"

Mercy didn't say anything for a moment. It wasn't that she was trying to find the right words to speak. She didn't know the answer to Irene's question. She didn't feel the same around Lennox. She felt different, special, better. She liked herself more in his company. He made her want to be a better person, kinder, more thoughtful, and understanding.

She felt like smiling around him and regardless of the weather, it always felt like a sunny day.

Yet she knew that every ounce of emotion she felt for Lennox Caitheart was going to demand a pound of grief. She could almost envision herself in New York, thinking back to this time. If given the same opportunity again, she would do exactly what she'd done last night. She would love Lennox regardless of the consequences. Even if it was unwise. Even if she did pay a price.

"Well?" Irene asked. "Were you playing him for a fool? You're not the first Macrory woman to stay the night and that didn't end well, either."

She stopped in the middle of the path and stared

at the older woman. The look Irene returned was one of acute dislike, no doubt born out of her loyalty to Lennox.

The question wasn't unfair. Nor was the look.

"No," she said. "I wasn't. Nor was he treating me badly. It simply happened."

She felt her face flame; the embarrassment was practice for what she was about to endure at Macrory House.

Irene folded her arms and studied her. "Things like that happen when people feel a certain way about each other."

"Thank you for the loan of the boots," Mercy said. "I'll leave them with Jean." She walked away from the older woman, unwilling to get into a discussion of her feelings. There was only one thing to do—continue as she'd planned and endure everything that she'd brought upon herself with courage.

She prayed she had enough.

"WHAT DO YOU mean, she's gone?" Lennox said, staring at Irene.

"Exactly that. She's left. Gone back to Macrory House."

He'd been checking on the damage the storm had caused to the chapel and the stable. The stable was in better condition than the chapel; it looked like the storm had melted another section of the roof. He would need to remove the rest of the pews and bring them into the Clan Hall to protect them.

"Why?"

Irene shrugged. "To get a carriage to take her to Inverness. To mend fences. To marry that fool man from America. What do I know?"

"Did she say anything?" he asked, knowing that he sounded like an idiot for asking. Did she impart some information that might mitigate this odd and unwelcome feeling of abandonment?

"Did she leave word for you? That she didn't. She was all for getting to Macrory House as quickly as her feet could carry her."

He knew. In that instant he knew what she'd done.

Without another word he left the kitchen, walked quickly down the corridor, and took the stairs two at a time. It wasn't that he didn't trust Irene. He wanted to see for himself.

He pushed open the door so hard that it bounced against the wall and stood staring at the tangled covers of the bed.

Marry me. If you won't marry me will you take me to your bed?

He should have seen it then, but he'd been shocked by her words, then overcome with desire, passion, lust—any word was acceptable. He should have known, but he hadn't, only seeing what he'd wanted to see.

He'd been manipulated. She hadn't wanted to marry Gregory so what was the easiest way to escape that marriage? Bed another man. Ruin herself. Lose her virginity. Gregory wouldn't want her then. In addition, she'd amused herself by bedding a Scot.

Why the hell hadn't he seen it?

Perhaps he should give orders that this room be locked, the door barred. An ax should be taken to the bed, regardless of its history. If nothing else, he should drag the mattress down to the courtyard, torch it, and watch it burn until it was nothing more than ash.

She'd used him. For a few hours he'd forgotten everything but her. He'd held her in his arms as she slept and marveled at her beauty. He'd loved her again in the dawn light, knowing he'd never forget those moments. In the morning he wanted to tell her things he'd never told anyone, show her the new plans he'd drawn for a few inventions, and share his thoughts.

He'd spent too many damn hours thinking about the woman and wondering about her. He should have seen who she truly was rather than who she'd portrayed herself to be.

What a fool he'd been.

She'd left him. Easily, simply, without a backward glance or an apology of any sort. She'd used him, then she left him.

Something in the corner caught his attention. He strode to the opposite side of the room and stood staring down at Mercy's valise. The valise filled with money. Had she thought to pay him for last night's services? He'd never felt anything like the rage that suddenly consumed him.

Bending, he grabbed the valise and made for the stairs, emotion blinding him to any thought but reaching Mercy.

Chapter Thirty-Nine

Things like that happen when people feel a certain way about each other.

Mercy thought about Irene's words all the way back to Macrory House. A certain way. What did she feel for Lennox? Was it love? If so, it didn't match any of the poetry or the novels she had read. There was nothing calming or sweet about this emotion. It swept all her thoughts away, made her act in ways she'd never envisioned, rendered her temporarily senseless. If this was love, then it needed another name, something violent and awe-inspiring.

She hesitated at the kitchen door. She didn't fool herself that she was going to be welcome inside Macrory House. She wouldn't be staying. Instead, she and Ruthie would leave today. If her relatives wouldn't agree to loan her a carriage, she'd ask directions to the village and walk there. Somehow, she'd find a way to Inverness.

Finally, she opened the door and walked through the kitchen, trying to ignore the looks from all the maids. Whispers followed her. They weren't unkind, merely speculative.

She glanced at the clock over the door. Nearly ten.

She'd wanted to get an earlier start, but it really didn't matter what time she returned to Macrory House. Her absence would no doubt have been noted regardless of the time.

She'd barely made it to the corridor when she heard Ailsa's voice.

"You must put a guard on the doors at night," she was saying. "Behavior of this sort will not be tolerated."

No doubt her grandmother was talking to McNaughton, who must have alerted Ailsa to the fact that Mercy hadn't been in the house last night. Why else would she be out of her room at this hour?

Mercy stopped and steadied herself, her hands at her waist. Her dress was nearly ruined from the rain and from being dried over the screen. Her petticoats were still limp and she hadn't laced her corset very tight. Her hair was a disaster since she hadn't had a brush or comb with her.

She was as reputable looking as she possibly could be, but she would certainly fail any inspection. Rather than delay, however, she squared her shoulders, reminded herself about courage, and followed Ailsa's voice.

Her grandmother was standing on one of the lower steps of the impressive staircase, attired in a scarlet quilted dressing gown. Her white hair was arranged in the usual coronet atop her head. She stood as straight as one of the balusters, her right hand on the banister. When she caught sight of Mercy, she nodded crisply at McNaughton who bowed slightly and turned.

Both of them frowned at Mercy.

"Where have you been?" her grandmother asked.

She didn't answer that question. Instead, she asked one of her own.

"May I borrow one of the Macrory carriages? I need to travel to Inverness."

At her grandmother's silence she continued. "I won't annoy you with my presence any further, Seanmhair. Ruthie and I will return to New York."

"Not until you're married."

Mercy took a deep breath, tilted her chin up, and kept her gaze fixed on her grandmother.

"I have no intention of marrying Gregory. Not today. Not tomorrow. Not in an eternity. You can yell at me. You can threaten me, but I will not say the words that bind me to that man. Nor will I allow you to dictate my life."

"Your parents have raised an incorrigible child."

She couldn't say that she was incorrigible. Perhaps determined was a better word. But she was most definitely not a child.

"It may surprise you to hear that I do not care about your opinion of me," Mercy said. "From the very moment I arrived here you've made it abundantly clear that you loathe and detest me. I can only admit that, regrettably, the feeling is mutual."

Ailsa's mouth was open in a perfect O. Had no one ever stood up to this woman before?

"You were with him, weren't you?"

She wasn't going to answer that question, either.

"You've been sniffing around Caitheart like a bitch in heat ever since you arrived in Scotland. We'll see what your fiancé has to say about that."

"Gregory is no longer my fiancé. Why are you so determined to marry me off to him? He's a Yankee, Seanmhair. You know, like my father? You've made your opinion of him well known, too."

"Who do you think you are to talk to me like that?"

"Someone without any respect for you, unfortunately. At the very least, I should value you because of your age. I find that I can't even do that. You've criticized my mother, my father, and me. You're determined to make me bend to your dictates. You'll pardon me if I don't participate."

"You're a whore and we don't associate with whores in this house. You'll stay in your room until your father arrives."

Mercy stared at her grandmother.

"Father is coming?"

"He left a week after me," Gregory said, stepping around the corner.

She'd never considered him the type who would eavesdrop, but evidently Gregory was not above all kinds of behavior.

"Why didn't you tell me earlier?"

"I didn't know that you would slink out in the middle of the night, Mercy."

She wasn't going to mention Lennox's name. Nor was it any of Gregory's concern where she'd been. She'd formally renounced their engagement. Just because he didn't agree wasn't a consideration.

"I'm disappointed in you, Mercy. I will, of course, forgive you."

"I don't want your forgiveness, Gregory. I don't need it. I don't want anything from you."

He only smiled, an expression that sent chills down her back.

Mrs. West suddenly entered the foyer and sent a wild look toward Mercy. Before she could ask what was wrong, Lennox appeared.

If her grandmother was angry, it was nothing to what Lennox was feeling at the moment. His eyes were narrowed, his jaw clenched. His grip on Mercy's valise was so tight that his knuckles were white.

She didn't get a chance to ask him why he was here before Lennox threw the valise at her feet.

"Did you think to pay me? I told you I wasn't going to take your damn money."

He didn't get another word out. Gregory was suddenly there, his fist planted beneath Lennox's chin. In the next instant, Lennox was flying through the air to land on the runner a few feet away.

He raised up on his elbows, shook his head, and in the next second was on Gregory.

Mercy couldn't tell where one body ended and the other began. The two men were a tangle of arms and legs, flying fists, and spraying blood.

Mrs. West attempted to get between Gregory and Lennox but was thrown back. McNaughton was the second one to try and he, too, couldn't stop them.

The fight was oddly silent except for the blows, wet, slapping sounds that made Mercy wince.

She'd never seen a fight before, especially one in which the combatants looked to be determined to kill each other. The spectacle was attracting a number of maids and male servants who crowded into the corridor behind Mrs. West.

The two men looked equally matched in size. She had to move out of the way, because they were rolling toward her.

"What in the bloody hell is going on here?"

Douglas stood there, his granddaughter beside him. Flora was wide-eyed and open mouthed.

The servants immediately dispersed, Mrs. West with them. Only McNaughton stood there, stiff backed with his nose in the air.

Lennox got to his hands and knees. Gregory stood and, in a move that was deliberately unfair, raised his boot and kicked Lennox in the side. Lennox reached out, grabbed Gregory's foot, and jerked him off his feet. In the next second he was sitting astride Gregory, pummeling his face.

"That's enough!" Douglas shouted. "Get off him, man!" he said to Lennox.

For a moment, she didn't think he was going to obey, but Lennox finally got to his feet. Lennox was holding his left side. In addition to a cut on his mouth and a bloody nose, Gregory was going to have a black eye. Lennox's shirt had been torn, but Gregory's was spotted with blood.

"Who the hell are you?" Douglas said to Gregory.

"The gentleman on the floor is a Mr. Gregory Hamilton," McNaughton said with his usual supercilious air. "Late from America, sir. I believe you know his Lordship, the Earl of Morton."

Douglas ignored Gregory in favor of Lennox. "What the hell are you doing in my home, Caitheart?"

"I returned some of Miss Rutherford's property," Lennox said. "A payment, if you will, for taking her virginity."

He turned to Mercy. "That's why you came to me last night, wasn't it? It wasn't to ask me to help you get to Inverness or even to buy a husband. You wanted to escape this marriage and you have."

She'd only heard his voice sound like that once, the morning of the accident. He'd been furious then, too.

He looked at Gregory, holding the back of his hand against the cut on his mouth. "She's used, isn't that what they say? She's known another man's touch."

His gaze swung back to Mercy. "Isn't that what you wanted? To be freed from marrying him?"

"Is that what you think?"

"That's what I know," Lennox said.

"Then you're wrong."

She could feel her lips curve into a smile, but it wasn't one filled with amusement.

"You don't understand, Lennox. Gregory has already forgiven me. You see, he doesn't care. I'm a commodity, a means to an end. Tell him, Gregory. It doesn't matter to you that I went to another man's bed as long as you can get your hands on all that lovely money of mine."

Gregory didn't say a word, but the look he gave her promised that he would exact payment for her comment in the future.

Her grandmother stretched out her arm and pointed at Lennox. "Get out of this house."

Lennox turned on his heel and went out the way he came without glancing once in Mercy's direction.

Gregory combed his fingers through his hair, nodded to Douglas, and said, "I'm Mercy's fiancé."

"No," she said in a firm voice, "he isn't. The man is exceedingly stupid. He doesn't seem to understand that I'm not marrying him. Ever."

Douglas looked from Gregory to Mercy and then to his sister. Mercy stole a glance at her grandmother. From Ailsa's expression, she wasn't going to remain mute for long. Any moment now and she would begin to lecture her again.

Mercy grabbed the valise, picked it up, and pushed past her grandmother to ascend the stairs. Only then did she see her aunt standing at the head of the stairs, her hand pressed to her mouth.

"Where do you think you're going, Hortense?" Ailsa asked.

"To my room."

"You'll stay there. I don't know how I shall be able to show my face in public after your antics. Have you no concept of decency? Do you not have a lick of sense?"

She didn't bother responding. Nor did she ask her great-uncle for the loan of his carriage. Her father was coming. The last thing she wanted to do was exacerbate the situation by escaping Scotland just as he arrived.

Her grandmother didn't need to tell her to stay in her room. Right now she didn't want to ever leave it.

Chapter Forty

*T*ears wouldn't help. In fact, they'd make everything worse. Her eyes would swell and she'd have a headache later. Plus, she always got a little nauseated when she was too emotional.

Emotional? Hah! She'd been emotional from the day she'd set foot in Scotland and it was all because of Lennox.

He wouldn't be happy if he knew that, would he? No, he'd blame her for that, too. For being insulted by him at first and then fascinated and finally—oh, what did she call what she'd done? Thrown her skirts over her head like some doxy and given in to every base impulse she had. The worst part was that she'd do it again willingly. Happily.

She'd hurt him. In turn, his words had been like acid, each separate word burning through her skin. She was more miserable than she could ever remember being.

Leaving him should be easier now, especially in light of his anger at her. She suspected, however, that it would still be difficult.

He'd always think that she'd used him and perhaps she had, only not in the way he thought. She'd wanted him to be the one who ended her innocence, who kissed her to madness and introduced her to loving. The memory of last night would stay with her forever, regardless of what he thought of her.

She should have gone after him. She should have raced after Lennox and explained. Leaving the valise at the castle had been an accident. Until Lennox appeared, she'd forgotten all about it.

Why hadn't she followed him? She'd stood there like a statue, watching as he walked away. The answer was difficult to accept: because the habit of remaining silent was still more comfortable for her than speaking out. Her fragile courage, nascent and barely used, had evaporated.

Those hours with him had been special. She'd never forget him or them. They would be tucked inside her heart in a secret place.

She'd awakened during the night and in the dying firelight watched as he slept. She'd felt gratitude and joy cascading through her and wanted, in some way, to thank him. No one could take those memories from her, not even Lennox.

What she felt for him confused her. It might be love, but then it was admiration, and perhaps a little awe. He was brave, undaunted by failure, resilient, amusing, kind, and thoughtful. He possessed character traits that set him apart from most men she'd met. She wanted to sit and talk with him about the subjects that interested her, including his castle and his family history.

She'd never understood, until last night, why her heart always beat faster when she was around him or why she was often breathless in his company. She knew why now. It was desire, something she'd never felt until Lennox. Oh, she'd known handsome men, and had been courted by more than a few charming and personable heiress hunters. Occasionally, she'd laughed too much or even giggled, charmed despite herself. She'd been flattered at their attention or felt her face warm at their compliments. But her body had never heated from the inside and she'd never felt as though she was melting when a man smiled at her.

Not until Lennox.

When had her fascination with him started? From that first moment when he'd peeled off the roof of the carriage? Or when he stitched her wound, assuming she wouldn't indulge in histrionics? Perhaps it had begun as early as that. Or when he'd written that letter that had so irritated her. Or when he'd plunged into the loch and her heart felt as if it had stopped at that exact moment. So many memories in just a few weeks.

She remembered an afternoon when her mother had reminisced about how she'd met Mercy's father. She'd been fourteen at the time, fascinated with the idea of romance, but not boys as much.

"I saw him," her mother said. "And knew right away. It took me a few days to convince him, however."

Her parents had exchanged a look, one that reassured Mercy that their relationship was one of mutual love and respect. What would they think to know that love had struck their daughter the same way?

How could she leave Scotland? How could she leave Lennox?

Somehow she must.

LENNOX DIDN'T REMEMBER walking back to Duddingston. He was filled with too many volatile emotions, like how he wanted to pay that bastard back for the sneaky kick to his ribs. While he was at it, he'd pummel the man a few minutes more, just to ensure Gregory remembered his visit to Scotland.

The Macrorys had proven themselves to be idiots as they always did. The old woman had ordered him out of the house and Douglas had demanded that the fight end. Not one person, from Flora to the woman at the top of the stairs, had said a damn thing in defense of Mercy. If she'd been cosseted in New York, she certainly hadn't had that experience in Scotland.

It was a sorry state of affairs when his conscience was more protective of Mercy than her relatives.

Once back at the castle he went to his bedroom, bathed his face, and inspected his wounds. He hadn't fought anyone since he was a boy and his opponent had been Robert. This experience, however, had been a great deal more painful. His cheek was bruised and would be discolored in a day or two. He had a cut near his eye that was minor enough not to need attention. The pain in his ribs, however, made him want to return to Macrory House and deliver the same blow to Hamilton. He tended to himself then descended the steps, purposefully avoiding Irene, and headed for the Laird's Room.

Once there he retrieved his drawings for his bubble shower. It was a new design, something that had occurred to him one night when he couldn't sleep. The bathing system mimicked a storm, where the water poured down from the top of the apparatus and was disposed of in a drain on the floor.

He'd heard of similar inventions, but he'd never seen one. Building it would keep his mind off other issues, things he didn't want to think about right at the moment.

Like how he was sure his ribs were, if not broken, then badly bruised. Or how Mercy had looked when he'd accused her of sleeping with him only to get out of marrying Gregory.

Had she been right? Was the bastard only after her money?

He closed his eyes and willed himself to stop thinking about her. Whatever she'd said or done no longer mattered. She'd be gone from Scotland shortly and he should wipe his mind clean of her memory starting now.

As soon as Connor got back to Duddingston, he'd outfit the airship with the new sails. He hoped the weather wouldn't slow Connor down because the wind was always higher around Ben Uaine after a rollicking storm. There, something else to anticipate and take his mind off Mercy.

He adjusted his stool, lit the lamp beside his sloping desk, and applied himself to his sketch. He thought that if he brought up the water to about seven or eight feet by the simple expedient of a pump, whoever was using the shower could simply turn a handle to release it or stop the flow.

It might even be possible, depending on where the shower was installed, to incorporate some kind of cistern with it. That would mean that there would be less pumping and more gravity at work.

He put the pencil down and scowled at the page. The design should work, but he wasn't interested in it as he always was when making something new. He couldn't see the shower for Mercy's face. Even now, alone in the Laird's Room, the scent of her delicate perfume seemed to linger in the air.

He shouldn't have said what he had. He shouldn't have humiliated her in front of her family. He'd been cruel and that wasn't like him.

How had she done it? How had she stripped him of his character to the extent he didn't recognize himself?

He tossed his pencil down onto the drawing board and decided that, ribs or not, he needed a visit to Ben Uaine.

Chapter Forty-One

*F*or three days Mercy remained in her room with Ruthie. The maid was in fine superstition form. Ruthie saw omens in everything, the latest a dropped fork which she swore meant that an unexpected visitor was about to appear.

Mercy told her about the news Gregory had delivered—that her father was on his way to Scotland.

"Oh, Miss Mercy," Ruthie said, sitting heavily on the side of the bed.

They exchanged a look.

James Rutherford didn't leave his empire lightly. Mercy was only too aware of the ramifications of her father's decision. She would be required to apologize for her behavior until the day he died.

"And the tea leaves, Miss Mercy. They told me that someone would be getting a letter."

On numerous occasions she'd tried to coax Ruthie out of believing that everything was a superstition. Now she didn't even try.

No doubt the letter would be from her mother, tear stained and filled with words that hurt to read.

Her grandmother had tried to gain admittance into Mercy's room more than once in the past three days.

On each occasion, Mercy had barred the door and claimed illness, which wasn't far from the truth. She was sick at heart.

She tried to act calm around Ruthie and most of the time was successful. At night, however, she stood at her window, wishing that it faced toward Duddingston Castle, and remembered every moment of that enchanted stormy night with Lennox.

Would she bear a child? The question should have paralyzed her with fear. Instead, she only felt a sense of waiting, knowing that the answer would reveal itself in due time.

Time slowed, each separate minute seeming to last ten times that. The days were interminable and not because she remained cloistered in her self-imposed prison. She was in pain, but it was unlike anything she'd ever experienced. It wasn't physical as much as emotional and seemed to grow worse with each passing hour.

She'd allowed Lennox to walk away. She couldn't forgive herself for that. Would his pride allow him to hear her out? Perhaps he would read a letter she wrote if Irene carried it back to him.

The knock on the door interrupted her thoughts. She opened it, thinking it was Ruthie returning from an errand. Instead, it was Mrs. West with the noon tray.

Since Lily was the one who normally brought her meals to her, Mercy was surprised. The housekeeper didn't normally perform such tasks. Unless, of course, she had some information to impart.

She opened the door for Mrs. West to enter and thanked the older woman when she put the tray on the table.

"Have you heard anything from Irene?" she asked.

"How are things at the castle?" In other words, was Lennox all right?

Mrs. West sent her a look that she understood what Mercy was asking.

"He's a bit bruised and battered," Mrs. West said. "Irene had to wrap his ribs after the fight. You would think that would have slowed the man down, but no, he's all set to drag that airship of his up Ben Uaine."

"He's going flying again?"

Mrs. West nodded. "Irene's as mad as I've ever seen her. He's in no shape to do something like that, even with Connor's help. She's worried about him. He's a stubborn fool when he wants to be."

"Can't someone stop him?"

"I don't know who could, Miss Mercy. The man has a head of rock on him when he wants."

She studied Mercy for a moment, almost as if she wanted to say something else.

"I heard what your grandmother said to you the other day, Miss Mercy."

She had grown so familiar with feeling embarrassed that she didn't turn away from Mrs. West's look.

"Do you remember your grandfather, miss?"

"Only a little," she said. "He died at the beginning of the war, but he was sick for a good while before that."

"I understand that he made something of himself in America."

Mercy nodded. "Their farm was very prosperous, at least before the war. And the house they built was beautiful."

"Do you know anything about his life in Scotland?"

"No," Mercy said.

"Well, I've a tale to tell you then. Cameron Burns

was a crofter who farmed a small patch of Macrory land. He barely made a living, but he was a handsome young man. Ailsa thought so, too. She took a liking to him. Many's the time she slipped out of the house to meet him. When her father found out he forbid her to see Cameron again. Ailsa and Cameron ran away to America."

Mercy had never heard that story.

"So when your grandmother goes on and on about your behavior, you might remember that. It was a great scandal. People whispered about her for years."

Mrs. West smiled kindly at her before turning and leaving the room.

Perhaps one day Scottish mothers would warn their daughters about her. *Let me tell you the tale of the foolish American girl and the earl.*

She ignored her meal for the moment. Instead, she went to the secretary and pulled out a piece of her stationery. Her pen hovered over the paper, but not one word came to mind. She should apologize for Gregory's actions and for the unfairness of his unexpected blow. She should most definitely explain about the valise. In addition, she would plead with him not to fly his airship now, at least not until he'd healed completely. She finally put the pen down and stared at the blank page.

If she wrote what she truly wanted to say, the letter would be completely different.

My Dearest Lennox,

Thank you for our night together. I never knew that such pleasure was possible. I never realized that I could feel as if I belonged to someone else as well as myself.

*Thank you for teaching me to kiss, for holding
me in your arms, and for making me feel as if I
was the most loved woman in creation.*

*I will remember you forever. No one else will
ever take your spot in my heart. Even if I live to
be an old woman I will never forget you.*

*Please be safe. And happy. Take the very best
care of yourself and if, some time, you think of
me, please be kind. I never meant to hurt you.*

I love you.

No, she wasn't brave enough to write those things.
Besides, she knew he wouldn't read it. He would forever think that she'd used him.

She turned her head, listening. The faint skirl of the
pipes seemed almost like a hallucination at first and
then the sound became louder.

Mercy stood, walked to the window that overlooked
the view of Ben Uaine. She could hear the pipes better
now. Her father had once hired someone to play for
her mother's birthday to honor her Scottish heritage
and Mercy had never forgotten the sound.

"They're not designed to be played indoors," her
mother had said later.

Here, though, was the perfect backdrop. The piper
stood on a rise in the glen. Ben Uaine absorbed the
sound yet somehow amplified it. The woods filtered
the notes and they sailed back to Macrory House.

Glancing down she saw the staff coming out to
watch. Not just the staff, but her relatives as well, all of
them standing straight and tall, silent and respectful.

The song was one she'd never heard before now. An
almost mournful melody, it tugged at her heart. This
was a different kind of music, almost savage and deeply

personal. The pipes reminded her of Lennox, alone, independent, and prideful.

"It's the mourning," Ruthie said, entering the room. "It's an annual event to mark Mary Macrory's death. They hire a piper and he plays a lament."

That meant that it was also the anniversary of Robert's death.

The sound of the pipes crept inside her heart, helping her make a decision. Perhaps it was unwise and potentially scandalous, but what did it matter now?

She had to go to him.

Chapter Forty-Two

$\mathcal{T}$he whole of Macrory House seemed to be involved in entertaining the piper. Or perhaps there was another ceremony marking Mary's death. Her relatives were in the family parlor along with McNaughton, Mrs. West, and the senior staff—information provided by Ruthie.

The other woman looked as if she regretted saying anything when Mercy explained her plans.

"I have to go and see him," she told Ruthie. "He shouldn't be flying his airship as long as he's injured."

"They've practically banished you as it is, Miss Mercy. Don't give them any more reason to be upset."

She turned and faced Ruthie. "You have always been such a wonderful support, Ruthie. I don't know what I would've done without you, but this is something I have to do."

"Then I should go with you," she said.

"I'm only going to talk to him. I'll be back in an hour or so."

How could she possibly explain herself? She couldn't, so she left the room before Ruthie said anything else.

No doubt Gregory had been invited into the family parlor with the rest of the family. Ever since he attacked Lennox, he'd been welcomed into the bosom of the family.

She slipped out the kitchen entrance, grateful that the maids in the kitchen were involved in meal preparation.

As she was heading for the walled garden something caught her eye. At first she thought it was the ghillie, the gamekeeper for her great-uncle, because of the shotgun he had slung over his shoulder. In the next instant she realized it was Gregory. She hugged the wall and watched as he kept to the path, glancing over his shoulder from time to time as though he was concerned about being followed.

Why was he acting so furtive?

Although her great-uncle had made a point of telling her about all the game that was raised on his land, she'd never known Gregory to have an interest in hunting. He tended to gravitate to those activities that required a group, but shooting sports had not been among them.

She followed him at some distance, curious. After cutting through the walled garden and reaching the other side, she saw him climbing the knoll the piper had used, descending to the other side, and heading toward Ben Uaine.

What was he doing?

Gregory preferred attending a play to walking in the garden. Even when he came to their country home, he would rather go to a social event than take the sailboat out or explore the nearby woods.

He wasn't a naturalist. Why, then, was he heading toward the mountain?

She kept to the edge of the woods, grateful that the ground had dried. She was wearing her only other pair of shoes, a sturdy black lace-up that was almost a boot. They were better than her kid slippers for tromping over the glen.

She couldn't figure out what Gregory was doing. Nor did she have any intention of calling out to him and letting him know that she was nearby. They were far enough away from Macrory House that they would be, essentially, alone. She didn't trust him. Nor did she feel safe in his presence.

He was parallel to the road now, still approaching Ben Uaine. She had reached the edge of the woods. If she wanted to remain unseen, she'd have to keep to the tall grasses.

Did he intend to climb the mountain?

She debated leaving Gregory to his task, whatever it was, and continuing on to Duddingston Castle. Lennox was of greater importance than her curiosity about Gregory.

A flash of white on the side of the mountain caught her attention. She stopped and stared, knowing what she was seeing. She hadn't been fast enough. Nor, evidently, had Irene been able to stop Lennox from his foolish flight.

Standing in the grasses, she watched as the sails unfurled and caught the wind. For a second her heart was in her mouth as the airship dipped then righted itself.

She'd been here before. Twice she'd looked up to see a birdlike object being launched from the side of Ben Uaine. Familiarity didn't lessen the fear she felt.

Gregory stopped in the middle of the road, abruptly knelt on one knee, removed the shotgun from its sling, and held it to his shoulder.

He was going to shoot Lennox out of the sky.

She began to run, wishing that she hadn't kept so much distance between her and Gregory. She stumbled more than once, caught herself, grabbing her skirts with both hands, uncaring if her unmentionables showed.

He raised the shotgun slightly, following the path of the airship's flight. Mercy ran as she never had before, her heart straining in her chest, her breath labored. One thought was uppermost—she had to save Lennox. She had to save Lennox.

She thrust her arms in front of her as she lunged at Gregory. The force of their collision was enough to knock them both over, the gun clattering to the road.

It took her a moment to get to her knees, but that was too long. Gregory had already retrieved the shotgun and was aiming it again. Reaching out, she wrapped her arms around one of his legs, pulling him off balance. He stumbled, but didn't fall.

Desperate, she got to her feet, grabbing for his arm. If she couldn't get the gun from him, at least she could make sure that his shot went wide.

Lennox's airship was getting closer and closer, low enough to be a perfect target.

Gregory struck her with the back of his hand. Pain exploded across her face, making her take a step back. He lifted the gun again. This time when she grabbed his arm she held on.

She saw the blow before it came. The next, however, was so fast that she didn't have a chance to anticipate it. Gregory's signet ring cut the corner of her mouth.

"What a pity I didn't know you were a whore, Mercy. We could have had some fun back in New York."

Lennox was landing, the boat-like carrier bouncing on the road behind them and then rolling some distance.

Let Gregory say whatever he wanted. At least she'd prevented him from firing at Lennox.

"What were you going to tell people, Gregory? That it was an accident? That you thought Lennox's airship was a bird? An eagle? Do you think anyone would have believed you? Or did you think that, because you're in Scotland you would have gotten away with murder?"

He moved toward her again. She held up her arms to block his blow, but he didn't get a chance to hit her. In the next instant he was on the ground, Lennox standing over him with what looked to be a piece of his airship.

"You bloody coward."

When Gregory looked as if he was going to get to his knees, Lennox shoved him with his foot, then put his boot on Gregory's back.

"Stay down or I'll hit you again."

Lennox turned to look at her. "Are you all right?"

She nodded.

Her hair had come free of its careful bun. Somewhere along the way she'd lost her snood and now tendrils blew across her face. She pulled at the hair and tried to tuck it behind her ears.

They made a strange tableau on the road. Lennox standing with one foot on Gregory's back, her standing a few feet away, none of them speaking.

"He hit you," Lennox finally said.

Gregory made a sound which made Lennox look down at him. He hefted the L-shaped piece of wood in his hands as if he wanted to hit Gregory again.

"Is that part of your ship?"

"It's a section of the tail. It seemed handy at the time."

He bent and retrieved the shotgun at Gregory's side. After inspecting it, he said, "This looks to be Douglas's. Is your fiancé taking on murder for the Macrorys now?"

"He isn't my fiancé."

He turned and looked at her.

"Don't tell me you married the idiot?"

She shook her head in exasperation, then turned and started walking.

He caught up with her, still carrying the shotgun.

"Mercy."

"You do have rocks in your head. You're the most obstinate, infuriating man I've ever met. He's not my fiancé. Nor is he my husband."

She kept walking.

"Mercy."

"I don't want to talk to you right now. I'm angry and I'm getting over being afraid."

"Why were you angry?"

She stopped and stared at him. "Why was I angry? Could you shake a few of those rocks loose? Gregory tried to kill you."

"Thank you," he said. "Thank you for saving my life."

She looked down at the road. It was so much easier than looking at Lennox.

"How did you know what he was going to do?"

"I didn't," she admitted. "I was coming to find you when I saw Gregory. I followed him."

"Why, Mercy?"

"Why what?"

"Why were you coming to find me?"

"Because I'd heard the piper," she said, giving him the truth. "I didn't want you to be alone today."

She started walking again, but he stopped her with a hand to her arm.

"Thank you for that, too."

"I was also going to fuss at you," she said. "You shouldn't have been in your airship today. Irene said you had to have your ribs wrapped. And what about your arm? You haven't given yourself time to heal."

"I'm a Scot. Do you think I've never hurt myself flying before?"

"Yes, you probably have. And you probably will again. For an intelligent man you can be very foolish." She pointed to the shotgun. "What are you going to do with that?"

"Throw it into the loch. I figure Douglas can fish it out if he cares enough."

"You really don't care if the feud continues, do you?"

"At this point," he said, "no. Especially after one of Douglas's guests tried to shoot me."

"He might not have known anything about it."

"Then he was lax in showing Gregory where the gun was kept."

There was that. She couldn't blame him for his irritation at Douglas or Gregory.

"You aren't supposed to be here," he said. "Why haven't you left Scotland? Or have you decided to extend your stay?"

"Are you wanting me to leave? Or hoping I'll remain?"

Chapter Forty-Three

$\mathcal{A}$t the moment he didn't know how to answer that question.

Irene had told him that Mercy was remaining in Scotland although the "whole of that family don't seem all that pleased she's still here."

"So the marriage plans fell through?"

She glanced at him. It wasn't a friendly look.

"Mercy."

He couldn't seem to think of anything cogent to say other than her name. So many emotions flooded through him. Fury—when he'd seen Gregory strike Mercy he'd been several dozen feet in the air and unable to help her. Gratitude—that she'd been able to keep Gregory from firing at him. Confusion—that despite what he'd said to her she'd come to his aid.

"Why were you afraid?"

"Are you jesting?"

"No. I want to know."

She just shook her head and walked away again.

"Mercy. Stop."

She didn't so he had no choice but to go after her.

"Why, Mercy?"

She halted, but didn't turn.

"Was it because of Gregory?"

"I'm thinking you need to shake your head a bit more, Lennox. The rocks have gotten stuck. No, it was because of you. You. Just because you're not afraid in that big, lumbering airship doesn't mean other people aren't afraid for you."

"It's not lumbering. It's a very sleek design."

She looked up at the sky, then shook her head.

He took advantage of her silence to come and stand in front of her. He placed his hands on either side of her face and gently turned her head to examine her. Her cheek was already swelling and the cut on her mouth needed to be treated.

"He hurt you." The words were said with calm, but it was the last thing he was feeling. He wanted to stride back to where Gregory was getting to his feet and bash the man over the head again.

"It's all right, Lennox."

"No, it isn't. It's not all right. He can't be allowed to do things like that." He stared at Gregory, now standing, long enough that Mercy put her hand on his arm.

"He's not worth it, Lennox."

The man deserved to be beaten into the ground.

"Please, Lennox."

He finally looked at her. "You're going to have a bad bruise."

"At least I won't need stitches," she said, smiling.

He admired her determined effort to find some humor in this damnable situation. He wasn't amused.

He took her hand and turned, walking down the road.

"This isn't the way to Macrory House," she said.

"No. No, it isn't."

She stopped in the middle of the road and pulled her hand back.

"I can't go to the castle, Lennox. That wouldn't be wise. My family is already going to be angry at me because I came after you. I've been lectured to death about how I've scandalized the whole of Scotland with my behavior."

He had probably added to the treatment she'd received with his parting words. The fact that she evidently didn't hold them against him was just one more indication of her character. A character a damn sight better than his own.

Neither of them had been innocent that night, but society punished the female more than the male in situations like this. No one had said a word to him about his actions. He certainly hadn't been told he'd acted scandalously.

Still, there were other important things to consider. Namely, Mercy's safety.

"I don't want you returning to Macrory House, not as long as Gregory is there. He struck you. If he did it once, he'll do it again and it doesn't sound like that family of yours would lift a finger to help you. If it's within my power to protect you, I will."

She blinked at him. That's all. She didn't say a word, only grabbed his hand and held it between both of hers.

"Do you remember why I came to Scotland?"

"To bring your grandmother some money from your mother, as I recall."

"That was just an excuse," she said. "The real reason was to obtain some freedom, if only for a little while. For once I wanted to do something on my own.

Not to please someone else. Not to keep someone from getting their feelings hurt. Simply on my own."

"And you think that I'm taking away your freedom if I ask you to come to Duddingston."

"I don't recall that you asked me," she said, her gaze not leaving his face.

"You're right. I didn't." Nor did he feel like asking her now, but it was a good point she made. "Will you come home with me? I want to make sure that you're safe, that no one will treat you badly."

She blinked at him again and this time he realized it was because she was trying not to cry. What had he done?

"Please, Mercy."

"I really shouldn't, Lennox."

"If your reputation is in tatters, as you say, what would it matter at this point? Connor can take you to Inverness tomorrow if you're set on leaving." He wanted to recall those words the moment he said them.

She shook her head. "My father's on his way to Scotland. That's why I haven't left."

That was information Irene hadn't provided.

"Then you can stay at the castle until he arrives. You'll be safer there. I'll send word to Douglas that you're going to be my guest and why. If it makes you feel better, I'll ask Irene to stay as well. Between her and Ruthie, you'll have enough chaperones."

"Are chaperones entirely necessary at this point?"

He sent her a quick glance. "Yes."

He'd wanted to kill Gregory when he'd seen the man strike her. Now he wanted to hold her close, keep her with him, and do whatever it took to ensure her happiness.

The fact that he felt that way was more frightening than launching himself off Ben Uaine. He pushed back that thought and concentrated on the problem at hand.

"I can't run away the moment my life becomes difficult."

He nodded. "I understand, but I'm not letting you go back there now, Mercy. If you want, we'll fight about it, but I won't have you mistreated. At Duddingston, at least I'll know you're safe."

When she didn't say anything, he added, "Please, Mercy."

She looked like she wanted to say something else, but all she did was nod.

He took her hand back as they descended the glen toward the castle.

"What are you going to do about your airship?"

He glanced back to where he had left it on the road. "Connor will bring it along, at least down to the bridge. We put a tow rope on the nose and pull it like a wagon. Once on the bridge, however, it takes two of us to lift it around to the back of the castle."

"Should you even be doing that?"

He smiled at her. "You needn't worry about me, Mercy. I'm a Scot."

"Stubborn, opinionated, and fond of whiskey. Is that it?"

"You've been listening to the English," he said. "We're also ferocious, loyal, and magnificent lovers."

He watched in wonder as her cheeks grew pink.

"There's something we have to get out of the way, before I take another step," she said, stopping and pulling her hand free. "Before I ever came to the castle that night I'd already told Gregory that I had no intention of marrying him. I told him in New York. He simply refused to listen. So whatever happened between us had nothing to do with him. The idea that I would pay you to take my virginity was stupid, Lennox. Simply stupid. And I forgot about the silly valise. I carried that thing all the way from New York. It never left my side. But that morning, with you? The very last thing on my mind was the valise."

He would have spoken, but she held up her hand.

"You're the one who said that you can't wrap everything up in a nice little bundle and put a bow on it. That's exactly what you did by thinking I left the valise there deliberately. That was stupid, Lennox."

"Here I was forgetting you were part Scot," he said. "You've got a bit of an opinion on you, too. Stupid? I wouldn't say it was stupid, Mercy."

"I don't know what you'd call it. I didn't pay you to take my virginity."

"I let my anger get away from me. I was feeling a bit used, what with your slipping away without a word."

"Why would I want to make things worse than they were, Lennox? I didn't want to say goodbye to you. It would have been too hard."

He hadn't considered that. "Will you forgive me?"

She already had or she wouldn't have come looking for him, but he wanted to hear the words anyway.

"Yes."

He looked down at her and the world seemed to drop away. Nothing or no one mattered in that moment but Mercy. He hoped her father took another month or so to arrive in Scotland.

Together they entered the castle and headed for the kitchen.

Irene sat at the table drinking tea. At the sight of them, she stood and came to stand in front of Mercy.

"What happened to you, lass?"

"Gregory," Lennox said, the man's name sounding like an oath. "She's not going back, Irene. They don't give a tinker's damn about her there and that Hamilton ass made a punching bag out of her. If that offends you, either you or Connor, then I'm thinking that Duddingston isn't the place for you."

"Are you daft?" Irene said. "It's the smartest thing either of you has done since you met."

With that, she went to get Lennox's medical bag herself, plunking it down on the table and looking at him expectantly. He'd evidently been given his orders, so he led Mercy to a chair, exchanging a smile with her as Irene bustled around the kitchen.

"It seems that every time I come to Duddingston it's to be treated."

"Not every time. You stitched me up, remember?"

"Are you certain your arm is healed?"

He nodded. "I've removed the stitches myself."

She didn't look convinced.

Bringing Mercy to Duddingston wasn't the best situation, but it was better than allowing Gregory within striking distance. At least this way he could be assured of her safety. Nor was he altogether certain that her family wouldn't try to marry her off to the idiot, just to prove a point.

There were bound to be ramifications, not to mention gossip, but at the moment Lennox was surprised to find himself oddly content. If not strangely—and disturbingly—happy.

Chapter Forty-Four

"What is that?" Mercy asked, wide-eyed.

He looked to where she was pointing. "A fox, I think."

"You think?"

"It could be a squirrel."

"It was no squirrel," she said. "And it was bigger than a fox. It could have been a bear."

"We don't have bears in Scotland," he said, grinning at her.

"Really?"

"Really. We don't even have many wolves nowadays."

"Wolves?" Her hand went to her throat.

He went to stand in front of her, trying to hide his smile and failing.

"I'll protect you," he said. "Even if we do encounter a wolf."

She put both her hands on his chest. He really should step back. At the very least he should ask her not to touch him. This past week he'd done everything in his power to treat Mercy like she was a guest. A stranger come to stay at the castle for a time and nothing more.

He hadn't gotten close to her. He hadn't remained alone with her despite the fact that they'd often found themselves deserted by Connor and Irene. He'd claimed the press of work, or needing to get back to his drawings, or some excuse to escape the temptation of her.

Today, however, he'd thought to take advantage of the beautiful weather and walk the other side of Loch Arn. All the wooded property was Caitheart land and he was thinking of taking an offer to cull some of the timber. It would provide him some much-needed cash. First, though, he wanted to pace off exactly how much land he'd agreed to strip.

He'd invited Mercy to accompany him, never realizing that even in the midst of a forest she would prove to be alluring.

Everything amazed her, from the height of the pines, to the shadowed stillness among the trees, to the animals scurrying away. More than once she'd asked a question that proved she'd never explored a forest.

"These aren't like the woods at home," she said. "This is almost a wild place."

Wild enough, since there was no village nearby or any other type of settlement.

He showed her where he and Robert had each carved their initials in adjoining trees. Robert's initials were much higher than his because his brother had been older—and taller—at the time.

Mercy didn't seem to care that her skirt occasionally dragged on the forest floor, picking up pinecones and feathery leaves. She'd brush them off from time to time but never fuss. Nor did she seem to mind that a bit of fluff that looked suspiciously like something from a squirrel's tail floated down from the upper branches.

"Stay there," he said, reaching out to pluck it from her hair.

"What is it?"

"A present from a tree," he said, holding it out for her inspection.

Her smile was a gift, one that warmed him.

For a moment they didn't speak. Her smile faded and his did as well. Tenderness washed over him, a feeling he'd rarely experienced. He wanted her, but he also wanted to protect her. Not only from woodland creatures, but from all the things that might harm her or hurt her. Or from the people who might wound her.

He wanted to create a home for her at Duddingston. He wanted to share this day and all his days with her, talk with her about things that mattered to him, and laugh with her. His life had been empty and he wanted it filled with Mercy.

All these thoughts cascaded through his mind as they looked at each other.

Her hands were warm, capable of burning through the linen shirt he wore.

He should have stepped back, away. He should have cautioned her with a look. Or told her that he was too susceptible to her touch. For the past week he'd kept his desire reined in, but now it was slipping free of its tether.

A foray through the woods had seemed an innocent occupation. More fool he.

She leaned toward him. He stayed where he was, waiting for his honor to reassert itself.

"Lennox," she said, his name a benediction on her lips.

He really shouldn't be around her as much as he was. He always wanted to touch her. To put his hand on her waist or cup her shoulder, lean close to smell the scent she wore, warmed by her skin.

A kiss would make everything worse.

Yet he was only human. His honor faded beneath his greater need. Slowly, he bent down, giving her the opportunity to move away and his better nature time to reassert itself.

His lips met hers. Pleasure lanced through him. His arms went around her, pulling her closer until their bodies were touching. He could feel her breasts despite the layers of clothing between them. His memory furnished the shape and feel of them cupped in his palms.

Her sigh was an aphrodisiac, a sound he'd forever remember.

His hands moved to her waist, then stole around to her back.

A bird flying close penetrated the fog of desire that surrounded him. He pulled back, ending the kiss but not the embrace. He didn't want to let Mercy go.

"Forgive me," he said a moment later, reluctantly dropping his hands. This was practice for a moment that was inexorably coming. One day, soon, her father would send word from Macrory House and he'd have no choice but to deliver her there, a last ride in his carriage, a short journey that would feel only seconds long.

There was nothing he could do to delay that moment. It was, like death, inevitable and on the horizon.

Mercy looked up at him, her hands still on his chest.

"Why haven't you come to my room?"

He gave a little laugh. "I've been trying to be honorable. You're a guest at Duddingston."

She nodded and only then did she move away.

"You've been very generous, Lennox. Thank you for your hospitality. You've been very proper." She smiled, and the expression looked more rueful than amused. "To my chagrin," she added, "we've always had a chaperone."

She walked a few feet away, then turned back to him. "These are my last days of freedom, Lennox."

He wasn't going to respond to that comment.

Instead, he forced a smile to his face, a more difficult task than it should have been. "I've been thinking of naming my airship *Dragon* in honor of you."

"Good. You'll have something to remind you of me."

As if he'd ever be able to forget her.

"Where to now?" she asked.

What would she say if he answered her honestly? To his bed. To Duddingston, to shock the entire world with their sin. To perdition, if necessary.

Instead, all he said was, "Just a little farther. Then we'll start back."

"I'm due to learn how to make scones," she said.

"Irene has agreed to teach you?"

She nodded. "I am, according to Irene, woefully ignorant in the kitchen."

"Do you really want to learn how to make scones, or is she browbeating you into doing it?"

She laughed. "No browbeating. I asked her to teach me."

"Why?"

"Why not? I love scones. I'm not entirely helpless, you know. I can tie my own shoes and do my own hair." She looked up at the canopy of branches above them. "Very well, maybe I can't do it as well as Ruthie, but it's a credible effort. And I have some talents. I can play the piano, for example, and sing. Dogs and cats don't howl when I do."

He reached over and hugged her, delighted with this side of her.

"Then I look forward to sampling some of your scones."

"You may not get any unless you kiss the cook."

She grabbed his shirt, stood on tiptoe, and kissed him. "There. I may ask for more of those."

He sincerely hoped she didn't. He was having a hard enough time keeping his hands to himself as it was.

His honor was intact—again—and he was determined that this errand would be performed without any more lapses in judgment.

Chapter Forty-Five

$\mathcal{E}$very morning when Mercy woke in the room she'd been given, the same one that held so many memories, all she felt was happiness because she knew she was going to see Lennox as soon as she dressed and went downstairs.

She wasn't going to tell him that, of course. She didn't want to seem needy or grasping. The worst thing in the world would be to admit loving a man who didn't have the same feelings for you.

Kindness wasn't love. Neither was protectiveness. Both qualities were natural to Lennox. He was a gentleman, unlike Gregory.

She hadn't agreed to come to the castle because she wanted to be agreeable. Or even because she thought Gregory would hurt her. He was the type of person who did things in secret, making her wonder if he was guilty of any of the reported atrocities in the war. At Macrory House she would have been surrounded by other people, making it difficult, if not impossible, for Gregory to see her alone. She'd accompanied Lennox to Duddingston for an entirely selfish reason. Her father was coming and when he arrived she would have no choice but to return to New York with him. Until then, she would take each day with Lennox like the gift it was.

In the future she would probably look back on these days with a sense of wonder. She would forever remember Lennox and their night together. Or when she'd helped him in the courtyard. Or when they sat together, dripping, in front of the fire. Or when she'd stitched his arm. But there would be other moments as well, like now as they walked hand in hand toward the chapel. So many treasured memories all pressed into a short amount of time.

When had her fascination with Lennox turned into something more? Maybe what she felt for him had always been there like a rosebud ready to burst into flower.

What a pity that he hadn't agreed to marry her. He might have considered it a marriage of convenience although it would have been so much more for her.

Society had arranged marriages all the time. Everyone knew that the parents of both parties had recognized the fiscal advantages of the merger and had communicated their wishes to their children.

Her parents had essentially done the same thing with Gregory. From the first they'd made no secret of their approval of the match.

She was absolutely certain that they wouldn't feel the same about Lennox. He didn't lust after her father's money or success like Gregory. Lennox wanted things out of life that couldn't be purchased. Influence didn't mean anything to him. What Lennox desired was to challenge himself, discover, invent, and create something tangible from a thought.

He couldn't be bought.

Such a man truly didn't care that she was an heiress. No, if she were to tempt Lennox into marriage, it would have to be because he wanted to spend his life with her. Her, not her fortune. Her, and not any coercion she could bring to bear because of her family name.

Lennox led her behind the castle, following a well-worn path around the curtain wall.

For the first time she saw the stable, empty but for the two Clydesdales. If Lennox would agree to marry her she could fill the empty stalls with horses.

"Is that the chapel?" she asked, pointing to a structure set apart from Duddingston and slightly higher. Built of the same weathered brick as the castle, it looked somehow older.

"It is," he said.

They headed up the gravel walkway leading to oak-banded double doors. He opened one and stepped aside so that she could precede him.

The first thing she noticed was the sunlight streaming in through the ruined roof.

"Oh, what a shame," she said, looking around her at the water damage from the recent storm.

"I've moved the really important, historical pieces into the castle," he said. "There's nothing I can do about the stained glass or the altar itself."

The altar was a massive piece of carved wood that must have been completed inside the chapel. Otherwise she didn't see how it could have been moved into the building. It had been covered with a tarp that Lennox removed now, revealing the artistry of the woodwork. She had never seen anything so beautiful and when she said as much to Lennox, he nodded.

"My ancestors were a good deal more religious than I am," he said.

"How lucky you are to be around such history every day. We don't have anything as old as the castle in America. You can trace your family's history here and feel it all around you."

"We've been here longer than the Macrorys, that's for sure."

She glanced at him. "Why do I think that the antipathy between the two families goes back a lot longer than Robert and Mary's romance?"

He grinned at her, such a charming expression that she wanted to see it over and over again. It made Lennox look almost carefree.

"You're right." He strode toward the altar, looking up at the ruined roof. "A Macrory man came along one day and stole a Caitheart daughter. She was due to marry another man, but lost her heart to him. It's been so long now that it shouldn't be a great conflict between the families, but history has a way of repeating itself."

Not only in the case of Robert and Mary, but with her and Lennox. Only his heart was not involved.

She wished it was. She wished, too, that there was something she could do to make him think of her as more than an American woman he'd once bedded. Wishing, however, never made someone fall in love. Wishes were for little girls dreaming of being a princess. Or a countess in a castle across the sea.

She turned and walked to the chapel doors, standing and looking over the expanse of Lennox's kingdom. The loch was turbulent today. The wind was creating whitecaps and bending the boughs of the pines on the opposite shore.

For some reason, Duddingston Castle had always

been a special place for her. Maybe it was the faint call of her Scottish blood.

Scotland had seemed so alien to her at first, but it had enfolded her in an embrace that felt warm and welcoming. Some people, like Irene and her sister, Jean, would forever remain in her memory. She would always be able to close her eyes and hear the sound of the bagpipes echoing through the glen. She'd recall the piercing beauty of that moment and how it had summoned her tears. She'd never forget how long the days were or how the sunlight looked glittering on Loch Arn.

She would miss this corner of the world and she hadn't counted on that.

Perhaps she could stay in Scotland, make a life here. It would be as easy here as in New York. It might even be easier here because no one would know who she was. She wouldn't be James Rutherford's daughter. Or an heiress. Just an American who'd fallen in love with the country.

"Is something wrong?" Lennox asked, closing the oak-banded door behind him.

She didn't know how to explain her abrupt, suffocating sadness, so she forced a smile to her face and shook her head.

"Do you want me to send a note to your grandmother?" he asked, surprising her.

The day she'd come to Duddingston, Lennox sent Douglas a letter explaining what had happened and why he'd issued an invitation to Mercy to stay at the castle. He'd advised Douglas that the authorities should be called about Gregory. He'd also asked for Mercy's belongings as well as requesting that Ruthie be allowed to accompany Irene back to the castle. So far, they hadn't heard anything from Douglas or any of the Macrorys.

It was entirely possible that Douglas was holding on to Mercy's luggage out of spite. She didn't care, and it surprised her how few items she really needed from day to day. Ruthie, however, was another matter. She and Irene had already discussed ways to spirit the other woman away from Macrory House. It was only a matter of time until Ruthie made it to the castle.

"A letter to my grandmother? She won't understand," Mercy said. "She's taken on the Macrory feud like it was her own. She didn't even live here when Mary and Robert eloped."

Lennox didn't respond, but what could he say?

Unfortunately, her grandmother wasn't one of those people she would miss and wasn't that a shame? Aunt Elizabeth was, but she'd been a ghost recently. Understandable, given her grief about her fiancé. Mercy didn't know how Elizabeth bore the pain of each day.

Together they descended the steps of the chapel and walked in silence to a door in the curtain wall. Surprisingly, it led to the courtyard where Lennox's airship was located.

She smiled at Connor who was sanding a piece of wood. No doubt it was for the tail assembly, since that had been damaged in the landing. Lennox had also taken part of it and used it as a weapon against Gregory.

"How do you get your airship into the courtyard?" she asked.

"There's a larger door," Lennox said, "but we do have to disassemble the wings in order to move it inside."

"Do you have work to do today? If you do, could you use an apprentice?"

She moved to stand in front of the airship. It hadn't been stripped of its wires or sails and she could see how complicated it was. Lennox was right; it wasn't a lumbering beast after all, but a sleek machine.

"I have accounts to do," he said, smiling. "Hideous accounts. I hate doing them, but they must be done."

"Then I'll take myself off," she said, determined not to be a bother. She'd ask Irene if there was anything she needed help with, an errand that she could perform or a task that needed doing. Perhaps she could learn to cook something else. Anything to take her mind off what she was feeling for a while.

If nothing else, she'd retire to her room. Perhaps she could rehearse her speech to her mother. Or the explanation she would give to her father.

Or the final words she would say to Lennox.

LENNOX REMAINED WHERE he was, debating whether he should follow Mercy and say to hell with his plans to go over the accounts. He'd rather spend the time with her, especially since their relationship would end as soon as her father got to Scotland.

Relationship. That was the word, wasn't it? Was it what they had? No, *relationship* didn't define what was between Mercy and himself. He didn't know what to call it, only that it confused him, threw him into chaos, and made his life miserable.

Yet he'd never felt more alive since the day she appeared on the road from Inverness.

He could still remember the moment he'd seen her in the ruined carriage, glaring up at him with her beautiful brown eyes. Eyes that looked as if they were smoldering with rage. What had she called him? Insane, that was it, and his airship had been a dragon. Well, she was right about one thing: he was daft about her.

He'd been a hermit before she'd arrived. Now? The notion of returning to his solitary life was repugnant. He wanted a brighter future, one to be shared with someone. No, not with anyone. He wanted a future with Mercy.

She was an heiress. He had nothing to offer her. A title and a castle might seem impressive on paper, but the title didn't garner him anything and the castle was ruinously expensive to maintain. He wasn't doing a good enough job of it. Look at the chapel alone. Then there were two other wings that had been allowed— grudgingly, due to the lack of funds—to fall into ruin.

The responsibility of Duddingston hung over his head every day.

He was close to perfecting his formula for flight— weight, lift, drag, and thrust—and if he could sell his airship he would be in a position to offer a woman a future with him. But that day was at least a year or so away. He couldn't ask Mercy to remain here until he became solvent.

Will you marry me? He could still recall how she looked that night, drenched and stubborn, her eyes begging him not to reject her. His pride demanded that he do no less. A damnable thing, the Caitheart pride. Other men might sell their title for a fortune, but he couldn't.

Irene thought he was a fool.

"It's evident she feels something for you, Your Lordship," she'd said a few days ago. "And I'd say you're the same. She's heaven sent, the answer to a prayer. A girl with a fortune, and a pretty girl at that."

"She's beautiful," he said. She wasn't just pretty. There was something different, unique, special about Mercy.

Irene smiled at him. "Then tuck your pride into the privy and tell the girl how you feel. And no more of this humiliating her in front of her family."

"You know about that?" He'd felt himself warm with shame.

"The world knows of that. Whatever were you thinking?"

"I wasn't," he said.

"Your feelings were hurt, then." She shook her head. "Men and their feelings. More damage has been done in this world because men didn't want to talk about their feelings."

She finished up their conversation by telling him that he was a stubborn, obstinate fool. She was probably right about her assessment. The problem was he didn't know how to correct the situation.

Mercy had forgiven him for what he said, though, even if she had taken a swipe at him by calling him stupid. At least he'd told her the truth. He'd felt used. That damnable pride again.

Chapter Forty-Six

$\mathcal{M}$ercy was in the kitchen with Irene trying to master the art of making oatcakes when the bell rang. Ruthie was upstairs, having volunteered to help Connor with some task. Although Ruthie's splint wasn't due to be removed until next week, she was adamant about being useful. Mercy thought she simply wanted to be around Connor. Since she felt the same about Lennox, she understood completely.

"It might be someone from the house," Irene said. "With more of your things."

For a week there had been no communication with Macrory House—other than the letter Lennox had sent by way of Irene. When Irene had visited the day before yesterday, Gregory was still there and Flora was waxing eloquent about how brave he was and how mistreated by the Earl of Morton.

According to Ruthie, who'd been allowed to come to the castle two days ago, Flora had expressed more than a little interest in Mercy's former fiancé. Gregory was no doubt fanning that flame. After all, Flora was an heiress.

Flora was more than willing to have him, with Mercy's blessings.

The bell rang again.

"I'll go," Mercy said, making her way to the pump and washing the oatmeal from her hands.

She should have known who it was as she made her way down the corridor and through the Clan Hall. She opened the heavy oak door and stared.

Her father stood there in the ruined tower of Duddingston Castle, looking as proud and defiant as any Scot.

"Daughter."

James Gramercy Rutherford had never addressed her in such a fashion. Whether it was an absence of minutes or hours, he always gave her a hug. Now his arms remained at his sides. That was one clue to his mood. His expression was another.

Her father was enraged.

He was one of the titans of New York with an appearance that was instantly recognizable. Mercy had lost count of the times he'd been called a pirate in the papers.

His hair was a uniform gray, no mix of black hair with silver threads. His pointed beard was black, however, as was his sweeping mustache. He squinted at her, a habit he had which either indicated that he wasn't fond of wearing spectacles or he was just naturally suspicious. She'd always thought it was the latter.

All he needed was a gold earring and an eye patch.

When he laughed, however, it was a booming laugh that made her think that's how God must sound.

He was tall and thin, because he often forgot to eat, being involved in his study of endless accounting ledgers and reports from the managers of all his various enterprises. More than once a maid had brought him a plate from the kitchen only to retrieve it hours later barely touched.

Her father's one passion was good whiskey. She had the errant thought that he'd come to the right country.

His character was such that he was focused forward. He never talked about the past and if he was disappointed about anything in his life, he never admitted it.

He looked down at the threshold and then up at her. "May I come in?"

Making a decision, she stepped back and opened the door fully. "Come in, Father."

Hopefully, Lennox would understand.

She led the way down the corridor and into the expanse of the Clan Hall. Her father stopped and looked up at the soaring ceiling, the mass of armaments and pennants on the walls, and the other artifacts nestled in the embrasures.

"An impressive room."

"Duddingston Castle is over four hundred years old. Lennox's clan settled this part of the Highlands."

Her father only nodded. She expected him to ask about Lennox, but he didn't. No doubt the Macrorys had already briefed him before this visit.

She led him to the throne-like chairs in front of one of the two massive fireplaces.

Lennox was in the courtyard, involved in making adjustments to the new airship design. She gave some thought to telling him that her father was here, and then just as quickly dismissed it. She and her father needed to talk privately.

He stood in front of the chair and she knew he wouldn't sit until she did. She took the adjoining chair, arranged her skirts, and dusted off a bit of flour from her apron.

"You are looking well," he said.

"As are you."

"Have you decided to become a scullery maid, Mercy?" He pointed to her apron.

"Not a scullery maid, Father. A cook, perhaps. I've become quite proficient at scones."

He frowned at her, but didn't say anything.

For a moment they just watched each other. She hadn't lied to him. He did look well, almost relaxed. Perhaps the ocean voyage had been the respite he needed. He always looked relaxed when they came back from their country home, but those breaks from work never lasted long.

"How is Mother?" she asked, knowing that she was opening a Pandora's box.

He didn't disappoint. "Heartbroken."

She nodded, half expecting that comment.

If this had been her home, she would have offered him some refreshments, but because it wasn't, she simply remained seated.

Whenever she'd been called to his library as a girl, guilty of some infraction or another, their meetings had been exactly like this. He doled out words like they were gold pieces, at least until he warmed to the subject. Any moment now he would let loose with a volley of accusations. She folded her hands together, waiting.

She had just as much patience as her father. Perhaps more, in this case, because she'd had some time to anticipate this meeting.

"Do you know how much we feared for you?" he finally asked.

She leaned back in the chair, her hands on the carved arms, her fingers curling around the lion's paws.

"I have always known how much you feared for me."

He frowned at her again. "What does that mean?"

"No one has ever been as protected, guarded, and wrapped in bunting as I have been, Father. I couldn't play with the neighbor's child because there were rumors of a disease sweeping through the city and she might be contagious. I couldn't go to the park because it might be cold in the afternoon. I could never play in the snow because I might get a chill. No one has ever been visited by so many physicians or examined by so many specialists. I had two nurses instead of one. As I grew I still had a nurse along with a governess. And then I had guards. I was accompanied by two people whenever I went anywhere and even my destinations were limited. I was twenty-eight years old and treated as if I was three. So, yes, I have always known how much you feared for me."

She hadn't meant for her tone to sound bitter but as she spoke, all the emotion that had been trapped for years flowed out of her.

"And so you ran away."

"Yes. I ran away. And I would do it again. I'm not an animal in a zoo, Father. Neither am I a hothouse flower."

"You don't understand, Mercy."

She sat up straight, her gaze never veering from his face. "I understand perfectly. Next you will tell me that it's because of your wealth that I was always so protected. Otherwise, I was in danger. If that doesn't work, you'll gently remind me of all those poor dead babies whose names I bear. If I'm still not suitably chastised, you'll bring up Jimmy. I understand perfectly. Which one will it be now, Father?"

To his credit, he looked taken aback. "All we wanted was for you to be safe."

"All I wanted was to live a life that wasn't constantly constrained."

"And you thought you had to come to Scotland for that?"

She looked away, her attention focused on the elaborate fireplace surround. "I wanted a taste of freedom. I wanted to be unguarded for a little while."

When he didn't speak, she leaned forward, wondering if there was a way to get her father to understand.

"These weeks in Scotland have been magic for me," she said. "For the first time in my life I'm not James Rutherford's daughter or Jimmy's sister or my mother's sole normal child. I'm simply Mercy. People don't care that I'm an heiress. My money is seen as a detriment, not an asset. I've been free as I never expected to be. I'm judged as Mercy. Who am I? What can I do? What do I want? I've had to answer all those questions for myself."

"What about Gregory? What about the wedding?"

She shook her head. "I don't care about Gregory. Or the wedding. I'm not going to marry him. I would just be exchanging one set of prison bars for another."

Her father sat like a king in his throne-like chair, his eyes flat. If he felt any affection for her at all it wasn't evident in his expression.

She'd failed. She'd tried to make him understand, but he didn't.

"Your behavior has not reflected well on your mother and me," he said. "Your Scottish relatives are not happy with you. Being here, for example, is scandalous. The only saving grace is it's Scotland. Hopefully, not a word of this will reach New York."

"And if it does?" she asked, unexpectedly weary. "Will it matter so much?"

"I will not have your mother hurt."

She left her chair, went to her father, and sank to her knees. Reaching up, she grabbed his hand and held it between hers.

"I don't want to hurt her, either. But I think I probably will, one way or another, simply by wanting to live my own life, away and apart from my parents. I love you both, but I can't bear to continue living the way I was."

"Gregory is a good match," he said. "He's a hero."

"He's a hero, Father, but he's not my hero. I didn't worry about him the whole time he was gone. The only emotion I felt was relief that he survived. Isn't that terrible? Elizabeth still grieves for the man she loved and all I felt was relief about Gregory."

"And Caitheart? How would you feel if something happened to him?"

Her life would be over. The thought came to her so fast that she was almost felled by it.

"Did Gregory tell you that he tried to kill Lennox?" she asked, sitting back.

"Or, more importantly, that he struck Mercy?"

They both turned their heads to find Lennox standing there. There was a look on his face that she had never before seen, and it was directed at her father.

James Rutherford wasn't a fool. He knew antipathy when he saw it. He stood and faced Lennox.

"Do you know who I am?"

"Mercy's father. Beyond that I don't care. That man

you think is such a good match struck your daughter more than once. Only a coward hits a woman."

The two men faced each other, implacable foes.

Mercy stayed where she was, wondering what she could say or do to ease the situation.

Her father reached into his vest and pulled out his pocket watch.

"It's now noon, Mercy. I will give you until four to gather up your belongings and say your goodbyes. At four I will be here to collect you. We'll stay the night at Macrory House and in the morning leave for the ship."

He didn't wait for her to speak, merely headed for the door, leaving her and Lennox to look at each other.

Chapter Forty-Seven

"What will you do?" Lennox asked.

He walked to where Mercy knelt and extended his hand. She stood, her gaze on the floor rather than him.

"What can I do?" she asked, her voice a monotone.

Without another word, she left him, crossing the Clan Hall and entering the corridor that led to the staircase.

He'd come to find her and had accidentally eavesdropped on her conversation with her father. He'd disliked Rutherford when he'd waxed eloquent about the Hamilton bastard. No doubt, coming from Macrory House, he'd been given an expurgated version of events. But any man who took Hamilton's side over his own daughter's was not a man he could respect.

With each step it felt as if she was moving farther and farther away from him. Not merely to another part of the castle, but halfway around the world.

Having her here had been both heaven and hell. He would turn and she'd be there, within arm's reach. Yet propriety dictated that he never touch her. Sometimes, she would smile at him across the room and he'd be frozen in that moment, seeing her and wanting to go to her, hold her, and tell her . . . what? That his life was better with her in it? That he couldn't imagine a time when she wouldn't be here? That it had been only days since she'd arrived and yet he couldn't remember living at Duddingston without her? At night, knowing that she was sleeping under his roof kept him awake and made him long for her even more.

Mercy spent time in the Laird's Room and, strangely enough, she didn't keep him from his work. She didn't touch things. She didn't barrage him with questions, but the ones she asked were insightful. She sat on the work stool, studying his drawings, interrupting her examination from time to time to send him a smile.

Last night she'd surprised him by standing on tiptoe outside the kitchen, after their evening meal shared with Irene, Ruthie, and Connor and kissed him lightly.

"There," she said. "I don't have to be honorable."

He watched her leave, wondering if she knew how much he wanted to follow her. If he had his way he'd dismiss everyone from Duddingston and keep her a beloved prisoner in his room. They wouldn't budge from his tower bedroom but for food.

Now he stood where he was long enough to be conscious of his immobility.

She couldn't leave, but what other alternative was there? He couldn't keep her here.

Irene stood in the doorway, her expression one he rarely saw. He wanted to tell her that she shouldn't pity him.

Instead, he headed for the Laird's Room.

MERCY SAT IN the bedroom that had been hers for the past week. The same room that still bore so many memories of Lennox.

What will you do? he'd asked.

What could she do but return to her prison and pretend to be a penitent escapee? She wouldn't marry Gregory and there was a chance she wouldn't marry anyone at all. Perhaps she'd become a little old lady living alone in the enormous gray house on the corner, becoming a legend or a source of speculation.

No, she never married, but I heard there was a lover in her past.

There's some tragedy there, I think. She never got over his loss.

They say she roams from room to room in that great house.

There was nothing she could do. She couldn't stay here. Even in the Highlands there was a certain type of behavior expected of people. For the past week she had defiantly—and gleefully—ignored all the rules of society.

She couldn't expect Lennox to give her safe harbor forever.

If she thought he would agree she'd ask him to marry her again, but he didn't want an American heiress. He didn't want *her*.

Time had flown by and now it was nearly four. Her father would be here shortly, and she was ready. Her trunk had been packed as well as the valises. Connor had already taken them and placed them outside Duddingston's iron door.

All that was left now was to descend the stairs, walk through the castle, and leave. How strange that it sounded so easily done, but it would be one of the most difficult tasks she would ever perform.

The truth was that she didn't want to go. She didn't want to go back to America, to a life she'd escaped. She didn't want to leave Lennox.

She'd always been loved; she couldn't fault her parents for that. Yet they'd trapped her in a web because of that love. She wouldn't be guilty of the same behavior. She wouldn't go to Lennox and tell him how she felt and ensnare him.

No, loving Lennox was her secret and she'd keep it.

She was probably going to anger him, but she wasn't going to take the valise with the money back to America. She had tucked it in the bottom of the armoire and left a note for Irene. In addition to thanking her for her friendship, the cooking lessons, as well as her kindness, she'd told the other woman about the money. She would pay her father back, making the greenbacks in the valise her gift to Lennox.

At least she would ease his life a little. He could have the chapel roof fixed or buy material for his airships.

She felt as if there was a hole where her chest should be. It seemed to be growing the closer she got to four o'clock. Hearts didn't break. Lives didn't really shatter. She would survive this, although she wasn't certain she wanted to. Part of her would always remain in Scotland.

Perhaps long after she was gone from life people would see her ghost walking in the glen or crossing the causeway and entering Duddingston Castle. Would she be a spirit haunting the castle itself? She could imagine the tales told about the forlorn woman who wandered through the kitchen and lingered in the Clan Hall.

She's looking for the earl, they might say. *She loved him, but she had to leave him forever.*

At ten until four there was a knock on the door. She'd expected it. Ruthie was always conscientious that way.

Leaving Connor would be as difficult for Ruthie as

leaving Lennox would be for her. Perhaps they could commiserate with each other on the voyage back to New York. During the trip she would confide her plans about the future to Ruthie. She hoped Ruthie would come to live with her. She didn't want to lose the only friend she'd ever had.

When Ruthie entered the room, Mercy knew something was different immediately. It took her a moment and then she began to smile.

"Your bandages are gone," she said. "And the sling."

Ruthie nodded.

Mercy stood and went to Ruthie's side.

"How does your arm feel?"

"A little strange, Miss Mercy," Ruthie admitted, holding it out.

It was paler than Ruthie's other arm, but that was the only change Mercy could see.

"Does it hurt?"

"Not at all. It does feel a little weak, but Lennox said that was to be expected since I hadn't used it."

"But you're sure it doesn't hurt?"

Ruthie shook her head.

When the other woman wouldn't meet her eyes, Mercy was sure she knew why.

"I'm sorry, Ruthie," she said. "I wish circumstances could have been better." How could she possibly ease the other woman's sadness? Words were sometimes useless. "I know you'll miss Connor."

Ruthie didn't respond. Nor did she offer up a suitable superstition or saying. Instead, she went to sit on the edge of the mattress.

"You've always been my friend, Miss Mercy, as well as my employer," she said, her attention on her clasped hands.

"I feel the same, Ruthie."

"I thought this trip to Scotland was filled with peril, Miss Mercy. All the omens said so. But I wouldn't have left you to travel alone."

"I know that, Ruthie. Thank you for coming with me. With any luck the voyage home will be as easy."

Ruthie glanced at her and then away. "Then we arrived and I met Connor."

Mercy remained silent.

"I think I fell in love with him from the first moment I saw him, Miss Mercy." Ruthie glanced at her once more. "I can't go with you. Connor asked me to marry him. Oh, Miss Mercy, I'm so sorry."

"Don't be sorry, Ruthie," she said, feeling a combination of envy and sadness. She didn't want to lose Ruthie, but neither would she stand in the way of the other woman's happiness.

"Won't you miss your family?" Mercy asked.

Ruthie nodded. "But Connor will be my family now."

Such a simple sentence and yet it had the power of a spear.

"Would you like me to take a letter back to your family?"

Ruthie nodded again. "Would you mind, Miss Mercy?"

"I would be privileged, Ruthie."

She went to the other woman and hugged her, wishing she didn't feel so close to tears. Sadness had its place in this farewell, but so did joy. She wanted the best for Ruthie and she'd known how the other woman felt about Connor.

For years Ruthie had been her sounding board, the one person who understood her life, the only person who heard her confidences and kept them private. Ruthie wouldn't be there any longer. That knowledge seemed to expand the hole in Mercy's chest.

"I'm so happy for you," she said. "But sad at the same time. I wish I could be at your wedding."

Even before she left, Mercy felt the separation. As if Ruthie were already stepping forward into her future, one that didn't include Mercy.

"You will write me, won't you?" Mercy asked. "I don't want to lose touch."

"I will. I promise."

After Ruthie left, she didn't give in to her tears. If she did, there was every possibility that she would keep weeping all the way back to America.

Her father arrived exactly at four. James Gramercy Rutherford was never late.

When she answered the door, the driver tipped his hat to her. No one else stood at the entrance of Duddingston Castle, but that was her doing. She'd asked Irene and the others not to come say goodbye. Her composure was hard won and seeing them all one last time would be too difficult. As far as Lennox, he'd left the castle earlier.

"I imagine he's gone to Ben Uaine," Irene had offered. "He goes there to mull things over."

She entered the carriage while her trunk and valises were being loaded.

Her father nodded in greeting. Mercy didn't look at him again as she settled into the seat and spent the next few minutes arranging the skirt of her blue-striped silk dress. When that was done, she stared out the far window, anything but look at Duddingston Castle as they pulled away.

The silence was a blessing. She didn't have anything to say to her father that she hadn't already said. He hadn't understood and she doubted that his opinion would change if she continued to try to explain.

No one was as stubborn as James Rutherford. She'd learned that lesson over the course of her life.

"Where is your maid?"

"She's decided to remain in Scotland," Mercy said. She didn't bother telling him that Ruthie had found a man who loved her as much as she loved him.

Some women were blessed in love. Others were cursed.

"Did Gregory really hit you?"

"Yes, he hit me."

"Such behavior doesn't sound like him."

She glanced at him. "Then don't believe me, Father. He didn't leave a scar when he struck me. Perhaps you would have believed me if he had."

He looked stunned by her comment.

"Do you hate me, Mercy?"

"No."

"Then why say such a thing?"

She looked straight at him. "Why not believe me? Why believe your idea of Gregory more than my words?"

"Have I done such a thing?"

She didn't say anything in response. Instead, she stared out the window again, wishing she didn't feel as if she had a gaping wound in her chest, one that was growing larger with each second they traveled away from Duddingston Castle.

"I will explain to Gregory that the engagement is off," her father said.

She shook her head. "Do you think I haven't already told him? More than once? I don't need my father to break my engagement."

"Then what function do you want me to perform in your life?"

"Love me. Believe in me. Have faith in me. Respect me. Don't think that you need to dictate my movements, my friends, or whom I am to marry. I have managed to live these past weeks, Father, without being wrapped in bunting and have thoroughly enjoyed it."

"Most people would want the life you have, Mercy. They would feel enormously privileged."

"They're welcome to it," she said.

She would prefer living in a half-ruined castle with a courageous, proud, and impecunious earl.

They didn't speak again all the way back to Macrory House.

Chapter Forty-Eight

Lennox made it to the top of Ben Uaine and stood there looking down at Duddingston Castle, the yoke that had been fixed around his neck after Robert died. He hadn't handled his responsibility as easily or as well as his older brother, but it hadn't been for lack of trying.

Along with that burden had come another: pride, the requirement that he never forget he was a Caitheart. If he'd practiced as a physician in Inverness, people wouldn't know where he came from and if they did, it wouldn't have mattered. He'd lost that anonymity when he'd been forced to come home.

Connor hadn't been able to sell his latest invention and Lennox hadn't come up with anything in the meantime. In a few months he'd have the income from the timber and some from fishing, but without something extra the next year would be difficult financially. He'd be able to pay Irene and Connor, but any additional expenses would be foolish to assume.

Like welcoming a bride to Duddingston.

How much was he supposed to give up for his birthright? How much sacrifice would it demand of him?

Mercy was going to leave him shortly and there wasn't a damn thing he could do about it.

What could he offer her? A half-ruined castle and an empty title. Hardly a promising future. She was accustomed to so much more. More than he could provide.

He moved to the north side of Ben Uaine, following paths he'd learned as a boy. From here he could see to the farthest point of Loch Arn. The wind was soft today, barely a breeze ruffling his shirt, carrying with it the scent of pine from the forest.

Many times he'd stood here in the midst of winter, feeling proud because he'd climbed Ben Uaine in spite of the ice and snow. Now in the middle of summer there was still a hint of the chill beneath the warm air. A reminder of what was to come.

Somehow he was going to have to let Mercy go back to America.

He felt empty. Was this how the rest of his life was going to be? He couldn't imagine living for decades like this. He'd accustomed himself to his hermitage until Mercy had come along. How was he supposed to forget her and retreat once more into that life, never seeing anyone but Connor and Irene? Never feeling joy or happiness.

She was an heiress.

He was a pauper.

She lived in a mansion.

He lived in a castle.

Her father was wealthy.

His had been an earl.

Her life had been constrained by love.

His had been dictated by his heritage.

But for wealth, their lives hadn't been all that dissimilar.

Was wealth going to be the only thing that stood between him and happiness?

His airship might garner him some attention, but realistically that probably wouldn't happen for a year or two. Or never. He could put aside his inventions and work toward reestablishing those industries that had begun to flourish under Robert's stewardship. He might be able to provide for a family, but not right away.

How long would he have to wait?

The future stretched out before him uncertain and unwritten. Yet here he was, standing on Ben Uaine, a place where he'd often come to challenge his courage. He believed in himself enough to throw himself off a mountain in a creation of wood and cloth. Why, then, didn't he trust himself enough to provide for Mercy? Yes, it might be difficult at first, but he could do it.

He didn't want to lose this chance at happiness. Not when it seemed Providence had literally put Mercy in his path.

He loved her. That was the most important point of all and it was going to be more than enough to start. He didn't want her money. After meeting Rutherford, he had the thought that she wouldn't remain an heiress for long, especially if she agreed to marry him. He didn't give a flying farthing if she came to him penniless. In fact, he'd prefer it.

Life might not be easy for them at first, but they'd have each other. Together, with Mercy, he would accomplish anything he attempted.

And he'd be happy while doing it.

Slowly he made his way down the mountain, smiling all the while. He was on a course that was probably foolish, but he didn't care. People had called him crazy for flying his airship. Let them call him crazy for being in love.

At the base of Ben Uaine, he stopped, surprised. Irene sat on a large rock, her eyes closed, her face turned up to the sun.

A surge of gratitude spread through him. She'd been more than a cook or housekeeper to him and Robert. Not quite a mother, but perhaps an older sister. She was loyal and fiercely protective, and genuinely sweet from time to time, although he suspected she'd be annoyed at that comment.

When he approached, she opened her eyes and looked at him.

"It's funny how people act the same over and over, isn't it? First Robert, now you."

He didn't say anything, knowing that Irene would explain. She never left him in doubt of what she meant.

"Mary Macrory was a bit more stubborn than your Mercy, I'd say."

When she didn't continue, he was forced to ask, "What do you mean?"

Irene smiled, almost as if she were a spider and he the fly and this conversation an intricate web.

She glanced toward Duddingston. "Robert used to climb to the top of the tower. Many a day I'd find him standing there looking toward Macrory House as if the answers to all his prayers were there. 'Irene,' he said to me once, 'pride is a damnable thing. It puts you on an island.' I didn't know what to say to him. Mary did, though."

Irene surprised him because she rarely spoke about Robert. For weeks after his brother's death he'd find her with red eyes, but she was careful never to cry around him. He suspected that Irene was devoted to maintaining the image of a woman with a crusty exterior.

"She came to Duddingston the day before they

eloped and shouted at him, 'I've never known a more stubborn man in my life, Robert Caitheart. You would turn your back on love for the sake of your pride. Well, I hope your pride keeps you warm at night, because it won't be me from now on.'"

Lennox glanced at her sharply.

"Aye," she said. "The past is the present once more. They were lovers. It was only Robert's stubbornness that stopped him from making more of it."

He frowned at her. "He was in love with Mary."

Irene nodded. "That he was, but did you forget? She was a wealthy widow. He told himself that he couldn't offer her anything, not compared to what she already had."

He had forgotten. Or he'd never thought of it.

"He knew she wasn't going to change her mind. Either he had his pride or he had Mary. So he took himself off to Macrory House and the two of them decided to elope then and there. It's a tragedy they died, but I'm glad they were together in the end."

He'd never realized that his brother had felt the same confusion he had.

"I always thought you were more like your brother than you knew. Now I know I was wrong all along."

He waited, certain the rest of her comment was coming.

"She's gone, Your Lordship," she said, standing. "Mercy has left Duddingston. By morning she'll be on her way to America. That girl is in love with you. Yer aff yer heid about her and yet you let her go without a word."

He went to stand in front of Irene. Then, when she was still fussing at him, he grabbed her by the shoulders, pulled her close, and kissed her forehead.

She pulled back and looked at him as if he had lost his mind. He probably had, but he'd never been happier in his insanity.

"Go and change your clothes, Irene. Something fancy, if you please."

She frowned at him. "And why would that be?"

"Because we're going to a wedding."

"Whose wedding?" she asked, her eyes narrowing.

Lennox smiled. "Mine."

Chapter Forty-Nine

$\mathcal{M}$ercy wanted to simply walk through Macrory House and make her way to the second floor and her bedroom. Instead, she guessed there would be a receiving line, of sorts, to let her know how far she'd strayed from propriety and what each member of the family thought about her.

She wasn't wrong.

The first to greet her was McNaughton, of course. The man actually bowed to her father, but spared a curl of his lip for Mercy. She brushed past him, entered the room where she and Ruthie had first been introduced to the surly butler, and headed for the stairs.

Only to be stopped by the imperious voice of her grandmother.

Mercy sighed, resigned to having this confrontation, and turned to greet Ailsa.

"You, Hortense, are a disgrace."

Mercy didn't respond. Nothing she could say would mitigate her grandmother's hostility. If she'd known that Ailsa had nothing but antipathy for her, she would certainly not have made the journey to Scotland. For that alone she should thank Ailsa. If she hadn't come, she'd never have met Lennox. However, she was not going to spare another scintilla of compassion for her grandmother.

Her aunt was another story.

Elizabeth stood beside her mother, her gaze carefully on the floor. Mercy understood. Elizabeth had no other place to live, or hope of another home. She was forced to endure Ailsa's tirades and judgments.

"The few hours you'll spend here are too long. I will celebrate the minute you leave this house and thank the Almighty that I'll never see you again. I rue the day I allowed your mother to marry that Yankee. She is an abomination as well, teaching you to flaunt authority. From this day forward, I have only one daughter."

"You'll not speak about my wife in that fashion."

Mercy glanced over her shoulder to see her father advancing on her grandmother. Ailsa had erred. Her father would never tolerate any word against Fenella.

"You'll not tell me how to address my granddaughter. She consorts with the enemy. She has done nothing but disobey me since her arrival."

Her father didn't answer, merely came to Mercy's side, cupped her elbow, and escorted her to the stairs.

"She has shamed this family!"

Mercy pulled free, turned, and addressed her grandmother. "Like you did, Seanmhair? Or did you think that no one would remember that you ran off and married a crofter? I never thought you were a hypocrite, but you're right in one way. Scandal does have a way of lingering, doesn't it?"

She really shouldn't have said anything. Ailsa looked apoplectic.

Turning, she avoided her father and walked up the stairs on her own.

It was a good thing they were leaving in the morning. The atmosphere at Macrory House was poisonous.

LENNOX TOOK THE steps two at a time and entered his tower bedroom. While he'd been talking to Connor, Irene had carried hot water up to the tower.

The woman was amazing.

He went to the armoire and removed the suit he hadn't worn since Edinburgh. He'd bulked up in muscle some, but it would still fit. The occasion was important, probably the most important thing he'd done in his life.

He removed his clothes, bathed, and wrapped the towel around his waist while he shaved and thought about the next few hours.

"I've a present for you," Irene said, startling him.

He glanced over his shoulder at her, wondering if he should duck behind the armoire doors or shriek like a maiden.

"I've seen it all before," Irene said with a smile. "Oh, not yours, of course, but they're all the same, aren't they?"

Was he supposed to answer that?

She came into the room and placed the bundle she was carrying on the bed. Slowly, she unwrapped the muslin, revealing a foot-high stack of carefully folded tartan.

"It's the Caitheart tartan," she said. "If you're getting married, Lennox, you should do so as a Scot."

"Have you kept it all this time?" he asked, going to the bed and fingering the fabric.

Robert had been a stickler for wearing a kilt, choosing to do so on every conceivable occasion. He'd been annoyed that Lennox hadn't done so as

well. He hadn't bothered telling his older brother
that life in Edinburgh wasn't as true to tradition as at
Duddingston. Nor had he taken to wearing it in the
past five years.

"He would have wanted you to wear it tonight,"
Irene said.

He nodded, agreeing. "Thank you, Irene."

She didn't respond, merely turned and walked back
to the stairs, leaving him alone with his memories.

He finished shaving, then went to the armoire for a
white shirt. At the bottom of the folds of tartan were
the knee-high socks that went with the kilt as well as
the sporran.

As he arranged the folds, he heard the echo of
Robert's voice instructing him in the art of wearing
a kilt. Robert had been more than his older brother;
he'd given him most of his life lessons. The only thing
Robert hadn't taught him was how to bury his beloved
brother, the last of his family, and endure that loss.

When he finished and donned a dark blue jacket,
he felt as if a metamorphosis was complete. Gone
was the man who'd once studied in Edinburgh. That
young man had been replaced by the Earl of Morton,
the last in a line of distinguished Highland Scots.

Leaving his tower bedroom, he headed toward the
oldest part of Duddingston, to the library. Here he felt
his brother's spirit the strongest.

He opened the door, then closed it again, taking in
the shadowed light, the desk that Robert had kept so
neat and which was always messy under his owner-
ship. All he felt was silence and a surprising sense of
peace.

"Forgive me," he said, speaking to Robert's spirit
as if it dwelled in this room. "For a time I hated you

for dying and leaving all this to me. I knew it wasn't your choice, but I resented my life having to change. I ascribed to you demands you never made. Forgive me for that."

He'd never experienced the joy and honor Robert had felt being the Earl of Morton. He'd never looked on Duddingston as a prize for being a Caitheart.

Instead, his life had been a facade, a faint replica of Robert's. He'd lived as a hermit in a world that felt alien to him. Only recently, after looking through Mercy's eyes, had he begun to see what Robert had known: the glory of the history of Duddingston Castle, the privilege of being its steward, the strength of the heritage that was his.

In the past five years he'd crafted his own life here. He'd carried on with his inventions and insisted on flying his airship. Yet neither Duddingston nor the earldom had ever required him to be a hermit. That he'd offered up as some sort of penance for not wanting to be here. A sacrifice for disloyal thoughts.

It had taken Mercy to show him, without words, how wrong he'd been.

Of course Robert had found love with Mary. Even Duddingston Castle and the Caitheart heritage wasn't worth continuing without the promise of love.

Not even the ability to fly was enough on its own.

"I never felt like I lived up to your example. Until now." He smiled. "Wish me well, brother."

He left the room and walked down the corridor to the Clan Hall. Connor and Ruthie were standing there waiting for him. Connor was attired in a kilt as well, the blue-green tartan reminding Lennox of the Black Watch. Ruthie had on a green dress with a clan badge that matched Connor's tartan on her bodice. It was as

distinctive as a sign saying that they were bound together and soon to be married.

Lennox greeted them and a few minutes later they
all walked toward the front entrance. Irene was standing there attired in a dark blue dress with a tartan
shawl, looking as festive as if she was on her way to
a party.

He wanted his friends around him when they entered Macrory House. They would be the witnesses to
his marriage.

He smiled and led the way to battle.

Chapter Fifty

A valise was sitting outside the room Mercy had been given. It was all she needed for tonight. The rest of her baggage was still in the carriage.

"We'll be leaving early," her father said. "Just after dawn. The ship is waiting for us and I don't want to hold it up."

Heaven forbid the captain be inconvenienced. Rutherford ships were occasionally known for setting speed records, but mostly for sticking to their schedules. Cargo was delivered when it was quoted. Passengers could anticipate arriving at their destination on the exact date printed in the timetable. An act of God, such as a storm, had no effect on a Rutherford ship.

Or on James Rutherford.

"I do not want to be gone from home any longer than I must, Mercy," he said, giving her a stern look.

"It was your decision to come to Scotland, Father. One that you made of your own free will. Something that I do not possess. If you're seeking an apology from me you won't get it."

"What has happened to you, Mercy? You were never rude before."

"Is it rude to speak the truth?"

"You need to be home," he said.

Home, where she could be watched and guarded. Home, where her days were strictly regimented.

Her freedom was gone. Her future was laid out before her. The message was clear: she'd better come to like it because it wasn't going to change.

Unless she changed it herself.

The decision had been long in coming, but it felt right. She'd return to New York with her father and live in the big gray house. Just long enough to set up her own establishment. She'd find a place to live, hire her own staff, and be the one to dictate her life. She didn't care if she shocked all of New York society. Or if she was held up as an object lesson of how not to behave.

She opened the door, her back to her father.

"You'll be ready?"

"Yes," she said, wishing her voice didn't sound as if it held unshed tears.

She turned to face him, a determined smile on her face. Her misery was her own and she wouldn't share it with anyone.

He looked hard at her before finally turning to leave. At least he hadn't asked her if she was well. She wasn't. Her heart was breaking. She'd never truly understood what that expression meant until now.

After closing the door, she leaned against it, both palms flat against the wood. The door felt solid, but she didn't. She felt as if she were in pieces, floating somewhere above her. She'd ceased to be herself the minute she'd left Duddingston.

She missed Lennox. She missed the person she'd become in the past weeks. She missed Ruthie.

The life she was heading back to was a mirage. This was her true life here.

The sad fact was that even if her father hadn't come, she would have had to leave Scotland. No one wanted her here. Not the Macrorys. And not Lennox.

He may have been her first lover, but he wasn't willing to be her husband.

She'd even thought about getting rid of all her money and coming to him penniless. Would that have made her more acceptable? How could her fortune make the difference? She was still the same person whether she was able to support herself or not.

One thing her parents had instilled in her was the idea that wealth didn't build character. It didn't make you a superior person. It didn't create goodness where there was none. She was expected to support the arts, to be generous to charities, to see the need in other people and use her money for good.

She didn't want to go home. Home. The gray mansion in New York with its six-foot stone wall didn't feel like home now. It was a showplace, an example of the magnificence that wealth could create. Her four-room suite was luxurious, featuring a sitting room, a bedroom, and a bathing chamber with a massive bathtub carved from marble, hot and cold running water, and fixtures from England. She had a separate dressing room with three armoires filled with the most recent fashions from England or France. Every want was satisfied almost before she voiced it.

For a prison it was magnificent.

However, her father was right. Most people would want the life she had. How strange that she didn't.

She wanted to climb Ben Uaine and explore the woods around Duddingston Castle. She wanted to learn about each of the artifacts in the Clan Hall and go to the dungeon Lennox said was beneath part of the courtyard. She wanted to see the Merry Dancers, the northern lights in the winter sky.

Foolish wishes. Wanting to remain in Scotland was foolish, too. Yet despite everything she couldn't regret coming to Scotland. Nor could she ever be sorry about meeting Lennox or loving him.

When someone knocked on the door, Mercy opened it. Lily entered the room bearing a tray and put it on the table beside the chair.

"Mrs. West thought you might be hungry, Miss Mercy."

"Thank you and tell Mrs. West I appreciate her thinking about me."

The housekeeper had always been kind to her.

"McNaughton said Ruthie wasn't with you."

She was surprised McNaughton had noticed. "No, she's staying here." Since the two women were friends, she told Lily that Ruthie and Connor were to be married.

"Oh, I'm so glad, Miss Mercy. She was up to high doh about leaving Connor."

Mercy interpreted that to mean that Ruthie had been upset.

When Lily left, she returned to the chair, the dinner tray having no interest for her. She wished for darkness, but the Highland sky would still be light a few hours from now.

Tears wouldn't come; they were as far away as New York.

All she felt was empty.

Somehow, she was supposed to go on with her life. How?

The day in the forest, love had shone in Lennox's eyes, for all that he would probably deny it. He wouldn't speak of what he felt because of pride. Or honor. Or whatever emotion he used to cloak it. He wasn't wealthy and for that one lack he doomed them both to heartache.

She'd fallen in love, but love hadn't been enough. How was that anything but a tragedy?

Standing, she walked to the window, staring out at the sight of Ben Uaine in the distance. The mountain was a sentinel on the landscape. It had been there for eons and would be there long after she left.

The beauty of Scotland had crept up on her, taking her unawares. Ben Uaine itself, the piney woods, the trails through the glen, the magnificent storms, and the wind that blew the scent of the loch to her—all these things would feature in her memories.

As would Duddingston Castle, a monument to Scotland's past and the fierceness of the people who'd built the fortress. And it's owner, Lennox Caitheart, Earl of Morton.

She welcomed the pain because at least it proved she could still feel something. Lennox was only a few miles away. How was she supposed to endure it with an ocean between them?

She'd once thought that she should tell Ruthie that there was no sense involving herself in a romance with no future. How foolish that was. She could no more have stopped Ruthie from falling in love than she could alter her own emotions.

Love shouldn't hurt. It shouldn't be almost physically painful. It shouldn't alter your thoughts, your mood, and your outlook. She couldn't imagine a future where she smiled or laughed or anticipated the start of another day.

The knock on the door was an intrusion, but she had no choice but to answer it.

Aunt Elizabeth stood there. "May I come in?" she asked.

"Of course," Mercy said, stepping aside.

Her relationship with both her grandmother and her aunt had undergone a change since she'd arrived in Scotland. Ailsa obviously didn't approve of her. As far as Elizabeth, she wasn't sure what her aunt thought.

She wasn't in the mood to hear criticism right now. Yes, she'd acted shockingly. Yes, she'd been the object of scandal. Yes, she'd shamed the family. The truth, however, was even more appalling: she'd do everything again if given the opportunity. She'd stay with Lennox. She'd take him as her lover. She'd be with him at every possible opportunity.

If pressed, she'd tell Elizabeth that.

She motioned to the chair and sat on the edge of the bed, folding her arms in front of her.

"How are you?" Elizabeth asked.

She hadn't expected the question or the genuine concern in Elizabeth's expression.

"I should probably say that I'm fine, but I'm not. I'm miserable."

"Of course you are."

That, too, was a surprise.

"Must you leave?" Elizabeth asked. "Is there no way you could stay? You love him. That's obvious to anyone who spares a moment to look."

"Yes," Mercy said. "I love him."

He doesn't love me, however. Or he's never said. She didn't want to talk about love right now. She didn't think she could bear it.

"Then don't leave," Elizabeth said. "Defy your father. Defy the world. Stay with him."

He doesn't want me. The words wouldn't come. She couldn't tell that brutal truth to Elizabeth.

"Love is not so easily found, Mercy, that you can afford to give it up."

How could Elizabeth think this was easy? This was the most difficult thing she'd ever done.

Elizabeth moved to stand in front of her.

"I don't want you to feel as I have this past year. My life is a burden, not a joy. Living is something I do because I don't die."

She didn't have a chance to answer. Three raps on the door made Mercy sigh. She knew it was her father because that's how he always knocked at home.

All she wanted was to be alone to grieve. She wanted to banish everyone, go to bed, and pull the covers over her. She might allow herself the first of her tears. How many years would it take to dispel her grief?

"Yes, Father?" she said, opening the door.

"Is Elizabeth with you?"

She nodded.

Elizabeth came to the door.

"Your sister asked me to give this to you," he said, holding out an envelope. "I apologize that it slipped my mind until just now."

Elizabeth took the envelope and thanked him.

He nodded to Mercy, then left, heading for the stairs.

She didn't close the door. "Thank you, Elizabeth," she said. "I know you want to go read your letter."

Perhaps her father was right and she was becoming rude, but she desperately wanted to be alone.

Elizabeth tucked the letter into the pocket of her skirt. At the door she turned to Mercy. "You will think about what I said, won't you?"

Mercy nodded. Not that any good would come of it. You couldn't beg someone to love you.

Chapter Fifty-One

No more than five minutes later, Mercy heard a woman scream.

At first she wasn't sure who it was, but when she emerged from her room it was to see Elizabeth standing in the corridor, holding the open letter in her hand.

She was crying, and at first Mercy thought she'd received some terrible news, but her face was radiant with joy.

"Mercy," she said, her voice tremulous. "It's a miracle! It's a miracle!"

Mercy went to her aunt's side. "What is it, Elizabeth?"

"Thomas. Thomas is alive. He's alive!" She waved the letter in front of her. "He was in a prison camp all this time. He's alive!"

Mercy hugged her aunt, tears coming to her own eyes. It *was* a miracle. For a year Elizabeth had believed that Thomas had been killed in the war and now he'd been returned to her.

"I'm so happy for you," she said. "What are you going to do?"

Elizabeth smiled. "I'm going home," she said. "I'm going to Thomas."

Everyone around her was being blessed and while she didn't begrudge them their happiness, Mercy wished a little of it would spread to her.

"I'll have to ask James if I can travel with you."

"Don't be ridiculous, Elizabeth. You're going nowhere."

They both turned to see Ailsa standing at the head of the stairs.

"But it's Thomas, Mother. He's alive."

The news should have been greeted with joy. Instead, Ailsa merely continued to look at her daughter without emotion, her eyes flat.

"You're not going anywhere, Elizabeth. Don't be a fool."

Elizabeth didn't say anything, merely folded the letter carefully and tucked it once again into her pocket.

Mercy glanced at her grandmother again. Why didn't she remember Ailsa as being so heartless? Had losing her farm and her house to the war changed her so drastically? Or had she always been this way and clung to those setbacks as a reason to be even more bitter? Even so, she had no right to deny Elizabeth happiness.

A few minutes earlier her aunt had given her advice. Now she turned to the older woman and said, "You must go to him, Elizabeth. You both have suffered so much. You deserve to be happy now."

"Don't interfere, Hortense."

"I have always hated that name," Mercy told her grandmother. "My name is Mercy. If you don't address me by that, I will not answer you."

"What an impudent little trollop you are."

"Don't listen to her," Mercy said, turning back to Elizabeth. "I'll repeat the same words you said to me. Love is not so easily found that you can afford to give it up. Go to him."

Elizabeth didn't say anything. She didn't even look at Mercy. It was as if all the life had suddenly left her.

Ailsa had won.

A HUNDRED YEARS earlier Lennox would have arrived at Macrory House armed with a cudgel, spear, and a hundred clansmen behind him. Or maybe he would have simply ridden in through the enemy's gates and made off with the daughter of the house riding pillion. For good measure he would have stolen a number of cattle as well.

Now he was accompanied by only three people, but he was in a reiver's mood. He was all for pillaging the house and laying waste to the whole of the ostentatious structure the Macrorys had built.

Perhaps there was something showing in his face, because McNaughton's expression changed when he opened one of the double doors. For a second there was real fear there before the man's expression shifted to his usual sneer.

He'd disliked McNaughton from the day the man had arrived in Edinburgh to bring him news of Robert's death. Douglas hadn't come himself, but Lennox had excused the man due to his age. However, he could have sent someone other than McNaughton, a dour man who'd made himself disliked in the village and beyond.

Lennox didn't bother asking for permission to enter. He gained admittance simply by pushing the other man out of the way and making his way into the house.

Connor, behind him, didn't utter a conciliatory word. A good thing, because Lennox wasn't concerned about making friends here. He was a Caitheart and this was a Macrory establishment.

In the annals of Scottish history, the Macrorys were newcomers.

He strode through the house, the others silently following. McNaughton trailed behind, continually talking.

"This is a breach, Your Lordship. You cannot enter without the Macrorys' permission. You do not have the right."

"You should save your breath," Lennox finally said, turning and addressing the older man. "Words aren't going to stop me."

McNaughton's face was as red as the tassels on the nearby curtains.

"Send for Douglas if you wish. I don't care."

The last time he was here, only a week or so ago, he hadn't paid any attention to his surroundings. Now he made note of the soaring majesty of the staircase, the shiny marble floor, and the tapestry hanging above the landing. The castle there looked too much like Duddingston. No doubt it had been commissioned to make the upstart Macrorys feel a little better about their lack of history.

Stopping in the middle of the foyer, he looked up at the second floor. He didn't know which room was Mercy's. He doubted McNaughton would tell him. Jean probably would, but he didn't want to get her in trouble.

He looked over his shoulder at Irene on the off chance that she knew, but she only shook her head.

Two maids poked their heads into the foyer, took one look at him, and disappeared. No doubt they went to announce his appearance to all and sundry.

When he'd been here last, he'd provided the staff with enough gossip for years. This visit was going to be even more entertaining. He wouldn't be surprised if news of his actions reached Edinburgh.

If necessary, he'd start knocking on every door in the house. It wasn't time to retire, so he wouldn't be guilty of rousting the Macrorys from their beds.

There was a faster way, however.

He shouted for her. "Mercy!"

Douglas walked out of a corridor to his left. "What are you doing here, Caitheart?"

Lennox didn't answer him. Nor did he say anything to the gorgon grandmother who suddenly appeared at the head of the stairs. Her expression revealed not one hint of human warmth, like she was the *Cailleach Bheur*, the old hag of winter. Was she going to order him out of the house again?

"Caitheart, what are you about?"

Most of their communication since Robert's death had been in tersely worded letters. Rather, Macrory had informed him of all the contracts he'd canceled in writing. Lennox hadn't bothered responding.

He turned and addressed Douglas. "I'm here to claim my life, Macrory."

He didn't care if the man didn't understand. It wasn't something he needed to explain.

Suddenly there she was, standing with another woman, one he didn't recognize.

Mercy was dressed as she'd been the last time he'd seen her, but somehow she looked different. As if more time had passed than a few hours. He'd never seen her so subdued, as if her emotions had been drained out of her and only the shell of the woman existed.

His heart leaped. His pulse raced. He wanted to jump over the space between them and enfold her in his arms and keep her safe. If nothing else, apologize for the hours that had passed since she left Duddingston.

Somehow, he should have known from the beginning how important she was to him. He should have kept her at Duddingston, a prisoner of love, refusing to let the world interfere.

What an idiot he'd been, thinking that pride mattered more than Mercy.

For a long stretch of time, minutes that might have been hours, they looked at each other. He didn't know what she saw, but he was facing his future. Life made whole by Mercy.

"Get back in your room, Hortense."

He glanced toward the gorgon who was evidently determined to interfere.

Mercy came to the railing and gripped it with both her hands. "Why are you here, Lennox?"

It had been only a few hours since he'd heard her voice, but it affected him in a surprising way. The sorrow in it tugged at his heart and at the same time angered him. He never wanted her to be sad. If it was within his power, he would prevent her from ever feeling anything but happiness.

He wanted to hear her laughter, see her smile at the beginning of the day and its end.

She looked past him to the bottom of the stairs where Irene, Ruthie, and Connor stood beside Douglas.

"Why are you here, Lennox?" she asked again.

"It does not matter, Hortense," the grandmother said. "McNaughton, see this . . . person out."

"Try it, McNaughton," Lennox said, not bothering to turn and look at the man. His gaze was on Mercy who was still looking at him quizzically.

Slowly, he walked up the stairs. When he came to the head, the grandmother blocked his way.

What a fool woman.

He grinned, grabbed her around the waist, and simply moved her.

She retaliated by slapping him.

He ignored her and stretched out his hand to Mercy.

Chapter Fifty-Two

"What is going on?"

Her father came to the foot of the stairs, followed by Flora and Gregory. They were certainly attracting attention. All they were missing was the rest of the staff.

"Mercy, get back inside your room," her father said.

For the first time in her life, she disobeyed him. Instead, she walked toward Lennox. She didn't know why he was here, but she was going to take advantage of any extra time she had with him. He took her hand and she looked up at him.

"You're wearing a kilt," she said. What a magnificent sight he was.

"That I am."

He gripped her hand as if he never wanted to let go. If only that was true. If only that was real.

"Caitheart, explain yourself," Douglas said.

She looked down at Uncle Douglas, then back at Lennox. He was smiling at her, and there was an expression in his eyes she'd seen in the forest just before he kissed her.

"Lennox?"

She held tight to his hand as he turned and headed

for the stairs. Her grandmother scowled at Lennox, but didn't try to stand in his way. They descended the steps followed by Ailsa. At the base of the stairs Lennox walked around her father and the others, ignoring them. He led her to the center of the foyer, just below the rotunda.

"I hadn't planned where to do this, Mercy, only that it had to happen."

"What must happen?"

He stood in front of her, taking her other hand and holding both in his.

"Just what are you about?" her father said. "You march in here like you own the place. You act like a barbarian and now you refuse to answer any questions."

Her father grabbed her arm and tried to pull her away from Lennox.

"Mr. Rutherford," Lennox said. "I mean you no disrespect, but this is between Mercy and me."

"My daughter wants nothing more to do with you."

"Is that right, Mercy?" Lennox asked.

She shook her head. "No, it isn't," she said.

"Then I'll ask you not to interfere, sir," Lennox said to her father before turning back to her and taking her hands once more.

No one ever spoke to James Rutherford in such a fashion. Mercy couldn't tell if it was rage or surprise that was keeping her father silent.

"I love you, Mercy. I have probably loved you from the moment you accused me of riding a dragon."

Time slowed until it didn't move at all. She stared up at Lennox, feeling as if her heart had stopped as well.

"No one has ever occupied my thoughts as much as you. I can't think. I can't concentrate. I can't devote myself to my calculations. Your face is always there."

"Oh?" She couldn't think of a thing to say, but what did words matter right at this moment?

"You're in my dreams. I stand at the top of the tower and stare toward Macrory House like a lovesick boy. I replay every conversation we've had. I touch things you've touched, wondering if I can feel you on them."

Her eyes widened.

"I can't let you go back to America."

"You can't?"

He shook his head. "You don't belong there anymore. You belong at Duddingston with me."

Words left her. All she could do was look at him. Lennox, blessed Lennox, her Scot, her earl, her love.

"I love you," she said, uncaring that everyone heard. She wanted to shout it from the top of Ben Uaine. "I thought my heart would break leaving you."

"Will you marry me, Mercy? Marry me. Live with me at Duddingston. Share my life."

"I'll disown her," her father said.

Lennox glanced at him. "Thank you. That would be a grand favor."

"What the hell do you mean by that?"

"I don't want your money. I love Mercy for Mercy, not your damn money."

"Would you like me to throw him out, sir?" Gregory asked her father.

Lennox shook his head and smiled down at Mercy. "If you'll wait a minute, Mercy, someone wants a skelping."

He dropped her hands and started to walk toward Gregory, who took a few cautionary steps back.

"Don't be a fool, Gregory," her father said. "And you, you need to leave."

Lennox nodded. "I shall, sir, in a moment."

Hostility permeated the air. Everyone hated everyone. Her grandmother hated Gregory and her father and her. Her father, Uncle Douglas, and Gregory hated Lennox. Elizabeth resented Gregory, and Flora no doubt sided with her grandfather.

Ruthie, Connor, and Irene seemed exempt from the swirling emotions.

Mercy didn't care about old grudges or sizzling resentments. All she cared about was the way Lennox was looking at her.

He loved her.

Returning to stand in front of her once more he asked again, "Will you marry me?"

"Yes. Yes. Yes," she said. Now the tears came, the same ones she'd held back for so long.

"Why are you crying?" he asked.

She shook her head, shrugged, then laughed through her tears.

"I don't know, Lennox. I don't know."

"I refuse to allow the marriage," her father said.

She glanced at him. "Oh, Father, you can't. Don't you see? I would live in sin with Lennox if he asked me."

She thought her grandmother gasped, but she wasn't sure. What did scandal matter when she was suddenly blissfully happy?

Irene, Ruthie, and Connor came to stand behind Mercy. She was so glad to see all of them.

"We have a way of marrying in Scotland, Mercy. It will garner me a fine, but it's as official as if a bishop was marrying us."

"Do something, Macrory," her father said, addressing Douglas.

"What the hell do you want me to do, man?"

She heard her grandmother in the background, as

well as Elizabeth. Everyone was speaking, but Mercy ignored all of them.

Lennox glanced at Connor who moved to stand beside him. At the same time Irene came to Mercy's side.

"Mercy, it is my intention that we shall live as man and wife. That you will be known as the Countess of Morton. That we shall live at Duddingston for the whole of our lives and that our children will be my heirs."

She couldn't stop the tears.

"Will you, Hortense Abigail Paula Sarah Gramercy Rutherford be my wife and my countess?"

"Yes," she said, almost before he finished the question. "Yes, Lennox. Yes."

He glanced at Connor. "Are you witness to the same?"

Connor nodded. "I am."

"And I am as well," Irene said.

Lennox bent forward and kissed her softly. "That's it," he said. "We're married."

"Is that all?" she asked when he pulled back.

"That's all."

"That can't be right," her father said. He glanced over at Douglas. "He isn't right, is he? You can't have such stupid laws in this country."

Douglas drew himself up to his not inconsiderable height and frowned at her father. Her great-uncle might be up in years, but right now he looked capable of engaging in a fight of his own. She sincerely hoped her father realized how insulting his comment had been. James Rutherford's character was not steeped in tact.

"It's right, he is," Douglas said, not looking all that pleased at the admission. Her grandmother looked as if she'd just eaten something sour.

"It can't be. They can't be married."

"I'm afraid it can," Irene said, sending him a smile. "It's our way."

"My father isn't happy," Mercy said, looking up at Lennox.

"I'd wager none of the Macrorys are, either."

She didn't care.

"We'll have a more proper ceremony later if you want."

"Do we need one?" she asked. "Will this one count?"

He grinned at her. "It'll count."

Uncaring about their audience, she stood on tiptoe, put her arms around his neck, and kissed him.

"How did you know all my names?" she asked a moment later.

He glanced toward Ruthie, smiling. "I got help."

Mercy turned to her friend and the two of them hugged.

"Oh, Miss Mercy, I'm so happy for you." Ruthie stole at glance at Mercy's father. "I'm sorry about Mr. Rutherford, though."

So was Mercy. She loved her father. She always had. He wasn't a bad man. Everything he'd done was for the right reason: to protect and guard her. Perhaps if she'd been a different type of person she would have enjoyed her life thoroughly, never seeing it as limited.

She wanted to go to him, but his expression indicated that he wouldn't be receptive to any of her overtures.

Her aunt surprised her by leaving her grandmother's side and going to stand in front of her father.

"May I travel with you back to America, James?"

"You won't leave Scotland, Elizabeth," her grandmother said, her voice strong and filled with fury.

Elizabeth ignored Ailsa.

Her father nodded. "I would be pleased, Elizabeth."

Mercy smiled at her aunt, delighted. Yes, Ailsa was going to be enraged, but Ailsa was often unhappy about the actions of other people. Perhaps she could restrict herself to controlling her own life and leaving other people alone.

Lennox took her hand and the five of them left before the simmering tensions gave way to outright warfare.

Chapter Fifty-Three

Mercy, Lennox, Irene, and Ruthie sat inside the carriage while Connor drove. Mercy held tight to Lennox's hand, half believing that she was imagining things and that the previous hour hadn't really happened. Any moment now she would come back to herself. Or wake up. But whenever she glanced to her left, there he was, smiling at her.

If they had been alone she would have snuggled up next to him. Or perhaps they could have talked about the one subject they hadn't mentioned: her wealth. But with the others in the carriage, it didn't feel appropriate.

She explained Elizabeth's news to the other women.

"I saw the letter, didn't I, Miss Mercy?"

She nodded. "Indeed you did, Ruthie."

"You will have to call her something else from now on, Ruthie," Lennox said. "She's no longer a miss."

Ruthie began to smile. "It's right, you are. Shall I call you Countess?"

Mercy shook her head. "Mercy will do just fine, Ruthie."

"Or Her Ladyship whenever you're annoyed with her," Lennox said. At Irene's look, he smiled. "It's what you do to me."

Although she had left her father without a farewell and there were, no doubt, hurt feelings there, Mercy was overjoyed. She didn't have a stitch of clothing to her name. Or any of her toiletries. She didn't care. She'd done without before and it hadn't mattered. Garments could always be purchased and she didn't need most of what she'd brought to Scotland anyway.

She had never realized that she could easily walk away from everything, but she had. Everything that really hadn't mattered, that is. Lennox was who mattered. Living at Duddingston Castle was what mattered.

The future stretched out before her, unwritten and unplanned. It was both frightening and exhilarating.

Soon enough, they were back at the castle. Instead of going around to the front, Connor drove into the stable. Lennox helped them all out of the carriage. Irene was the first to disappear, citing a need to get home to her little cottage. Before she left, however, she came to both of them, put one hand on Lennox's arm and the other on Mercy's.

"I thought the two of you would suit from the first moment I saw you together. May God grant you joy, wisdom, and long life." With that, she kissed both of them on the cheek, then turned to leave, but stopped before she made it to the stable doorway.

"I didn't tell him about the money, Mercy. It's still where you left it." And then she was gone, vanishing into the Highland summer night, now only gradually succumbing to darkness.

Lennox turned to look at her. "The money?"

She shook her head. She would tell him later.

As Connor was removing the harness from the horses, aided by Ruthie, Lennox thanked them both, then grabbed Mercy's hand, and pulled her from the stable.

If they had been married in a formal ceremony, followed by a dinner, it would have been hours until they were alone. She wanted, very much, to be alone with Lennox. Her husband. Lennox was her husband.

"I just realized I've added one more name," she said and recited all of them. She stopped on the path and kissed him. "Caitheart, the best name of them all."

"Wife," he said.

"Husband," she countered, then kissed him again.

A moment later she asked, "Are we terribly rude? Should we have offered them all tea? Or whiskey?"

"Let them get their own," he said. "I want to be alone with my wife."

She felt exactly the same way.

She hadn't given it any thought, but when he led her through the Clan Hall, down one corridor door and then to another, she realized that he was headed for the tower.

"We're going to your bedroom," she said.

"It's not just mine, Mercy. It's ours from now on."

So many different emotions cascaded through her at once. Gratitude, that this wasn't a dream or her imagination. Joy, that they were married. Excitement, that she would soon be in his arms.

They slowly climbed the curving tower steps. Once in the tower room, Mercy moved away from the staircase and looked around. The bed, double the size of hers in New York, sat against one curved wall. A screen concealed the bathing and dressing area while an armoire and bureau made up the rest of the furnishings. Two windows faced the loch, revealing a view of the water and beyond, to Ben Uaine.

She stood there marveling at the sight. Just think, she'd wake to this view every morning. The thought brought a smile to her face.

"Will you mind being disinherited?" Lennox asked, coming up behind her. He wrapped his arms around her and she leaned back against him. This moment couldn't be any more perfect—except for one thing.

"I have a confession," she said, turning in his arms. "I don't think you're going to be happy about it."

One of his eyebrows arched upward. "A confession? Are you already married?"

She shook her head.

"That's the only thing that matters, isn't it?"

"I hope you feel that way after I tell you," she said.

"Then what is it?"

"It doesn't matter if my father disowns me."

"I concur," he said, bending to kiss her.

A minute later she shook her head. "No, I mean it really doesn't matter. My grandfather already left me a fortune."

He pulled back and stared at her.

"I could give it all up, but wouldn't that be foolish, especially since the chapel needs a roof? Wouldn't it be better to use it to repair the castle?"

"Just how large is this fortune?"

When she told him, he actually flinched.

"I didn't marry you for your money, Mercy."

"Oh, everyone knows that, Lennox. If anything, you married me despite my fortune. But it seems a shame not to use it, don't you agree?"

Before he could answer, she continued. "And Lennox, another thing."

"What now?"

"You should always wear a kilt," she said. "You have spectacular legs."

If she didn't know better, she would think that Lennox was embarrassed. He glanced away and then back again, his face deepening in color.

"I've been outmaneuvered," he said. "Outfoxed. I had all these grand plans about how I was going to support you."

"You could consider it my dowry. After all, you're an earl and I'm just a commoner."

"I've never met anyone less common than you," he said. "Very well, Your Ladyship, I will accept your fortune and do with it as you wish."

"Perhaps we could build a dock next to the tower," she suggested. "And add on to the kitchen."

She wasn't able to tell him any further ideas because he was kissing her. Every thought flew out of her head, replaced by pleasure.

She had been thirsty before. Or hungry for food. She had never craved touch like she did now. For a week she'd wanted Lennox to touch her, to stroke his hands over her skin, and explore her intimately.

It was a race to see who could get their clothes off first.

Chapter Fifty-Four

"You cheated," she said when Lennox simply pulled a few folds loose and the kilt fell to the floor.

Her eyes widened.

"Never ask a Scot what he wears beneath the kilt," he said with a grin.

His jacket was next, followed by his shirt and there he was, standing naked but for his shoes and socks.

The Highland night had not yet fallen which meant that there was ample light to see him.

"You're beautiful," she said.

"You've got to stop saying things like that, Mercy," he said, shaking his head.

"I think not. You are beautiful, in a masculine sort of way, of course."

"You're the one who's beautiful." He came and stood in front of her, his fingers working her buttons so much faster than she could.

She stood motionless as he stripped her, dropping her garments on the chair beside the bed.

"I'll have to borrow your shirt," she said. "I've none of my baggage."

He stopped what he was doing. "An heiress with no clothing. You're a continual paradox, Your Ladyship."

"That sounds so odd," she said. "I think I like *wife* better."

"What about *my love*?"

Her heart turned over in her chest. "That's even better."

He bent to remove her stockings and a minute later she was completely naked. He took her hand, but instead of leading her to the bed, he twirled her in front of him.

"You're beautiful everywhere, my love."

"As are you."

She had no idea if other couples divested themselves of their modesty along with their clothing. It seemed so natural for her to allow Lennox to look his fill. They were husband and wife. He had already labeled her his love and that's exactly what he was to her. Why should there be any reticence between people who loved each other?

He still held her hand as he walked to the four-poster. Instead of using the small set of steps, he put his hands on her waist and lifted her up to the mattress.

As she sat in front of him, she reached down and touched him, her curiosity growing as he did.

"I've seen naked men before," she said, "but only in statue form." Her lips quirked. "Most of the time they had fig leaves in strategic places. Except once. One day my parents took me to a museum. We walked into a large room with a soaring arched ceiling. The space was filled with three rows of Grecian and Roman statues. The third statue I saw was a man who'd been depicted standing, legs apart, holding a discus. My mother took one look at the statue and whisked me out of the room."

"I take it there was no fig leaf in evidence?"

"Exactly," she said, smiling at him. "I was, however, able to get a good look, which was very educational. Although I have to say, Lennox, that it wasn't sufficient preparation for you."

She wrapped both hands around Lennox.

"Mercy." His voice sounded different, almost strained.

"Am I doing something wrong?" she asked, her gaze fixed on her hands.

"I've wanted you to touch me for a week, but perhaps it would be better if you didn't do that right now."

She looked up at him. "A week, Lennox?"

He nodded.

"We could've eased each other," she said. "I wanted you to come to my room, but you were too honorable."

"But there's no restriction now, my love. You and I can stay in this bed for a week if we wish."

"Wouldn't that be lovely?" She reluctantly released him, scooted back on the bed, and lay down.

He was instantly there, covering her. She reached up, wrapped her arms around his neck, and smiled in welcome.

"I was so miserable," she said. "I was trying to figure out how I could possibly live without you."

"Now you don't have to."

"I know. It's my miracle. Elizabeth has hers and I have mine. You're my miracle."

"I love you, Mercy Caitheart. I don't think I expected to love anyone, but there you were, glaring up at me, giving me all sorts of orders."

"I thought you were exceedingly handsome," she said. "Too handsome. All the exceedingly handsome men I had met in the past were so filled with their own consequence. Not you, though. You were interested in things other than yourself. I was fascinated by you from the beginning."

"Then I thank your parents for protecting you too much," he said. "Because if you hadn't wanted your freedom you would never have come to Scotland."

"And if you hadn't been flying your airship, you would never have crashed into us."

"Fate," he said.

"Destiny," she countered.

He kissed her then and all thoughts of how they met vanished from her mind. All she knew was that it was Lennox, her love, and life was suddenly special and exciting.

He palmed her breasts and found her nipples. With each touch, her body thrummed, the sensations building. The core of her was an inferno, a fire that he effortlessly stroked. She wanted him with her, in her, but every time she urged him, he kissed her lightly and whispered, "Soon."

"Don't tease," she said.

He only kissed her again and she could feel his lips curving in a smile.

What she was feeling wasn't quite pain, but it was more than pleasure. Need soared through her, making every inch of skin ache. Her nipples grew harder, seeming to summon his lips.

She stroked her hands from his shoulders, down his arms, loving the feel of him, savoring each flexed muscle as he hovered over her. Even his back was beautiful, and she discovered that his buttocks were soft pillows for her hands.

"Now who's teasing?" he asked.

He nibbled at her throat, then continued the biting kisses down to her breasts.

He moved to the side, propping himself up on one forearm, one hand dancing across her stomach, and then gently combing the hair at the apex of her thighs.

"Mercy," he said, as his fingers played among her folds. Just her name, spoken with his beautiful voice, his Scottish accent amazingly seductive.

She widened her legs, curved the rest of her body toward him, needing that connection, wanting his touch.

Reaching down, she slid her fingers over his length, glorying in his muttered groan. Good. She hoped he felt like she did, out of control, her will buried beneath her body's needs. She was overwhelmed with sensations: heat, the pounding of her heart, breathlessness, and above all this driving need to have him ease these feelings and complete her.

The first time they'd loved, she'd been awash in wonder and a little trepidation. Their joining had been pleasurable, but marked by a little discomfort. The second time was glorious and tonight would be no different.

She would be able to love Lennox every night of her life. She would grow to know his responses as well as learning her own. She already knew, for example, that stroking her nails along his back made him shiver. His buttocks were sensitive and he liked to be touched, almost as much as she did.

Lennox was capable of great restraint, however, much more so than she. She wanted him now. She wanted him five minutes ago. Yet he continued to tease her with his fingers and lips.

She pulled his head down for a kiss, nibbling on his bottom lip in mock punishment for his teasing.

"Now, Lennox," she said, speaking against his lips. "Soon."

"Please. I want you inside me."

She grabbed him and squeezed gently. She could tease him, too.

"Lennox. Please."

Suddenly he was over her again. She spread her legs wide, invitation without a word spoken. Then he was inside her and she groaned in pleasure.

No wonder mothers cautioned their daughters a hundred ways to keep themselves inviolate. If the daughters truly knew what they were missing there wouldn't be a virgin left in the world.

As for Mercy, she was exceedingly glad that she was no longer a virgin, that her wedding night wasn't spent in worrying about what came next. She knew exactly what was going to happen and it was why she raised her hips, wrapped her feet around Lennox's calves, grabbed his shoulders, and surrendered to his kiss.

Bliss was different, she discovered. Before it had been a pleasant explosion of feeling. Tonight it was as if the world rocked, the bed shuddered beneath her, and in those long moments of cataclysmic pleasure, she shattered and was put together again.

Colors danced behind her closed eyelids. She lost her breath and gained it. She was certain her heart stopped in that instant of completion then raced to catch up. Lennox made a sound in the back of his throat, stiffened, and held her tight to him.

She wanted to weep or scream with pleasure. Some sound to mark what they had created between them. All she ended up doing was holding tight to him, her cheek against his heated skin, hearing the booming sound of his heart and knowing that hers matched his beat for beat.

Her prayer was simple and heartfelt, a few words of thanks to a generous God who'd put them in the same place to find each other.

Chapter Fifty-Five

*T*oward dawn, Lennox woke, staring up at the ceiling.

The sun wouldn't make an appearance for at least an hour if he'd awakened at his usual time. He turned his head, for the first time not being alone in the ancestral bed. Now he knew why it was so large. It had been designed for a man and his wife. He could even imagine their children joining them in a few years, clambering over the end of the mattress, their excited smiles revealing impish mischief or solemn wisdom.

He wasn't given to second sight, but he knew that his life would be full and joyful and that he would repeat this moment of deep gratitude for the rest of his life.

Mercy was asleep, a palm tucked under her cheek. Even asleep she was beautiful, her long lashes sweeping down over a delicately colored complexion. His wife. His very surprising wife. His very stubborn wife. His wealthy wife.

He grinned.

Slowly, so as not to wake her, he got out of bed, went behind the screen, and took care of his morning ablutions. Grabbing his trousers, he donned them and then, barefoot, went up the stairs to the top of the tower.

Normally, when he viewed his kingdom it was with thoughts of responsibility. Things had changed since yesterday. Not just his wedding, but his realization that he had narrowed his life himself. No one had demanded it of him.

Suddenly, he wasn't blessed with an albatross around his neck as much as a legacy to protect and defend. A legacy for his children and their children and hopefully a bloodline that stretched far into the future.

A noise made him turn and there she was. His wife. The Countess of Morton. The beautiful Countess of Morton.

She was dressed in his shirt, and that was all, the sight bringing his desire to life again.

"We have to find you some clothes," he said, smiling. "But not right this moment."

She threaded her fingers through her hair as she walked toward him. "And your brush," she said. "I have absolutely nothing, and not for the first time. Isn't that amazing?"

"Amazing?"

"That I don't care," she said. "Not one whit. I have everything I need," she added. "You."

He took her into his arms, smiling down at her. Such a comment required a kiss. A few minutes later he pulled back, knowing that he was going to take her back to their bed. They might stay there the whole day, driven out only by hunger.

For now, he turned with her to view his domain. Dawn was creeping over the horizon almost apologetically as if not wishing to disturb them.

Mercy stood in front of him, his arms wrapped around her. The morning breeze was filled with the scents of growing things. The far woods were dense, the woodland creatures beginning to stir. Life was waking to the day, a panorama that had often been presented to him, but one he had not appreciated as much as he did this morning.

She leaned back against him, her head resting on his chest.

He wanted to accomplish so much in his life; that hadn't changed. He wanted to learn, to master flight, to expand his knowledge. With Mercy beside him as his partner, his companion, his love.

He dropped his arms, took her by the hand, and led her back to their bed.

*F*OUR HOURS LATER they were roused from slumber by the bell beside his bed. He'd rigged a wire, trailing it though some of the loose bricks leading down to the kitchen. Instead of having to come to his tower bedroom, Irene could simply tug on the rope he'd installed near the kitchen window.

Mercy sat up, and looked at him wide-eyed. "What is that?"

He rolled over, kissed her, and told her about the bell. "It's hidden behind the bedside table," he said.

"What does it mean?"

"That Irene needs me." He sat on the edge of the bed and looked over at her. "She wouldn't use the bell unless it was important."

Mercy surprised him by getting out of bed and donning her clothes.

"There's no need for you to get dressed," he said, smiling at her.

"I'm starving," she admitted. "Maybe some toast and tea?"

He made a mental note to obtain some coffee for Mercy since she preferred that to tea.

They descended the steps a few minutes later. He was attired in clean clothes while Mercy had to wear what she'd worn the night before and not for the first time. They needed to solve her clothing issue as soon as possible.

Irene greeted them in the corridor.

"Your father is here," she said to Mercy. "And your aunt. I've put them both in the Clan Hall."

With that, she left them.

"Would you like me to see to them?" he asked.

Mercy sighed. "No. That would be the coward's way out. Besides, I want to say goodbye to my aunt and see if my father and I can't come to some type of arrangement."

"I won't let him browbeat you, Mercy."

"Of course not," she said, smiling. "I'm the Countess of Morton."

They walked to the Clan Hall hand in hand. At the door he stopped, surveying his two guests for a moment before they knew they were being observed.

Elizabeth was standing in front of a display of battle flags, reading the inscriptions. Rutherford was examining the vaulted ceiling as if he expected it to fall down on top of him.

Mercy squeezed his hand, then released it, and strode into the room.

Elizabeth stepped forward to embrace her niece. Rutherford held back, a scowl indicating how he felt about this meeting.

To his surprise, the older man didn't greet his daughter. Instead, he addressed Lennox.

"I hear you fly airships," he said. "Why would you do such a fool thing?"

"Because I can," Lennox answered. Rutherford had already struck him as the kind of man who wouldn't be convinced of anything easily. However, he was under no compunction to try and make the man understand why flight fascinated him.

"You're arrogant," Rutherford said.

Lennox only inclined his head, neither agreeing nor disagreeing. He had Mercy to think of. He didn't want to hurt her by clashing with her father.

"I'll buy your invention."

"In the hopes that I'll go away and leave your daughter alone? Too late. We were married by the laws of Scotland whether you accept it or not."

"No, you damn fool. Not because I want you to go away and leave my daughter alone. It's too late for that. Because she's my daughter, that's why."

"In an effort to appear less arrogant, Rutherford, I have to tell you that while I appreciate the offer, my invention is not for sale. Nor am I."

"I have heard you actually fly the thing."

"So far, I've created little more than a glider. I'm experimenting with thrust, velocity, and lift."

"I have people working on the same thing," Rutherford said.

Perhaps the offer to buy his airship was genuine.

"I hear you're an inventor as well. And a physician."

"I don't practice as such."

"However, you've loaned your talents to people in the village when necessary."

"Whoever has told you about me is well informed."

"I have been plagued by people who want to tell

me about you, Caitheart, from every member of the Macrory family to each of their servants. I have to admit that the servants have a better opinion of you than the family."

Lennox smiled, genuinely amused.

"There's been bad blood between the Macrorys and the Caithearts for generations."

"Then I would be about mending fences if I was you, Caitheart."

"Why is that, Rutherford?"

Despite himself, he was enjoying sparring with the older man and, if he didn't mistake it, Rutherford was feeling the same way.

"Because I've made Macrory an offer on his house. It's big enough that he and Mercy's grandmother can live there as long as they wish, but I need a place for my wife and me to stay when we come to Scotland."

That was a surprise.

"You're welcome to stay here," he said. "As my father-in-law, it would be expected."

"This is a moldering dump," Rutherford announced.

"It is not," Mercy said, her voice indignant. "It's a four-hundred-year-old castle, Father. With a history of a family, one that I married into. I would appreciate your demonstrating a little respect. All it needs is a new roof over the chapel and a few repairs here and there."

"Which you'll do, no doubt," her father said.

Rutherford didn't look all that angry. In fact, he appeared rather pleased with himself.

"I do have my grandfather's money," she said.

"And mine," he added. "In due time, Mercy."

"Your father wants to buy my airship," Lennox told her.

"Does he?"

She glanced at her father and smiled. "I think that shows a remarkable amount of vision."

"I'm not going to sell," Lennox said.

She didn't look surprised. "My husband is a genius, Father, but he's also very stubborn."

"I've already determined that."

Rutherford studied Lennox. "You won't get her to yourself, you know. Her mother and I will be here often enough. We'll be back on the next ship." He turned to Mercy. "I've a mind to bring Jimmy with us rather than leave him home."

Mercy looked surprised but didn't comment.

"She's my daughter and we love her."

"In your position I'd do exactly the same," Lennox said.

"Good, just so we understand each other."

Lennox only smiled.

Rutherford turned to Mercy. "I've brought your baggage. I'll have the rest of your things sent to you. And your mother will, no doubt, be shopping for everything she thinks you'll be lacking. Look for a ridiculous amount of trunks to arrive in the next few weeks."

"Thank you, Father."

He nodded.

When she went to him, he opened his arms, hugging her. His eyes closed and in that moment, Lennox realized that he might come to like Mercy's father.

Rutherford pulled back, smiling. "You realize, of course, that you will deprive your mother of the event of the season. However, you have spared me having to attend such a spectacle. Still, I don't think she'll be pleased." He looked at Lennox. "The only saving grace is your being an earl. That will mollify her somewhat. She can tell all her friends that her daughter is a countess."

"What about Gregory? Tell me he's going back with you."

Rutherford had the strangest expression on his face. "Well, now, that's another story. It seems that Hamilton has developed some feeling for your cousin."

"She is, after all, an heiress," Elizabeth said, exchanging a knowing glance with Mercy.

Mercy came to him and linked her arm with Lennox's, evidently uncaring that her aunt and her father were witnesses.

"Right now I'd love for everyone to be as happy as I am," she said. "Even Gregory."

Lennox decided that he didn't care if the world watched. He picked up his wife and twirled her in the light streaming in through the stained-glass windows.

Then, as she was laughing, he kissed her.

Epilogue

"*I*t's a blustery day, Lennox," Connor said.

"That it is."

"A perfect day to fly," Mercy added.

Lennox frowned at her and gently urged her away from the edge of Ben Uaine. He hadn't been in favor of her coming to see him off. He would much rather have her waiting in the glen. Or on the road. Or even on the tower. She would have had a much better vantage point from there.

"I'd like to fly with you," she said.

"What?"

"You've made the cabin large enough for two people. Why shouldn't one of them be me?"

"Because it's dangerous."

She raised one eyebrow and stared at him. "Is it any less dangerous for you?"

They'd been married only a month. A month that had totally changed Lennox's life. He had taken Mercy to Edinburgh and shown her his favorite sights. It had been illuminating to see the city as she did.

She'd already consulted with experts to repair the roof over the chapel. She'd hired four men to expand the kitchen garden, asking Irene about the types and number of plants she needed and wanted. She'd hired two girls from Macrory House, Lily and another girl that Ruthie had recommended to help Irene with the upkeep of the castle.

All this in a month. He couldn't imagine what she'd accomplish in a year.

She had taken over Robert's library, pouring through books on Duddingston to ensure that she knew everything there was to know about her new home. He'd never considered that she would come to love the castle as much—or even more—than Robert had.

Douglas hadn't yet agreed to sell Macrory House to Rutherford, but according to Mrs. West he was giving it serious thought, especially if he and his sister could continue to live there for the rest of their lives. Elizabeth had returned to North Carolina and was planning to marry her long-lost love while Flora had agreed to become Mrs. Gregory Hamilton, living in New York and, no doubt, becoming a fixture in society.

It was like the families changed places. That was fine, as long as he and Mercy continued to live at Duddingston. He would welcome the Rutherfords because they were Mercy's family, but he would be happy with only his wife as company. Part of that was his hermit-like nature reasserting itself. The rest of it was the fact that he was deeply in love.

He had never realized that the emotion could so effortlessly change his life. Nor had it ever occurred to him how miserable he'd been in the past five years. Mercy taught him that and it looked like she was in the midst of teaching him another lesson. He couldn't help but wonder if she knew it or if it was accidental.

He wasn't going to risk her life. Flying off Ben Uaine wasn't suicidal, exactly, but it was dangerous. In the past, he'd had the challenge of flight to goad him to such behavior. Now he had so many other things to restrain him and that knowledge was startling.

He didn't want to injure himself. He didn't want to die. He had too much to live for.

"I really do want to fly with you, Lennox."

The idea was so preposterous that he wouldn't even entertain it.

"No," he said with so much force that she looked surprised.

Connor backed up. He was probably going to disappear in the next moment. Connor had become less conciliatory since he and Ruthie had married two weeks earlier. Now it was as if he knew better than to get between a husband and wife.

"Why not?"

"Because I love you," he said. "I won't take a chance with your life."

"Yet you'll take a chance with your own."

"You're going to be like that, aren't you?"

"Be like what?" She folded her arms in front of her.

"Protective. Determined. You're going to worry about me, aren't you?"

She nodded. "Constantly. Endlessly. You're my cause, Lennox. You're my abiding interest."

"What if I feel the same about you?"

"That would only be fair," she said.

She had a point. A very good point.

He had already learned as much as he could about acceleration by launching his airship from Ben Uaine. He had given some thought, lately, to stretching wires between the mountain and the tower. It would still be a descent, but a controlled one and certainly less dangerous. He could test the aerodynamic qualities of a design that way and it didn't even have to be a manned flight.

When he explained what he was considering, Mercy nodded from time to time. Her questions were astute, and he realized that her understanding of his plans was based on her memory of his diagrams.

Perhaps he should show her his newest ideas and get her feedback.

"Connor and I are going to have to drag this down to the bottom of the mountain," he said, looking at his airship.

"Does that mean that you're not going to launch it?"

There was such hope in her voice that he realized that she'd truly been afraid for him.

"I can always kick it off the mountain," he said. "But then I would have to build it again."

"Whatever is safer for you, Lennox. I don't think I would want to live if anything happened to you."

There it was, the knowledge that had been there all along: the burden of love, the depth and breadth of it. It wasn't a free emotion. It demanded that a price be paid. To care about another was to give of oneself. In his case, to know that his well-being was Mercy's happiness and vice versa.

He walked back from the edge of the mountain. The airship could wait. He led the way down Ben Uaine, glancing back from time to time to reassure himself of Mercy's safety. As they reached the bottom and started for home together, Lennox realized something else. He would never be alone again. Instead, Mercy would be with him.

His American. His heiress. His love.

Author's Note

$\mathcal{L}$ennox's experiments in flight were based on the work of Sir George Cayley (1773–1857), sometimes called the Father of Aviation. Cayley was the first to identify the four key requirements of successful flight: lift, weight, thrust, and drag. His paper "On Aerial Navigation" changed the then current design of airships from the ornithopter model to fixed-wing aircrafts. Cayley was also the first to build a successful glider (1849) that looked a little like one of Lennox's airships. The ten-year-old son of a servant became the first person to fly in one of Cayley's airships. There are no records of Cayley ever piloting one of his own crafts, however.

Seanmhair is the Celtic (and more formal) word for grandmother. It's pronounced shen-a-var.

The Otis passenger elevator was installed in a New York City department store in 1857. I think, with James Rutherford's unlimited wealth, that he could have heard of such an invention and had one installed in his own home.

Duddingston Castle was loosely based on the general shape and size of Urquhart Castle. However, Urquhart was a ruin around the end of the seventeenth century.

Some Scottish phrases used in the book:

> She's up to high doh—She's upset.
>
> Yer bum's oot the windae—You're not making any sense. (Your bottom's out the window.)
>
> Yer aff yer heid—You're crazy. (You're off your head.)
>
> Skelping—Thrashing.

Keep reading for an excerpt from
the first book in

Karen Ranney's
ALL FOR LOVE

series,

To Love a
Duchess

Undercover as a majordomo, spy Adam Drummond has infiltrated Marsley House with one purpose only—to plunder its mysteries and gather proof
that the late Duke of Marsley was an unforgivable
traitor to his country. At the same time, Adam is
drawn to a more beguiling puzzle: the young and
still-grieving duchess—a beauty with impenetrable
secrets of her own. For Drummond, uncovering
them without exposing his masquerade will require
the most challenging and tender moves of his career.

That a servant can arouse such passion in her is
too shocking for Suzanne Whitcomb, Duchess of
Marsley, to consider. Yet nothing quickens her pulse
like Drummond's touch. It's been two years since
the duke lost his life in a tragic accident—and even
longer since she's been treated like a woman. But
when Drummond's real mission is revealed, and the
truth behind Suzanne's grief comes to light, every
secret conspired to tear them apart is nothing compared to the love that can hold them together.

Chapter One

September 1864
Marsley House
London, England

*H*e felt the duke's stare on him the minute he walked into the room.

Adam Drummond closed the double doors behind him quietly so as not to alert the men at the front door. Tonight Thomas was training one of the young lads new to the house. If they were alerted to his presence in the library, they would investigate.

He had a story prepared for that eventuality. He couldn't sleep, which wasn't far from the truth. Nightmares often kept him from resting more than a few hours at a time. A good thing he had years of practice getting by with little sleep.

He'd left his suite attired only in a collarless white shirt and black trousers. Another fact for which he'd have to find an explanation. As the majordomo of Marsley House, he was expected to wear the full uniform of his position at all times, even in the middle of the night. Perhaps not donning the white waistcoat, cravat, and coat was an act of rebellion.

Strange, since he'd never been a rebel before. It was this place, this house, this assignment that was affecting him.

For the first time in seven years he hadn't borrowed a name or a history carefully concocted by the War Office. He'd taken the position as himself, Adam Drummond, Scot and former soldier with Her Majesty's army. The staff knew his real name. Some even knew parts of his true history. The housekeeper called him Adam, knew he was a widower, was even aware of his birthdate.

He felt exposed, an uncomfortable position for a man who'd worked in the shadows for years.

He lit one of the lamps hanging from a chain fixed to the ceiling. The oil was perfumed, the scent reminiscent of jasmine. The world of the Whitcombs was unique, separated from the proletariat by two things: the peerage and wealth.

The pale yellow light revealed only the area near the desk. The rest of the huge room was in shadow. The library was *ostentatious*, a word he'd heard one of the maids try to pronounce.

"And what does it mean, I'm asking you?" She'd been talking to one of the cook's helpers, but he'd interjected.

"It means *fancy*."

She'd made a face before saying, "Well, why couldn't they just say *fancy*, then?"

Because everything about Marsley House was ostentatious.

This library certainly qualified. The room had three floors connected by a circular black iron staircase. The third floor was slightly larger than the second, making it possible for a dozen lamps to hang from chains affixed to each level at different heights. If he'd lit them all it would have been bright as day in here, illuminating thousands of books.

He didn't think the Whitcomb family had read every one of the volumes. Some of them looked as if they were new, the dark green leather and gold spines no doubt as shiny as when they'd arrived from the booksellers. Others were so well-worn that he couldn't tell what the titles were until he pulled them from the shelves and opened them. There were a great many books on military history and he suspected that was the late duke's doing.

He turned to look at the portrait over the mantel. George Whitcomb, Tenth Duke of Marsley, was wearing his full military uniform, the scarlet jacket so bright a shade that Adam's eyes almost watered. The duke's medals gleamed as if the sun had come out from behind the artist's window to shine directly on such an exalted personage. He wore a sword tied at his waist and his head was turned slightly to the right, his gaze one that Adam remembered. Contempt shone in his eyes, as if everything the duke witnessed was beneath him, be it people, circumstances, or the scenery of India.

Adam was surprised that the man had allowed himself to be painted with graying hair. Even his muttonchop whiskers were gray and brown. In India, Whitcomb had three native servants whose sole duties were to ensure the duke's sartorial perfection at all times. He was clipped and coiffed and brushed and shined so that he could parade before his men as the ultimate authority of British might.

His eyes burned out from the portrait, so dark brown that they appeared almost black, narrowed and penetrating.

"Damn fine soldiers, every single one of them. All mongrels, of course, but fighting men."

At least the voice—surprisingly higher in pitch than Adam had expected—was silent now. He didn't have to hear himself being called a mongrel again. Whitcomb had been talking about the British regiments assigned to guard the East India Company settlements. He could well imagine the man's comments about native soldiers.

What a damned shame Whitcomb had been killed in a carriage accident. He deserved a firing squad at the very least. He wished the duke to Hell as he had ever since learning of the man's death. The approaching storm with its growling thunder seemed to approve of the sentiment.

As if to further remind him of India, his shoulder began to throb. Every time it rained the scar announced its presence, the bullet wound just one more memory to be expunged. It was this house. It brought to mind everything he'd tried to forget for years.

Adam turned away from the portrait, his attention on the massive, heavily tooled mahogany desk. This, too, was larger than it needed to be, raised on a dais, more a throne than a place a man might work. A perfect reflection of the Duke of Marsley's arrogance.

The maids assigned this room had left the curtains open. If he had been a proper majordomo he would no doubt chastise them for their oversight. But because he'd been a leader of men, not of maids, he decided not to mention it.

Lightning flashed nearby, the strike followed by

another shot of thunder. The glass shivered in the mullioned panes.

Maybe the duke's ghost was annoyed that he was here in the library again.

The careening of the wind around this portion of Marsley House sounded almost like a warning. Adam disregarded it as he glanced up to the third floor. He would have to be looking for a journal. That was tantamount to searching for a piece of coal in a mine or a grain of sand on the beach.

This assignment had been difficult from the beginning. He'd been tasked to find evidence of the duke's treason. While he believed the man to be responsible for the deaths of hundreds of people, finding the proof had been time consuming and unsuccessful to this point.

He wasn't going to give up, however. This was more than an assignment for him. It was personal.

One of the double doors opened, startling him.

"Sir?"

Daniel, the newest footman, stood there. The lad was tall, as were all of the young men hired at Marsley House. His shock of red hair was accompanied by a splattering of freckles across his face, almost as if God had wielded a can of paint and tripped when approaching Daniel. His eyes were a clear blue and direct as only the innocent could look.

Adam always felt old and damaged in Daniel's presence.

"Is there anything I can do for you, sir?" the young footman asked.

"I've come to find something to read." There, as an excuse it should bear scrutiny. He could always claim that he was about to examine the Marsley House ledgers, even though he normally performed that task in his own suite.

"Yes, sir."

"I think we had a prowler the other night," Adam said, improvising. "One of the maids mentioned her concern."

"Sir?"

Daniel was a good lad, the kind who wouldn't question a direct order.

"I'd like you to watch the outer door to the Tudor garden."

"Yes, sir," Daniel said, nodding.

"Tell Thomas that I need you there."

"Yes, sir," the young man said again, still nodding.

Once he, too, had been new to a position. In his case, Her Majesty's army. Yet he'd never been as innocent as Daniel. Still, he remembered feeling uncertain and worried in those first few months, concerned that he wasn't as competent at his tasks as he should be. For that reason he stopped the young man before he left the library.

"I've heard good reports about you, Daniel."

The young man's face reddened. "Thank you, sir."

"I think you'll fit in well at Marsley House."

"Thank you, Mr. Drummond."

A moment later, Daniel was gone, the door closed once again. Adam watched for a minute before turning and staring up at the third floor.

The assignment he'd been given was to find one particular journal. Unfortunately, that was proving to be more difficult than originally thought. The Duke of Marsley had written in a journal since he was a boy. The result was that there were hundreds of books Adam needed to read.

After climbing the circular stairs, he grabbed the next two journals to be examined and brought them back to the first floor. He doubted if the duke would approve of him sitting at his desk, which was why Adam did so, opening the cover of one of the journals and forcing himself to concentrate on the duke's overly ornate handwriting.

He didn't look over at the portrait again, but it still seemed as if the duke watched as he read.

At first Adam thought it was the sound of the storm before realizing that thunder didn't speak in a female voice. He stood and extinguished the lamp, but the darkness wasn't absolute. The lightning sent bright flashes of light into the library.

Moving to the doors, he opened one of them slightly, expecting to find a maid standing there, or perhaps a footman with his lover. He knew about three dalliances taking place among the staff, but he wasn't going to reprimand any of them. As long as they did their jobs—which meant that he didn't garner any attention for the way he did his—he wasn't concerned about their behavior in their off hours.

It wasn't a footman or a maid engaged in a forbidden embrace. Instead, it was Marble Marsley, the widowed duchess. She'd recently returned from her house in the country, and he'd expected to be summoned to her presence as the newest servant on the staff and one of the most important. She hadn't sent for him. She hadn't addressed him.

He had to hand it to the duke; he'd chosen his duchess well. Suzanne Whitcomb, Duchess of Marsley, was at least thirty years younger than the duke and a beautiful woman. Tonight her dark brown hair was arranged in an upswept style, revealing jet-black earrings adorned with diamonds. Her face was perfect, from the shape to the arrangement of her features. Her mouth was generous, her blue-gray eyes the color of a Scottish winter sky. Her high cheekbones suited her aristocratic manner, and her perfect form was evident even in her many-tiered black cape the footman was removing.

Did she mourn the bastard? Is that why she'd remained in her country home for the past several months?

From his vantage point behind the door, he watched as she removed her gloves and handed them to the footman, shook the skirts of her black silk gown, and walked toward him with an almost ethereal grace.

He stared at her, startled. The duchess was crying. Perfect tears fell down her face as silently as if she were a statue. He waited until she passed, heading for the staircase that swooped like a swallow's wing through the center of Marsley House, before opening the door a little more.

Glancing toward the vestibule, he was satisfied that Thomas, stationed at the front door, couldn't see him. He took a few steps toward the staircase, watching.

The duchess placed her hand on the banister and, looking upward, ascended the first flight of steps.

He had a well-developed sense of danger. It had saved his life in India more than once. But he wasn't at war now. There weren't bullets flying and, although the thunder might sound like cannon, the only ones were probably at the Tower of London or perhaps Buckingham Palace.

Then why was he getting a prickly feeling on the back of his neck? Why did he suddenly think that the duchess was up to something? She didn't stop at the second floor landing or walk down the corridor to her suite of rooms. Instead, she took one step after another in a measured way, still looking upward as if she were listening to the summons of an angel.

He glanced over at the doorway, but the footman wasn't looking in his direction. When he glanced back at the staircase, Adam was momentarily confused because he couldn't see her. At the top of the staircase, the structure twisted onto itself and then disappeared into the shadows. There were only two places she could have gone: to the attic, a storage area that encompassed this entire wing of Marsley House. Or to the roof.

He no longer cared if Thomas saw him or not. Adam began to run.

Where the hell was the daft woman?

Adam raced up the first flight of stairs, then the second, wondering if he was wrong about Marble Marsley. He'd overheard members of the staff calling her that and had assumed she'd gotten the label because she was cold and pitiless. A woman who never said a kind word to anyone. Someone who didn't care about another human being.

In that, she and her husband were a perfect pair.

But marble didn't weep.

He followed the scent of her perfume, a flowery, spicy aroma reminding him of India. At the top of the staircase, he turned to the left, heading for an inconspicuous door, one normally kept closed. It was open now, the wind blowing the rain down the ten steps to lash him in the face.

He'd been here only once, on a tour he'd done to familiarize himself with the place. Marsley House was a sprawling estate on the edge of London, the largest house in the area and one famous enough to get its share of carriages driving by filled with gawping Londoners out for a jaunt among their betters.

Not that the Marsley family was better than anyone else, no matter what they thought. They had their secrets and their sins, just like any other family.

He kept the door to the roof open behind him, grateful for the lightning illuminating his way. If only the rain would stop, but it was too late to wish for that. He was already drenched.

In a bit of whimsy, the builder of Marsley House had created a small balcony between two sharply pitched gables. Chairs had been placed there, no doubt for watching the sunset over the roofs of London.

No one in their right mind would be there in the middle of a storm. As if agreeing with him, thunder roared above them.

The duchess was gripping the balcony railing with both hands as she raised one leg, balancing herself like a graceful bird about to swoop down from the top of a tree.

People didn't swoop. They fell.

What the hell?

He began to run, catching himself when he would have fallen on the slippery roof.

"You daft woman," he shouted as he reached her.

She turned her face to him, her features limned by lightning.

He didn't see what he saw. At least that's what he told himself. No one could look at the Duchess of Marsley and not be witness to her agony.

He grabbed one of her arms, pulling her to him and nearly toppling in the process. For a moment he thought her rain-soaked dress was heavy enough to take them both over the railing.

Then the daft duchess began to hit him.

He let fly a few oaths in Gaelic while trying to defend himself from the duchess's nails as she went for his eyes. Her mouth was open and for a curious moment, it almost looked like she was a goddess of the storm, speaking in thunder.

He stumbled backward, pulling her on top of him when she would have wrenched free. He had both hands on each of her arms now, holding her.

She was screaming at him, but he couldn't tell what she was saying. He thought she was still crying, but it might be the rain.

He pushed away from the railing with both feet. He'd feel a damn sight better if they were farther away from the edge. As determined as she was, he didn't doubt that she would take a running leap the minute she got free.

The storm was directly overhead now, as if God himself dwelt in the clouds and was refereeing this fight to the death. Not his, but hers.

He was a few feet away from the railing now, still being pummeled by the rain. Twice she got a hand free and struck him. Once he thought she was going to make it to her feet. He grabbed the sodden bodice of her dress and jerked her back down. She could die on another night, but he was damned if he was going to let her do it now.

He made it to his knees and she tried, once more, to pull away. She got one arm free and then the second. Just like he imagined, she made for the railing again. He grabbed her skirt as he stood. When she turned and went for his eyes again, he jerked the fabric with both hands, desperate to get her away from the edge.

The duchess stumbled and dropped like a rock.

He stood there being pelted by rain that felt like miniature pebbles, but the duchess didn't move. Her cheek lay against the roof; her eyes were closed, and rain washed her face clean of tears.

He bent and scooped her up into his arms and headed for the door, wondering how in hell he was going to explain that he'd felled the Duchess of Marsley.